Arthur stilled, his heart pounding in his chest as he felt the lass's gaze sweep over the crowd of soldiers, and then—bloody hell—return to him.

Instinctively, his hand tightened around the handle of his sword. A cold sweat slid down his spine.

This time there was no helm to shield his face, and he felt the intensity of her scrutiny full force. He stilled when a small furrow appeared between her brows.

For one long heartbeat he waited for her to unmask him. For her voice to ring out with the words that would condemn him to death . . . and to failure.

But the furrow only deepened.

And then in one reckless moment he knew what he had to do. He had to be sure.

Slowly, he lifted his gaze to hers.

He didn't move. Didn't breathe. Didn't blink as their eyes collided unhindered for the first time. Gazing into her eyes, as dark and deep a blue as the sea, he felt himself drowning. Lost, if only for an instant.

When she gasped, he knew it was all over.

BY MONICA MCCARTY

The Ranger
The Chief
The Hawk

Highland Warrior
Highland Outlaw
Highland Scoundrel

Highlander Untamed
Highlander Unmasked
Highlander Unchained

THE Ranger

A HIGHLAND GUARD NOVEL

MONICA McCARTY

BALLANTINE BOOKS • NEW YORK

A Ballantine Books Mass Market Original

Copyright © 2010 by Monica McCarty

Published in the United States by Ballantine Books, an imprint of The Random House Publishing Group, a division of Random House, Inc., New York.

BALLANTINE and colophon are registered trademarks of Random House, Inc.

ISBN 978-0-345-51826-2
eBook ISBN 978-0-345-51827-9

Cover design: Lynn Andreozzi
Cover illustration: Franco Accornero

Printed in the United States of America

www.ballantinebooks.com

9 8 7 6 5 4 3 2 1

To Andrea and Annelise who are always ready with champagne, pom-poms, or words of wisdom. In other words: bartender, cheerleader, and Obi Wan Kenobi all rolled into two fabulous agents. Thank you for everything.

ACKNOWLEDGMENTS

A special thanks to the entire team at Ballantine without whose support along each step of the way—from art, to sales, to editorial, to production, and publicity—this book would not be possible. Taking point on all this, of course, is my fabulous editor, Kate Collins, whose enthusiasm and thoughtful feedback are invaluable. Can you believe it's been three years and six books?

Contrary to popular belief, writing is not a solitary endeavor. I am fortunate to have a wonderful group of writer friends to rely on when I need to bounce around ideas, come up with a solution for a plot issue, or flesh out characters. From daily phone calls (Jami Alden, stand up) to group lunches and emails (it's your turn Bella Andre, Veronica Wolff, Barbara Freethy, Carol Culver, Penelope Williamson, Tracy Grant, and Anne Hearn), I don't know what I'd do without you. My good fortune in writing friends has extended to the very highest peaks. Catherine Coulter is not only one of the all-time great romance authors, but also a fabulous hostess. Thank you for the delicious food, a beautiful view, and excellent company—your lunches are the best! When I feel the need for a little jump across the pond, I know exactly whom to call—fellow "Onica" Veronica, I can't wait for Mommy Abandonment

Tour 2010: The Yanks are Back (and our chance to redeem ourselves at the pub quiz). When it comes to navigating the business side of writing and learning about the industry, RWA national has become a fun barroom classroom where I get to learn from the best: Barbara Samuel and Christy Ridgeway, I'm already looking forward to next year!

Thanks to Emily and Estella at Wax Creative not only for a beautiful website, but also for keeping up on the latest and the greatest so that I don't have to.

And finally to Dave, my constant source of inspiration (seriously, I'm not laughing . . . it's really more of an over-enthusiastic smile with sound), and Reid and Maxine who never miss the opportunity to promote my books by yelling across the bookstore, "Mom, they have your book!"

THE HIGHLAND GUARD
Winter 1307–1308

With King Robert Bruce:

Tor "Chief" MacLeod: Team leader and expert swordsman

Erik "Hawk" MacSorley: Seafarer and swimmer

Gregor "Arrow" MacGregor: Marksman and archer

Eoin "Striker" MacLean: Strategist in "pirate" warfare

Ewen "Hunter" Lamont: Tracker and hunter of men

Lachlan "Viper" MacRuairi: Stealth, infiltration, and extraction

Magnus "Saint" MacKay: Mountain guide and weapon forging

William "Templar" Gordon: Alchemy and explosives

Robert "Raider" Boyd: Physical strength and hand-to-hand combat

Alex "Dragon" Seton: Dirk and close combat

With the English:

Arthur "Ranger" Campbell: Scouting and reconnaissance

FOREWORD

The Year of Our Lord thirteen hundred and seven. The tide has turned, but Robert the Bruce is still far from being able to claim victory in his quest to claim the Scottish throne.

With England in turmoil following the death of his greatest foe, King Edward I of England, Bruce turns to vanquishing the enemies within. Many of his own countrymen still oppose him, foremost among them the Comyns, the MacDowells, the Earl of Ross, and the MacDougalls.

With the help of his secret band of elite warriors known as the Highland Guard, Bruce continues his revolutionary strategy of "pirate" warfare, cutting a swath of destruction across the lands of his enemies that will be remembered for generations.

He subdues the MacDowells in Galloway before starting the march north into the Highlands. After securing temporary truces with Ross and the MacDougalls, Bruce attacks the Comyns at Inverlochy, Urquhart, Inverness, and Nairn.

But just when victory seems to be in his grasp, Bruce is struck with a strange sickness, leaving the would-be king hovering near death. The enemy becomes cold and hunger, as his men are forced to wait out the winter in uncertainty.

The year before, when all seemed lost, and Bruce was forced to flee from his kingdom a fugitive, he turned to the warriors of the Highland Guard to help him survive. Now, to defeat the powerful nobles who stand in his way, he will need them more than ever.

Prologue

St. John's Church, Ayr, Scotland, April 20, 1307

Arthur Campbell wasn't there—or at least he wasn't supposed to be. He'd told King Robert Bruce about the silver changing hands at the church tonight on its way north to the English garrison at Bothwell Castle. His part of the mission was over.

Bruce's men were concealed in the trees not fifty yards away, waiting for the riders to appear. Arthur didn't need to be here. In fact, he *shouldn't* be here. Protecting his identity was too important. After more than two years of pretending to be a loyal knight to King Edward, he'd invested too much to risk it on a "bad feeling." It wasn't just explaining himself to the English that he had to worry about. If King Robert's men discovered him, they would think he was exactly what he appeared to be: the enemy.

Only a handful of men knew Arthur's true allegiance. His life depended on it.

Yet here he was, hiding in the shadows of the tree-shrouded hillside behind the church, because he couldn't shake the twinge of foreboding that something was going to go wrong. He'd spent too many years relying on those twinges to start ignoring them now.

The clang of the church bell shattered the tomb of darkness. Compline. The night prayer. It was time.

He held perfectly still, keeping his senses tuned for any sign of approaching riders. From his initial scouting of the area, he knew that Bruce's men were positioned in the trees along the road approaching the church. It gave them a good view of anyone arriving, but left them far enough away to be able to make a quick escape in the event the occupants of the church—which was serving as a makeshift hospital for English soldiers—were alerted by the attack.

Admittedly, St. John's wasn't the ideal place to stage an attack. If the wounded English soldiers inside weren't enough of a threat, the garrison of soldiers stationed not a half-mile away at Ayr Castle should give Bruce's men pause.

But they had to operate with the intelligence they had. Arthur had learned that the silver would change hands tonight at the church, but not by which road it would leave. With at least four possible routes out of the city to Bothwell, they couldn't be certain which one the riders would take.

In this case the reward was worth the risk. The silver—perhaps as much as fifty pounds—intended to pay the English garrison at Bothwell Castle could feed Bruce's four hundred warriors hiding in the forests of Galloway for months.

Moreover, capturing the silver wouldn't just be a boon to Bruce, it would also hurt the English—which was exactly what these surprise attacks were calculated to do. Quick, fierce attacks to keep the enemy unsettled, interfere with communication, take away the advantage of superior numbers, weaponry, and armor, and most of all, to instill fear in their hearts. In other words, they would fight the way he'd always fought: like a Highlander.

And it was working. The English cowards didn't like to travel in small groups without an army to protect them, but Bruce and his men had been giving them so much trouble, the enemy had been forced to use furtive tactics in attempting to sneak the silver through by using a few couriers and priests.

Suddenly, Arthur stilled. Though there hadn't been a sound, he sensed someone approaching. His gaze shot to the road, scanning back and forth in the darkness. *Nothing.* No sign of riders approaching. But the hairs at the back of his neck were standing on edge, and every instinct warned him otherwise.

Then he heard it. The soft but unmistakable crackle of leaves crushed underfoot, coming from behind him.

Behind.

He swore. The couriers were arriving via the path from the beach, not the road from the village. Bruce's men would see them, but the attack would be much closer to the church than they wanted. They'd been trained to expect the unexpected, but this was going to be close . . . very close.

He hoped to hell the priest didn't decide to come out and investigate. The last thing he wanted was a dead churchman on his soul—it was black enough already.

He listened harder. Two sets of footsteps. One light, the second heavy. A twig cracked, and then another. They were getting closer.

A moment later, the first of two cloaked figures came into view on the path below him. Tall and bulky, he stomped forcefully up the winding path, pushing branches out of the way for the soldier trailing behind. As he strode past, Arthur could just make out the glint of steel and the colorful tabard beneath the heavy folds of wool. A knight.

Aye, it was them all right.

The second figure drew closer. Shorter and slimmer than the first, and with a much more graceful step. Quickly dismissing him as the lesser threat, Arthur started to turn back to the first when something made him stop. His gaze sharp-

ened on the second figure. The darkness and hooded cloak
blotted out the details, but he couldn't shake the feeling
that something wasn't right. The soldier almost seemed to
be gliding along the path below him. There was something
under his arm. It looked like a basket—

His stomach dropped. *Ah, hell.* It wasn't the courier, it
was a lass. A lass with *extremely* bad timing.

Arthur's senses hadn't failed him. Something bad was
going to happen all right. If the lass didn't get out of here,
he had no doubt Bruce's men would make the same mistake he had. But they wouldn't have time to correct it.
They'd be attacking as soon as she and her knightly companion came into view—which would be at any moment.

He tensed as she swept right by him, the faint scent of
roses lingering in her wake.

Turn back, he urged her silently. When she paused and
tilted her head slightly in his direction, he thought she
might have heard his silent plea. But she shook it off and
continued along the path, walking right into a death trap.

Christ. What a damned mess. This mission had just gone
straight to hell. Bruce's men were about to lose their element of surprise—and kill a woman in the process.

He shouldn't interfere. He couldn't risk discovery. He
was supposed to stay in the shadows. Operate in the black.
Not get involved. Do *whatever* he had to do to protect his
cover.

Bruce was counting on him. The prized scouting skills
that had landed him in the elite fighting force known as the
Highland Guard had never been as valuable as they were
now. Arthur's ability to hide in the shadows and penetrate
deep behind enemy lines to gather intelligence about terrain, supply lines, and enemy strength and positions, was
even more important for the surprise attacks that had become a hallmark of Bruce's war strategy.

One lass wasn't worth the risk.

Hell, he wasn't even supposed to be here.

Let her go.

His heart hammered as she drew closer. He didn't get involved. He stayed in the shadows. It wasn't his problem.

Sweat gathered on his brow beneath the heavy steel of his helm. He had only a fraction of an instant to decide . . .

Bloody hell.

He stepped out from behind the trees. He'd been playing a knight for so long he must have started to believe it. He was a damned fool, but he couldn't stand by and let an innocent lass go to her death without trying to do something. Maybe he could intercept them before they came into view. Maybe. But he couldn't be sure where all of Bruce's men were positioned.

He moved stealthily through the shadows, coming on her from behind. In one smooth motion, he slid his hand around to cover her mouth before she could scream. Hooking his arm around her waist, he jerked her hard against him.

A little too hard. He could feel every one of her soft, feminine curves plastered against him—particularly the nicely rounded bottom saddled against his groin.

Roses. He smelled them again. Stronger now. Making him feel strangely lightheaded. He inhaled reflexively and noticed something else. Something warm and buttery, with the faint tinge of apple. Tarts, he realized. In her basket.

Her struggles roused him from the momentary lapse. "I mean you no harm, lass," he whispered.

But his body was responding to her in a manner that might be construed otherwise, crackling like wildfire at her movement. A hard shock of awareness coursed through him. She had a tiny waist, but he could feel the unmistakable heaviness of very full, very lush breasts on his arm. A rush of heat pooled in his groin.

He couldn't remember the last time he'd had a woman. Hell of a time to think about it now.

Her guardsman must have heard the movement. The knight spun around. "M'lady?"

Seeing her in Arthur's hold, he reached for his sword.

"Shhh . . ." Arthur warned softly. He kept his voice low, both to avoid being heard and to disguise his voice. "I'm trying to help. You need to get out of here." He relaxed his hold on her mouth. "I'm going to let go of you, but don't scream. Not unless you want to bring them down on us. Do you understand?"

She nodded, and slowly he released her.

She spun around to face him. In the tree-shrouded moonlight, all he could see were two big, round eyes staring up at him from under the deep hood of her cloak.

"Bring who down on us? Who are you?"

Her voice was soft and sweet, and thankfully low enough not to carry. He hoped.

Her gaze slid over him. He'd traveled lightly tonight as he always did when he was working, wearing only a blackened habergeon shirt and coif of mail, and gamboissed leather chausses. But they were fine, and from his helm (which he'd lowered to cover his face) and weaponry, it was clear he was a knight. "You're not a rebel," she observed, confirming what he'd already guessed of her sympathies. She was no friend of Bruce.

"Answer the lady," her companion said, "or you'll feel the point of my sword."

Arthur resisted the urge to laugh. The knight was all brute strength and moved about as deftly as a barge. But cognizant of the situation, he didn't want to take the time to prove the soldier wrong. He needed to get them out of here as quickly and quietly as possible.

"A friend, my lady," he said. "A knight in the service of King Edward."

For now at least.

Suddenly, he stilled. Something had changed. He couldn't describe how he knew, other than a disturbance in the back of his consciousness and the sensation that the air had shifted.

Bruce's men were coming. They'd been discovered.

He cursed. This wasn't good. No more time to convince her gently. "You must leave now," he said in a steely voice that brokered no argument.

He caught the flare of alarm in her gaze. She, too, must have sensed the danger.

But it was too late. For all of them.

He gave her a hard shove, pushing her behind the nearest tree moments before the soft whiz of arrows pierced the night air. The arrow meant for the lass landed with a thud in the tree that now shielded her, but another had found its mark. Her guardsman groaned as a perfectly shot arrow pierced through his mail shirt to settle in his gut.

Arthur barely had time to react. He turned his shoulder at the last moment as the arrow meant for his heart pinned his shoulder instead. Gritting his teeth, he grabbed the shaft and snapped it off. He didn't think the arrowhead had penetrated deeply, but he didn't want to risk trying to pull it out right now.

Bruce's men thought he was one of the couriers. An understandable mistake, but one that put him in the horrible predicament of battling his compatriots to defend himself or betray his cover.

He could still get away.

Maybe they would realize it was a lass? But he couldn't make himself believe it. If he left, she would die.

Arthur barely had time to process the thought, for in the next moment all hell broke loose. Bruce's men were on them, bursting out of the darkness like demons from hell. The lady's guardsman, still staggering from the arrow, took a spear in the side and a battle-axe in the head. He toppled to the ground like a big oak tree, landing with a heavy thud.

Arthur heard a startled cry behind him and, anticipating

the impulse, blocked the lass's path before she could rush
forward to help the fallen soldier. He was past help.

But one of Bruce's men must have caught the movement.

Arthur's next move was nothing but instinct. It was too
fast to be anything else. A spear hurdled through the air,
heading straight for her. He didn't think, he reacted.
Reaching up, he snatched the spear in his hand midair,
catching it only a few feet from her head. In one swift
movement he brought it down across his knee and snapped
it in two, tossing the splintered pieces to the ground.

He heard her startled gasp but didn't dare take his eyes
from the score of men rushing toward him. "Get behind
the damned tree," he shouted angrily, before turning to
block a blow of a sword from the right. The man left him
an opening, which Arthur didn't take.

He swore, fending off another. What the hell should he
do? Reveal himself? Would they believe him? He could
fight his way out, but there was the lass to consider . . .

A moment later the decision was taken from him.

A man's voice rang out from the trees, "Hold!" The warriors seemed confused but immediately did as the new-
comer bid, stopping in their tracks. Seconds later, a
familiar figure stepped out of the shadows. "Ranger, what
in the hell are you doing here?"

Shaking his head with disbelief, Arthur stepped forward
to greet the black-clad warrior who'd emerged from the
trees. Gregor MacGregor. That certainly explained the perfect arrow shot he'd noticed earlier. MacGregor was the
best archer in the Highlands, giving proof to the *nom de
guerre* of "Arrow" chosen by Bruce to protect his identity
as a member of the Highland Guard.

Arthur wasn't sure whether or not he should be grateful
to see his former enemy turned Highland Guard partner,
and at one time, the closest thing he had to a friend. That
had changed when Arthur had been forced to leave the
Highland Guard over a year and a half ago. At the time,

none of his fellow guardsmen—including MacGregor—
had known the truth. When they'd heard he'd joined with
the enemy they'd thought him a traitor. Though they'd
eventually learned the truth, his role had kept him apart.

They clasped forearms, and despite his initial hesitation,
Arthur found himself grinning beneath his helm. Damn, it
was good to see him. "I see that no one's messed up that
pretty face of yours yet," he said, knowing how much
MacGregor's renowned good looks bothered him.

MacGregor laughed. "They're working on it. It's
damned good to see you. But what are you doing here?
You're lucky I saw you catch that spear."

Arthur had once saved MacGregor's life doing the same
thing. It wasn't as difficult as it looked—if you could get
past the fear. Most couldn't.

"Sorry about the arrow," MacGregor said, pointing
toward Arthur's left shoulder where blood was oozing
from around the splintered staff, an inch of which was still
protruding from his arm.

Arthur shrugged. "It's nothing." He'd had worse.

"You know this traitor, Captain?" one of the men asked.

"Aye," MacGregor said, before Arthur could caution
him. "And he's no traitor. He's one of ours."

Damn. The lass. He'd forgotten about the lass. Any hope
that she might not have heard MacGregor or grasped the
significance was dashed when he heard her sharp intake of
breath.

MacGregor heard it, too. He reached for his bow, but
Arthur shook him off.

"It's safe," he said. "You can come out now, lass."

"Lass?" MacGregor swore under his breath. "So that's
what this is about."

The woman moved out from behind the tree. When
Arthur reached to take her elbow, she stiffened as if his
touch offended. Aye, she'd heard all right.

Her hood had slid back in the chaos, revealing long,

shimmering locks of golden-brown hair falling in thick, heavy waves down her back. The sheer beauty of it seemed so out of place, it temporarily startled him. And when a sliver of moonlight fell upon her face, Arthur's breath caught in a hard, fierce jolt.

Christ, she was lovely. Her tiny heart-shaped face was dominated by large, heavily lashed eyes. Her nose was small and slightly turned, her chin pointed, and her brows softly arched. Her lips were a perfectly shaped pink bow and her skin . . . her skin was as smooth and velvety as cream. She had that sweet, vulnerable look of a small, fluffy animal—a kitten or a rabbit, perhaps.

The innocent breath of femininity was not what he was expecting and seemed utterly incongruous in the midst of war.

He could only stare in stunned silence as MacGregor— the whoreson—stepped forward, peeled off his nasal helm, and gallantly bowed over her hand.

"My apologies, my lady," he said with a smile that had felled half the female hearts in the Highlands—the other half he'd yet to meet. "We were expecting someone else."

Arthur heard the lass's predictable gasp when she beheld the face of the man reputed to be the most handsome in the Highlands. But she quickly composed herself and, to his surprise, seemed remarkably lucid. Most women were babbling by now. "Obviously. Does King Hood make war on women now?" she asked, using the English slur for the outlawed king. She eyed the church up ahead. "Or merely priests."

For someone surrounded by enemies, she showed a surprising lack of fear. If the fine ermine-lined cloak hadn't given her away, he would have known she was a noblewoman from the pride in her manner alone.

MacGregor winced. "As I said, it was a mistake. King Robert makes war only on those who deny him what is rightfully his."

She made a sharp sound of disagreement. "If we are done here, I've come to fetch the priest." Her eyes fell on her fallen guardsman. "It is too late for my man, but perhaps he can still give release to those who await him at the castle."

Last rites, Arthur realized. Probably for those wounded in the battle of Glen Trool a week's past.

Though the helm covered his face, he kept his voice low, to further mask his identity. His cover had been jeopardized enough—he didn't want there to be any chance that she would be able to identify him.

She had to be related to one of the nobles who'd been called to Ayr to hunt Bruce. He'd make sure to stay away from the castle—far away. "What is your name, my lady? And why do you travel with such a paltry guard?"

She stiffened, looking down her tiny nose at him. With the adorable little upturn, it should have been ridiculous, but she managed a surprisingly effective amount of disdain. "Fetching a priest is usually not a dangerous task—as I'm sure even a spy can attest."

Arthur's mouth fell in a hard line. So much for gratitude. Perhaps he should have left her to her fate.

MacGregor stepped forward. "You owe this man your life, my lady. If he hadn't interfered," he nodded toward her fallen guardsman, "you both would have been dead."

Her eyes widened, and tiny white teeth bit down on the soft pillow of her lower lip. Arthur felt another unwelcome tug beneath his belt.

"I'm sorry," she said softly, turning to him. "Thank you."

Gratitude from a beautiful woman was not without effect. The tug in his groin pulled a little harder, the lilting huskiness of her voice making him think of beds, naked flesh, and whispered moans of pleasure.

"Your shoulder . . ." She gazed up at him uncertainly. "Is it hurt badly?"

Before he could form a response, he heard a noise. His gaze shot through the trees to the church, noticing the signs of movement.

Damn. The sound of the attack must have alerted the occupants of the church.

"You need to go," he said to MacGregor. "They're coming."

MacGregor had seen firsthand Arthur's skills too many times to hesitate. He motioned his men to go. As quickly as they'd arrived, Bruce's warriors slipped back into the darkness of the trees.

"Next time," MacGregor said, before following them.

Arthur met his gaze in shared understanding. There would be no silver tonight. In a few moments the church would be swarming with men and lit up like a beacon, warning anyone who approached of the danger.

Because of one lass, Bruce would not have the silver to provision his men. They would have to rely on what they could hunt and scavenge from the countryside until another opportunity came.

"You had best go, too," the lass said stiffly. He hesitated, and she seemed to soften. "I'll be fine. Go." She paused. "And thank you."

Their eyes met in the darkness. Though he knew it was ridiculous, for a moment he felt exposed.

But she couldn't see him. With his helm down, the only openings in the steel were the two narrow slits for him to see and the small pinpricks for him to breathe.

Still, he felt something strange. If he didn't know better, he'd say it was a connection. But he didn't have connections with strange women. Hell, he didn't have connections with anyone. It kept things simpler that way.

He wanted to say something—though hell if he knew what—but he didn't have the chance. Torches appeared outside the church. A priest and a few of the wounded English soldiers were heading this way.

"You're welcome," he said, and slipped back into the shadows where he belonged. A wraith. A man who didn't exist. Just the way he liked it.

Her sob of relief as she threw herself into the arms of the priest followed him into the darkness.

He knew he should regret what happened tonight. In saving her life, he'd sacrificed not only the silver, but also his cover. But he couldn't regret it. There would be more silver. And their paths were unlikely to cross again—he'd make sure of it.

His secret was safe.

One

Please, let him be dead. Please, let it finally be over.

Anna MacDougall set her basket down and knelt at her father's feet, praying to hear the news that would put an end to the war that had marked every day of her life.

Literally.

Anna had been born on a momentous day in the history of Scotland: the nineteenth of March, the year of Our Lord twelve hundred eighty-six. The very day that King Alexander III had ignored the advice of his men and raced to Kinghorn in Fife on a stormy night to be with his young bride—sliding off a cliff and falling to his death on the way. The king's lust had left his country without a direct heir to the throne, resulting in twenty-two years of war and strife to determine who should wear its crown.

At one time there had been fourteen competitors for the throne. But the true battle had always been between the Balliol-Comyn faction and the Bruces. When Robert Bruce took matters into his own hands two years ago and killed his chief competitor, John "The Red" Comyn—her father's cousin—he'd made a blood enemy of the MacDougalls forever. Only their MacDonald kinsmen were despised as much as Robert Bruce. Bruce's actions had forced the MacDougalls into an uneasy alliance with England.

Even Edward Plantagenet was better than having a Bruce on the throne.

And it was Bruce's death that she prayed for now. Ever since word had arrived that in the middle of his campaign north he'd taken to his sickbed with a mysterious illness, she'd prayed for the ailment to claim him. For nature to vanquish their enemy. Of course, it was a terrible sin to pray for a man's death. *Any* man's death. Even a murderous scourge like Robert Bruce. The nuns at the abbey would be horrified.

But she didn't care. Not if it meant the end to this bloody, godforsaken war. The war that already had claimed her brother and fiancé, and had taken its toll not only on her aging grandfather, Alexander MacDougall, Lord of Argyll, but also on his son—her father, John MacDougall, Lord of Lorn.

Her father had barely recovered from the most recent bout of chest pains. She didn't know how much more he could take. Bruce's recent success had only made it worse. Her father hated to lose.

It was hard to believe that a little over a year ago "King Hood" had been on the run with only a handful of supporters, his cause all but lost. But the fugitive king had returned and, thanks in large part to the death of Edward I of England, resurrected his bid for Scotland's throne.

So sinful or not, she prayed for the death of their enemy. She would gladly do the penance for her wicked thoughts if it meant protecting her father and clan from the man who would see them destroyed.

Besides, as the nuns had told her countless times before, she'd never been destined for the life of a nun anyway. She sang too much. Laughed too much. And most importantly, had never been as devoted to God as she was to her family.

Anna studied her father's face, gauging it for any reac-

tion, as he tore open the missive and read. In his anxious-
ness, he hadn't even bothered to call for his clerk. She'd
been fortunate to find him alone in his solar, having just
finished a council with his men. Her mother, usually found
anxiously fussing at his side, had gone to the garden to
oversee the picking of herbs for a new tincture suggested by
the priest to help clear the bogginess from her father's
lungs.

She could tell right away that the news was not good. A
dangerous flush reddened his well-lined face, his eyes grew
bright as if with fever, and his mouth fell in a thin white
line. It was a look that struck fear in the hearts of the most
hardened of warriors, but in Anna it only provoked concern. She knew the loving father beneath the gruff warrior's exterior.

She clutched the arm of the thronelike chair upon which
he sat, the carving biting into her palm. "What is it, Father? What's happened?"

His gaze lifted to hers. She felt a flash of fear, seeing the
rising anger. Her father's apoplectic rage had always been a
terrifying sight—rivaling the infamous Angevin temper of
the Plantagenet kings of England—but never more so than
after his attack. Anger is what had caused the pains in his
arm and chest last time. Pains that had frozen him, cut off
his breath, and put him in bed for nearly two months.

He crumpled the parchment in a ball in his fist. "Buchan
has fled. The Comyns have been defeated."

She blinked. It took her a moment to comprehend what
he'd said as it seemed impossible. John Comyn, the Earl of
Buchan—kinsman to John Comyn the murdered Lord of
Badenoch—was one of the most powerful men in Scotland.

"But how?" she asked. "Bruce was hovering near
death."

Her father had always encouraged his children to ask
questions. He deplored ignorance, even in women, which
was why he'd insisted that all his daughters be educated at

the convent. But seeing his face flame and body stiffen with rage, she almost wished her question back.

"Even from his sickbed the scourge manages miracles," he said disgustedly. "The people already think him some kind of hero—like the bloody second coming of Arthur and Camelot. Buchan had the bastard pinned near Inverurie, but his men faltered when they saw 'The Bruce' at the head of the army." He slammed his fist down on the table beside him, sending wine sloshing from his goblet. "The Comyns ran like cowards at the sight of a sick man being carried into battle. They fled from a damned invalid!"

His face turned so red that the veins in his temples started to bulge.

Fear clutched her chest. Not because she feared his anger, but because of the danger to his health. She fought back the tears that sprang to her eyes. Her fiercely proud father would see her tears as a sign that she thought him weak. He was a powerful warrior, not a man who needed to be coddled.

But this war was killing him as surely as a slow poison. If she could just get him through this trouble with Bruce, everything would be all right. Why couldn't the false king have just succumbed to illness the way he was supposed to? This would all be over.

She had to calm him. Instead of using tears and pleas, she took his hand and forced a teasing smile to her face. "You'd better not let Mother hear you talk like that around me. You know she blames you for my 'unmaidenly' vocabulary." For a moment she feared her words had not penetrated, but slowly the haze of anger started to dissipate. When he finally looked at her as if he really saw her, she added innocently, "Perhaps I should I call for her?"

He let out a sharp bark of laughter, muddled by the heaviness in his lungs. "Don't you dare. She'll force another one of those revolting potions down my throat. Lord knows your mother means well, but she would drive a saint to perdition with her constant worrying." He shook his head, giving her a fond look that told her he knew exactly what she had done. "You've nothing to fear, you know. I'm perfectly hale." His eyes narrowed. "But you are a shrewd lass, Annie-love. More like me than any of the others. Haven't I always told you so?"

Anna dimpled with pleasure at the compliment. "Yes, Father."

He continued as if she hadn't responded. "Since the day you toddled into my solar with your thumb in your mouth, took one look at the battle map, and moved our men to the perfect place to attack."

She laughed, having no memory of the day but having heard the story many times before. "I thought the carved figures were toys," she said.

"Ah, but your instincts were pure." He sighed. "But I fear it will not be so simple this time. Buchan writes that he will seek refuge in England. With the Comyns defeated, the usurper will turn to us."

Us? She swallowed hard. Dread settled over her. "But what about the truce?"

Months ago, when Bruce had first started his march north, he'd turned his eye briefly to battling the men of Argyll, threatening them by land and by sea. Her father, ill and undermanned, had agreed to a truce—as had the Earl of Ross to their north. She'd hoped the truce would mean an end to the fighting.

"It expires on the Ides of August. The day after, we can expect to see the fiend at our gate. He's chased off the MacDowells in Galloway, and with the Comyns gone . . ." Her father frowned his disgust again.

Sensing a return of his anger, she reminded him, "The Earl of Buchan has never been a good battle commander. You've said so many times before. King Hood would not have been so lucky against you, which is no doubt why he sought a truce in the first place. Dal Righ is still too fresh in his memory."

Her father fingered the chunky silver brooch he wore at his neck. The large oval crystal surrounded by tiny pearls was a talisman of just how close he'd come to capturing the fugitive king. They'd had Bruce in their grasp—literally—the brooch coming off in the struggle.

She could tell by the hint of a smile around his mouth that her words had pleased him. "You're right, but our previous victory will not stop him this time. We're all that's left between him and the crown."

"But what of the Earl of Ross?" she said. "Surely, he will fight with us?"

Her father's mouth tightened. "Ross cannot be counted on. He will be reluctant to leave his lands unprotected. But I will try to persuade him that we must join forces to defeat King Hood once and for all."

There was nothing reproachful in her father's manner, but Anna felt a twinge of guilt nonetheless. Persuading Ross might have been made easier if she'd accepted the proposal of his son Hugh last year.

"I will call my barons and knights and send word to Edward requesting aid. He is not half the king that his father was, but perhaps Comyn's defeat will finally force him to see the imperative of sending more men north."

But he didn't sound hopeful. Anna knew as well as her father not to expect much help from Edward II. The new English king had too many troubles of his own to worry about Scotland. Though English soldiers were still garrisoned in many key castles around Scotland—especially along the borders—Edward had recalled many of his commanders, including Aymer de Valence, the new Earl of Pembroke.

She bit her lip. "And if help does not arrive?"

She knew better than to ask her father whether he would submit. He would see them all dead before he kneeled to a

Bruce. "To Conquer or Die." The MacDougall motto lived
strong in her father.

Despite the warmth of the solar, she shivered.

"Then I shall defeat the bastard alone. I nearly had him
at Dal Righ—coming damned near to killing him in the
process. This time I intend to finish the job." His eyes narrowed dangerously. "By the end of summer, Robert Bruce's
head will be on my gate with vultures plucking at his eyes."

Anna ignored the twinge of discomfort. She hated when
her father talked like that. It made him seem cruel and
ruthless, not the father she adored.

She gazed up at him, seeing the firm resolve set on his
grizzled features, and did not doubt him for a moment. Her
father was one of the greatest warriors and military commanders in Scotland. Fate might be moving against them,
but John of Lorn would stop it.

Maybe an end to the war was in sight after all. The uncertainty, the death, the destruction, the deceit—it would
all be over. The poison that was killing her father would be
gone. Her family would be safe. She would marry and have
a home and children of her own. Everything would be
blissfully *normal*.

She couldn't let herself contemplate the alternative. But
sometimes it felt as if she were trying to hold back a waterfall with a sieve or swimming against a whirlpool that was
determined to drag them all under: her parents, her sisters
and brothers, her little nephews and nieces.

She couldn't let that happen. Whatever it took, she
would protect her family. "What can I do?"

Her father smiled, giving her an indulgent pinch on the
cheek. "You're a good lass, Annie-love. What say you of a
visit to my cousin the Bishop?"

She nodded and started to get to her feet.

"And Anna," he paused, giving her an amused look as
she picked up her basket. "Don't forget the tarts." He
laughed. "You know how fond he is of them."

Near Inverurie, Aberdeenshire

A full moon hung over the ancient stone monument, but gauzy plumes of smoke from the nearby fires filtered the light in a ghostly haze. Victory tasted acrid on Arthur's tongue and burned the back of his throat. It was near midnight, but the distant sounds of revelry and rampant destruction still filled the smoky night air. Bruce had taken William Wallace's lessons to heart, scorching the earth, leaving nothing in his wake that could be used by his enemies. Comyn had been chased from Scotland, but the harrying of Buchan would not be over for some time.

The single shard of granite in the clearing seemed to point to the heavens at an angle that could only be purposeful. To what purpose he could only guess. Too many years had passed and the intent of the mystical druid stones had been lost. But as the stones were often placed in isolated locations, they served as convenient meeting places.

Arthur watched the clearing from the shadows of the circle of trees that surrounded it, uncharacteristically impatient for the men to appear. He hoped this was finally the end of the deception. He was tired of living a lie. After years of pretending, sometimes it was hard to remember what side he was on.

Other than across the battlefield, this would be the first time he'd seen the man he'd been fighting for in nearly two and a half years—since the day he'd been forced to leave his training as a member of the Highland Guard to "join" the enemy. The fact that the king was risking meeting with him in person was what made him think his days as a spy might be at an end.

Arthur had done his job well, providing key information before the battle at Inverurie that had enabled Bruce and his men to defeat the Earl of Buchan and send him scurrying to England with his tail between his legs. With the Comyns defeated, Arthur hoped to take his place among the other members of the Highland Guard—they were the best of the best, an elite band of warriors handpicked by Bruce for their skills in each discipline of warfare.

He stilled, his gaze shooting to a break in the trees to the right. The faint scurry of a rabbit or squirrel was the first sound to signal their arrival. Being attuned to the smallest details, the slightest observations, were what set him apart. Soundlessly, he cut a diagonal path through the trees, coming up on them from behind.

Once he confirmed their identity, he identified himself by the hoot of an owl.

The three men spun around, swords drawn, obviously startled.

His brother Neil was the first to recover. "God's bones, even better than I thought! We're still at least fifty paces from the clearing." He turned and grinned at the tall, fearsome-looking man beside him. "You owe me a shilling."

Tor MacLeod, the captain of the Highland Guard, made a sharp sound of disgust, murmuring a few choice words.

Neil ignored him and strode forward to greet Arthur, not bothering to hide his pleasure. "You've gotten even better, brother." At Arthur's questioning glance toward MacLeod, Neil explained, "I bet that stubborn barbarian over there that you would find us before we reached the clearing—no matter how quiet we were. You've put a nick in that steely Highland pride of his."

Arthur had to bite back a smile. Tor MacLeod was the greatest warrior in the Highlands and Western Isles; his pride didn't get nicked. But clearly Arthur had impressed his captain—and his brother.

Neil, his eldest brother, was nearly twenty-four years Arthur's senior, and in many ways like a father to him. Even though Arthur now towered over his older brother by nearly half a foot, he would always look up to him. If there was anyone responsible for who he was today, it was Neil.

He'd picked Arthur up out of the mud as a boy more times than he could remember when his other brothers were trying to make a warrior of him. Neil was the one who'd encouraged Arthur to hone his skills, not to bury them. To be proud of the abilities that had made everyone else in his family uncomfortable.

He owed his brother more than he could ever repay. But he'd never stop trying.

MacLeod came forward to greet him, grasping his hand and forearm in the same manner that his brother had. "I've not had a chance to thank you for what you did," he said, his expression strangely intense. "Without your intervention my wife—" He stopped. "I am in your debt."

Arthur nodded. Two years before, right before Bruce had made his bid for the crown, Arthur had prevented MacLeod's wife from being killed. He'd been in the right place at the right time, only recently "kicked out" of the guard.

"I hear congratulations are in order, Chief," Arthur said using the war name given to him to protect his identity.

The stone-faced captain of the Highland Guard broke out into a rare smile. "Aye," he said. "I have a daughter. Beatrix, named after her aunt."

Neil laughed. "I don't think he held her for a week—he was afraid of breaking her."

Tor scowled at him, but didn't argue.

The third man stepped forward. Shorter than the other two, he was still an impressive figure. Wide-shouldered, with the thick, heavy muscles of a warrior despite the recent illness that had taken its toll on his health, he wore a full suit of mail and a gold tabard emblazoned with the red rampant lion beneath his dark cloak. Even if the rough-cut features and dark pointed beard were not visible beneath his steel bascinet, Arthur would know him by the majestic aura that surrounded him.

He dropped to his knee and bowed his head before King Robert Bruce. "Sire," he said.

The king acknowledged his fealty with a nod. "Rise, Sir Arthur." He came forward to grasp his forearm with a shake. "So that I may thank you for the service you have done us at Inverurie. Without your information we wouldn't have mounted an immediate counterattack. You were right. Buchan and his forces were ill-prepared and collapsed with barely a nudge."

Arthur scanned the king's face, seeing the gray pallor and lines of strain. MacLeod had surreptitiously come up beside the king, subtly giving him support, but Arthur was surprised to see the king walking at all. He suspected there were men waiting not far away to help carry him back to camp. "You are well, my lord?"

Bruce nodded. "Our victory against Comyn has been a far better cure than any tinctures the priests have cooked up. I am much improved."

"The king insisted on thanking you himself," MacLeod said, a note of censure in his tone.

But the king didn't seem to mind. "Your brother and Chief are as protective as two old crones."

MacLeod led the king to a low rock for him to sit on, and said unrepentantly, "It's my job."

The king looked as if he might argue, but realized the futility and turned to Arthur. "That is why we are here," he said. "I have a new job for you."

This was it. The moment he'd been waiting for. "You wish for me to rejoin the Guard," he finished.

There was an awkward pause.

The king frowned; obviously it wasn't what he'd been about to say. "Nay, not yet. Your skills have proved too valuable working for the other side. But we've been made aware of a new opportunity."

New opportunity. He wasn't returning to the Guard. If

Arthur felt any disappointment at the king's news, he didn't admit it.

It was better if he stayed on his own. He'd never been comfortable in groups anyway. He liked the freedom of making his own decisions. Not having to explain himself or account for himself to anyone. As a knight in his brother Dugald's household, he could pretty much come and go as he pleased.

As was the case for many families in Scotland, the Campbells had been split apart by the war. Arthur's brothers Neil, Donald, and Duncan were for Bruce, but his brothers Dugald and Gillespie were aligned with the Earl of Ross and England.

The division in his family had made placing him in the enemy camp that much easier.

"What kind of opportunity?" he asked.

"To infiltrate the very heart of the enemy."

Infiltrate. That meant getting close. Something Arthur tried to avoid. It was why he'd never attached himself to a noble as most knights did. "I work better alone, my lord." On the outside. Where he could blend in and stay in the background. Where he could go unnoticed.

Neil, who knew him well, smiled. "I don't think you'll mind this time."

Arthur's gaze snapped to his brother's. The satisfaction he read there made him realize what this meant.

"Lorn?" The single word fell with the force of a smith's hammer.

Neil nodded, a smile of anticipation curling his mouth. "This is the chance we've been waiting for."

MacLeod explained. "John of Lorn has put out the call to his barons and knights. Your brothers will answer. Go with them. Find out what the MacDougalls are planning, how many men they have, and who will join them. They're getting messengers past our men and I want you to stop them. We want to keep them as isolated as possible until the truce expires. I have Hawk watching the seaways, but I need you on the land."

It was land that Arthur knew well. Argyll was Campbell land. He'd been born at Innis Chonnel, a castle in the middle of Loch Awe, and had lived there until the MacDougalls had stolen it.

Arthur felt a rush of pure anticipation course through him. This was the moment he'd been waiting for for a long time. Fourteen years, to be exact. Since the moment John of Lorn had treacherously stabbed his father right before his eyes. Arthur hadn't seen it coming. It was the only time his senses had failed him.

Even if Neil hadn't asked it, even if Bruce hadn't offered him lands and the promise of a rich bride to fight on his side, Arthur would have joined Bruce for the chance to destroy John of Lorn and the MacDougalls.

Blood for blood was the Highland way. He wouldn't fail his brother the way he had his father.

Mistaking the source of his silence as objection, MacLeod continued. "With your knowledge of the terrain, there is no one better suited for the job. You've spent over two years establishing your false allegiance for just this type of mission. Lorn might not like having Campbells around, but with the feud ended by Edward and your brother Dugald reconciled to him some time ago, he has no reason to think you are anything other than what you seem."

"Hell, Lorn's uncle fights with us," Bruce added, referring to Duncan MacDougall of Dunollie. "Divided families are something he knows well enough."

"John of Lorn doesn't know what you saw, brother," Neil said quietly, referring to Arthur's witnessing of their father's death. "Do what you always do. Lie low and observe. For someone so big," he said with a fond smile, recalling that it hadn't always been that way, "you're amazingly adept at going unnoticed. Stay out of Lorn's way. And have care—he might be suspicious initially, so don't turn your back on him."

He knew that better than anyone. But Arthur didn't need to be convinced. Any resistance he might have had to infiltrating the household of the enemy had vanished at the mention of Lorn.

"Well?" Bruce said.

Arthur met his gaze, a slow, deadly smile spreading across his face. "How soon can I leave?"

He'd see John of Lorn destroyed and enjoy every bloody moment of it.

Nothing was going to stand in his way.

Two

❧

Less than three weeks after the meeting with the king near the standing stone, Arthur Campbell was here. In the belly of the beast, the den of the lion, the lair of the devil: Dunstaffnage Castle, the formidable stronghold of Clan MacDougall.

Gathered in the Great Hall with the other knights and men-at-arms who'd answered the call, awaiting their turn before the dais, Arthur tried not to think about the importance of what was to come. If there was a time that John of Lorn would focus his attention on him, this would be it.

He scanned the room with his usual intensity, taking note of all the the potential ways in and out. Not that escape would be likely. If Lorn learned what he was about, Arthur would be hard pressed to make it out of there alive. But instinct was also habit—it was better to be prepared. For anything.

Taking in the details of the room, he had to admit he was impressed. The castle was one of the finest he'd ever seen. Built about eighty years ago, Dunstaffnage was strategically situated on a small promontory of land where the Firth of Lorn met the southern shore of Loch Etive, thus guarding a key western seaward approach into Scotland. Constructed on a base of rock, the massive lime-coated walls extended about fifty feet up from the ground, with round towers on three of the four corners. The largest of these towers, next to the Great Hall, served as the donjon, housing the lord's private chambers.

The design and architecture of the castle reflected the power of the man who'd built it. Still part of Norway at the time it of its construction, its builder, Duncan, son of Dugald, son of the mighty Somerled, had been invested with the title of *ri Innse Gall*, King of the Isles. A title the MacDougalls still took to heart.

The castle did indeed befit a king. The Great Hall took up the entire first floor of the eastern range, spanning about one hundred feet by thirty feet. The wood-beamed ceilings had to be at least fifty feet at the highest point. Intricately carved wooden paneling fit for the nave of a church adorned the eastern entrance wall, while the others were plastered and decorated with colorful banners and fine tapestries.

A massive fireplace on the inner long wall of the castle provided heat, and two double lancet windows on the opposite outer wall allowed for an unusual amount of natural light. Trestle tables and benches lined the main floor of the room, and a dais had been erected at the end of the room opposite the entrance. In the middle of the massive wooden table that spanned its length was a large wooden throne.

Though Alexander MacDougall, Lord of Argyll, the chief and head of Clan MacDougall, still occupied that chair, it was the cold-hearted bastard seated to his right who wielded its power. Alexander MacDougall was an old man—at least seventy by Arthur's reckoning; years ago, he'd delegated his authority to his eldest son and heir, John, Lord of Lorn.

This was the closest Arthur had been to the man who'd killed his father in years, and the intense hatred that gripped him surprised him. He wasn't used to such fierce emotion, but his chest burned with it.

He'd been waiting so many years for this moment, he thought it might be anticlimactic. It wasn't. If anything, he was surprised by how anxious he was to see it done. It would be easy—and damned tempting—to surprise him with a dirk in his back. But unlike his enemy, he would kill him face-to-face. On a battlefield.

And killing Lorn wasn't part of his mission. Yet.

His enemy had aged, he realized. Gray now streaked his dark hair and the lines that marked his face had started to sag. Arthur had heard rumors of an illness and wondered if there might be some truth to them. But the eyes were the same. Cold and calculating. The eyes of a despot who would stop at nothing to win.

Afraid of what he might unconsciously reveal, or that MacDougall would somehow be able to sense the threat, Arthur forced his gaze away from the dais.

He had to be careful. *Damned* careful to give nothing away. If he was discovered, Arthur knew the best he could hope for was a quick death. The worst was a long one.

But he wasn't overly concerned. There were at least a score of knights and five times that many men-at-arms who'd answered Lorn's call. He wouldn't be noticed. Neil was right; he was good at fading into the background and not drawing attention to himself.

Though he wished he could say the same for his brother. He winced as Dugald let out a loud bellow of laughter, cuffing his squire in the jaw with the back of his hand. Blood dripped from his lip.

Arthur felt a twinge of sympathy for the lad, having been on the bad side of his brother's fist more times than he could count when he was a youth. But sympathy wouldn't do the lad any good. Not if he wanted to be a warrior. It was part of the lad's training, intended to toughen him up.

Eventually he would learn to stop reacting. Not feeling would take longer.

"What lass is going to notice a whelp like you with me around?" Dugald laughed.

The squire blushed hotly, and Arthur felt even sorrier for him. The lad was going to be miserable until he learned to control his emotions. Dugald would hone in on that weakness until it was pounded out of him. Like their father, being a warrior—a fierce warrior—was all that was important to him. Except for the lasses.

Dugald might be an overbearing braggart at times, but it was not without cause. Though not quite as tall as Arthur, his brother was powerfully built and undeniably a formidable warrior. He was also reputed to be the most handsome of the six brothers and took to his role with relish.

"I didn't think they'd look at me," the squire said, his deep red face matching the color of his hair. "I just wondered if they'd be as fair as they are reputed to be."

"Who?" Arthur said.

"St. Columba's bones, little brother." For a moment, Dugald looked as if he wanted to cuff Arthur, too. But Arthur wasn't a lad anymore. He would fight back. Though he'd been careful to keep his skills hidden—initially as a means of self-preservation, and now to not have those skills used against his compatriots—he wondered if Dugald sensed that the balance of power had shifted between them. He pushed him, but only so far. "Where have you been living? In a cave with King Hood?" Dugald laughed even louder, drawing a few eyes in their direction. "Lorn's daughters are reputed to be rare beauties—particularly the middle one, the fair Lady Mary."

Arthur wasn't the least bit intrigued. Reports of noblewomen's beauty were often exaggerated. Besides, he doubted any of them could hold a candle to MacLeod's wife. He'd seen Christina Fraser only once, but he'd thought her the most beautiful woman he'd ever seen.

Another face flashed before his eyes—this one more
sweet than classically beautiful—before he pushed it away
with a frown. Strange that he still thought of the lass from
the church though more than a year had passed. The king
had been furious to lose the silver—especially when they
learned it was double the amount they'd originally
thought—but had understood why Arthur interfered.

"They have one fatal flaw," he pointed out.

The squire looked confused, but Dugald understood. His
brother's expression fell, his mouth tightening in a hard
line. His ambitious brother might have seen the advantage
of siding with Ross and King Edward—and by necessity
the MacDougalls—but Dugald didn't like Lorn any better
than Arthur did. "Aye, you're right about that, little
brother."

"What flaw?" the squire ventured to ask. The lad had
courage, Arthur thought, knowing what was to come.

Dugald clopped the boy again. "You'd better hope it's
blindness, if you want any of the lasses to notice you."

Another hour of his brother's loud conversation passed
before it was their turn. At last, Arthur followed his
brother forward to pledge his sword to MacDougall. As
the head of the family, at least as far as England and the
Earl of Ross were concerned (his three older brothers having been declared rebels), Dugald spoke for them all.
Alexander MacDougall handled the formalities, but
Arthur sensed Lorn's immediate interest.

"Sir Dugald of Torsa. . . ." Lorn left off contemplatively.
"One of Colin Mor's sons," he said, giving him a long,
steady look. "Not the eldest, though."

His quick-tempered, hotheaded brother replied with surprising equanimity. "Nay, my lord. My eldest three brothers fight with the rebels." As Lorn well knew. "And your
uncle," Dugald added with just the right tinge of sarcasm.

Lorn's mouth thinned; he obviously didn't appreciate the
reminder of his traitorous kinsman. "I remember your

brother Neil," he said, looking his brother straight in the eye. "He fought well at the battle of Red Ford."

Red Ford. The battle between the MacDougalls and Campbells over their lands in Loch Awe. The battle where their father had been cut down in cold blood. By Lorn.

Lorn—the bastard—was baiting them. Dugald knew it. Arthur knew it. But only Arthur wanted to kill him for it. Dugald hadn't seen what he had. The great Colin Mor Campbell had died like a warrior on the battlefield, but only Arthur had witnessed the treacherous manner in which he had been killed. It would have been his word against Lorn's. Neil was right to have protected him. He would never have been believed.

"I suppose you would have been too young," Lorn said offhandedly.

Dugald nodded. "I was a squire at the time with the MacNabs."

His point was taken. The reminder of Dugald's bond with the MacDougalls' closest allies and neighboring clan was enough. Lorn seemed satisfied, and Arthur felt himself relax.

The hardest part was over. They'd passed initial scrutiny and had been accepted into the fold. With any luck, this would be the last time Lorn noticed him.

They were about to move away, when the door flew open and the sound of laughter floated across the room.

A girl's laughter. Light and full of uncomplicated joy. It was a laugh unlike any he'd heard in a long time, and it filled him with a strange sense of longing.

He glanced over his shoulder, but with the crowd of soldiers filling the hall, he couldn't see the source.

Suddenly the crowd parted like the Red Sea, creating an aisle down the middle of the room. The loud, boisterous din of men's voices evaporated into stunned silence.

A moment later, two girls came rushing forward toward the dais. The first was one of the most beautiful creatures

he'd ever seen—a blond-haired rival to MacLeod's wife.
The circlet of gold and pale blue veil that she wore did not
fully hide the riotous mass of white-blond curls that tumbled down her back. With her pale skin, perfectly formed
features, and bright blue eyes, she looked like an angel.

He heard his brother suck in his breath and mutter
something between a prayer and an oath. A sentiment
Arthur understood completely.

But it was the second lass who drew his eye. There was
something about her . . .

She laughed again, tossing back her head and revealing
long locks of golden-brown hair beneath a pale pink veil.
His gaze fell on her face. Her cheeks were pink with cold
and her big, deep-blue eyes bright with laughter. Had he
ever been that happy about anything? That free?

It took him only an instant for recognition to hit.

His heart dropped like a stone. *Dear God, it couldn't be!*

But it was she. The lass from the church.

He heard Lorn say, "Mary, Anna, you've returned."

Arthur swore there was actual delight in the hard-
hearted bastard's voice.

Both lasses ran forward, but Arthur had eyes for only
one. She threw her arms around Lorn's neck, planting a big
kiss on his cheek.

"Father!" she said excitedly.

Father. Arthur felt as though a dirk had just lodged in his
gut.

He'd saved Lorn's daughter. If it weren't such an unmiti-
gated disaster, he might laugh at the bitter irony.

If she recognized him, his head would be hanging above
the castle gate by nightfall. Dying didn't bother him. But
failure did.

He tried to motion to his brother to leave, wanting to get
the hell out of there. But Dugald seemed in a trance, staring at Lady Mary MacDougall as if she'd just descended
from the clouds.

Arthur had shifted his gaze from the women, but out of the corner of his eye he saw the second lass startle. For the first time, she seemed to look around the room and realize the number of eyes on them.

She bit her lip. It was an innocently erotic gesture that might have affected him before he realized she was Lorn's daughter. Nonetheless, he adjusted his sword—the steel one.

"We've interrupted something." She turned to the other lass, presumably her sister. "Come, Mary, we shall tell Father of our journey later."

Lorn shook his head. "Nay, there's no need. We're almost finished here."

Arthur stilled, his heart pounding in his chest as he felt the lass's gaze sweep over the crowd of soldiers, and then—bloody hell—return to him.

Instinctively, his hand tightened around the handle of his sword. A cold sweat slid down his spine.

This time there was no helm to shield his face, and he felt the intensity of her scrutiny full force. He stilled when a small furrow appeared between her brows.

For one long heartbeat he waited for her to unmask him. For her voice to ring out with the words that would condemn him to death . . . and to failure.

But the furrow only deepened.

And then in one reckless moment he knew what he had to do. He had to be sure.

Slowly, he lifted his gaze to hers.

He didn't move. Didn't breathe. Didn't blink as their eyes collided unhindered for the first time. Gazing into her eyes, as dark and deep a blue as the sea, he felt himself drowning. Lost, if only for an instant.

When she gasped, he knew it was all over.

But she quickly dropped her gaze, and a soft pink blush spread over her cheeks.

Arthur nearly sighed with relief. The lass hadn't recognized him. She was simply embarrassed to be caught staring.

His relief, however, was short-lived. The girl might not have denounced him as a spy, but she'd unwittingly done exactly what he'd hoped to avoid: brought him to her father's attention.

"Which brother are you?" Lorn asked, his dark, beady eyes having missed none of the exchange.

Dugald answered for him. "My youngest. Sir Arthur, my lord. Beside him is my brother Sir Gillespie."

Both men nodded, but Lorn was focused on him—like a cur with a meaty bone. "Sir Arthur . . ." he murmured, as if trying to recall the name. "You were knighted by the king himself."

Arthur met his enemy's gaze for the first time, giving no hint of the hatred seething inside him. "Aye, my lord, King Edward knighted me after Methven."

"De Valence—Pembroke—thinks much of you."

Arthur bowed as if the praise pleased him, though it did anything but. Knowing, as he did, that the English commander's praise had come at the expense of his friends. He did what he could to avoid battling Bruce's men, but at times it was inevitable. To stay alive and to maintain his cover, he had no choice but to defend himself—sometimes to the death. It was the part of his mission he didn't think about but that stayed with him nonetheless.

Lorn gave him a long look, before finally turning his gaze.

The next group of men stepped forward and Dugald led them away. But Arthur could feel the weight of eyes on his back the entire way. The girl's, he thought, not Lorn's. But neither was good for his mission.

One thing was certain: He needed to stay far away from the lass.

Anna MacDougall. His mouth hardened with distaste. Nothing killed a bit of unwanted lust like learning that the woman who'd fired his blood was the daughter of the man who'd killed his father.

Three

Anna wasn't watching where she was going. She'd returned to the castle with barely time to bathe and change her gown for the feast. A feast that had been her idea as a way to welcome the baron, knights, and men-at-arms who'd answered her father's call to Dunstaffnage.

With war hovering on their doorstep, a celebration might seem strange to some—such as her brother Alan, for example—but Anna knew how important it was to put aside the doom and gloom if only for one night. To remember what they were fighting for. To feel normal, if just for a little while—or what passed for normal in the midst of war.

Fortunately, her father agreed and thought the feast a fine idea. She suspected he was also anxious to show his men that he'd recovered fully from his illness. But whatever the reason, Anna couldn't have been more excited. There would be decadent amounts of food and drink, music, a *seannachie* to regale the crowd with a history of the clan, and dancing. Dancing! It had been so long since she'd danced.

She and her sisters had spent hours deciding what to wear, planning every last detail.

And now she was late.

Not that she regretted it. Beth's new baby was adorable,

and Anna knew how much her recently widowed friend needed help. She felt a pang of sympathy for the child who would never know her father. There were so heartbreakingly many of them. Yet one more reason why she couldn't wait for this blasted war to be over.

She heard the first chords of the harp and muttered one of her father's favorite oaths under her breath. Darting out of the sunlight into the darkened entrance of the Hall, she ran headlong into a wall.

Or at least she thought it was a wall until it reached out and caught her from falling backward. Saving her, she suspected, from a hard landing on her bottom.

She gasped with surprise. First at the impact, and then at the heady sensation of being held in a rather strong and muscular—extremely muscular—pair of arms.

"Are you all right?"

Lord, what a voice! It wrapped around her as firmly as his embrace. Deep and rich, with just the right amount of huskiness. It was a voice to resonate from halls and hilltops. She might have listened more intently to this morning's sermon if Father Gilbert had a voice like that.

"I'm fine," she said dazedly. Actually she felt a little lightheaded. She looked up, blinking to clear the stars from her eyes, and gasped again.

It was the young knight she'd noticed a few days ago. The one who'd caught her staring at him. Sir Arthur Campbell.

Her cheeks fired. She didn't know what had caught her attention that day, but she felt it all over again. The strange little spike in her pulse. The flash of warmth that spread over her skin. The nervous flutter in her stomach.

There was something different about him. A feeling she couldn't quite describe. It was as if there were an undercurrent of intensity emanating from him.

He was undeniably handsome, although she hadn't noticed it right away. Sir Arthur's quiet, unassuming good looks were not as immediately apparent as his brother's. His brother had the kind of bold good looks that were impossible *not* to notice.

Like that gorgeous man from the night at the church a year ago—the one who'd called off the attack when he'd recognized her "rescuer." Even with the black smudges on his face, she didn't think she'd ever seen a man so exceptionally well formed. But he was a rebel, so his appeal had tarnished quickly.

Strange that she'd thought of that night again. It was the second time this week. She thought she'd put that terrifying episode behind her and had stopped looking at every man as if he could be the one. The man who was both a traitor and her savior. *Ranger.* What kind of name was that? Rangers were men who roamed across the countryside to protect and instill law and order—hardly fitting for a spy.

Or was it? From her account and description of that night, her father suspected the two men might have been part of Bruce's secret band of phantom warriors. Part bogeyman, part mythological hero, the warriors had sent waves of terror through the English and their Scottish allies.

Right now all she could think about was the man holding her. He smelled divine. Warm and soapy from the bath he must have just taken. His dark hair was still damp, curling in loose waves at his neck and forehead. He'd shaved, although she could still see the shadow of his beard along his strong, chiseled jawline.

Chiseled described him well. All hard angles and rough cuts. Blatantly masculine in a way that had never appealed to her before. She preferred men more refined in manner and appearance.

She didn't usually look at warriors. They reminded her too much of war.

But he was undeniably a warrior. Build like a siege engine, if the steely muscles in his arms were any indication.

Funny that she hadn't noticed how tall and muscular he was the first time she'd seen him. But then again, with all that mail and armor, knights pretty much all looked the same to her.

Anna wasn't particularly short for a woman, but she had to crank her head back to look up at him. Heavens, he must be at least four inches over six feet! And his shoulders were nearly as wide as the entry into the hall.

Their eyes met.

She felt a shock reverberate through her. She'd never seen eyes that color before. Amber with flecks of gold. Not brown, as she'd thought. And framed by ridiculously long, soft lashes to inspire envy in any woman's heart.

She saw the flicker of recognition before he released her.

Dropped her, actually. So suddenly that she avoided that hard landing on her bottom by only the narrowest and most ungainly of margins. She stumbled back, waved her arms like some kind of clucking chicken, and—thankfully— managed to find her balance.

So much for impressing him with her grace. Not that his expression indicated the slightest chance of impressing him.

A young man had never looked at her with such . . . blatant indifference. Good thing she wasn't vain. Or at least she hadn't thought she was, but she had to admit feeling a little sting of something right now.

Realizing she was looking up at him like some moon-struck girl right out of the convent, she quickly lowered her gaze. He couldn't have made his disinterest more plain. He'd nearly dropped her, for heaven's sake! Maybe he'd missed the gallantry part of knight's training.

Trying to muster some semblance of composure, she smiled and said, "I'm sorry, I didn't see you standing there."

He gave her a long look that seemed to hold a hint of arrogant impatience. "Obviously."

Her smile fell. She furrowed her brow, not sure what to say next. Awkward moments were uncharted seas for her. Apparently, he wasn't much of a conversationalist. "I was late," she explained.

He stepped back to allow her to move past him. "Then don't let me detain you any further."

Though he kept his voice neutral and there was nothing wrong with his words on the surface, she felt the distinct nip of coldness.

He doesn't like me.

Suddenly feeling like a fool, Anna hurried past him. What did she care if he liked her or not? A warrior was the very last type of man to interest her. She'd had enough war to last her a lifetime. Peace. Quiet. A happy home and a husband whose conversation didn't revolve around war and weaponry. Children. That's what her future held.

Right before getting swallowed up by the large crowd swarming the Great Hall, she chanced a glance over her shoulder.

His gaze flickered away. But he'd been watching her.

Arthur was counting the minutes until he could leave.

He wasn't much for feasts and drunken celebrations under normal circumstances, but thanks to Anna MacDougall, he was finding it difficult even to pretend to relax and enjoy himself.

He was the one who watched and observed, *not* the other way around. He didn't need keen awareness or razor-sharp senses to feel her eyes on him. He was seated in the back corner of the hall, about as far away from the dais as possible, but he might as well have been right beside her, so intently did he feel her scrutiny. Feminine interest, and something far more dangerous—curiosity. And he didn't like it.

Why wouldn't she stop looking at him? And worse, why was he finding it so damned hard not to look back?

She was pretty—beautiful even. But beautiful women weren't such a rarity that he should be struggling to ignore her. He wasn't having any trouble keeping his gaze from her sister Mary, and she was one of the most beautiful women he'd ever seen.

But something about Anna MacDougall drew the eye. Even in a room full of hundreds of celebrating clansmen with plenty of attractive young lasses vying for attention, she sparkled like a diamond among glass.

Beauty wasn't it—or all of it, at least. Her appeal went deeper. It wasn't only male gazes that followed her; women watched her, too. There was something infectious about her laugh, endearing in her smile, captivating about the twinkle in her deep-blue eyes, and delightfully naughty in her dimples. Dimples. Of course she had to have dimples. What adorable sprite did not?

But other than a quick glance or two, he assiduously avoided looking at her. Restraint. Control. Discipline. These were the traits he prided himself on. They were what made him an elite warrior.

His pride took a blow, however, when the dancing started. One glance at her flushed cheeks and laughing eyes, and he'd been just as entranced as the rest of them. She was vivid and vivacious, brimming with youthful strength and vitality.

It sounded so damned trite, but her joy of life was written on her face. For a man who'd known nothing but death, destruction, and turmoil for as long as he could hold a sword, who'd lived in the shadows for years avoiding the attention she reveled in, who'd never experienced that kind of joy in his life, the light was nearly blinding.

He tried to focus on her imperfections. But alas, he could find no stray hairs or unsightly moles to mar the smoothness of her skin. Her nose was perhaps a little pert. Her mouth a bit wide. Her chin a tad pointed. But it all added up to adorable and sweet.

Despite his initial impression being exactly that, he told himself she was probably spoiled and haughty. Or calculating and cunning like her father.

He'd just about convinced himself when he saw her stumble. He was almost out of his seat before he caught himself. Her feet slid out from under her, and she landed with a hard thud on her bottom.

The music stopped, followed by a stunned silence.

From the horrified look on the young clansman's face who stood behind her, Arthur figured it was his bump that had sent her sprawling.

Arthur waited for the tears or angry diatribe at the man who'd caused her embarrassment. He was to be disappointed.

Anna MacDougall took one look at herself on the floor and broke out into laughter. After her partner had helped her to her feet, he could see her teasing the horror from the young clansman's face.

So much for spoiled and haughty. He picked up his goblet of ale and took a long swig, feeling the sudden urge for drink.

He could have watched her for hours. But he forced his gaze away, knowing he was playing with fire. He sure as hell didn't want her to catch him looking at her.

Given who she was, his fascination with the chit angered him. He should be repulsed by her name alone. She was Lorn's daughter, for Christ's sake.

But when she'd tumbled in his arms earlier, repulsion was not what he'd felt at all.

He'd felt hard. Aroused. Hot.

He'd wanted to sink into that softness. Press her body closer to his. Feel the fullness of her breasts on his chest and her hips on his cock. The intensity of his reaction had startled him, causing him to let go of her too quickly.

But lust, though annoying, was easily controlled. It was nothing compared to the danger her interest in him posed.

He'd been doing this long enough to know that the only thing he could count on with every mission was that something would go wrong. But fending off unwanted attention from a beautiful lass wasn't the kind of problem he'd anticipated.

Arthur's experience with women was limited to more primal relations. Although he was not as ridiculously fine of face as MacGregor—thank God—Arthur could attract far more female admirers if he wanted. But his demeanor did not encourage them. Which was how he preferred it.

Women in general were far more perceptive than men. Usually they sensed something different about him, and instinct warned them away.

Usually. But with Anna MacDougall he'd been forced to take harsher measures. His attempt to discourage her, however, hadn't worked. Unless succeeding in making himself feel like an arse counted. Charm and gallantry might not come naturally to him—that was his brother's domain— but neither did outright rudeness. His cold treatment of her didn't sit well, even if it had been necessary.

He shook his head. What the hell was the matter with him? Anna MacDougall was the last lass in the world who should concern him. A few curt words was nothing compared to what he'd come here to do.

Her world was about to be destroyed.

Not that you'd know it by the jubilant smiles on the faces of the people around him. Didn't they know that the tide had turned? That their most powerful allies—the Comyns and England—had deserted them? That Bruce would be coming as soon as the truce expired?

Hell, even his brother was acting as if he didn't have a care in the world, he and his men laughing and jesting as loudly as the rest of them. Louder, perhaps.

"Don't you like the ale, Sir Arthur?"

He turned to see Dugald's squire beside him on the

bench. "Well enough," he said with a wry turn of his mouth. "Though perhaps not as much as my brother."

The lad smiled. He leaned closer and lowered his voice. "I couldn't help noticing the lady, sir." Arthur didn't need to look to know to whom he was motioning. "She's been watching you. Perhaps you will ask her to dance?"

Unfortunately, he hadn't lowered his voice enough—or Arthur's brother wasn't as drunk as he'd thought. Dugald interrupted loudly. "Don't waste your time, Ned. My brother would rather dance with his sword than a young, marriageable lady." The others laughed, not missing the ribald jest.

Though Dugald had finished eating, he still held the horn hilt of his eating knife in his hand. Arthur noticed the squire stiffen, his eyes widening anxiously, when Dugald started to toss the knife up in the air, catching it with one hand. Unconsciously, the lad started to rub his hands and inch forward on the bench.

Arthur understood the squire's reaction only too well. One glance down at his own hands—scarred by dozens of knife marks—said why. It was Dugald's idea of a game. He'd toss the knife—or dagger or spear—around for a while, and then suddenly throw it at someone, expecting that person to catch it. It was supposed to improve reflexes and build alertness, awareness, and readiness.

It did, albeit with a considerable amount of pain and blood.

God, how he'd dreaded that damned knife—a sentiment shared by the squire if the ashen, edgy look on his face was any indication.

"He hasn't courted a lass since he was a pissant squire like you," Dugald continued. "What was her name, brother?"

Arthur slid his finger over the rim of his goblet carelessly. Dugald was prodding him, but he wouldn't bite. "Catherine."

"What happened, sir?" the squire asked Arthur, casting furtive sidelong glances toward Dugald—never completely taking his eyes off the five-inch steel blade.

Arthur shrugged. "We didn't suit."

Dugald laughed. "After you scared her senseless. By God, you were a strange lad." Thankfully, he didn't explain, but looked back to the squire. He made a quick motion with his hand, faking a throw of the dagger, chuckling when the lad flinched. "He was even more of a hapless fighter than you. A runt, if you can believe it." From the way the others turned to him in astonishment, it was clear they couldn't. "Puny and weak. He could barely lift a sword until he was twelve. We all despaired of ever making him a warrior."

Except for Neil. Neil had always believed in him.

"But look at him now," Dugald said. "A knight our father would be proud of." With a deft sleight of hand, he tossed the dagger high in the air, caught it, and immediately flipped it toward the squire. Arthur would have knocked it down, but the lad was ready. Eyes fixed on the flashing blade, he managed to get enough of the handle to catch it. Dugald let out a belly roar of laughter. "Ha! Mayhap there's hope for you after all."

The others laughed.

The offhanded compliment about Arthur's warrior skills mattered more than he wanted it to. He and Dugald would never be close, but they were brothers. On *opposite* sides, he reminded himself.

The squire moved away, and the rest of the men returned to their drink, but Dugald quietly looked around the room. Arthur knew what—or who—he was looking for. The Lady Mary MacDougall had captured his brother's attention—a rarity for any lass.

"It's a damned shame," Dugald said roughly.

He nodded. "Aye, brother, that it is."

John of Lorn's daughters were not for them.

Four

Anna had even more flaws than she'd realized. After today, she would have to add arrogance and vanity to the list, which already included her well-known stubbornness (it was she who'd threatened—nicely—to tie her father to his bed if he attempted to get up), outspokenness (women weren't supposed to have opinions, let alone voice them—but she wouldn't take the full blame for that; it was her father's fault for encouraging her), and the very unmaidenly penchant to repeat her brothers' and father's favorite oaths (which she wouldn't add to her sins by giving examples of).

Now, she'd discovered a rather perverse need to be liked. Surely it was the height of arrogance to think that *everyone* should like her? Of course it was. Even if they usually did. It shouldn't bother her that the young knight never once looked at her. Not once. All night.

But it did. Especially when she found herself doing nothing *but* look at him.

As she laughed until her sides split, danced until her feet hurt, ate until her belly ached, and drank until her head swam, she found her gaze drifting around the room with anything but aimlessness, searching for the darkly handsome knight who couldn't have made his disinterest in her more plain.

She frowned. Why didn't he like her?

She'd been perfectly friendly, smiling and attempting to make conversation. She didn't have warts on her nose, hairs sprouting from her chin, or rotting teeth. Actually, she'd been told many times before—and not just from the men in her family—that although she certainly wasn't as beautiful as Mary (who could be?), she was quite pleasing to look upon.

Thus, her descent into vanity.

Perhaps it was lingering animosity from the old feud between the Campbells and the MacDougalls? She'd been only a child at the time and knew little of the circumstances. She could always ask her father. Though *why* she was so desperate to find an explanation for his apparent disregard, she didn't know.

It shouldn't matter. She didn't even know him. And he was a warrior—there was nothing refined about him at all. That should be enough.

What was one man? Plenty of men liked her. Including Thomas MacNab, a perfectly pleasant scholar, who'd just gone to fetch her a goblet of the sweetened wine that she loved while she recovered from their energetic dance—and her embarrassing fall—near the open window. She'd like to say she wasn't usually so clumsy, but she couldn't. She didn't consider it a fault, more of an affliction.

She leaned against the stone sill, inhaling fresh breaths of air as her gaze traveled around the Great Hall. The room was sweltering, heated not by the peat fire but by the lively energy of the celebrants swirling all around. If the smiles and laughter on the faces of the men and women were any indication, the feast had been a resounding success.

Her smile fell. Except for one person.

Don't look . . .

But of course she did. She supposed she should add an appalling lack of self-control to the list. Her gaze immediately went to the figure in the far right corner of the room.

He was still there—which was surprising, since he seemed to be watching the door as if he couldn't wait to leave. In her experience, warriors were always anxious to leave. Eager to get to the next battlefield.

Unlike the other men around him, Sir Arthur wasn't availing himself of the MacDougall wine and ale. His flagon had barely moved from the table in front of him.

Seated with his back to the wall and a blank expression on his face, he'd positioned himself with a view to the entire room. She wondered if it was intentional. Though he seemed perfectly at ease—leaning back against the wall and occasionally cracking a smile at something one of his companions said—she sensed a watchfulness to him. As if he were constantly assessing and always on guard. It was so subtle she didn't notice it at first. But it was there, in the steadiness of his gaze and the stillness of his position.

Though he sat with a group of other warriors, including his two brothers whom he'd been with the first day, he seemed more of an observer than an active participant in the conversation. He seemed detached. Apart. And something about it bothered her.

She didn't like to see anyone left out. Maybe she should see if—

Before she could finish the thought, she found herself lifted off the ground from behind and spun around in the air.

"No one to dance with, brat?" he teased. "Should I order one of my men to partner you?"

She laughed with delight, knowing exactly who it was. Though it had been a long time since she'd heard the teasing lilt in his voice. "Don't you dare. I can find my own partners." She pushed at his thick arm, trying to wriggle out of his bearlike hold. "Let go of me, you big oaf."

He set her feet back on the floor and spun her around to face him, a stern look on his face. "Big oaf? You need to show proper respect to your elders, little one."

"Did I say big oaf?" She batted her eyes innocently. "I meant *Sir* big oaf."

He chuckled, the same blue eyes as hers crinkling at the edges.

Her heart swelled to see the smile on his face. It was the happiest she'd seen her brother since his wife had died giving birth to their third child, nearly a year ago.

Though Alan was only ten years her senior, the recent months had aged him. The affection he'd borne for his wife was etched deeply in the lines on his face. His dark-blond hair had receded at the temples, and perhaps thinned a little on top, but he was still a handsome man. Especially when he smiled—which wasn't often for the serious heir of Lorn and Argyll.

He reached down and wriggled her nose between his thumb and forefinger the way he used to do when she was a child. "You were right, you know."

"What was that?" She put her hand to her ear. "It's so loud I can't hear you."

He shook his head. "Brat. You know exactly what I'm talking about. The feast. This is exactly what we needed."

She beamed. She couldn't help it. Her brother's opinion meant much to her. It always had. "You really think so?"

He nodded. "I do." He bent down and kissed the top of her head. Though not as tall as a certain young knight, Alan was a formidable man. Nearly six feet in height, he had the thick, bulky build of their father and grandfather. Ewen and Alastair, her two other brothers, were slimmer in stature.

A shadow of sadness passed over her. Somhairle had been somewhere in between. Tall, broad-shouldered, and packed with lean muscle, he'd cut an impressive figure. The quintessential warrior. Not unlike Sir Arthur (why did she keep thinking of him?). But Somhairle, her second-eldest brother, had died fighting alongside Wallace at the Battle of

Falkirk almost exactly ten years ago. He'd been twenty years old.

Not wanting to spoil Alan's rare good humor, she pushed aside the sad thoughts.

"Where are all those men who've been flocking around you all night?" her brother asked with an overprotective gleam in his eye.

She rolled her eyes. "If there were any, I'm sure they scattered when they saw you coming."

His mouth curved in a satisfied grin. "As well they should."

She harrumphed. "Thomas MacNab went to fetch me some wine; I'm sure he'll return when you leave."

Alan folded his thick arms across his chest and frowned. "That pretty—" He stopped himself. "Any man who lacks courage to face one harmless brother . . ."

She snorted. "*Three* overbearing brutes, you mean. I saw all of you glaring at him earlier."

He gave her a chastising look and continued as if she hadn't interrupted. ". . . isn't worthy of you. You want a man who will stand down dragons and crawl on his knees through the fires of hell to protect you."

Anna wrapped her arms around his broad chest and gave him a big squeeze. Alan didn't understand her preference for a quiet, scholarly man like Thomas MacNab— who wouldn't know what to do with a sword even if he could carry one—when an impressive knight like Sir Hugh Ross had wanted to marry her. "I thought that's what I have you, Father, Alastair, and Ewen for."

He squeezed her back. "Aye, Annie-love, that you do." He held her back to look at her. "Is there no one else but the tutor who interests you?"

Without thinking, her gaze flickered to the back corner of the room, landing momentarily on Sir Arthur Campbell. It was long enough. Her observant brother took note. "Who were you looking at?"

"No one," she said quickly.

Too quickly. Her brother's eyes narrowed as he glanced in the direction where she'd looked. "Campbell?"

Drat her fair skin! She could feel the flush creep up her cheeks.

He looked surprised. "Sir Dugald? He's a fine warrior." He frowned. "A bit too popular with the lasses, though."

She wasn't about to correct him. It didn't matter. She was a bit attracted to Sir Arthur, that was all. His indifference had only tweaked her womanly vanity.

"Careful, love. If he tries anything—"

Anna scooted him away. "I know just who to call. Now, why don't you go over there and ask Morag to dance. She's been casting glances at you all night."

She expected an immediate refusal and was surprised to see instead a speculative glint in his eye.

"She has?" His gaze settled on the pretty young widow. He didn't say anything more, but the flicker of interest gave Anna hope that her brother's coma-like existence might be at an end. He'd mourned his wife deeply. Though his sadness was a testament to his love for her, he had not died with her.

She looked over the crowd for Thomas and held out at least another thirty seconds before glancing back toward the corner. She was just in time to see three young clanswomen—who happened to be pretty, buxom, and the most notorious flirts in the castle—approach the Campbells' table.

Anna's fingers clenched the soft velvet of her skirts. She felt a spike of something vaguely resembling irritation. *Extreme* irritation. It didn't help that she knew it was irrational. Of course the girls were interested in them. Why shouldn't they be? The newcomers were knights, handsome, and as far as Anna knew, unmarried. An irresistible combination to any young unmarried lass.

Nor was she surprised when the girls were quickly

welcomed to join them. But when one of the women—Christian, the lovely raven-haired, blue-eyed daughter of her father's henchman—sat beside Sir Arthur, Anna's spine stiffened. The room seemed to grow even warmer. A hot flush rose to her cheeks, and her heartbeat took a sudden erratic jump. She told herself it was none of her business, but she couldn't force herself to look away.

She needn't have worried. After a few flirtatious advances went unappreciated—including coquettish smiles and a not-so-subtle dip forward to give Sir Arthur a good view of her ample bosom—Christian gave up and turned her attention to one of his companions.

Though Anna was more relieved than she wanted to admit, something about the interaction made her frown. Had she jumped to the wrong conclusion? Maybe it wasn't her at all. Maybe Sir Arthur hadn't meant to be rude, but was simply gruff like her father. Or shy around women, like her brother Ewen?

As much as she wanted to convince herself that was it—so she could forget about him—she couldn't. Earlier he hadn't acted shy at all. Actually he'd acted annoyed. A little angry, even. As if she were bothering him. Like a midge in summer or a recalcitrant pup under his heels.

She *had* slammed into him, of course, but it was an accident. And he certainly looked strong enough to weather a little jostling from a woman. Lord, he looked as if he could weather a blow from a sledgehammer!

She might not have noticed his size at first, but she was noticing now. Despite the loose, bulky fit of his wool tunic and relaxed posture, the man was built like a rock. All tight, steely hard muscle. Why, he'd barely even moved when she'd come barreling into him.

And when he'd held her in his arms, she'd felt an overwhelming sense of safety and security. As if nothing could possibly harm her with this big, powerful man holding her.

Before he dropped her, that is.

He pushed back from the table and bent over to say something to his brother Sir Dugald.

Her heart took a strange jump when Sir Arthur started to walk toward the door. He was leaving. Leaving! But it wasn't even dark yet. The feast would go on for hours.

He couldn't leave. He hadn't even danced yet.

She glanced to her left, seeing Thomas threading his way back through the crowd, and then back to the young knight.

Before she realized what she was doing, she was striding purposefully toward the door. Not running, but not exactly walking, either.

He was only a few feet from the entry where she'd crashed into him earlier, when she cut in front of him.

He didn't look happy to see her.

The forbidding glower on his face gave her a moment's pause, but it was too late to turn back now. She'd always preferred the straightforward approach, though, she thought with a belated flush of embarrassment, it usually didn't involve chasing after strange men.

She wasn't chasing . . . exactly. It was her duty to see that all their guests enjoyed themselves, wasn't it? Moreover, she couldn't shake the thought that she might have misjudged him.

Ignoring his expression, she smiled. "I hope I am not the cause of your early departure?"

If the lift of a brow was any indication, she'd managed to surprise him.

She smiled teasingly and explained, "I feared you might be nursing bruises from my clumsiness earlier."

His mouth quirked, but only for a moment. "I believe I shall recover," he said dryly.

Lord, when he smiled he was a handsome devil. She felt that same funny flutter in her stomach and jump in her pulse, but it was even worse standing so close to him. She'd been surrounded by tall, muscular men her entire life, but never had she been so acutely aware of a man's masculinity and her own femininity.

He unnerved her. Made her feel nervous. Discombobulated. Flush with impulses she didn't understand. She wanted to move closer. Put her hand on his chest and feel the strength underneath. Stare at his face and memorize every hard angle, every line, every scar. It was outrageous to the point of ridiculous.

She'd been attracted to a handsome man before, but this was unlike anything she'd ever experienced. Nothing like the fondness she'd felt for Roger, her former fiancé. It was deeper. More intense. More visceral. It reached inside and pulled, compelling her to him.

He was waiting for her to say something. Clearly he wasn't going to make this any easier on her. "Then I hope it is not the food and entertainment?"

He shook his head. "It's a fine feast, my lady." His gaze flickered to the door in a none-too-subtle indication of his wish to leave.

She stepped to the side, putting herself firmly in his path. "Don't you like to dance?"

When he arched his brow again, she blushed, realizing how forward her question had sounded. It sounded as if she wanted him to ask her to dance. Which she did, but it was hardly ladylike to solicit it so brazenly.

But perhaps it was what he needed. She hated to think of anyone being left out of the fun.

"Sometimes." He hesitated, and for a moment she thought he would ask her. But then his gaze flickered over her shoulder, and he tensed. If she hadn't been watching him so carefully, she wouldn't have noticed the steely cold glint in his eye.

He turned back to her, letting his gaze slide down the length of her body.

She sucked in her breath. No one had ever looked at her so boldly. It might have been a little exciting if it weren't also utterly dispassionate—as if she were a horse at market. And not a very impressive one at that.

"But not today."

His meaning couldn't have been more clear. He didn't want to dance with her. She hadn't misjudged him or misinterpreted anything. It wasn't his brusque warrior's manners.

The stab of hurt she felt by his rejection was surprisingly sharp for someone she'd just met. For a man who shouldn't have interested her at all.

This shouldn't be so bloody difficult. But standing there, watching the emotions flit across her face as easy to read as words on a page, Arthur felt as though he was being twisted in a vise or splayed out on the rack.

He didn't like hurting her—or any woman, he corrected. But when he'd caught Lorn watching them, he knew he had to put an end to this. Whatever *this* was.

He couldn't believe he'd actually been considering dancing with the chit. Her genuine friendliness and innocent-kitten expression were not without effect. But her father's interest had brought him harshly back to reality.

He hoped his crude glance cured her of any romantic illusions.

It had. Her eyes widened, taking on a stricken look that made him feel like a clod who'd just stepped on her fluffy white tail.

"Of course," she said softly, her cheeks pink with embarrassment. "I'm sorry to have bothered you."

She lowered her gaze and took a step back.

He felt it again. That strange compulsion that he'd experienced at the church. The inability to let her walk away.

He dragged his fingers through his hair, trying to fight the urge, to calm the sudden restlessness teeming inside him. It didn't work.

Ah, hell. He reached out. "Wait," he said, grabbing her arm.

She stiffened at his touch, not looking at him, color still high on her cheeks.

He dropped his hand.

When he didn't say anything, she finally lifted her chin and tilted her face slightly toward him. He wished the soft candlelight had hid the quiver in her chin.

"Yes?" she asked.

Their eyes met, and Arthur cursed himself for a bloody fool. What the hell had he thought to say? *I'm flattered, but it would never work; I'm here to destroy your father.* Or how about, *I can't dance with you because I'm afraid you might realize I'm the spy for Bruce who saved you at the church.*

She eyed him expectantly.

"I have a job to do," he blurted, feeling like an idiot. He didn't blurt anything. And why the hell was he explaining himself?

He sensed her scrutiny, felt the penetration of her gaze, and had the uncomfortable suspicion that she was seeing far more than he wanted her to.

"And nothing more," she filled in.

He shrugged. "I've little time for anything else."

A wry smile turned her mouth. "Are knights not permitted one day of entertainment and fun?"

Her response was lighthearted; his was not. "Nay. Not me, at least. Not with war on the horizon."

He almost regretted his honesty when he saw the flash of alarm in her too-expressive big, blue eyes. It was clear the harsh reality of her father's situation was not something she wanted to think about. Could she really be that naive, or was she living in some kind of fantasy world? A world of feasts and celebrations, happily ensconced in the bosom of her family, while war reigned in chaos beyond their gates.

His words had succeeded in doing what he'd wanted to do from the first. When she looked at him again, he didn't detect even a hint of feminine interest in her gaze. She was looking at him as if he were any other warrior who'd come to serve her father. He hadn't realized how differently she'd been looking at him until the look was gone.

"Your devotion to your duty is to be commended. I'm sure my father is fortunate to have a knight like you in his service."

Arthur felt like laughing. If she only knew. Fortune was the last thing he would bring John of Lorn.

He wasn't a knight, he was only playing one. He was a Highlander. The only code he lived by was win. Kill or be killed.

Suddenly, an older, plumper version of her sister Lady Mary appeared at her side.

"There you are, darling. I've been looking for you every-where."

"What is it, Mother?"

The note of worry in Anna's voice bothered him. She shouldn't be upset.

"The men are talking about that horrible Robert Bruce again." The still-beautiful older woman twisted her hands anxiously. "Your father is getting angry." Fear crept into her voice. "You need to do something."

Anna muttered something under her breath that sounded like "St. Columba's bones." When a frown gathered be-tween her mother's eyes, in an expression distinctly like her daughter's, Arthur realized he'd heard her right. "Don't worry," Anna said, giving her mother's hands a pat. "I'll take care of it."

He suspected she took care of quite a lot.

Her mother glanced over at him, seeming to realize she'd interrupted. She flashed him an apologetic grin. "I'm sorry, sir, you'll have to wait for the next dance."

There wasn't a hint of embarrassed color in Anna's

cheeks when her gaze slid over him. "There is no dance," she said firmly. "Sir Arthur was just leaving."

Though there was nothing discourteous in her voice, Arthur knew he had just been dismissed. Without another glance, Anna followed her mother through the crowd.

He watched her longer than he should have, telling himself he should be happy. This was what he'd wanted. It would be for the best.

But it wasn't happiness he felt at all. If he didn't know better, he'd think it was regret.

It was hours later when Anna knocked on the door of her father's solar.

He bid her enter, then upon seeing it was her, dismissed his *luchd-taighe* guardsmen.

She waited for the clansmen to leave before coming forward. "You wished to see me, Father?"

John MacDougall, Lord of Lorn, was seated behind a large wooden table and motioned for her to sit in the chair opposite him. After the exhaustion of the feast, she did so willingly. It had to be near midnight.

Her father's serving man had caught her just before she retired for the evening. Though she could barely keep her eyes open, and every bone in her body ached, she didn't think about refusing. A summons by her father could not be ignored. So she'd donned a velvet fur-lined robe to cover her chemise and hurried to his solar, wondering why he wanted to see her so late. Maybe, like Alan, he wanted to praise her for her efforts tonight?

He gave her a long look. "I have something I should like you to do for me."

She tried not to feel disappointed. Her father had too many things on his mind, too many people to worry about, to concern himself with the feast. She knew he appreciated her; he didn't need to tell her. She should have realized it would be something important to call for her this late at night.

"Of course," she said without hesitation. "Do you wish me to visit your cousin the Bishop of Argyll again?"

He shook his head, a wry smile curving his mouth. "Nay, not this time." He paused, giving her a knowing look. "I noticed you speaking with one of the new knights earlier."

She bit her lip uncertainly. "I spoke to many of the men. Did I do something wrong? I thought you would wish me to help welcome the new arrivals."

He brushed off her worries. "You did nothing wrong. Before your mother sent you over to distract me with all those foolish questions . . ." He gave her a forbidding frown, but she simply grinned, not bothering to deny it. They were foolish, but she couldn't think of anything other than food on the spur of the moment. ". . . I noticed you talking to one of the Campbells."

Her smile fell. *That* new knight. "Sir Arthur," she provided, keeping her voice even.

But she felt a prickle of unease, suspecting what her father wanted her to do. She might not be able to wield a sword or join her brothers on the battlefield, but Anna did what she could to help put an end to the war in other ways. Including, on occasion, keeping an eye on knights or barons whom he didn't trust. It wasn't spying . . . exactly.

"What do you think of him?"

The question didn't surprise her. Her father often asked her impression of visitors or new soldiers. Most leaders wouldn't deign to ask a woman's opinion, but her father was not most men. He believed in using whatever tools he had at his disposal. Women were more perceptive than men, he believed, so he took advantage of their skill.

She gave a little shrug. "I spoke with him only briefly. Not more than a few words. He seemed . . ." Rude. Aloof. Cold. "Dedicated to his duty."

He nodded as if he agreed. "Aye, he's an able knight. Not

as lauded as his brother, perhaps, but an accomplished warrior. Was there nothing else?"

She could feel her father's scrutiny and fought the flush that threatened to climb her cheeks. She'd noticed the knight was handsome and built like a rock, but she wasn't going to mention that. She thought back to the feast. "He seems to prefer to keep to himself."

His eyes sparked as if she'd said something to interest him. "What do you mean?"

"I noticed at the feast that he didn't seem to talk much, even to his brothers. I don't think he even has a squire. He barely drank, he wasn't interested in flirting with any of the lasses or dancing, and he left as soon as he could."

His mouth twisted to the side. "You seem to have noticed quite a bit about him."

This time she couldn't prevent the heat from flooding her face. "Perhaps," she admitted. "But it's no matter."

"Why's that?"

"I don't think he likes me very much."

Her father couldn't hide his amusement, which she thought a bit unfeeling in the circumstances.

"Actually, that's why I called you here."

"Because he doesn't like me?"

"Nay, because I think it's just the opposite, and I wonder why he's going to such an effort to pretend otherwise."

Anna thought her father seriously misread the situation, but she didn't bother arguing. Like most fathers, he thought it inconceivable that any man would reject one of his beloved daughters. "Perhaps it's the old feud," she suggested. "His father died in battle with our clan, didn't he?"

A strange look crossed his face, before he gave a dismissive wave of his hand. "Aye, many years ago. That could be some of it, but I don't think all of it. Something about the lad bothers me. I can't put my finger on it, but I want you to keep an eye on him. Just for a while. It's probably nothing, but with the truce coming to an end, I don't want to take any chances. But neither can I afford to give offense. The Campbells are formidable warriors and I need all the men I can get."

Her stomach dropped. It was as she'd feared. After their conversation earlier, the last thing she wanted to do was keep an eye on Sir Arthur Campbell. "Father, he has made it clear—"

"He's made nothing clear," he snapped. "You are wrong about Campbell's interest in you." Then in a milder voice, he added, "I'm not asking you to seduce the man, just watch him." He gave her a hard look. "I do not understand this reluctance. I thought you wished to help. I thought I could count on you."

Chastened, she said hurriedly, "You can."

His eyes narrowed. "Did something happen you are not telling me about? Did he touch you—"

"Nay," she insisted. "I told you everything. Of course I will do as you bid. I was just suggesting it might not be easy."

Whatever qualms she had paled in comparison to her vow to do whatever she could to see an end to the war and a victory for the MacDougalls. Even if it meant pursuing a man who did not want to be pursued. Even if it meant her pride was about to take a severe lashing.

Her father smiled. "I think it will be much easier than you imagine."

She hoped he was right, but she suspected there wasn't anything simple about Sir Arthur Campbell.

Five

❧

Arthur had almost made it. The gate wasn't fifty feet away. Another minute and he would have been riding out on his way to gathering more information for Bruce.

"Sir Arthur!"

The soft, sweet feminine voice made every muscle in his body tense. *Not again.* He eyed the distance to the gate. He wondered if he could run for it.

Already he could hear the men around him start to snicker as the achingly—and he meant achingly, even his teeth had begun to hurt—familiar face appeared at his side.

She was smiling. She was *always* smiling. Why the hell did she have to smile so much? And why did it have to light up her entire face, from the soft curve of her too-pink lips to the bright twinkle in her deep-blue eyes? If he were prone to ruminating like a lovesick bard about poetic allusions to eye color, he would say they were like dark sapphires. But he had a hell of a lot more important things to do, so they were dark blue.

Sapphires . . .

He jerked his gaze way. He should have kept his eyes on her face, but he made the mistake of dropping his gaze and had to smother a grunt of pain. The persistent throb between his legs jerked hard. A state to which he was growing painfully accustomed.

One look at her gown and he felt like dropping to his knees and begging God for mercy.

Was she trying to kill him?

Probably. Her flirting and increasingly bold overtures were getting harder to ignore. Seeking him out at meals, insisting on helping the healer when he'd taken a blow on the arm from a sword a few days ago (he'd been distracted, damn it, by her flouncing around the garden, laughing with her sisters), showing up at the stable at the same time he was due to ride out in the morning, and now this. Her sunny yellow satin surcote was fitted tight in all the wrong places. He didn't know how she could breathe; it clung to her chest and slim waist as if she'd dampened it in the loch.

But that wasn't the worst part. The worst part was how low the square neckline dipped on her chest. Her ample— mouthwateringly, prodigiously ample—chest.

Christ's bones, he couldn't take his eyes off the soft, pale flesh swelling—nay, spilling—over the bodice. *Ripe* and *lush* were two words that came to mind. But that didn't even begin to describe the perfection of her magnificent breasts.

He'd just about chop off his left arm to see them naked. And he was having a damned hard time doing anything but imagining how they would look. How they would taste. How they would bounce when . . .

Ah, hell. He jerked his gaze away. His body was on fire under his armor. From lust, aye, but also from an irrational flare of anger. If she were his, he'd keep her locked up in his room for a week for wearing that gown in public. *After* he ripped it off her and burned it.

He couldn't remember the last time a woman had gotten him so . . . bothered.

Unaware of his violent thoughts, she gazed up at him eagerly. "I'm so glad I caught you," she said, her breath coming in short gasps. Gasps that made him think of swiving. Hell, just about everything she did made him think of swiving.

She must have sprinted from the tower when she saw him ride out from the stable. It wasn't the first time. He'd been wrong about discouraging her the night of the feast. Dead wrong. If anything, she'd only redoubled her efforts since then.

He'd been living on edge all week, never knowing when she would show up. It seemed wherever he went, she was there. His brothers and the other men thought it was hilarious.

He, not so much.

He wasn't as immune to her as he wanted to be. It was hard not to like the chit. She was so . . . fresh. Like the first flower in spring.

He cursed inwardly. What the hell was happening to him? He was beginning to sound like a bloody bard.

"If you have a moment, there is something I should like to speak with you about," she added.

He tried to smile, but his teeth were grinding together, and he suspected it was more of a grimace. "I'm riding out for the day. It will have to wait."

Her smile fell. He braced himself, told himself he wasn't going to feel it again, but he did. Like an arse. The way he'd felt most of the week. Stepping on fluffy kitten tails apparently never got any easier.

"Of course. I'm sorry." She blinked up at him so innocently, he felt those little kitten claws digging into his chest. "I don't want to bother you, it's just that this is important—"

"Go on, Arthur," his brother said, unable to hide his smirk. "The lady says she needs you. You can ride out with us another time."

Arthur just might have to kill his brother. Dugald was

doing it purposefully—backing him into a corner, making it impossible to refuse—just to see him suffer.

Dugald's attitude toward Lorn's daughters had softened in the week since the feast. But Arthur knew that Dugald, the bloody bastard, was just as motivated by the enjoyment he got out of seeing Arthur squirm, guessing—although by this point it was probably obvious—how uncomfortable he was about the lass's attention.

This was quickly becoming the longest week of his life. He'd almost rather go through MacLeod's two weeks of warrior's training, not-so-jokingly dubbed Perdition, than another day of this.

Anna's eyes brightened and the smile returned to her face. "Are you sure it's all right?" She didn't wait for Arthur to disagree. "That would be wonderful. Where were you going?"

"It's not important," Arthur lied, biting back his anger. It was the first opportunity he'd had to scout out the terrain on the north side of Loch Etive. Now, he would have to look for another excuse. It wasn't the first time the lass had gotten in the way of his mission the past week.

He'd managed to follow a few priests and keep a short surveillance on the castle chapel and the nearby priory, but most of his time had been spent dodging Anna.

This had to stop.

"Have fun, little brother," Dugald said, not bothering to hide the amusement in his voice. "See you when we return."

Arthur watched them leave. He didn't usually engage in petty forms of sibling revenge, but he was reconsidering.

He jumped down off his mount and started to lead the swift and agile Irish hobby that had given the lightly armored "hobelars" horsemen their name back to the stable.

Anna pranced happily along beside him. He was careful to keep a certain distance between them. The lass was prone to touch his arm when she talked and each time she did it, he felt like he was jumping out of his damned skin. Pure defensive warfare, but he wasn't ashamed. At this point it was about survival.

He'd been trained to be one of the most elite warriors in Scotland. A secret, lethal weapon who would do whatever he needed to protect his cover. He could slip behind enemy lines, steal through an enemy camp, single-handedly take down a dozen warriors, and kill a man without making a sound. But there was one thing he hadn't been trained to do: dodge an overenthusiastic lass.

He didn't understand it. Most women were wary of him, sensing something about him that wasn't quite right. Sensing the danger. But not her. She looked at him as if he were *normal*.

It was bloody unsettling.

He kept his eyes straight ahead so he wouldn't notice how the sun picked up the golden strands in her long, silky hair. Or the softness of her skin. Or how incredible she smelled. The chit must bathe in rose petals.

Damn. He shouldn't think about her bathing. Because if he thought about her bathing, he would inevitably think of her naked, and then he would think of her breasts. But he wouldn't stop there.

His gaze dropped to her chest, where it had rested too many times this past week. To the soft, creamy mounds of flesh straining and spilling out of her bodice.

He'd think of cupping those spectacular breasts in his hands. Lifting them to his mouth and sucking them.

Ah hell. He jerked his eyes away, feeling the hard swell of heat in his loins.

"I hope you are not too disappointed to miss your ride," she ventured conversationally.

He shrugged and grunted unintelligibly.

She appeared not to notice his lack of enthusiasm. He couldn't quite tell whether she was purposefully ignoring his obvious disinterest or just so happy and good-natured that she wasn't aware of it.

He handed off the horse to one of the stable lads and turned to face her. "What is it you would like to talk to me about?"

A crease appeared between her brows. "Wouldn't you like to go inside? I can have one of the servants bring us something cool to drink—"

"Here is fine," he said sharply.

Defensive warfare, he reminded himself. The Hall would be quiet inside at this time of day. A yard full of people milling about was much safer.

Thank God MacGregor and MacSorley weren't around to see this. He would never hear the end of it.

Apparently he did have a cowardly bone in his body. He'd have to tell his brother Neil the next time he saw him.

She pursed her mouth, trying to look disapproving. But it failed miserably, only making her nose wrinkle up— adorably, damn her.

"Very well." She didn't sound happy about it. "Your brother mentioned you were good with a spear."

Dugald didn't know the half of it. Arthur carefully kept the extent of his skill hidden, not wanting it turned against his friends. With his enemies he was good—but not so good as to attract notice. He downplayed his scouting skills even more. Dugald still liked to prod him about the "freakish" abilities he'd displayed as a lad. Only Neil knew they hadn't disappeared but had actually been honed sharper.

"What does my ability with a spear have to do with anything?" His voice held the edge of impatience.

"I thought you might help organize the tests of skill for tomorrow's games."

He frowned. "What games?"

"Since we weren't able to hold the Highland Games this year, I thought it would be fun to put together a series of challenges for the men. They can compete against one another instead of other clans. My father thought it was a wonderful idea."

Arthur stared at her incredulously. "*This* is what is so important?" This was what she'd made him miss his ride for? Fun? Games? He fought to control his temper, but he could feel it slipping away. He didn't have a temper, damn it. Nonetheless his fists were clenched tight. The chit was living in a fantasy world with no idea of how precarious her father's situation was. "Do you know why the games weren't held this year?"

Her eyes narrowed, not missing the patronizing tone. "Of course I do. The war."

"And yet you devise games while men are trying to prepare for battle."

He saw a spark in her eye. Good. He hoped she was angry. She might not want to think about the war, but neither could she ignore it. Maybe she'd see how ridiculous this was.

Just like it was ridiculous for him to be noticing how long and feathery her lashes were, or the delicate arch of her brow.

"It *is* training. The games are only a means to enliven it. The competition will be good for them, and it will be fun."

"There is nothing fun about warfare," he said angrily.

"Perhaps not," she said softly, seeming to pick up on something in his voice. Then she did it again. Touched him. The gentle press of her hand on his arm made every nerve-ending blast off like one of William "Templar" Gordon's explosions. Their eyes met and he could see her sympathy. He didn't want it—or need it. It wasn't him she should worry about but her father and clansmen. "But sometimes going into battle is not all about warfare. What of the men's spirit? Is that not important as well?"

He didn't say anything. He didn't completely agree, but he didn't completely disagree either.

He could feel her eyes scanning his face. "If you do not wish to help me, I can find someone else."

He clenched his jaw, knowing he should deny her. Let her torture some other poor fool. But he liked that idea even less. Instead he found himself asking through gritted teeth, "What do you need?"

She beamed, and the force of it hit him like a blow across the chest. He nearly staggered.

As he listened to her excited voice explain what she wanted him to do, Arthur knew he should have run for it when he'd had the chance.

The day of the "Games" dawned bright and sunny. A good portent, as it turned out, for the games themselves.

Anna had been right, she thought with a smile that might have held a twinge of smugness. This was good for the men. No matter what *he* said.

Thus far, the games had been a rousing success. Not just for the knights and men-at-arms participating in the challenges, but for the occupants of the castle and the villagers as well. Hundreds of clansmen had followed the warriors' progress in the challenges of skill and strength, cheering for their favorites whether they won or lost.

In the morning the spectators had gathered near the galley house—which housed her father's ships—to watch the boat races and swimming contests in the bay behind the castle. They'd moved to the *barmkin* for the sword and archery contest before the lavish midday meal, and now they'd clustered on patches of grass mixed into the rocky knoll just beyond the castle gates for the final event: spear throwing.

"There's your knight," her sister Mary teased, pointing to the group of warriors lining up below.

Anna winced. If Mary had noticed, *everyone* must have noticed. Her normally blissfully unaware sister defied their father's rule that women were more perceptive than men.

"He's not my knight," she quipped.

Too adamantly, she feared, judging by her eldest sister Juliana's grin. "It certainly looks like you want him to be. A little sisterly advice, though"—Anna could tell she was trying to hold back her laughter—"you might want to be a little more . . . uh, subtle."

Anna pursed her mouth. She'd tried that. It hadn't worked.

She lifted her chin, pretending not to know what her sister was talking about. "I'm merely trying to be a good hostess. Being friendly to *all* the knights who have answered Father's call."

That caused both of her sisters to burst out into peals of hysterical laughter. "Lud, I hope you aren't that friendly to *all* of them," Juliana said. She leaned over Anna, who was seated on the plaid between them, to address Mary. "Did you see that dress she wore yesterday? It must have been five years old. It wouldn't fit Marion," she said, referring to their petite twelve-year-old niece.

"Mother was furious," Mary nodded, her eyes sparkling with mischief. "You should have seen her face when she saw Anna come in for the midday meal. It was the angriest I've seen her since Father fell ill."

At least one good thing had come of Anna's humiliation. It had been wonderful to see her mother cast aside her worry, if only for a moment, to berate her. Lord knows, nothing else had come of it. She could have been wearing a sackcloth for all Sir Arthur took notice of the gown.

She knew she should be ashamed, stooping to such wanton lengths as donning an indecent dress to get his attention. But desperate times called for desperate measures. And after a week of making a fool of herself, chasing after a man who didn't want to be chased, she was at her wit's end. Sir Arthur Campbell was almost as much of a mystery to Anna as the first time she'd bumped into him. She knew that he was an able knight, who was focused on his duty and liked to keep to himself—but she'd known all of that before.

He was an impossible man to read. Faith, he was an impossible man to get in the same room! Inventing reasons to be near him wasn't easy, and Anna had been growing increasingly frustrated in her efforts to keep an eye on him. None of the other men had ever been this much trouble. Probably because they hadn't been trying to avoid her.

So far, she'd seen nothing to warrant suspicion—unless being monosyllabic and unforthcoming were reasons for suspicion. He had to be the most difficult man she'd ever tried to converse with. Sir Arthur was the master of the short reply, not to mention as prickly and cantankerous as a bear roused from its winter slumber. If this was an indication of his interest in her—not that she gave any credence to her father's claim—she couldn't imagine what he was like when he *wasn't* interested.

Yesterday, however, she'd made an important discovery. She'd learned how to make him talk: Get him angry. Perhaps she'd been going about this all wrong.

Her eyes narrowed on the enigmatic knight, currently moving with the other participants to the far end of the field. Though he'd done nothing suspicious, she couldn't quite shake the feeling that he was hiding something. Whether this was due to her powers of womanly perception or simply her pricked pride, however, she didn't know. But there was definitely something different about him.

When her sisters had finally stopped laughing, Juliana said, "I must admit I'm surprised by your *friendliness* toward the knight." She bit back another laugh. "He's handsome enough, but you usually avoid men of his sort."

Warriors, her sister meant. She was right.

"His brother is the far more handsome of the two," Mary interjected, her gaze fastened on Sir Dugald's impressive form below.

Anna didn't agree, but she certainly wasn't going to give them any more reason to tease her.

"And Sir Arthur is not nearly as popular with the ladies, either," Juliana pointed out as a way of warning to Mary.

She spoke from experience. Juliana had been widowed years before, but her marriage had not been a happy one. Her husband Sir Godfrey de Clare, an English baron, had blamed her for their inability to produce an heir and according to her sister, lifted every skirt he could find to try to prove it.

Anna desperately hoped Juliana's next husband was a man her sister could love. Though love usually had nothing to do with how marriages were arranged, the sisters were more fortunate than most. Three marriageable daughters was a treasure trove for any nobleman seeking to enrich his lands and connections, but their father was not unreasonable. He took their wishes into consideration when finding them potential husbands.

Juliana had wanted to marry Sir Godfrey—at least initially. Just as Anna had wanted to marry Roger.

Sir Roger de Umfraville had been the third son of the old Earl of Angus's younger brother. They'd met when Anna had accompanied her father to Stirling Castle a few years back for Parliament. She'd been immediately drawn to the quiet young scholar with the winsome smile and dry sense of humor.

Educated at Cambridge, Roger had been considered a great scholar and promising politician. He abhorred bloodshed. As a third son, he should have been safe from the war. But when his two elder brothers died—one at Falkirk and the other from a fever—Roger had felt it his duty to take up the sword. Anna had been heartbroken when he'd died after a seemingly insignificant wound he'd suffered at Methven festered.

Unlike her sisters, Mary had yet to settle on a husband. That her father hadn't pressed, Anna suspected, was because he hoped for an important alliance—preferably English—from her beautiful sister. Once Bruce was subdued, her father would be able to find them all husbands.

Her chest squeezed. *When the war was over.*

"I thought Father was going to arrange a match with Sir Thomas or some nice, staid English baron for you when King Hood is brought to heel?" her sister said.

"Faith, Juliana, this has nothing to do with marriage! I barely even know the man," Anna said truthfully. She was attracted to him—perversely intrigued by his indifference, even—but a Highland warrior wasn't the husband for her. A life of quiet and peace, a father who would know his children, *that* was what she wanted.

But why did Thomas MacNab's face suddenly seem . . . womanly? *Pretty* Alan had called him. She bit her lip, suddenly agreeing.

She was tempted to tell them what it was really about, but her father wished for her to keep her tasks on his behalf between them. Probably so her mother wouldn't find out.

Whether her sisters believed her explanation or just decided to give up teasing her because the challenge was about to start, she couldn't be sure, but she was grateful when they turned to the field below. Their seat on the edge of a rocky hillside gave them a perfect vantage of the entire field below.

It had been Sir Arthur's idea to have the entrants not simply toss the spears at a different range of targets but do so in armor from horseback at a full gallop.

In his terse, matter-of-fact tones, he'd quickly and efficiently helped organize the different challenges. She suspected it was partly in the effort to be finished with her as soon as possible. What she'd hoped would take all day had taken only a few hours. He'd also elicited plenty of help from other men-at-arms, probably to avoid being alone with her.

Sighing, she turned her attention back to the field. One

by one, the men urged their mounts to a gallop down the path and threw their spears at the straw buttes secured to a post. If this were the real Highland Games, there would be both spear throwing and thrusting. For the latter, a longer spear was used and the rider would position the spear under his arm in the manner of a joust.

The challenge was harder than it looked, as evidenced by the number of spears that went wide or fell short of the target. But a few of the contestants were quite good, including her brother Alan. She cheered along with her sisters when his spear landed with precision in the center of the target. Only Alexander MacNaughton, the keeper of the royal Frechelan Castle on Loch Awe, had done as well.

Sir Arthur brought his steed around to the start, and Anna found herself inching forward on the rocks. As did the other contestants, he wore a steel helm, full mail, and a tabard emblazoned with his arms to match his shield. All of the Campbell arms had the gyronny of eight in or and sable—basically a pie of alternating black and gold triangles—but his was individualized by the bear in the middle, a reference no doubt to the Gaelic *artos,* from which his name was derived.

He held the spear in his left hand, the reins in his right, and started forward. Being left-handed, he would be at a disadvantage. Unlike the other contestants, he would have to throw across his body to the target.

Anna's pulse spiked as he picked up speed. An avid rider herself, she noticed right away that he was an exceptional horseman. Strong and powerful, he moved with remarkable fluidity, as if he were one with his mount.

He neared the target.

Her breath caught high in her throat as, never hesitating, he heaved the weapon in one smooth motion toward the butte. It landed with a definitive thud a few inches below the center of the target. Her breath released in an excited cry as she joined the other cheers. It was an excellent shot.

Not as good as her brother's or MacNaughton's, but it was still only the first round.

The field of competitors narrowed with each round. By the end of the third, however, the result was the same. Though Anna knew it was unwarranted, she felt a twinge of disappointment. For some reason, she'd expected him to win. It was silly—based on nothing but a feeling. He'd acquitted himself exceptionally well, coming in third behind MacNaughton and her brother.

Yet it was strange. He seemed to miss by precisely the same amount each time—a few inches off where her brother's or MacNaughton's had landed.

The men had taken off their helms and had handed off their mounts to the stable lads. Rather than stand around and accept the congratulations of the crowd, Sir Arthur looked as if he intended to follow his horse back to the stables.

Anna stood up quickly, wanting to rush down and catch him before he could escape. Perhaps she'd insist the top competitors join the high table on the dais for the evening meal tonight? That ought to make him angry enough for a few sentences at least.

She stepped around Mary, who was taking her sweet time getting up from the blanket.

"Where are you going in such a rush?"

Anna's cheeks grew hot. "I wish to congratulate Alan, don't you?"

She picked her way along the rocky path on the edge of the cliffside, trying not to look down as she silently urged the crowd of spectators down the hill faster.

"Are you sure it's not the young Campbell you wish to congratulate, Annie-love?" Juliana teased from behind her. "Don't look now," she whispered, though with the boisterous crowd it was unnecessary. "But I think he's looking at you."

Of course she looked.

Anna turned over her left shoulder and gazed down.

She sucked in her breath. Juliana was right. He was staring right at her. Their eyes met in a sudden jolt that reverberated like a powerful shock through her body. For the first time, he wasn't looking at her with indifference. Actually, it looked like alarm.

Too busy gazing at him, she wasn't watching where she was going.

"Anna, watch out!" Mary warned.

But it was too late.

She stepped on a rock. Her ankle twisted and she started to lose her balance (which even in the best of circumstances wasn't very good). Propelled backward, she stepped back to catch herself—which would have been fine if it wasn't the edge of the hillside and if the rocks hadn't given way beneath her foot.

"Anna!" Mary shrieked, reaching for her.

Oh God! For one horrifying moment time seemed to hold still as she hung in midair.

Then she was falling.

She could see her sisters' horrified faces swimming above her as momentum carried her backward. A loud rush of air drowned out the cries of the crowd and for a moment it was eerily quiet—as if she were in a strange, airless tunnel.

Ten feet.

Twenty.

No time to shift her position to try to land on her feet.

She braced herself for impact and hit the ground.

But she didn't hit the ground.

She gasped, realizing she wasn't lying in a painful mass of twisted limbs and broken bones. Nay, she blinked up into the handsome visage of Sir Arthur Campbell.

My God, he'd caught her! But how? How could he have gotten there so quickly?

"Are you all right?"

She nodded, because she couldn't speak. It's wasn't fear from her fall that caught her tongue, but something else.

His voice. The look in his incredible eyes.

It wasn't indifference.

At the first crack in his steely facade, a flutter of awareness shuddered through her. Maybe her father wasn't wrong after all.

Six

Arthur inhaled deeply, letting his lungs fill with the pungent air.

Freedom, even reeking of cow shite, still smelled sweet. Five days away from the castle, patrolling (or in his case surreptitiously scouting) the eastern borders of Lorn's lands, and now, courtesy of the good friar, he'd bought himself a couple days more.

In other words, he would have an entire week of freedom from the blue-eyed, honey-haired enchantress who'd tormented him with her innocent flirting and pushed him to the end of his tether.

It wasn't until she'd fallen—and he'd caught her—that he knew he had to get the hell out of there. So much for his plan to go unnoticed; the entire castle could speak of nothing else. Even the devil's spawn Lorn had thought to honor him by insisting that Arthur sit beside him at the lord's table that night. He might as well have been eating nails—that was all he'd tasted. It had taken every ounce of his skill at deception to mask his hatred throughout the long meal.

Apparently, the cold-hearted bastard had a weakness: his daughters. It seemed even the devil could care about something. Arthur had detected the fear in Lorn's eye when the story of Anna's tumble off the hillside was relayed to him, and his gratitude toward Arthur had been real enough.

Though Lorn accepted his account of the day's events, Anna MacDougall wasn't as easy to fool. He knew she didn't believe his "I was just lucky enough to be in the right place when she fell" explanation. The lass was entirely too perceptive, and that meant dangerous. The last thing he needed was for Dugald—or worse, Lorn—to start asking questions.

What a mess! Bad luck heaped upon bad. First, the lass he rescued—the one woman who could unmask him—happens to be the daughter of the man he intends to destroy. Then, for some God-knows-why reason, she sets her fancy on him. And worse, she takes a tumble off a cliff, forcing him to betray the abilities that could draw even more unwanted attention his way and making him the MacDougalls' latest hero—not to mention giving the men another source of amusement. He didn't know how many times over the course of the journey one of the men had climbed up on a rock and pretended to jump off while yelling dramatically, "Catch me, Sir Arthur!" in a high voice.

Hilarious. Almost made him miss MacSorley.

The "Games" themselves hadn't been as much of a waste of time as he'd thought. She'd been right: The competition had been good for the men's spirit. Moreover, he'd learned much about the caliber of the enemy soldiers and would be able to pass on the information to Bruce.

But knowing he needed to tread carefully around the lass—or better yet, tread far away from the lass—he'd jumped at the first opportunity to leave. That it also provided an opportunity to scout Lorn's lands for Bruce was even better.

He needed to focus on his mission. He was one of the most elite, highly trained warriors in the country, in the middle of the most important mission of his life, but at times he felt as though he were playacting in some school-girl's farce.

He'd never had this kind of trouble before. It was why he liked to work alone. On the outside. Infiltration was too personal. Too close.

His spot of good fortune continued when on the way back to the castle with his brothers and the other men who'd gone on the patrol—mostly MacNabs and MacNaughtons—they'd come upon Friar John near Tyndrum. The good friar had come from St. Andrews and was walking across Scotland through Lorn on his way to the Isle of Lismore. Lismore, the small, narrow island just off the coast, was the traditional seat of the Bishop of Argyll—who just happened to be a MacDougall and a kinsman of Lorn.

Having long suspected that the MacDougalls were passing messages through the churches, Arthur volunteered to escort the friar as far as Oban—just south of the castle—where he would catch the ferry. It was the direction he was headed anyway, Arthur insisted. The friar could ride behind him. Though they would travel at a much slower pace than the others, he was in no hurry to return. He got a few snickers at that.

When the friar tried to refuse, it made Arthur even more hopeful that he was on to something. Perhaps he'd found the source of the MacDougalls' messages?

He frowned. The only misfortune was that at the last minute, Dugald had decided to go as well. Probably to torment him to death with the constant talk of the spear contest.

"If you'd aimed a bit higher and let your wrist snap down like I've told you, you might have won."

Arthur gritted his teeth and kept his gaze fixed on the path before him. "I did my best," he lied, not knowing why Dugald's attempts to improve his skills were grating on him.

He could have bested either man if he'd wanted. But preserving his cover was all that mattered.

He'd "lost" many times before. He didn't know what the hell was wrong with him. He sure as hell didn't care about impressing the lasses—or any one lass in particular. Pride could get him killed.

"Which wasn't good enough to win," Dugald pointed out, just in case he'd forgotten.

He hadn't.

"The next church is just across the river," the friar said, in a welcome change of subject.

They'd just come through Ben Cruachan, the highest mountains in Argyll, along the narrow, steep-sided pass of Brander or *Brannraidh,* place of ambush. Appropriately named, he thought. Opposite them lay the relatively flat, grassy land on the southern bank of Loch Etive.

"You mean Killespickerill?" Arthur asked. The ancient church in Taynuilt had once been the seat of the Bishop of Argyll.

"Ah, you know of it?"

Arthur exchanged a look with Dugald. The good friar was obviously unfamiliar with the history between the Campbells and MacDougalls. "A bit," he said in an understatement. The small village of Taynuilt was located at the key juncture of Loch Etive and the river Awe, which connected three miles downstream to Loch Awe. Lorn's lands, but close to Campbell lands. His jaw clenched. The former Campbell lands, that is.

"If you wish to make Oban by nightfall we shouldn't stay long. We've still a good twelve miles to travel."

At this pace it would take them another two days. It seemed as if they'd visited every church between Tyndrum and Loch Etive. Not that Arthur was complaining. It gave him more of an opportunity to scout the area. When Bruce and the rest of the men marched west to Dunstaffnage to face Lorn, they would pass through this same countryside.

Their slow pace would also delay his return to the castle, which was fine by him.

But joining the friar hadn't brought him any closer to discovering how messengers were slipping through King Robert's net. They had to be churchmen, but so far not *this* churchman. He hadn't seen the friar slip anything in or out of the leather sporran he wore around his waist. Nor had he discovered anything last night while the friar slept, when he'd taken the opportunity to make sure.

"Brother Rory makes the best pottage in the Highlands," the friar said. "You won't want to miss it."

The last church had had meat pies, the one before that jam. Arthur suspected the stops at the various churches were more about tasting the local specialties than ministering to the faithful. Not that you would know it by the lance-thin churchman. He was more bone than flesh, and hearty of temperament rather than girth.

They crossed the river at the bridge of Awe and followed its banks, skirting the edge of the forest to the south. Simple gray stone cottages peppered the landscape, becoming more numerous and closer together as they drew nearer the village.

A few minutes later, nestled in the center of the lazy village on a small rise, the old stone church came into view.

There were a few people about, mostly women, and the light sounds of laughter and children playing ruffled through the air.

He stilled, hearing the traces of a song. A woman's voice. His senses buzzed as if a bee had just passed behind his neck.

"Is something wrong?"

The friar, seated behind him, was close enough to pick up on his reaction. Arthur waited. His gaze flickered back and forth, but there was no sign of anything unusual, nor did he pick up the unmistakable air of danger.

He shook his head. "Nay, nothing."

They continued on into the churchyard to the small building behind, where the priest slept and ate.

Friar John was good to his word. Brother Rory's pottage was indeed one of the best Arthur had ever had. After two bowls he would have been content to sit on the bench in the priest's garden and enjoy the crisp summer afternoon, but they needed to be on their way.

As he pushed back from the table, he heard it again. Singing. Louder this time. The sweet, musical tones were stunning in their beauty, filling him with a sense of awe like that which occurred when beholding a natural wonder. Like a perfect sunset. Or the mist upon a loch at dawn.

"Who's that?" he asked almost reverently.

Brother Rory gave him a strange look that shook Arthur out of his trance. He'd spoken without thought, not adjusting for his keen hearing.

The priest listened and seemed to realize what he'd heard. "Ah, the lady is visiting from the castle today. She must be singing to Duncan—he loves nothing better since he returned than to hear the lady sing."

Arthur froze. His senses no longer buzzed, they clamored. It couldn't be.

Oblivious to Arthur's reaction, Brother Rory continued. "Her visits are looked forward to by everyone. She brings such cheer." His chest puffed with pride. "The lady never forgets us, or the people who have served her grandfather."

"What lady?" Dugald asked.

"The Lady Anna. The Lord of Lorn's youngest daughter. An angel sent from heaven, that's what she is."

More like sent by the devil to torment Arthur.

Dugald took one look at Arthur's face and burst out laughing. "Sounds like the lass has tracked you down."

Arthur couldn't believe it. She couldn't have found him . . . could she? The other men would have returned yesterday.

He shook it off. Nay, it was impossible. A coincidence. An *unfortunate* coincidence.

Brother Rory looked confused by Dugald's jest. "The lady comes every other Friday. As dependable as mist on the mountaintops. Do you know her?"

"A little," Arthur said, before Dugald could respond.

Even more anxious to leave than before, he hurried to the post in the garden where they'd tied their horses.

Unfortunately, Lady Anna chose this moment to leave the small cottage she'd been visiting.

She stepped out on the path, not more than fifty yards away, and turned to wave goodbye to the woman and two small children who stood in the doorway. The sun caught her hair in a halo of golden light.

He felt a strange skip in his chest. He'd thought about her more than he wanted to admit, and he'd be damned if seeing her didn't make him feel a brief flash of . . .

Hell. It felt like happiness. As if he'd actually missed her. But of course he hadn't missed her. She was a nuisance. An *adorable* nuisance.

Her gaze turned in his direction.

He saw her startle and knew she'd seen him. But she pretended not to, spinning around and heading quickly down the path toward the loch.

Away from him, her guardsman following trustily behind.

Arthur frowned. Not because she's just ignored him, he told himself. Nay, because of her guardsman. Her *solitary* guardsman.

Before he could think better of it, he shouted, "Lady Anna!"

He could see her shoulders lift to her ears from here. Why that particular movement irritated him, he didn't know, but it did.

Ignoring his grinning fool of a brother, he retied his horse to the post and strode toward her.

She seemed to stiffen—*stiffen,* damn it—straightening her spine and bringing her basket closer to her side, almost as if she were preparing to do battle.

"Sir Arthur," she said in that soft, breathless tone that he'd forgotten. *Right.* She looked past his shoulder to his brother. "Sir Dugald. What a surprise."

It didn't sound like a pleasant one. What the hell was the matter with her? Had her interest drifted already?

That's what he wanted, blast it.

He stopped right in front of her, perhaps a step too close. If he didn't know himself better, he'd say he was trying to intimidate her. Using his size to block an escape. But he wasn't a barbarian—he didn't do things like that.

"Where are the rest of your men?" he snapped.

Her brows furrowed, creating those little lines atop her nose. "What men?"

He tried to sound patient but failed. "I see but a solitary guardsman," he said, with a nod of acknowledgment to the young soldier.

She smiled. "Robby always accompanies me on Fridays. He was raised in this village."

Arthur's nonexistent temper started to rise again. Robby, though tall, couldn't be more than ten and eight, and he sure as hell wouldn't stop anyone intent on harming her.

Satan's stones, there was a bloody war going on! What in Hades was Lorn thinking to let her wander like this?

He turned to his brother. "I'll take the friar to Oban. You return to the castle with Lady Anna."

Ah hell. He saw his brother's eyes narrow and knew she'd done it again. She'd made him do something without thinking. He'd just given an order to his captain. He didn't make mistakes like that.

"I'll take the friar," Dugald said, a hard edge to his voice. "*You* can take the Lady Anna."

The lady in question seemed to pick up on the sudden

tension between the two brothers. "No one needs to take me anywhere. I'm perfectly fine with Robby."

Arthur felt himself backed into the corner again. He knew his brother: Dugald had dug in his heels and would not retreat. Arthur had challenged his authority, and he couldn't afford to get in a pissing match with his brother. If someone was going to accompany her, it would have to be him.

But that would mean giving up on a chance to see whether the friar was one of Lorn's messengers.

He should just let her go. Most likely she'd be fine.

Most likely.

The days were long. It probably would still be light when she returned.

Probably.

His fists clenched as the frustration coiled inside him. "I'm sure you are fine," he said, to preserve the lad's tender pride. "But it would be my honor to see you back to the castle, my lady."

Anna wasn't happy to see him at all.

After weeks of avoiding her—leaving at the first opportunity—*now* the contrary man decides to anoint himself her stalwart protector?

Of course, she hadn't forgotten what he'd done for her. When she'd looked up into those amazing dark golden eyes and realized that he'd caught her, realized that he'd saved her, realized he was cradling her in his arms . . .

It had been the most romantic moment of her life.

The most romantic *single* moment. Because the next he'd set her on her feet, told her to be more careful, and left her standing there gaping at him.

How had he reached her so quickly? She remembered the flash of alarm in his eyes. It was almost as if he knew she'd been about to fall. Which of course was ridiculous . . . wasn't it?

But unconsciously she tucked her basket closer to her side. The man was entirely too watchful; she would have to think of something to distract him.

"Come along then, if you insist." She spun on her heel and started back down the path.

His hand on her elbow, however, stopped her in her tracks. Her heart stopped as well, before kicking into a sudden race. He wasn't gripping her hard, but she could feel every one of his fingers burning into her skin. A blast of awareness flooded her skin with heat.

She'd told herself she'd exaggerated the intensity of her reaction to him. But she hadn't. Why *him*? Her attraction to him was inexplicable.

"Where is your horse?" he demanded. "The castle is in the other direction."

"I'm not yet returning to the castle. I've still a few more villagers to visit."

"It will be dark soon."

Lud, he had a forbidding frown. She carefully extracted her elbow from his hand. "It won't be dark for at least four hours. I've plenty of time."

And before he could argue, she started off down the path, waving her quick goodbyes to Brother Rory, the friar, and Sir Dugald.

From his disapproving expression, she could tell that Arthur wasn't pleased with the arrangement, but he followed along beside her like a brooding, unwelcome shadow.

They visited three more homes. The first belonged to Malcolm, who'd lost his sword arm fighting against the rebels at Glen Trool and was having a difficult time adjusting to life away from the battlefield.

Yet covered in scars and missing an arm, Anna knew he'd give another one if only he could go back. She didn't understand this love some men had for war, and probably never would. She was tired of scars, of missing limbs, of wives without husbands and children without fathers.

Her nose wrinkled and she cast a surreptitious glance at the man in the corner. Not all scars bothered her, it seemed. Some were rather . . . attractive.

He had scars. One along his jaw that stood out when he clenched his teeth—which around her he seemed to do often—and a small nick on his right cheek. His hands were littered with them. He probably had some on his arms. And on his chest.

Her body flooded with heat as an image of his broad, powerfully muscled chest sprang to mind. Naked.

Nails to the cross, what was wrong with her? Fantasies—were she to engage in any—were utterly inappropriate in the middle of the day while trying to read to an injured man.

She might not be able to put a stop to the war, but she would do what she could to help, no matter how small. Malcolm's wife, Seonaid, said he drank less *uisge-beatha* after she read to him, so Anna continued to bring her prized copy of Thomas of Britain's *Tristan*. The old warrior loved the doomed tale of love between the knight and the Irish princess almost as much as she did.

She ignored the man brooding near the door, but she could feel him watching her.

It wasn't until they'd left that he said, "You know how to read."

She shrugged, knowing it wasn't common in the Highlands. "My father thought it important that all of his children be educated." She met his gaze, challenging him to say something. "Even the girls."

He gave her a long look—frowning again—but didn't comment.

The next house she visited belonged to the village healer. Afraig was getting old and didn't travel around the countryside as easily as before, so whenever she visited, Anna brought a few herbs and plants that she'd collected in the forest near Dunstaffnage.

Anna saved the most important stop for last. Her recently widowed friend Beth had been left with five children, including baby Catrine—Cate—born not three months ago, six months after the poor babe's father had been killed in an ambush by Bruce's men near Inverlochy Castle, right before it fell to the rebels.

The death of her husband had only hardened Beth's resolve. Like Anna, she would do what she could to help defeat King Hood and put an end to the war.

Anna hoped Sir Arthur would get bored with their chatter and find something else to do, but he seemed content to sit by the door with Robby and wait. Watching her with that too-intense, too-perceptive, golden-eyed gaze of his. It was almost as if he knew she was up to something.

She could see the older children kicking a ball around outside through the two small openings in the stone. The wooden shutters had been pulled back to allow the fresh summer air to breeze through the long single-room building. Suddenly, the play stopped, and she had her opportunity.

She looked at Sir Arthur over the head of the sleeping baby nestled in her arms. "It looks like the children's ball is stuck on the roof of the barn again. Would you mind—"

"I'll get it," Robby said, jumping up as if he'd been waiting for any excuse to leave. She had to bite back a smile at his eagerness. Perhaps she'd gone a little overboard in asking Beth to describe—in detail—Cate's recent digestive problems, including the rainbow of colors that ended up on her cloths.

Right result, wrong man.

"I suppose we should be getting on." She stood up, intending to give the sleeping child back to Beth.

But then she had another idea and had to fight back the smile that rose to her lips. She knew just how to distract him.

"I almost forgot," she said to Beth. "I've brought you some tarts."

"And I have some fresh sugared buns for you as well," Beth said, catching on.

Before he realized what she intended, Anna placed the sleeping baby in Sir Arthur's lap and picked up her basket.

The look on his face was full of such abject horror, it took everything she had not to burst out into laughter. His expression was almost worth the trouble he'd caused her. *Almost.*

He immediately tried to hand the baby back to her. "I don't know anything—"

"There's nothing to it," Anna said sweetly. "Just keep your arm under her head like that and she'll be fine."

He, on the other hand, looked decidedly ill.

All the jostling had caused the baby to stir, and she started to emit a series of little grunts and cries.

The fierce knight who looked as though he could single-handedly take down an army gazed up at Anna, begging for mercy.

Despite her amusement, there was something oddly arresting about the sight of the tall, muscular warrior cradling the tiny infant in his arms, awkwardly but with a gentleness that made her heart take a funny little skip.

Their eyes met, and something strange passed between them. A primal awareness of the attraction sizzling between them. An acknowledgment of the possibility that between a man and a woman such blessings might come. What would it be like to see him holding *their* child?

Embarrassed by the fanciful direction of her thoughts, Anna dropped her gaze. Envisioning possible offspring with a man she barely knew was definitely something new for her.

"Rock her a little," she encouraged, feeling a bit sorry for him. "She likes that. We won't be long."

And with that she followed Beth to the far end of the room, where the kitchen stood.

And Cate, bless. the wee angel, did her part. Her soft cries and progressively louder wails covered up their quick exchange.

By the time Beth returned to claim her baby, Sir Arthur looked as if he'd just been dragged through hell behind Satan's chariot.

"Now that wasn't so bad, was it?" she said as they were leaving the small cottage.

His eyes narrowed dangerously. He looked as though he very much wanted to throttle her. Dragging a reaction from him was certainly proving enjoyable.

Anna said goodbye to the children, promising to return soon. Robby had brought the horses, and it wasn't long before they were on their way.

She knew she should try to use the opportunity to learn more about him, but she was tired from her long day at the village, and, if she were truthful, not in the mood to be rejected.

That strange moment at Beth's had made her feel . . . vulnerable. She didn't want to think of him that way. She didn't want her heart to wander. She was merely keeping an eye on him for her father, not pursuing him in truth.

They rode single-file for the first few miles, but when the road widened, Sir Arthur dropped back from his position in the lead and pulled alongside her.

She was surprised when he spoke. Initiating conversation? This was a first.

"Why do you do it?" She looked at him uncertainly, and he explained, "Surround yourself with such . . ." He struggled to find the word. "Things."

"You mean the fruits of war?" she challenged.

She wasn't surprised that he didn't know how to speak of what he'd seen. Warriors focused on the glory, on the honor of the battlefield, not on what happened when it went wrong. Missing limbs and fatherless children weren't something a man wanted to go into battle thinking about. She understood blocking out such thoughts was necessary, but it didn't mean it wasn't the reality.

"I thought you didn't like it, yet . . ." He shrugged.

"I hate war," she said harshly. "And I can't wait for it to be over, but it doesn't mean I don't want to do my part. This is what I can do. If a few songs and stories, or holding a child for a while so her mother can have a moment of peace, bring a few moments of cheer, then that's what I'll do."

He gave her a hard, assessing look. "You have a soft heart." It didn't sound as if he thought that was a good thing. "The soldier was not deserving of your time. He's killing himself with drink."

She heard the disgust in his voice. She suspected he thought the man weak. "Perhaps," she admitted. "But Malcolm fought for my father with honor and loyalty for years. Does he not deserve a few moments of my time for his sacrifice?"

"It's his duty."

"As this is mine."

"You make it your duty."

This time it was she who shrugged.

He frowned at her again. "You're exhausted."

She realized she must be getting used to those forbidding looks, because she merely laughed. "I am."

"What were you and your friend whispering about?"

The sudden change of topic caught her off guard. She startled but composed herself quickly. "Women's things."

"What kind of women's things?"

Her eyes twinkled as she gave him a pointed look. "Do you really want to know?" she dared.

He turned away quickly. "Perhaps not."

My God, he's blushing! She hadn't thought it possible. But the tiny chip in his steely facade only added to his appeal. It was charming. *He* was charming. Not in the gallant, sweep-her-off-her-feet manner of a courtier, but in a far more subtle way. It was as if he'd just lifted the curtain a little and shown her a part of himself that he did not often reveal. The hint of boyishness was so unexpected, and *that* charmed her.

The knot in her chest clenched a little tighter.

Anna knew she was in trouble. Sir Arthur intrigued her, and that was dangerous. It was better to think of him as just a simple warrior, the type of man she could understand—and dismiss. She didn't want to learn things about him. She didn't want to see a different side of him. She didn't want to be curious. And she didn't want to be so blasted *attracted* to him.

She had her life all planned out. When the war was over, her father would find her a good man to marry. They would have a house full of children, hopefully in the Highlands close to her family, and they would live a life of peace and happy quiet. She wouldn't need to worry about everything she knew, everything she loved, being destroyed. *Stability.* That was what she wanted.

He might have surprised her, but it didn't change one fundamental problem: Sir Arthur was a warrior. A man who looked like he'd been born with a sword in his hand—and would die the same way. He could never give her what she wanted.

For Anna knew that a man who was always looking at the door as though he wanted to leave would inevitably walk through it.

Arthur didn't like what he was learning about Anna MacDougall. It was far easier to dismiss her as a naive, pampered princess, living in a fantasy world, with little understanding of what was going on around her.

But that wasn't the case at all. She knew what was happening around her, maybe even better than he did. Like most warriors, Arthur distanced himself from the repercussions of war. He didn't want to think about what happened afterward. Seeing war through her eyes . . .

The death. The devastation. Men without limbs dulling the pain with drink. Women left to fend for themselves. Children without fathers. The reality.

He frowned. How many times had he passed by these things and not seen them? Ridden by a burned-out castle or farm and never thought about the people who lived there?

He'd been fighting almost his entire life, but all of a sudden he felt exhausted.

"Why don't you like me?"

The directness of the question disarmed him—though perhaps it shouldn't have. Anna didn't shy away from anything. Open and outgoing, she spoke her mind with the confidence that came only from a lifetime of being loved, cherished, and encouraged. It was one of the things that was so unusual—and so entrancing—about her.

He hesitated, not sure how to respond. "I don't dislike you." From her expression he could tell that she didn't believe him. "It's as I told you before, I'm here to do a job. I don't have time for anything else."

"Is it because of the feud?"

He tensed, not liking where this was going. This wasn't a conversation he wanted to have with anybody—especially not her. "The feud has been over for many years."

"So it's all in the past? You aren't angry about your land or the castle on Loch Awe."

He checked the reflexive surge in his pulse. He was angry. But not at her. "That land would have belonged to my brother Neil—not me. It would have been forfeit after Methven. King Edward recompensed us for the loss and has rewarded my brothers and myself for our loyalty."

"Then is it because of your father?"

He stilled. *Christ.* It must be a MacDougall trait to instinctively aim for the gullet. Though intended kindly, her words eviscerated. "My father died in battle."

"At my father's hand," she said quietly. "It would be understandable if you hated me for it."

He wished he could. But Anna was not to blame for the sins of her father. "I don't hate you." Far from it. He wanted her. More than he'd ever wanted a woman in his life. "What happened is in the past."

He could feel her gaze on him, but he kept his face straight ahead. "Why are you really here?"

"What do you mean?"

"What do you want?"

Justice. Revenge. In this case, they were the same thing. "What most knights fight for: land and reward."

In his case, Bruce had promised to restore Innis Chonnel to his brother and had dangled the promise of a rich bride for Arthur—the richest in the Highlands, Christina MacRuairi, Lady of the Isles.

"And nothing else?"

"An end to the war."

"Then we want the same thing."

She didn't know how wrong she was. An end to the war for him would see Bruce on the throne and the MacDougalls destroyed.

He gave her a sidelong glance. She was so beautiful she made his chest hurt. But that beauty had deceived him. He'd seen the innocent freshness of her face and sweetness of her smile, but not the strength. For a man who prided himself on perception and observation, it was disconcerting to have been so wrong.

In light of what he'd seen today, her actions over the past two weeks—the feast, the games—took on a different cast. Perhaps it wasn't fantasy, but a means of protection: doing what she could to preserve a way of life that was tumbling down around her ears.

Though he admired her, he was also sorry for her. She

was fighting a losing battle. And there was a fragility to her strength that made him wonder whether she knew it as well.

He wished he could protect her. Which was both ironic and ridiculous, given that he was here to destroy that which she was trying so desperately to hold on to.

He was surprised how much it bothered him.

Whether he liked it or not, Anna MacDougall was the enemy.

Seven

They rode in silence for a few miles before Arthur spoke again. "There's a burn ahead where we can stop to water the horses and have a bite to eat if you are hungry." He inhaled the caramel scent of butter and sugar. "The smell of those buns is making me hungry."

He thought her cheeks paled a little, but perhaps it was the fading light. "Please, don't stop on my account. The horses will be fine until we—"

She stopped, peering through the trees to the bank of the small river ahead. "What are those boys doing?"

Arthur heard a muffled, frantic barking. From the thrashing bag slung over one of the boys' shoulders, he could guess. "Come," he said. "We'll stop at the next burn."

Her eyes narrowed and then widened in horror when she realized what was happening. "No!" she shouted, galloping forward as the boys started to lower the bag into the water. "Stop!"

The lads, ranging from about ten to fifteen, looked up in stunned awe as she approached. Arthur could only imagine their incredulity at seeing a nymph spring from the forest like a crusading Valkyrie.

"What do you have in that bag?" she asked as they stared up at her dumbly.

The eldest boy found his tongue first. " 'Tis only a pup, m'lady. The sickly runt of the litter."

The little cry of despair in her throat tugged strangely in Arthur's chest.

"Let me see him," she demanded.

One of the younger boys said, "You don't want him, m'lady. His own mother don't want him. He'll starve if we don't get rid of 'im."

She made another one of those cries and the pain in his chest sharpened. Arthur feared he'd do just about anything never to hear that sound again.

"Show the lady," he said sternly.

The boys started to shuffle their feet as if they'd been caught doing something wrong, although they'd only meant to do the pup a kindness.

The eldest boy dropped the bag on the ground and loosened the tie. He folded back the edge of the bag, revealing the skinniest, ugliest puppy Arthur had ever seen.

"He's adorable!" Anna exclaimed, jumping from her horse before either Arthur or Robby could help her.

The boys gazed at her as if she were daft.

She kneeled down and scooped the pathetic-looking ball of matted gray-and-black fur in her arms. "The poor little thing is terrified." She looked up to Arthur for sympathy. "Look how badly he's shaking."

Arthur could see right away that the young deerhound did not have long for this world. He was small and painfully thin. His mother had probably refused to feed him since he'd been born.

"The lads are saving the pup from a far worse death," he said gently. "He won't survive."

Anna narrowed her eyes and pursed her mouth, giving him a glimpse of stubbornness that he suspected could be every bit as formidable as his own.

"I'll take him."

Her generous heart was preventing her from seeing reality. "How will you feed him?"

She lifted her chin, giving him a glare that chastised him for daring to talk about realities. "I'll think of something."

He heard the determination in her voice and knew she wouldn't be dissuaded. For someone who looked as threatening as a kitten, she could certainly be stubborn.

"He's not worth it, my lady," one of the boys said. "He'll never make a good hound. If you want a dog, you can have one of his brothers."

As if he knew he'd found his champion, the pup burrowed his head into her arm. She shook her head and smiled. "I don't want another one, I want *him*."

I want him. Her words resonated. Hell, for a second he'd almost envied a damned dog.

The lad shrugged as if to say *What can you do?* Clearly, he thought the lady was foolish, but she was the lord's granddaughter so he wouldn't argue with her.

Arthur took one look at her cooing gently to the dog in her arms and wanted to agree—mostly because he didn't want to see her go through the frustration of trying to nurse the creature back to life—but he couldn't.

A long time ago he'd been that runt.

Odd that he was even thinking about it. He never thought about the past. The struggles of his boyhood had made him the warrior he was today. He'd worked harder. Trained harder. Taken the abilities that had set him apart and honed them into something extraordinary. He'd forged his own destiny. He might not have been born a warrior, but he'd made himself one of the best.

It had been his focus for so long, he hadn't thought of anything else.

But it hadn't always been so.

Arthur watched her fuss over the small, pathetic creature in her arms and felt a stirring of . . . something.

He turned harshly away, irritated by the twinges of sentiment provoked by the lass's compassion. She was the enemy, he reminded himself. But it rang hollow even to his own ears.

Sir Arthur had retreated back into his shield of silence and indifference, but Anna was too busy trying to soothe the squirming ball of dark fur in her arms to notice. Well, perhaps she'd noticed, but she *was* busy. The pup seemed to have realized he'd escaped danger, and his terrified shaking had turned to whimpers of hunger.

They were only a few miles away from the castle when she asked to stop. She had to try to feed him; his pathetic little cries were tearing at her heart.

Though the sun would not set for at least a half hour, deep inside the thick forest that sat to the east of Dunstaffnage it was dark already. She didn't like the forest at night and was suddenly grateful for Sir Arthur's insistence on accompanying her.

He and Robby saw to the horses while she saw to her new charge. She'd wrapped the pup in the plaid she'd brought in case the summer evening drew chill and used it to make a little bed for him as she went about trying to fashion something for him to eat. Pulling off her thin leather glove and tying it at the wrist, she filled it with water from the stream. She wished she had milk, but water would have to do for now. Using a needle from her basket, she poked a hole in one of the fingertips. Then, after tearing a few pieces of bread from one of the rolls, she turned back to the pup.

Bollocks! She muttered one of Alan's favorite oaths. The little scamp had wandered off. Lying the glove and pieces of bread down in the blanket, she gazed around frantically.

There. She smiled. He hadn't wandered far, she could see him just beyond a big tree.

She called to him but he ran from her, obviously still

frightened. His little paws scooted through the leaves and dirt like wooden pegs. But he was too weak to go far, and Anna caught up to him after a few minutes.

Scooping him up in her arms, she cradled him against her chest. "Naughty little boy," she cooed. "I won't hurt you. Don't you want to eat?"

He licked the tip of her nose in answer, and she giggled.

"Then I'd better get you back." She looked around, realizing that she'd gone farther than she thought. She hurried her step, anxious to return to the stream, trying not to notice that the shadows were growing darker and more menacing as the forest closed in around her.

Her heart jumped when Sir Arthur suddenly stepped out in front of her. Dear Lord, he'd come out of nowhere! She hadn't heard a sound.

"Where the hell did you go?" he demanded.

Anna's eyes widened. The coarse language even more than the glint in his eye surprised her. He looked concerned. Worried. Definitely *not* indifferent. It was the same way he'd looked when he'd caught her. She'd almost convinced herself that she'd been imagining it.

She nuzzled the puppy in her arms, planting a soft kiss on his head. "I put him down to get some food and he wandered off."

To her surprise, he reached down and stroked the puppy under his chin. The unconscious gentleness made her heart catch.

His touch on her would be just as gentle, and the sharp pang of yearning that hit stunned her. She'd never craved a man's touch before. But she wanted to feel those big battle-scarred, callused hands on her skin. Her face. Her neck. And . . .

Her breasts.

Heat rose to her cheeks. Saints preserve her, where had that come from?

Their eyes caught, but she quickly looked away, fearing he would read her wanton thoughts.

"Next time let me know where you are going," he said roughly. There was something tight and husky in his voice that she didn't understand. "It isn't safe—"

He stopped suddenly and stilled as if he'd heard something. Anna listened, but didn't hear a sound. Indeed, it was oddly quiet.

She clutched his arm, instinctively moving closer to him. "What is it?"

"We need to get back to the horses. It's the puppy."

He pulled at his sword and tucked her against him. Despite the sudden hammering of her heart, she felt safe. Protected. And something else. He felt familiar.

"What's wrong?" she asked breathlessly, trying to keep up with him. "What do you mean, 'It's the puppy'?"

He didn't answer her, but pushed her along faster. "Hurry, they're coming."

"What's coming?" Her voice betrayed her fear. "I don't hear anything."

"Wolves."

She gasped, looking around wildly. "I don't see . . ." She pulled the puppy closer to her chest. "I won't leave him."

He gave her an exasperated look. "I know." But then he swore. He pushed her against a large tree, tore the dog from her arms, and then used his body as a shield in front of her. "Stay behind me," he ordered. "If I tell you to run, do it."

"I won't—"

He gave her a fierce glare. "You will. I will do my best to save your dog, but I won't let you be killed for him."

Anna didn't understand. How could he be so certain? She didn't hear or see anything.

Then she heard it. The faintest sound of movement. Running. Coming toward them.

How had he known . . . ?

The pack sprang out of the trees with bloodcurdling swiftness. Wolves were shy by nature and usually avoided humans. *It's the puppy*. That's what he'd meant. They wanted the puppy.

At first she thought there were a dozen of them, but when her mind cleared to finally enable her to count them, she could see it was only half that many.

"Robby?" she asked.

Sir Arthur shook his head. "I ordered him to stay with the horses."

She sighed with relief. She didn't want the young guardsman to unknowingly stumble on them and startle the wolves into attacking him.

Sir Arthur held his sword out, turning from side to side. The wolves snarled, fur standing on end, their eyes pinned to the puppy Sir Arthur had tucked under his arm. Was it her imagination, or did they look hungry?

They seemed to be sitting back, shrewdly assessing their opponent, trying to find his weakness and waiting for the right moment to spring. Though she couldn't see his face, she knew Sir Arthur was doing the same.

The biggest wolf took a step forward, as if trying to draw Sir Arthur to him. He was, she realized. The other wolves had started to circle behind them. God, how smart they were. The wolf wanted Sir Arthur to move toward him and then the others would attack from the rear.

Instead, Sir Arthur held the puppy out by the scruff, daring the biggest wolf toward him.

"What are you doing?" she cried.

"Hopefully getting rid of the leader. Be ready," he warned.

When she didn't respond, he looked at her. "Anna!"

She nodded quickly, not wanting him distracted. Sir Arthur had just turned back when the biggest wolf attacked, leaping through the air for the wriggling pup.

Sir Arthur moved faster than she would have thought

possible. She'd never seen reflexes like that. Anna smothered a scream in her hands as he tucked the puppy out of harm's way with one arm and sliced through the air with the other.

She turned her gaze after seeing the line of red appear across the wolf's throat. A second later, she heard the thud of its body hit the ground. Without their leader, the wolves seemed to shrink back. Sir Arthur took a few steps forward, swinging the magnificent great sword back and forth in the air effortlessly, though because of the pup he was using only one hand. His right, she noticed. Not even his strong arm.

One more wolf ventured tentatively forward, but a hard hit by the side of the sword cured him of bravery. As quickly as they'd appeared, the wolves fled, disappearing into the darkness.

It had lasted no longer than a minute, but it had been the longest minute of her life. Arthur lowered his sword and turned back to her.

She didn't know who moved first, but she was in the circle of his arms, pressed up against the hard shield of his chest. She burrowed her head for a moment—not unlike her puppy was doing in the other arm—and let the fear slide from her body.

"Are you all right?"

She looked up at him. His face was so still; the only sign of how affected he'd been was the heavy beat of his heart. She wanted to say she was fine, that she'd never felt more safe, but his mouth was so close that all she could think about was how much she wanted him to kiss her. How much she *needed* him to kiss her.

He was so handsome, with his dark, wavy brown hair and strange golden-amber eyes. She liked the dent in his chin and the slight crookedness of his nose where it had probably been broken. But it was his mouth, wide and undeniably sensual, that she could not look away from. It looked so soft, while the rest of him was so strong.

He was strong. And safe.

He made a harsh sound in his throat and pressed her closer to him. His gaze lowered to her mouth and she knew he was going to kiss her.

His hand fell to her face. The rough pads of his fingers cupped her chin. Her heart strummed like the strings of a harp. So incredibly gentle. Just like she'd imagined.

His eyes darkened with something hot that made her body flutter in naughty places. He was staring at her mouth as if he wanted to devour her. The sensations were so strong—so palpable—she could almost feel his mouth on hers. The soft caress of lips. Her stomach flipped. The heady taste of spice.

She was so convinced he was going to kiss her that when he released her instead, her legs wobbled.

He looked away for a moment, as if he were fighting some invisible battle, every inch of his body drawn up as tight as a bowstring.

Abruptly, he turned back to her, the heat in his eyes gone. He handed her back the puppy. "We need to get back."

This time the remote indifference stung. Confused by the intensity of her body's reaction, by her weakness, his control felt like a slap. He might want her, but he wasn't going to act on his desire.

Desire. That was what she was feeling. That was what had made her pulse race and her body heat when she thought he was going to kiss her. And that was the disappointment that was crashing through her now.

She squeezed the puppy in her arms and nuzzled his warm, furry head. At least *he* liked her.

Heat prickled her eyes, but she pushed it back angrily. The emotion was because of the wolves, she told herself. She was feeling vulnerable because of the attack—not because of his rejection.

She drew a deep breath, trying to get hold of her tangled emotions. Like him, she was determined to pretend as if that moment had never happened.

He'd come to her rescue once more, and she'd nearly forgotten to thank him. He tried to lead her away, but she stopped him. "Thank you," she said.

He shrugged off her gratitude. "It was nothing."

A modest knight? She didn't think such a thing existed. But perhaps she should have guessed he'd be that way. He seemed determined not to draw attention to himself.

"I know you probably won't believe me," she said, "but I'm not usually this in need of rescue."

One side of his mouth lifted. "This time it wasn't you, it was him." He pointed to the puppy in her arms.

"We were both fortunate to have you looking out for us. Our very own knight in shining armor."

She was only teasing, but his expression returned to serious. "Don't believe in faerie tales, Lady Anna. You'll only be disappointed."

She heard the warning, but he was wrong. "You were amazing. I've never seen anyone react so quickly. It was as if . . ."

Her brows drew together. The moments before the attack were coming back to her. How did he know the wolves were going to attack? It was the same as at the cliff. It was almost as if he knew what was going to happen, as if he'd sensed it before he should have.

Dear Lord, *he had*. Her eyes widened, and her gaze jerked to his. Did that explain the strange intensity she'd sensed simmering under the surface? She'd attributed it to watchfulness and keen observation, but was it something more?

She took a step backward and covered her mouth with her hand. "You *knew*."

*   *   *

Arthur tensed, muscles clenched, as he braced himself for the fear. For the revulsion that always came on the rare occasions when someone caught a glimpse of his unusual abilities. Even his own parents had looked at him like that.

As a boy, he'd tried to pretend he wasn't different. He'd tried to explain. Tried to make them understand that he wasn't some kind of freak—that his senses were sharper, his awareness heightened, his skill at observation and perception keener, but that was all. He didn't see the future. He didn't have premonitions.

It was more an inkling.

But after a while he'd stopped trying to explain. It was easier not to deal with it at all. So he kept to himself, and didn't allow people close enough to give them a chance to guess.

He was different, he knew now. He'd been blessed with extraordinary abilities. Being alone didn't bother him— hell, he preferred it that way.

But Anna MacDougall wouldn't let him be. He was trying to resist, but she kept dragging him in. And now she'd seen something that she shouldn't have.

Though he was prepared for her reaction, her involuntary step back stung. His lungs filled with fire. He pretended not to hear her question and started back toward the horses.

What the hell did he care what she thought? He should be glad to be rid of her.

"Wait," she said, chasing after him. "Why are you angry?"

He didn't look at her, but kept walking. "I'm not angry."

He only sounded that way.

"Wait," she repeated, grabbing his arm. "I want to talk about what just happened."

Why the hell did she always have to touch him? He jerked his arm from her grasp but made the mistake of glancing down at her face.

"God damn it, stop looking at me like that," he growled.

His vehemence startled her, which was good, as it got rid of the hurt.

"How am I looking at you?"

"Like I just stepped on that puppy of yours."

She lifted her chin, her eyes sparking dangerously. "You'll have to forgive me; I didn't realize you had such a strong aversion to my touch. I'll try to remember it in the future."

Was the lass daft? He'd laugh if he wasn't so furious. Aversion to her touch? It should be the other way around. She should be cringing away from him, not touching him. And certainly not looking hurt for him jerking away. What the hell was the matter with her?

She wasn't acting the way she was supposed to. Even Catherine, the woman who'd professed to love him, had refused to be in the same room with him after he'd pushed her out of the way of a stone corbel that fell where she'd been standing a moment before.

Perhaps Anna hadn't guessed.

"I didn't mean to make you uncomfortable; it's just that what you did back there was remarkable."

She'd guessed all right. But that sure as hell couldn't be admiration he read in her gaze.

He clenched his jaw. "I fought off a few wolves—anyone could have done as much. You make too much of it. Come. Robby will be wondering what has happened to us."

If he'd thought to put her off, he'd failed. "It was more than that and you know it. The wolves were too far away for you to have heard them. Yet you knew they were coming. You sensed it before any normal—"

He flinched. Even after more than twenty years of it, he still flinched. That angered him more than anything else. He grabbed her arm and hauled her close to him, bringing her mouth only inches from his. Even through the anger he felt the bolt of gut-wrenching, mind-numbing lust.

She was pushing him from every direction—her incessant flirting, her sweet face and sinful body, her tantalizing scent, her bloody questions—and she didn't know how close he was to giving her what she was asking for. He didn't flirt. He didn't dance. He didn't play around. If a woman offered, he took. Simple and uncomplicated.

And he kept it that way.

"Look," he said tightly; fighting the urge to ravish her senseless had stripped him of niceties. Throwing her up against that tree was looking too appealing. "I don't know what the hell you think you saw, but you're mistaken. I heard the wolves and reacted. Just because you didn't hear them, don't start imagining things."

"I couldn't have heard them," she persisted. "They were too far away."

"For you. You aren't trained to look for the signs. The unnatural silence, their scent in the wind."

But she wasn't listening to his explanations. He could feel her eyes on his face and regretted their closeness. "What are you trying to hide?"

"Nothing." He let go of her. Not very gently.

Her scrutiny intensified, and he had to fight the urge not to turn away. God damn it, he didn't turn away from anything.

"I think you're lying," she said softly. "I think you keep to yourself so people won't see what I just saw. I think you're pushing me away right now for the same reason."

Arthur stilled. Everything inside him chilled except for a small place in the very deepest part of him. *That* was burning.

He didn't want her compassion, damn it. He wasn't a puppy that needed rescuing.

He reacted the only way he knew how. His gaze met hers. "Did it ever occur to you that I'm pushing you away because I don't want you?"

She gasped, flinching from the bald cruelty of his words.

She blinked rapidly, and he felt the burning in his chest squeeze and squeeze. But he wouldn't comfort her. This was for the best.

Still, her wobbly smile nearly broke him. "Much to my shame, it didn't. I'm sorry for any embarrassment that I may have caused you."

As regal as any queen, she turned on her heel and walked away.

And despite the fire eating away in his chest, he let her.

Eight

It was the longest ride of Anna's life. She'd never been so humiliated in her life. But by the time they'd returned to the castle, that humiliation had turned to anger.

"*. . . I don't want you.*"

He'd *lied*.

She'd seen it in his eyes when he'd held her—he did want her. But for some reason he wanted her to think differently.

Determined to prove that she hadn't been imagining it, when Robby came over to help her down from her horse, she handed him the puppy instead.

"Sir Arthur," she said with exaggerated sweetness. "If you would be so kind."

He gave her a blank look, but she was beginning to be able to read those "blank" looks and saw the flicker of suspicion.

It was warranted.

When he took her hand to help her down, she leaned too far forward, forcing him to catch her to prevent her from falling.

For one long heartbeat, she was stretched out against him, her arms laced around his neck, and her hands brushed against the thick, wavy hair that was every bit as silky soft as it looked. She wanted to dig her fingers into it and pull his face down to hers.

He made a sharp sound at the contact—a groan. That's what it was. A deep, masculine groan. And when she looked into his eyes, she knew he was lying. He did want her. And if the white lines around his mouth and the tic twitching under his jaw were any indication, it was rather badly.

She wasn't unaffected herself. Despite the fact that it was hardly a surprise where she'd ended up, she gasped and her heart thumped wildly against the hard, cold steel of his chest—mail or flesh, it was hard to tell the difference.

When her head stopped spinning, she unlaced her arms, allowing her body to slide down his before letting go. He was as hard and unyielding as a rock, every muscle pulled taut. She could feel the tension licking off him like flames from a fire.

"So sorry about that," she said with a careless smile. "I don't know what's wrong with me."

His eyes narrowed, but she didn't care. She'd proved her point. She knew it, and more importantly, *he* knew it.

"Have care, my lady," he warned in that dark, smoky voice of his. "You wouldn't want to get hurt doing something foolish."

"How sweet of you to be concerned." She almost gave him a fond pat on the cheek but thought that might be rubbing his nose in it a little too much—she had her victory. "But you needn't worry, I know *exactly* what I'm doing."

She took her dog from Robby and swept into the castle. Though she was tempted, she didn't look back. She'd seen that dark glower enough to know what it looked like.

Anna might have been content to leave it at that—female pride intact—if he hadn't made her curious. Why was he so determined to be rid of her? Was he hiding something, or did he merely seek to avoid the entanglement?

It was almost as if he'd been purposefully trying to be

cruel in the forest. As if she'd hit some kind of nerve. She'd merely wanted to thank him for what he'd done—and the extraordinary abilities he'd demonstrated—but he'd reacted as if she'd accused him of being unnatural.

She bit her lip. Was that it? Was he worried about how other people would react? She supposed it was understandable. Differences weren't tolerated well in today's society, provoking fear and revulsion.

He'd pretended that he hadn't done anything out of the ordinary.

Had he? She bit her lip, no longer certain. It certainly had felt that he had at the time. It had all happened so fast. Had he read signs that she missed, or had it been something more?

Whatever it was, it seemed he didn't want to acknowledge it as anything special. Later, he'd explained to her father what had happened in much the same way as the fall from the cliff, severely minimizing her version of the story with an explanation for everything. Her father had scolded her for putting herself in such danger over a dog and expressed his gratitude to Sir Arthur once again.

Anna didn't understand why Sir Arthur was downplaying what had happened. His skills could be put to great use against the rebels. With his keen abilities, Bruce and his band of pirates would be hard-pressed to wage their ambush-style attacks.

But when she suggested to her father that he take advantage of Sir Arthur's skills, making him a tracker—or better yet, a scout—you'd have thought from the knight's reaction that she'd suggested that he clean out the garderobe. Sir Arthur had been furious at her. Each time their eyes met over the next few days, she felt the hot intensity of his gaze bore into her.

Keeping an eye on him turned out to be easier this time around. For that, she had to thank Squire. It seemed her new puppy had developed an attachment to his rescuer. As soon as Anna's back was turned, Squire—that's what she'd taken to calling him after she heard the men teasing Sir Arthur that he finally had a squire—would make a beeline for the knight. Whether he was in the yard practicing with the men, in the hall eating, or even in the barracks, the dog would find him. If Sir Arthur went out riding for the day, the puppy would sit whinging by the gate until he returned.

It might not have been so bad, if the poor little thing didn't get so excited that whenever he saw the knight he peed. The last time, he'd nearly done so on Sir Arthur's foot.

To say that the puppy was an annoyance to the knight was an understatement. Sir Arthur ignored him, shooed him away, and snapped at him, but no matter how hard he pushed him away, the puppy couldn't get enough.

Squire was a glutton for punishment.

Anna knew the feeling. It seemed she and the pup both had a weakness for ruggedly handsome knights with wavy dark-brown hair, gold-flecked brown eyes, and dents in their chin.

She was drawn to him. Perhaps like the puppy, she sensed that Sir Arthur needed someone. His distance she saw as loneliness, his remoteness as a shield that she was determined to pierce.

Though exactly what she hoped to find, she didn't know. And as the days passed with no cause for suspicion, her excuse for watching him began to wear thin. But if she wasn't watching him for her father, for whom was she?

It was a question that she asked herself as she made her way to the Great Hall for the evening meal. Her father would be expecting a report soon, and she would have to give it to him. She'd found nothing. The knight's greatest offense was a propensity to keep to himself and a keen ability to ignore her.

She knew it was time to put an end to her spying. But why was she so reluctant to let him go?

Sir Arthur was nothing like the men who normally attracted her. But she could not deny she was attracted to him—deeply attracted. More than she'd ever been attracted to a man in her life. Almost enough to make her forget how wrong he was for her.

Aye, it was time to put an end to this.

She was about to exit the spiral stairwell of the donjon into the passageway that led to the Great Hall when a yapping ball of gray-and-black fur went speeding past her feet. Nearly tripping, she muttered an unladylike curse, realizing she must not have securely latched the door to the chamber she shared with her sisters and Squire had managed to escape again.

But thankfully the closed door at the bottom of the stairwell had trapped him. When she caught up with the naughty little thing he was standing at the door, barking and wagging his tail excitedly.

She picked him up and he licked her face. "Where do you think you're going?" she asked. "Let me guess, Sir Arthur?" He barked, seemingly in the affirmative, and she laughed. "You are a fool, little one. When are you going to accept that he doesn't want you around?"

The puppy whinged and cocked his head as if he hadn't heard her right.

She sighed and shook her head. Perhaps she should listen to her own advice. "All right, all right, I'm sorry." She put him down and opened the door. "But don't say I didn't warn you."

She expected the puppy to head for the Great Hall, but he made for the stairs that led to the courtyard instead.

With a sigh, she followed him outside. The cool sea breeze and descending mist cut right through her thin wool summer gown, making her wish she'd brought a plaid—although she hadn't anticipated an evening promenade when she'd gone down to eat. It was dark, and except for the guards along the walls, the *barmkin* was deserted. Everyone would be inside eating.

So why wasn't Sir Arthur?

Squire ran past the well in the center of the courtyard, past the kitchens to the northwest range. Apparently, the knight was in the barracks. The puppy stood by the door waiting for her.

It was quiet out there. Eerily so. And dark in that corner of the courtyard. The men had yet to light the torches near the entry.

She felt a prickle of apprehension as she approached, suddenly wondering if this was a good idea. Tracking him down to the barracks in the middle of the day was one thing, alone at night was another. The puppy seemed to be having second thoughts himself, because he'd stopped barking and was looking at her uncertainly.

"You got us into this," she mumbled. "Too late to turn coward now." Whether she was talking to the dog or herself she didn't know.

She cracked open the door and peeked inside. Her eyes scanned the darkened room, lit only by the simmering embers of the peat fire on the opposite wall.

Squire, apparently having found his courage, darted past her feet into the empty room. She muttered another choice oath, tempted to leave him there, but instead followed him inside.

The door closed behind her with a slam that made her jump.

She forced her pulse to calm, not knowing why she was so jittery. "Squire," she called in a hushed voice, though why she was whispering she didn't know. No one was there.

The puppy ignored her and tore down to the far end of the long, narrow wooden building, jumping on the pallet that she knew must belong to Sir Arthur.

Her pulse spiked again as she drew near, seeing the pile

of belongings strewn across the pallet. Wherever he'd gone, it wouldn't be for long.

She bit her lip, debating. If she'd ever wanted a chance to learn about Sir Arthur Campbell, this was it. Pushing aside the prickle of guilt, she started to go through his things carefully, not knowing exactly what she was looking for. Aside from his mail, gamboissed chausses, a few extra sets of clothing, an extra plaid, and a silver brooch that she'd never seen before, there was little else—certainly nothing personal in nature. Knights traveled light; she didn't know what she'd hoped to find. Something that might help unlock the mystery, perhaps.

Squire was digging at his mail shirt, trying to get to something underneath the pallet. She didn't have time to investigate, however, because at that moment she heard a sound that stopped her blood cold.

The door opened and closed.

Footsteps. The glimmer of a candle.

Nails to the cross, he was back!

Guilt made her panic. Rather than stand there and think of a plausible explanation for being in the barracks, she snatched the puppy off the pallet and looked around for a place to hide. Seeing a large wooden post in the far corner, she ducked behind it just as the circle of light edged into view.

She seemed to have stopped breathing. Too late, she realized the foolishness of hiding. The dog could betray them at any time. But Squire seemed strangely attuned to her nervousness and had buried his head into the crook of her arm.

Sir Arthur set down the candle beside his pallet, giving her a clear view of what he was doing.

Her eyes widened when he tossed a drying cloth he had looped around his neck down on the bed. His hair and shirt were wet. Too late, she realized what he must have been doing and why his mail and belongings were strewn across his bed. He'd been bathing.

She smothered a startled gasp when he grabbed the edges of his wet shirt and yanked it over his head, tossing it down beside the drying cloth.

Her mouth went dry, taking in the rippling mass of muscles that covered him from waist to shoulders.

My God, he was incredible! Broad shoulders, lean waist, thickly built arms, and layer upon layer of muscle that stretched across his stomach. She'd never seen anyone so impossibly . . . cut. He might have been chiseled from stone, his body as perfectly sculpted as a statue. Except that he was flesh and blood—*warm* flesh and blood.

She'd been right to suspect that he would bear the marks of his profession. Scars were liberally strewn across his belly and arms. A large gash across his side and an ugly-looking star-shaped one on his shoulder seemed to be the worst.

She frowned. Below the scar on his upper arm was a strange black mark. She peered in the darkness, unable to make out the design of what appeared to be a tattoo. Although she knew the marks weren't unusual among warriors, she'd never seen one up close and was curious.

A little too curious. She leaned forward, and Squire seemed to take that as an invitation. He jumped out of her lap and raced for the half-naked knight.

When Arthur realized that he wasn't alone, he was furious. When he realized who was there, and that she'd managed to sneak past his defenses, he was livid. No one had surprised him in years, and the fact that it was Lady Anna made it that much worse.

It seemed proof of just how badly the lass had distracted him. Her interference had already put him at risk, drawing too much attention to him. The lass had no idea of what

she was meddling with. It was because of her that he was
now a scout for Lorn, for Christ's sake!

He ignored the annoying pup jumping at his heels and
stared into the darkness, letting her know she'd been discovered.

A moment later, she stepped out from behind the post.
"Sir Arthur," she said brightly, but her hands twisting in
her skirts gave her away. "What a surprise! Squire and I
were just going for a walk and . . . uh, the door was open,
and he must have wanted to see you because he came in
here before I could stop him, and—"

She stopped, gazing up at his face. Her cheeks paled before filling with a nervous flush.

Until that moment, he'd forgotten that he wasn't wearing a shirt.

But the foolish lass didn't have the good sense to look away
or at least pretend not to notice; she stared—blatantly—
and he could read exactly what she was thinking.

Jesus.

The air between them went hot. He could feel her awareness, not just in embarrassment but in something far more
potent: arousal.

She stooped to pick up the dog. "Y-y-you're busy. We
were just leaving—"

"Stay," he ordered the infernal beast, before it could
jump into her arms. The mangy little blighter had better
not try to piss on him again.

Both Anna and the dog froze at the sound of his voice.
And both of them looked at him with that blasted innocent
expression on their faces. He didn't know which one of
them was more trouble.

But it was the lass who concerned him now. He caught
her arm and hauled her up against him. "What were you
really doing here, Lady Anna?"

"Nothing, I . . ." Her gaze dropped guiltily to the pile of
things on his bed.

His blood went cold. He glanced down to where he'd left the map, relieved to see that it was undisturbed. Some of his other things, however, looked askew.

Suddenly it hit him. Was that what this was about? Had her interest in him merely been a pretext for spying? God's blood, it made perfect sense now. Lorn had used his daughter to keep an eye on him. He'd laugh at the irony, if he weren't so furious.

"You were spying on me," he said flatly. "Is that why you've been shadowing me since I arrived? Did your father ask you to watch me?"

She gasped. A pink flush rose to her cheeks—guilt or outrage, he didn't know. "I don't know what you are talking about." She swallowed nervously. "I haven't been shadowing you, and I certainly wasn't spying."

She was lying. If she were a man she'd be dead right now for what she'd done. He could snap her neck with one hand. God, did she think this was some kind of game? If she were to somehow learn the truth . . .

He was supposed to protect his cover at all costs, so he'd better damn well make sure that never happened. He could never hurt her.

He inched her closer, feeling her tremble against him. Even through the mist of anger he could smell the soft, heady perfume of her skin. Desire closed around him like a vise.

The lass had no idea of the danger she was in—and not just from her spying. She was completely at his mercy. She didn't know how damned close he was to taking advantage of the situation. They were alone. In the candlelight. Her body was pressed against his naked chest and the bed was right there—ready for them to fall on. If he was inclined to use a bed. Right now the wall was looking good.

His muscles tensed. Restraint was getting harder and harder to hold on to. "Then is there another reason I find you in my bed?"

Her eyes widened. "I wasn't in your bed," she replied indignantly. "You weren't here. Squire was anxious to see you and I was merely curious." Her chin lifted. "Perhaps if you were more forthcoming, I wouldn't be so curious."

Arthur was stunned. Had the chit actually managed to blame him for her nosing through his things? The adeptness of a woman's logic would never cease to amaze him.

"Did you appease your curiosity?"

She ignored his sarcasm. "Nay." Her gaze dropped to his arm. "Is that a tattoo on your arm?"

It was a testament to his control that the curse that came to his head didn't slip out of his mouth. The Lion Rampant on his arm was the one outward link he had to the Highland Guard, intended as both a bond between the warriors and a means of identification should the need ever arise. He kept it hidden to prevent questions and tried to bathe and change his underclothing when others weren't around.

The last thing he needed was for Anna MacDougall to see it.

But she had. Knowing the harm had already been done, he said, "Aye. A remnant of my days as a squire."

"I've never seen one before."

Before she could examine it further—and, God forbid, touch him again as she looked as though she was about to do—he released her, leaned down, pulled a clean shirt from the pile of clothing, and jerked it over his head.

Covering his nakedness should have eased some of the tension, but the innocent lass didn't have the good sense to mask her disappointment, and his blood heated all over again.

"You shouldn't be here," he said roughly.

"Afraid I'll trap you in a compromising situation, Sir Arthur?"

He knew she was teasing, but he was in no mood for games. The lass put far too much store in his honor as a knight. He was a Highlander—he played by his own rules. And right now it was taking everything he had not to teach her a lesson about the limits of a man's restraint.

"Have care what you ask for, Lady Anna. You just might get it." The intensity of his gaze left no doubt of his meaning. "It wasn't me who showed up uninvited to *your* chamber."

The tiny pulse at her neck quickened, and a soft flush rose to her cheeks. But her eyes, her beautiful, deep blue eyes, still challenged. "You don't want me, remember?"

He stilled. Every instinct rose up hard inside him. He was one hair's breadth away from proving her wrong.

But something in his expression made her bravado falter, and she bid a hasty retreat. "Besides, it was Squire who wanted to come." She bent down to pet the puppy, who was rolling around on his pallet. "Isn't that right, boy?"

The puppy barked playfully and started digging his head in the plaid.

Oh hell. The blasted dog wasn't playing; he was trying to get at something.

"Off," Arthur said, trying to shoo the troublesome mongrel away. But it was too late. She'd seen it.

"What do you have there?" she said to the dog.

Before Arthur could stop her, Anna pulled the corner of the small piece of parchment the puppy had uncovered from beneath his pallet.

He cursed, wanting to rip it out of her hands, but he forced himself to feign nonchalance. How the hell was he going to explain a map of her father's lands? He knew he'd better think of something.

"It looks like a drawing." She gazed up at him. "Did you do this?" He didn't say anything. She looked at it again, her fingers tracing over the lines of ink etched by the quill. "It's exquisite."

The admiration in her voice affected him more than he

wanted it to. He remembered how much his mother had
loved the chalk drawings he'd done for her as a boy. Once
he'd started training, he no longer had time for such things.
Then she'd died, and it no longer mattered.

He shook off the memories. God's blood, the lass had
done it again. Distracted him. Instead of figuring out a way
to save his skin, he was acting like that cursed beast of hers,
lapping up her praise.

"It's nothing," he said sharply.

She looked at him, those far-too-observant eyes taking in
more than he wanted her to. He betrayed nothing, his expression implacable, but somehow she sensed his discomfort.

Fortunately, she misinterpreted it. "You need not be embarrassed," she said with a gentle smile, placing her hand
on his arm.

Why did she have to be so damned sweet and smile at
him like that? His life was uncomplicated. Just the way he
liked it. He didn't want to be drawn to her. But her warmth
and kindness were impossible to resist.

"I think it's wonderful. The way you captured the countryside . . . You have an artist's eye for perspective and detail."

His chest tightened. With relief, he told himself. She
obviously thought it only a sketch, and that he was embarrassed to have been caught engaging in such an unwar-
riorly pastime. He was damned lucky to have just started
the map. Although that was why it wasn't in his sporran,
where it should have been. But if she turned it over . . .

He'd be hard-pressed to find an excuse for the notes he'd
made about the number of men, knights, horses, and the
stores of weapons.

He cursed his carelessness in not putting the document
away properly before he'd gone to the loch. He'd thought
to be undisturbed. But he should have known better. It
seemed there was no place he could be free of her.

His face was hard as he took a step toward her and held out his hand.

She hesitated—obviously not eager to relinquish the map—and looked at it again, holding it up to the candle he'd placed on the table beside his bed. "What are these marks?"

His stomach dropped, realizing she was seeing the shadow of the writing on the back. He caught her wrist in his hand before she could turn it over.

"Leave it alone, Anna."

Leave me alone.

She gazed up at him, their eyes locking in the flickering candlelight. "I can't." Her words seemed to shock her as much as they had him. A befuddled frown gathered between her brows. "Don't you feel it?"

He didn't want to hear her, didn't want to acknowledge what was impossible. She was Lorn's daughter. They were on opposite sides. Damn her, he didn't feel anything. "I thought I made myself clear on the ride back from the village."

Her eyes flashed. "I heard what you said. But I felt something different."

He felt a spark of rage and jerked her against him. "What you felt was lust." He molded her to him, letting her feel the hard power of his body. "Is this what you want, Anna?"

She gasped and tried to break free, like a bird fluttering in a cage, but he wouldn't let her go. Not this time. She'd tormented him long enough. She needed to learn that this was not a game. That her interference was dangerous in more ways than one. It wasn't just the threat to his mission. She was a lady, and what he wanted from her was something she could not give.

"Let go of me." Her eyes searched his face wildly. "You're scaring me."

He slid his hand around her throat, quieting the flutter of

Nine

Arthur crushed her mouth to his, kissing her hard, wanting to punish her for doing this to him. Tempting him. Distracting him. For being so damned sweet. He wanted to teach her a lesson.

But at the first touch of her lips, he felt as though he'd been slammed in the chest with a hammer. The hard shock of sensation felled his anger in one swift stroke. Desire washed over him, filling him with an intense yearning.

Jesus. She tasted like heaven. Her lips were so damned soft. Her skin so damned fragrant. And her hair—God, her glorious hair—he let the silky waves wind through his fingers. It was unreal.

She was unreal. An angel sent to torment him.

He groaned and relaxed his hold, softening his kiss, and eased into her again. Slow and easy this time. Cradling her against him and molding his lips to hers gently. Drawing. Tasting. Savoring the exquisite sensation of her mouth moving under his.

It was incredible. Even sweeter than he could have imagined—if he'd ever dared let himself imagine this. From the first moment he'd cast eyes on Anna MacDougall he'd wanted her, but he'd refused to allow himself to think it possible.

Hell, it wasn't possible. It was wrong. Dangerous. Doomed. He shouldn't be doing this. But he couldn't make himself stop.

It was only a kiss, he told himself. Something he'd done countless times before. Nothing he couldn't control.

But it didn't feel like any kiss he'd had before.

Feel. That was the difference. Usually he didn't. For him, a kiss was a means to an end—something expected before the main act, not something to evoke pleasure in itself.

But kissing her was bringing him pleasure. Too much pleasure.

Something was wrong with him. His body wasn't reacting the way it should to a simple kiss. He was on fire. And why the hell was his heart beating so fast?

Lust was something that could be controlled. Managed. Other women had made him hot, but not even when he'd been a squire about to swive his first maid had he been this consumed by need. He was hard. Aching. Hotter than he'd ever been in his life.

At least lust was understandable. What he didn't understand was this other feeling. The feeling that swelled in his chest and made his heart feel as if it were going to explode. The feeling that gave him the overwhelming urge to protect her. To treasure and take care of her.

The feeling that made him want to hold on to her and never let go.

The intensity of his reaction should have warned him. But he was too busy reveling in sensation, inhaling her sweet perfume, winding his fingers through her silky locks of hair, and savoring the softness of her skin against his, to listen.

All he could think about was the woman melting in his arms who could never be his.

For one heart-stopping moment Anna feared she'd pushed him too far. The look in his eyes before he'd kissed her had terrified her. She caught a glimpse of a man she'd never seen before. Not the remote, controlled knight, but a wild, untamed warrior. A man who was far more dangerous than she'd realized.

The fierceness of his kiss shocked her. It was as if all the dark energy she'd sensed simmering under the surface and held in check exploded in one fell embrace. She could feel his anger in the punishing harshness of his mouth.

Perhaps she should have been scared, but even if he were angry and out of control, she knew he would never hurt her. How she could be so certain she didn't know, but she was.

Then before she could react, before the shock had faded from her limbs, before she could think how good he tasted—like cloves and something dark and distinctly male—everything changed.

He groaned, and it was as if all the anger seeped out of him. The kiss meant to punish now entreated. The embrace meant to crush now cradled her as gently as if she were a babe. Where he would have ravaged with passion, now he devastated with a tenderness of which she could never have imagined this big, fierce warrior capable.

It was . . . perfect. *He* was perfect.

Each stroke of his mouth on hers unleashed a firestorm of new sensation. The brief kisses she'd exchanged with Roger were nothing like this. They didn't make her feel as if she'd just walked into the bread oven. They didn't make her tingle in places she shouldn't think about. They didn't make her heart flutter and her knees weaken. And they certainly didn't make her think of ripping off his shirt and splaying her hands over the bare skin that would be forever etched in her memory.

He was so big and powerful, his muscular body hard and imposing as a wall of granite. The proof of his warrior profession was branded on every steely inch of flesh. But she'd never imagined how good steel could feel pressed up against her. How warm a man's chest could be. How safe and protected she would feel. How she wanted to sink into him and never let go.

And what he was doing with his mouth . . .

It felt like a dream. His lips were too soft. His kiss too tender. Surely this wasn't the same man? How could the implacable warrior who looked at her with such indifference kiss her with such feeling?

He even smelled like something from a dream. Like soap with a hint of salt from the loch.

But it wasn't a dream. In her dreams she didn't feel so strange. She didn't know what was happening to her. She felt faint. Drenched with heat. Sensitive and achy. Every nerve ending on edge. It felt as if her body was not her own.

Pleasure had taken hold and would not let go. All she could think about was how good it felt. His talented mouth. The subtle scratch of his jaw against her chin. The weight of his hand on her waist. The gentle caress of his fingers. With each teasing brush of his lips on hers, the sensations only intensified. Building. Making her yearn for something more. Something she didn't understand but desperately wanted.

Arthur was trying to take it slow, but the little sounds she was making were driving him half-crazed. But even more than he wanted to sink into her, he wanted to bring her pleasure. So instead of ravishing her senseless, he coaxed with long, slow strokes of his mouth.

And she responded.

God, she responded. Tentatively at first, and then with his persuading, more boldly.

With an enthusiastic little moan that went straight to his groin, she slid her arms around his neck and opened her mouth.

A growl of pure masculine satisfaction tore through him at the instinctive response.

He wanted nothing more than to plunge into her mouth, to take what she offered, but conscious of her innocence, he slid the tip of his tongue between her lips for one deft flick before quickly retreating. He felt her shock but didn't give her time to think. His tongue swept inside her mouth again, longer this time, letting her get used to the sensation. And then when he felt her relax against him, he showed her what he wanted. Circling his tongue against hers, he slid deeper and deeper into her mouth.

Her eager response nearly broke him. Desire, held long at bay, broke free in one torrential storm. He could feel her nipples harden against his chest, digging into him, egging him on.

He groaned, feeling the demanding tug in his groin, and sank into her.

She kissed him back, molding her sweet little body to his. The instinctive movement of her hips against his cock was almost too much. The sensation too intense. His blood spiked. His heart hammered. The reins of control began to slip through his fingers as desire took over.

His kiss grew wilder. Harder. More insistent. He covered her breast with his hand, her startled gasp smothered by his groan. The spike of pleasure was beyond belief. He'd been dreaming about her breasts for weeks, and now to have them in his hands . . .

They were incredible. Big, soft, and full in his palm. Rubbing his thumb over the taut peak of her nipple, he teased and plied until a soft moan escaped from between her lips and her back arched into his hand. Naked. He wanted her naked.

God, she was sweet. So responsive. He couldn't seem to get enough.

He was spiraling down a tunnel of sensation. Quickly moving to a place of no return. He wanted to make her come. He wanted to touch her with his hands, taste her with his mouth, and fill her with his cock. He wanted her weak and wet.

He wanted to make her his.

He liked to think he would have come to his senses— that he would have managed to find the control that had never eluded him before—but he would never know.

The dog did it for him. Probably deciding he'd been neglected for too long, the puppy started to whinge. It was enough to penetrate the haze.

The shock of reality was like a bucket of cold water. All at once, Arthur realized the madness of what he was doing. He broke the kiss, pushing her away more harshly than he intended.

She gasped in surprise.

For a moment, they simply stared at each other in the candlelight, the heaviness of their breathing damning proof of what they'd just done.

Christ. Disbelief mixed with incredulity. What the hell had just happened? He'd never lost control like that, ever.

A kiss, damn it. That was all it was supposed to be. A simple kiss to teach her a lesson. It didn't mean anything. He'd kissed dozens of women. It was nothing that should have affected him, and nothing that should make him feel this . . . rattled.

And he *was* rattled, more rattled than he wanted to admit. Touching her had been a mistake. What the hell had he been thinking?

He hadn't been thinking. He'd been angry. Tormented. Pushed beyond reason by her teasing and flirting.

But even as he was condemning himself as a fool, when he looked at her swollen lips and flushed cheeks all he could think about was doing it again.

And that rattled him even more. Enough to make damned sure it never happened again. "Was that enough to satisfy your curiosity, my lady?"

She blinked, confused. "W-what do you mean?"

He took a deep, ragged breath, trying to calm the fierce pounding in his chest. "It means that you have that dog to thank for letting you leave here with your virtue intact." He held her gaze, his eyes hard and unyielding. "But I can damn well assure you that if you keep up this game of yours, the next time you might not be so fortunate."

She flinched as if he'd struck her. "How can you say that? How can you kiss me like that and act as if it doesn't mean anything? As if you didn't feel—"

"What I felt was lust. Don't make the mistake of thinking it's something more."

He wouldn't.

He couldn't.

She took a step back, her eyes dampening with tears. His chest started to throb and burn.

"Why are you doing this? Why are you deliberately trying to be cruel?"

His fists clenched against the nearly irrepressible urge to comfort her. He was doing it for her own good—for them both—protecting her from an impossible situation. "I'm merely giving you a warning. Your little game is over. Whatever you were doing here, it ends now."

She gazed up at him mutely, searching his face for something she would never find.

"Take your dog," he said, his voice oddly rough, "and go."

Without another word, she scooped up the puppy and fled. He watched her, feeling as if the room had suddenly grown darker.

Only belatedly did he remember the map. He looked down. It was there, at his feet, where it must have slipped from her hand—landing the wrong side up. Had she looked down, she would have seen the notes on the back. But somehow the disaster that he'd avoided didn't seem to come close to the one that he hadn't.

* * *

Anna barely made it out the door before the tears of hurt and humiliation burst through the dam of pride. She wouldn't let him see how badly he'd hurt her. Devastated— not only by the kiss, but also by the cruel rejection that followed—she took refuge in her chamber. She was fortunate that everyone seemed to be at the evening meal, as she was in no state to see anyone.

Pleading a headache to her maid—who took one look at her face and must have known she was lying but was friend enough to go along with the pretense—Anna feigned sleep when her sisters returned. The last thing she wanted to do was answer questions or talk about what had happened. She didn't even want to think about what had happened.

God, he'd been right. Horribly right. She'd been a hair's breadth—or in this case, a puppy's whinge—away from doing something disastrous.

His kiss. His tongue. Dear Lord, the incredible sensations of his hands on her breasts. They'd felt too good. She hadn't wanted it to stop. She'd been swept up in desire far beyond her experience to resist. Instinct had overtaken caution, pleasure had overtaken reason, the primal urge to join with him had drowned everything else in its wake.

Her body had been tingling for him. Flushed and eager for his touch. The place between her legs had been—her cheeks heated—*damp*.

He could have taken her innocence with little resistance. Tears poured from her eyes and a harsh sob tore from her chest. Nay, with *no* resistance.

Her heart squeezed at the appalling truth. She'd wanted him. Enough to do something inconceivable. Something rash and foolish that could never be undone.

But it hadn't been just about lust. At least not for her. When he'd held her in his arms and kissed her, Anna had been overwhelmed with emotion. What she felt for him was intense . . . powerful . . . *different*.

Yet the kiss that had meant so much to her had merely

been some cruel lesson to him—a means of discouraging her "shadowing him."

The accusation was all the more humiliating for its truth. She *had* been chasing after him, and if it had been only about her father's request, it might not have been so bad. But after what had just happened, she was forced to admit the truth: it hadn't been about just doing a job for her father. Her interest in him had been just as much about her as it had her father. Perhaps more so.

His cruel lesson worked. The next morning, with the tears if not the hurt that spawned them behind her, Anna reported her findings to her father. Sir Arthur Campbell was exactly as he appeared: an able, ambitious knight focused on the upcoming battle. Any lingering doubts that he was hiding something, she pushed aside.

Satisfied by her estimation, her father instructed her to cease her efforts. Her attention in the young knight had been remarked upon and her father didn't want Sir Arthur to grow suspicious.

Anna didn't tell him that it was too late for that.

Relieved to be free of her duty, she kept to her room for the remainder of the day. Though she loved nothing more than to be surrounded by her family and a brimming Hall full of clansmen, today was the rare occasion when she wanted to be by herself. She also feared her low spirits would be obvious and didn't want to draw unwanted concern from her well-meaning mother and sisters. Moreover, she was still feeling far too vulnerable after that kiss to chance running into him.

It was cowardly, perhaps, but she needed time to think. She'd replayed what had happened over and over in her mind, and each time she became more convinced that she hadn't been wrong.

He couldn't kiss her like that and not feel *something*. He'd wanted her to think it had been only lust, but in her heart she knew it was something more.

Yet, for some reason he was intent on pushing her away. His coldness and cruel words seemed calculated to do just that.

But why?

And more importantly, why was she so desperate to find a reason?

Because she cared, and it seemed she was harboring some silly, childish hope that maybe he hadn't meant what he'd said. That maybe he cared, too.

It shouldn't matter. He was all wrong for her. A cold, remote warrior who didn't care about anyone or anything other than fighting the next battle.

But as much as she wanted to put him in that box, he didn't quite fit.

He wasn't nearly as unfeeling as he wanted her to think. She had seen glimpses of emotion when he'd caught her after she'd stumbled off the hillside, and when he'd saved her and Squire from the wolves. Then, the way he'd kissed her had left no doubt that he was a man capable of deep emotion.

She'd never been attracted to warriors before, but with Arthur it was just the opposite: she'd never been so attracted to a man—or his body—in her life. Who knew muscles could be so . . . arousing? His battle-hard physique should represent everything she hated about war, but in his arms she'd never felt so safe and protected.

And the sketch. That had been the most surprising thing. That the same hand that wielded a sword and spear with such devastation could draw with such deft skill and beauty . . .

Arthur Campbell wasn't a typical warrior. There was more to him. From the first she'd sensed something different about him. Not just that he kept to himself, but the strange intensity simmering under the surface that set him apart.

Perhaps it was also the hint of loneliness and sadness

that drew her. Even with his brother and the other men he'd seemed like a contented outsider—a man who didn't need anyone.

But everyone needed someone. No one could actually want to be alone.

Maybe he just didn't know any better.

Anna felt a flicker of possibility break through the hurt. She hugged the puppy curled up in her lap to her chest, kissing the soft fur on his head. Maybe, like Squire, he only needed someone to give him a chance. Someone to give him a little affection.

By the next morning, Anna was feeling more like herself. She returned to her seat beside her brother Alan on the dais to break her fast.

Her pulse spiked each time someone walked in the room. She was ready to see him. She wanted to see whether she was right. When their eyes met for the first time, she was certain she would know whether he cared for her, whether cruelty was merely his way of keeping her at a distance—just like he did everyone else.

As the meal drew on and Arthur didn't appear, Anna grew increasingly uneasy. When his brothers and the rest of the Campbells appeared, the fierce pounding in her chest took a sudden dive.

Unfortunately, her odd behavior had not gone unnoticed.

"He's not here," Alan said, putting his hand on hers.

She startled, jerking her gaze away from the entry. "Who's not here?" But the hot flush that rose to her cheeks gave her away.

He squeezed her hand under his, gently. "Campbell."

Obviously, he'd figured out the correct one.

She managed a wan smile, not bothering to feign ignorance. Her interest in the knight had not gone unnoticed by her overprotective brother. "I merely wished to ask him a favor. Squire has been moping around all morning, and I wondered if Sir Arthur might take him with him when he goes out riding this morning."

Her brother gave her a look that suggested he was not fooled by her feeble excuse.

"You'll have to find someone else to exercise your hound for a while."

A sick feeling dropped in her chest, settling uneasily in her stomach. Her voice quivered. "What do you mean?"

She braced herself, but part of her already knew what Alan was going to say.

"Campbell left with Ewen to patrol the southern borders between the castles at Glassery and Duntrune—father suspects the MacDonalds are up to something again. He'll be gone for days, probably weeks."

Gone. He's gone.

How could he have left her without a word, after what they'd shared? Her chest constricted, tighter and tighter until she thought she would burst from the pressure.

"I see," she whispered.

She was a fool. Because it felt special to her, she'd convinced herself it must be special to him. She'd known what he was, and still she'd convinced herself that maybe he was different.

Alan's gaze narrowed. "Did something happen? Did he do something—"

She shook her head furiously. "Nothing. Nothing happened."

Nothing significant. She drew her hand from under her brother's and folded her arms over her belly. She wanted to curl up in a ball and fall apart, but she wouldn't. He wasn't worth it.

"What is he to you, Annie-love? Do you care for him? I thought you were doing a favor for Father."

She hadn't been aware that Alan knew of her unusual activities, but perhaps she shouldn't have been surprised. With their grandfather's age and their father's illness, Alan had assumed more and more responsibilities. She wondered how much he knew. She suspected not all, or he wouldn't be so calm.

"I was," she assured him. Taking a deep breath, she forced the air back into her lungs. "He's nothing to me," she said, and meant it.

Her first impression had been correct: Arthur Campbell was a man with one foot out the door. He would never give her the stability that she craved. If she let him, he would only break her heart.

Ten

"You look like shite, Ranger. What the hell's the matter with you?"

Arthur tried not to let his annoyance show, but the brash seafarer had an uncanny ability to hone in on a sore spot. There was nothing wrong with him, damn it. Nothing that a restful night of sleep wouldn't cure.

But in the ten days since he'd left Dunstaffnage, he hadn't had one night of peace. His dreams had been invaded by a lass with big blue eyes and honey-gold hair. A lass whose expression when she'd fled the barracks still haunted him.

She was always so damned happy. It was one of the things that had drawn him to her from the first. But he'd made her sad. Actually, she'd looked as if he'd crushed her. He hoped to hell she wasn't harboring tender feelings for him. That would be foolish. *Very* foolish, he reminded himself.

His jaw hardened. Obviously, it wasn't just his dreams she'd invaded but his thoughts as well. Anna MacDougall had gotten under his skin.

He didn't understand why he couldn't stop thinking about her. He'd left—what he always did when a woman started to think about more than the bedchamber—but this time it wasn't working. If anything, it had made him more on edge. He was sure this irritating inability to focus would stop, if only he could see her and assure himself she was all right.

He should be able to push her out of his head. Focus on his task. And it infuriated him that he couldn't.

But he sure as hell wasn't going to explain any of this to MacSorley. He'd never hear the end of it.

"Good to see you too, Hawk." He studied the big Islander in the moonlight, noticing the lines of strain etched on his face beneath the smudges of ash. In addition to blackened armor and dark plaids, the warriors of the Highland Guard darkened their skin, enabling them to blend in to the night and move stealthily through the shadows. "Perhaps I should be asking you the same question?"

The man standing beside Erik "Hawk" MacSorley made a sharp sound—reminiscent of a laugh, but with scorn rather than amusement. "Hawk's wife has him by the bollocks. She'd due to have a child any day now, and he jumps at every sound, thinking it's the damned messenger." Lachlan MacRuairi, known by the war name of Viper among the Highland Guard, shook his head with disgust. "It's bloody pathetic."

Hawk grinned. "My wife can hold my bollocks anytime she wants. And we'll see how calm you are when your time comes."

A dark look came over MacRuairi's face, his slitted, piercing gaze glowing like a wildcat's in the moonlight. And people thought Arthur was eerie.

"It'll be a cold day in Hades before that time comes. I've had a wife. I'd rather have my bollocks cut off and stuffed through my nose than have another."

Of all the members of the Highland Guard, MacRuairi was the only one whom Arthur didn't like—or trust. The West Highland descendant of the mighty Somerled, King of the Isles, had a black heart, a vicious temper, and a biting tongue. Like the cold-hearted snake from which his war name had derived, MacRuairi also had a deadly, silent strike.

From the first Arthur's senses had flared, cautioning wariness. But while it didn't take any unusual abilities to sense the anger emanating from MacRuairi—nay, rage— what bothered Arthur was the darkness that went with it. Darkness that had only grown deeper since the king's wife, daughter, sister, and Bella MacDuff had been captured by the English on MacRuairi's watch. Getting them back was all he cared about. He'd tried a few months back to free Bella from her cage hung high above Berwick Castle, but it proved an impossible task, even for the elite warriors of the Highland Guard. She'd been freed from her cruel prison recently, but no one knew where she was.

But MacRuairi had his uses. Aside from expertly wielding the two swords he wore crossed over his back, he could get in and out of anywhere. A lack of conscience also came in handy for unpleasant tasks. To win this war, they would all need to get their hands dirty. MacRuairi's were just dirtier than most.

Only MacRuairi was more of an outsider in the Highland Guard than Arthur. Most of the men were wary of the hostile Islander—and rightly so. The leader of the Guard, Tor MacLeod, tolerated him, having come to some kind of understanding with his former blood enemy, but only William Gordon and MacSorley genuinely seemed to like him.

"Never say never, cousin," MacSorley said. "Your problem was marrying the wrong woman. One of these days the right one will come along." He paused and gave him a sly look. "If she hasn't already."

Arthur suspected MacSorley was referring to Bella MacDuff, Countess of Buchan. She'd taken an immediate dislike to the infamous cateran pirate. Arthur thought the dislike was mutual, but he hadn't been around enough to know whether MacSorley spoke true.

But if he were MacSorley, he'd watch his back for the next few days. MacRuairi looked as if he wanted to kill him. "You don't know what the fuck you're talking about."

MacSorley only grinned. "Such crude language. Could I possibly have hit a nerve, cousin?"

Not a few days. Arthur would watch his back for a week. MacRuairi looked ready to strike. "I'm just damned sick and tired of hearing about it. You're like a priest trying to convert the pagans. Spread your poison about the joys of marriage somewhere else; I'm not interested."

MacSorley's wide grin only seemed to make his kinsman angrier.

Arthur couldn't believe he was hearing the swaggering seafarer exalt the virtues of marriage and "the right woman." MacSorley's bigger-than-life personality and bold charm drew almost as many women as MacGregor's pretty face. Hawk loved women and they loved him. Hard to think of him settling down with one. She had to be a stunner. The big Viking always had a bevy of bold beauties with lush figures at his command.

Knowing MacSorley wouldn't stop needling his kinsman until they came to blows, Arthur changed the subject. "Why did you need to see me? I assume it must be important to risk meeting like this."

To preserve Arthur's cover, the king had taken great precautions. Meetings were arranged only on an as needed basis, by leaving coded messages at one of the numerous stone monuments that littered the countryside, such as the stone circle where they'd gathered tonight. King Robert relished the connection with Scotland's ancient past, and the mystical stones seemed a fitting allusion for his secret guard of the greatest warriors in Scotland.

Most communications were by messenger—only rarely did Arthur risk meeting with his fellow guardsmen. After infiltrating the MacDougalls, it had become even more dif-

ficult. He'd lost much of the freedom of movement he'd enjoyed working on his own. Tonight, he'd had to sneak out
of Duntrune Castle in the middle of the night and hope to
hell no one discovered he'd gone.

MacSorley sobered. "Aye, we received word last week
that you'd come south. I'm glad you saw our message."

Arthur tried to check the monuments as often as he
could. When he'd seen the three smaller stones arranged in
a triangle in the center, he'd known: it was the code to
come as soon as possible. It was the same message he'd left
at the cave north of Dunollie Castle before he'd gone
south. With its access to the sea, the cave was the safest
place for Bruce's men to venture and only a few miles south
of Dunstaffnage. "I assume since you knew where to leave
it that you received mine?"

MacSorley nodded. "We were surprised to hear you'd
left Dunstaffnage."

Arthur schooled his features, not betraying the hint of
guilt that crept up his consciousness. He hadn't forgotten
his mission, damn it. He'd just needed to get away.

"It couldn't be avoided," he said, offering no further explanation. "Lorn fears that Angus Og is up to something.
I've accompanied his son Ewen to see what we can find
out."

"My cousin is always up to something," MacSorley said
about the powerful MacDonald chief. "He's mobilizing his
fleet for the battle against the MacDougalls."

"I thought as much." The attack against the MacDougalls from the sea would be every bit as important as the
attack from land. Bruce would press Lorn from both directions. It was one of the reasons that MacSorley's skills were
so valued. He would be the one to lead the attack by sea.

"Lorn is well informed," MacRuairi said.

Arthur grimaced. "Aye, he is. But I've been unable to
find out how he's doing it. There have been no strange
churchmen about, nor have I seen any messengers."

MacSorley smiled. "That's why we sent for you. I intercepted one of Edward's messengers on his way north with a message for Lorn. It's one Lorn has been waiting for, though not the news he hoped for." He grinned. "King Edward has declined Lorn's request to send additional men north. And thanks to my cousin here, we know where the messenger was heading."

Arthur didn't need to ask how MacRuairi had got him to talk. MacRuairi always got them to talk.

"Ardchattan Priory," MacRuairi said.

Arthur felt a tingle of excitement. The priory was close to Dunstaffnage, right in the heart of Lorn. This was it: the chance they'd been waiting for.

"So they are using churchmen," Arthur said. It was as he'd suspected.

"So it seems," MacSorley agreed. "All you need to do is keep an eye on the church and see who comes to pick it up. As one of Lorn's knights, your presence, should you be discovered, won't be remarked upon. How soon will you be able to get away?"

"I'll leave in the morning."

"You will be able to explain your sudden need to return to the castle?" MacRuairi asked.

"Someone needs to report back to Lorn. I'll volunteer to go."

With his mission clear, Arthur was anxious to be on his way, but he took a few minutes to catch up on the other guardsmen.

MacSorley and MacRuairi were the only two members of the Highland Guard in the west, watching the seas. MacKay, Gordon, and MacGregor were in the north, keeping the roads clear of messengers and wreaking havoc on Ross for what he'd done to the women, and the rest of the team were in the east with the king.

Robert "Raider" Boyd and his partner, Alex "Dragon" Seton, had returned recently from a successful mission in the southwest, with Sir James Douglas and Sir Edward Bruce, the king's sole remaining brother. King Robert had lost three brothers in one year—two at the hands of MacDowell, the man they'd sent scurrying from Galloway. Seton, too, had lost a brother.

"Have Raider and Dragon finally figured out they are fighting on the same side?" Arthur asked. The ill-fated pairing between Seton, an English knight, and Boyd, the man who hated all things English, had been one of the biggest hurdles in the early days of the Guard.

"It's gotten worse." MacSorley frowned, so Arthur knew it had to be serious. "Dragon has changed since the death of his brother. He's angrier, and most of that anger is directed at Raider." The smile returned to his face. "But there is some good news. Guess who they brought back with them, captured near Caerlaverock Castle in Galloway?"

"Who?" Arthur asked.

"My old companion, Sir Thomas Randolph."

Arthur swore, not hiding his surprise. "What did the king do?"

The news that his young nephew had gone over to the English the year before had been a bitter blow to the king who was attempting to regain his kingdom. Switching sides was regrettably all too common—King Robert had done it himself many times in the early years of the war—but Randolph's defection had come at a particularly difficult time for the king. At the very lowest point in his struggle.

MacSorley shook his head in disgust. "He forgave him. Too easily, in my opinion. Especially after the pup had the nerve to criticize his uncle for not fighting like a knight but like a pirate."

"Apparently Hawk failed to make an impression on him," MacRuairi said dryly.

"Perhaps so," MacSorley said. "But I'll get another

chance. The king has vowed to send him to me again for training."

Arthur lifted a brow. "Why do I have a feeling the young knight will have his punishment after all?"

MacSorley shrugged not so innocently. "I'll make a Highlander out of the lad yet." He gave Arthur an amused look. "I hope you haven't forgotten, *Sir* Arthur. You're looking very fine in your knight's garb."

The jest hit a little too close to the truth. "Sod off, Hawk. Care for a demonstration?"

MacSorley chuckled. "Perhaps another time. My wife would have my bollocks if the messenger comes and I am not there. And you should get back to Duntrune Castle before they discover you're gone."

They'd already said their farewells when Arthur remembered. "Here," he said, taking out the map that he'd finished a few days ago. "It's for the king."

MacSorley held it up to get a better look at it in the moonlight. "Damn, this is good. The king will be pleased. He'll need it for the march west. I'll send a messenger right away."

Arthur nodded. "And I'll send word as soon as I have something."

"*Airson an Leòmhann,*" MacSorley said.

For the Lion. The symbol of Scotland's kingship and the battle cry of the Highland Guard.

Arthur repeated the words and slid into the shadows, not knowing when or if he would see them again. In war, nothing was certain.

Arthur was in place less than twenty-four hours later. From his position behind a grassy knoll to the east of the priory, he had a clear vantage of the approaches to both the cross-shaped stone church and the square cloister that housed the monks to the south.

Established by Duncan MacDougall, Lord of Argyll,

about seventy-five years earlier, Ardchattan Priory was one of only three Valliscaulian monasteries in Scotland. He didn't know much about the rare order of monks, except that they reputedly followed a strict code.

Just six miles to the east of Dunstaffnage on the north side of Loch Etive, Ardchattan was the perfect place from which to route messages—especially since the prior was a MacDougall. It was one of the first places he'd focused on upon arriving a month earlier. But although he'd kept it under surveillance for a few days, except for a couple of women from the village, the monks had very few visitors.

Now, with the trap set, all he had to do was wait and he would finally have some answers. Answers that would put him that much closer to fulfilling his mission for King Robert and seeing John of Lorn pay for what he'd done to his father.

Fourteen years was a long time, but he still remembered it as if it were yesterday. At twelve, he'd been desperate to impress the man who seemed like a king to him.

He could still remember the way the sun had caught his father's mail in a halo of silvery light as Cailean Mor, the Great Colin, gathered his guardsmen in the *barmkin* of Innis Chonnel Castle, readying for battle.

He'd looked down at the son who most of the time he tried to ignore. "He's too small; he'll only get himself killed."

Arthur started to say something in his own defense, but Neil cut him off with a glance. "Let him come, Father— he's old enough."

Arthur felt his father's gaze fall on him and tried not to shuffle under the weight of his scrutiny, but in all of his twelve years he'd never felt so lacking. Small for his size. Skinny. Weak. And on top of it, unnatural.

I'm not a freak. But in his father's eyes, that's what he saw.

"He can barely lift a sword," his father said.

The shame in his voice cut like a knife. Arthur could see what he was thinking: *How could this odd, puny whelp of a lad be of my blood?* Blood that had forged some of the fiercest, toughest warriors in all the Highlands. Campbells were born warriors.

Except for him.

"I'll watch over him," Neil said, putting his hand on Arthur's shoulder. "Besides, maybe he can be of help."

His father frowned, not liking the reminder of Arthur's strange abilities, but nodded. The hint of possibility in his gaze gave Arthur hope. "Just make sure he doesn't get in the way."

Arthur had been so excited, he'd barely been able to contain himself. Maybe this was his chance. Maybe he'd finally be able to prove to his father that his skills could be of use, as Neil said.

But it didn't work out that way. He was too nervous. Too excited. Pressing too hard and wanting it too much. And too damned emotional. His senses weren't responding the way they usually did.

They were nearing the border of Campbell and MacDougall territory, having just passed the eastern edge of Loch Avich approaching the string of Lorn—the old route through the hills of Lorn used by drovers and pilgrims on their way to Iona. He and Neil had ridden ahead with the scout, anticipating a surprise attack by their enemies along the narrow pass.

They rode over a ford in a small burn and stopped near Loch na Sreinge. "Do you feel anything yet?" Neil asked.

Arthur shook his head, his heart pounding fiercely in his chest and sweat beading on his brow as he tried to force his senses to sharpen. But it was his first battle, and now that the excitement had worn off, fear and anxiety had invaded. "Nay."

Then they heard it. Behind them, not fifty yards away on

the other side of the forested hillside. The sounds of an attack.

Neil swore and ordered him behind a tree. "Stay here. Don't move until I come for you."

To his horror, Arthur's eyes filled with tears, only adding to his self-loathing. How could he have failed? How could he not have sensed them? This was all his fault. He'd been given a chance to prove himself—to show his skills—and instead he'd let the one person who believed in him down. "I'm sorry, Neil."

His brother gave him an encouraging smile. "It's not your fault, lad. This was only your first time out. It'll be better next time."

His brother's faith in him only made it worse.

He wanted to go after them, but his father was right, he would only get in the way.

It seemed like hours before the sounds of battle began to fade, and still Neil hadn't come for him. Fearing that something might have happened to his brother, Arthur couldn't wait any longer. He carefully crept through the trees, making his way toward the battle.

Suddenly, he came to a stop. The senses that had so deserted him flared to life.

The clash of steel on steel seemed to be all around him—indiscernible, but something made him turn to the left. He felt a flash of panic and started to run toward the sound. His sword dragged through the leaves and dirt, and he struggled not to stumble as he wound through the trees and scrambled up a small rise, taking refuge behind a large boulder.

Then he saw them. Two men, a short distance from the rest, hidden from view by the bend of the hillside, were waging a fierce sword battle at the base of a small waterfall. It was his father and a man he'd seen only once before from a distance: their enemy, John MacDougall, Lord of Lorn, the MacDougall chief's son.

Arthur held his breath, watching as the two men, both in the prime of manhood, exchanged blow after powerful blow. When it seemed it couldn't go on much longer, his father swung his sword with both hands over his head and sent it crashing down on his opponent. Arthur nearly cried out with relief, seeing Lorn sent to his knees by the force of the blow, his sword ripped from his hands.

Arthur's blood froze with fear. He knew he was about to see his first death on the battlefield. He wanted to shield his eyes, but he found himself unable to turn away. It was as if he knew that something important was about to happen.

The sun flashed off Lorn's steel helm. His father lifted his sword. But instead of a death knell, he rested the point on Lorn's neck.

The men were too far away. The waterfall should have drowned out their voices. He shouldn't be able to hear them. But he could.

"The battle is over," his father said. "Call off your men; the Campbells have won the day." Arthur glanced at the other side of the bend, near the ford in the burn, and saw that his father spoke true. The bodies of their enemy littered the grass along the bank of the burn, turning the stream red with blood. "Surrender," his father ordered, "and I will let you live."

Behind his nasal helm, Arthur could see Lorn's eyes burning with hatred. His mouth was twisted with rage. It took him a long time, but eventually he nodded. "Aye."

The Campbells had won! Arthur was filled with pride. His father was the greatest warrior he'd ever seen.

Great Colin lowered his sword and started to walk away.

Arthur felt a flicker of premonition, but his cry of warning was too late. His father turned around, only in time to have the blade of John of Lorn's dirk find his stomach instead of his back.

He froze in stunned horror as his father's eyes found his from his hiding place behind the boulder. His father staggered, fell to his knees, and in harrowing slowness the lifeblood drained out of him. His father's gaze held his the entire time, and in it Arthur read his silent plea: *Avenge me.*

Lorn shouted, and a few of his men came around the bend to answer his call. Seeing the mighty Campbell chief fallen at their leader's feet, they let out a fierce battle cry of victory. Lorn pointed to the hillside in Arthur's direction. Arthur knew he couldn't see him, but Lorn must have heard the cry that had alerted his father. When they started to come toward him, Arthur turned and ran.

He didn't remember much of what happened afterward. He'd hid in the trees and rocks for nearly a week, too terrified to move. When he'd finally made his way back to the castle, Neil said he was half-dead. Arthur told his brother immediately what had happened, but by then it was too late to counter the MacDougalls' version of events. Even if it could be explained how he'd heard the men from so far away, Neil knew that Arthur would not be believed. The MacDougalls had won the day, with Lorn taking credit for defeating the powerful Campbell chief.

Not long afterward, Lorn laid siege to Innis Chonnel and the Campbells had been forced to surrender.

From that day, Arthur had vowed justice for his father. Vowed to destroy MacDougall for the treacherous murder. Vowed to never let emotion get the better of him.

For fourteen years he'd bided his time, working to become one of the greatest warriors in the Highlands—a warrior his father would have been proud of—and now he had his chance. He couldn't let anything interfere. He had to stay focused.

He'd failed his father once—his senses had let him down—and he would not do so again.

But he wished . . .

Hell, it didn't matter what he wished. There were some things that even he could not change. The lass was Lorn's daughter. No matter how much she made him wish differently.

He leaned back against a nearby tree. As there was still an hour or so until nightfall, he figured he had some time to relax. After the breakneck pace of his journey north, it felt good to sit down. Though his instructions were simply to identify the messenger and not interfere—thereby not alerting MacDougall and allowing Bruce to intercept future messages—he needed to be prepared for anything.

But he was wound as tightly as a spring and relaxing proved impossible. It wasn't only the trap for the messenger tying him up in knots, he knew, but the prospect of returning to the castle.

He would see her again.

The surge in his chest betrayed him. He told himself that it was merely because he wanted to assure himself that she was all right—not because he *wanted* to see her. Not because he couldn't stop thinking about her. And sure as hell not because he missed her.

He couldn't be that much of a fool.

Another month, he told himself. *Stay away from her for a few more weeks and this will all be over.* Once he had the identity of the messenger, he would see what he could discover of the MacDougall battle plan. But when the battle started, his mission would be done. He would leave and never look back.

Realizing he hadn't eaten since morning, he took out a piece of dried beef and oatcake, ate it, and washed it down with the water from the stream where he'd filled his skin. Absently, he scanned the grassy landscape.

His heart jerked to a violent stop. For a moment he stood transfixed. Hunger rose hard inside him, a yearning so intense it claimed his breath. Like a starving man, he watched as the lass he'd been thinking about for the past week seemed to materialize out of his dreams. Though she was still a good distance away and wore a hooded cloak over her golden hair, he knew it was her. He felt her nearness in his bones. In his blood.

Every nerve ending stood on edge as he watched her alight from a small skiff and begin to make her way up the grassy pathway from the small jetty to the cloister.

He struggled to catch a glimpse of her face in the fading daylight. The need to see her, to assure himself she was well, almost made him forget where he was. He took a step forward before realizing what he'd done.

Swearing, he slipped behind the tree before anyone noticed him standing there like a love-struck fool.

What the hell was she doing here?

She had that basket with her, and once again, only a solitary guardsman accompanied her. The lass had a singular ability to be in the wrong place at the wrong time. Just like at the church in Ayr—

He went utterly still. The truth struck him right between the eyes.

Nay, it wasn't possible.

But he didn't believe in coincidence. Either Anna MacDougall had an uncanny knack for showing up exactly where she shouldn't, or she was the messenger.

She's the messenger.

The messages were in her basket, buried in the tarts or whatever else she carried with her. He recalled how jumpy she'd been at the village. How she'd handed him the baby and taken the basket with her to the kitchen. How she'd paled when he mentioned that the smell of the rolls was making him hungry.

And she'd been the one to pick up the silver in Ayr.

The truth had been right under his nose the entire time. How could he have been so blind?

His mouth hardened. He knew how: he'd underestimated her. Twice. Because she was pretty and young and innocent, because she seemed so vulnerable and sweet, because she was a lass, he'd never questioned her presence that night—even after he'd learned that she was spying on him.

Damn, it was brilliant. Using women as couriers. He thought of the women he'd seen coming and going from the churches. He'd never given them a second thought. They'd slipped right through his net.

He might have admired it, had he not been consumed by a far greater realization. His blood chilled to a trickle sliding down the back of his neck.

God's wounds, how could her father use her like this? If Arthur wasn't already planning it, he could kill MacDougall for putting her in such danger. Didn't they realize what would have happened to her that night had he not been there to save her from MacGregor and his men? She could have been killed.

His heart pounded fiercely as she approached the door. He clenched his fists, struggling not to rush over there, toss her over his shoulder, and get her the hell out of here. He felt a primal urge to take her someplace safe, where he could lock her up and protect her.

Not your job. Not your responsibility.

Not yours.

A cold sweat had gathered on his brow. When he thought of the risk she was taking, it nearly drove him mad with . . .

He flinched at the realization. Jesus, it was fear.

He hadn't felt like this since Dugald tried to cure him of his aversion to rats by locking him in a dark storage shed crawling with them—without a weapon.

She knocked on the door. A moment later a priest answered. Though Arthur kept his ears pinned, they spoke in low tones and he couldn't hear what they said. But from the monk's apologetic expression and the shake of his head, Arthur knew he was telling her there was nothing. Her shoulders seemed to droop. They exchanged a few more words, and then she quickly returned to the skiff.

Arthur watched her go and knew that his mission had just gotten a whole hell of a lot more complicated.

Bloody hell, why did it have to be her?

He fought against what he had to do. But staying away from Anna MacDougall was no longer an option. No matter what his instincts warned him against, his mission demanded that he stay as close to her as possible. He needed to keep apprised of the MacDougalls' plans.

A battle was about to begin. But for once, Arthur questioned his ability to escape unscathed.

Eleven

Anna pushed back her hood as she entered her father's solar. After setting down her basket on the table, she joined him and her mother beside the smoldering peat fire. Even in summer, the stone walls of the castle kept it cool and drafty inside.

Her mother glanced up from the new silk banner she was working on and frowned. "Where have you been, Annie-love? It's late."

Anna leaned down and gave her a kiss. "I took some tarts to the monks at the priory."

She met her father's gaze. His expression darkened. A small shake of her head had answered his unspoken question.

Before her mother could voice further objection, her father coughed. Though Anna knew it had been done purposefully, the raspy, wet sound concerned her.

"Didn't you mention something about a new herb brew Father Gilbert recommended to help clear the bogginess from my lungs?"

Her mother gasped and jumped to her feet, tossing aside her embroidery. "I'd forgotten. I shall ask Cook to prepare it right now."

As soon as the door closed behind her, her father said, "King Edward has not responded?"

Anna shook her head. "We should have heard from him by now."

Her father stood up and started pacing before the hearth, his anger growing with each step. "Bruce's damned brigands must have intercepted it. It seems like over half our messages are not reaching their destination—even with the help of the women." His mouth fell in a hard line. "But as we've heard no word of soldiers on the march, I think we can assume that none will be forthcoming. Young Edward is too busy trying to save his own hide to worry about ours."

After all her father had done for the first King Edward, Anna couldn't believe the new king would abandon him like this.

Lay down with dogs . . .

The old adage slipped to mind but she pushed it away; it seemed somehow disloyal. Her father hadn't had a choice. The first King Edward had been too powerful. After Wallace's defeat at Falkirk, it was either ally with the English king or see their lands forfeited. When Bruce had stolen the crown, the alliance had become even more necessary. With Bruce and the MacDonalds on one side, the MacDougalls could stand only on the other—with England.

"Should we try to send another message?"

"There isn't time," her father snapped, clearly annoyed by what he perceived as a foolish question. "The English move slowly. With all their household plate and furniture, it would take them weeks to march this far north. Even were Edward to change his mind, he would need time to gather the men. King Hood and his murderous band of marauding cateran will be here before the English have time to load the carts with all their finery."

Anna tried not to take her father's anger personally. He had every right to be short-tempered. Their enemy was bearing down on them and no one was coming to their aid. Like King Edward, the Earl of Ross had yet to respond to their pleas to join forces.

It was becoming painfully clear that they were going to be left on their own to face Bruce—eight hundred men to the usurper's reported three thousand.

Fear closed around her throat. The MacDougalls were fierce fighters, and her father was one of the best battle commanders in Scotland, but could they overcome such odds? Her father had nearly defeated Bruce before, but then the outlaw king had been on the run with only a few hundred men to her father's much larger force. This time the MacDougalls would be the ones greatly outnumbered.

It didn't matter, she thought fiercely. Her father would win anyway. One MacDougall was worth five rebels.

But no matter how many times she told herself that John of Lorn could overcome even the gravest of odds, she couldn't deny the faintest, tiniest possibility her loyal heart would allow that they could . . . lose.

Lose.

A shudder ran through her. Even thinking the word seemed the vilest of blasphemies. She couldn't let that happen. The ramifications were too hideous to consider. But everything that she held dear, all her dreams of a happy future, seemed to be balanced on the point of a pin—or in this case, a sword. The barest nudge could send it all careening over the edge.

The thick stone walls of the castle suddenly felt like thin panes of glass, ready to shatter.

Their situation was dire—desperate even. But there was a way she could make it less so.

Time seemed to still. Dread formed a tight knot in her stomach. The anxious flutter in her chest quickened as she realized what she would have to do. The answer had been lurking in the back of her mind for months, but she hadn't wanted to consider it.

Her fingers clenched the folds of her cloak as if she were grasping for a rope to hold on to. "What of Ross?" she asked softly. "There is still time for him to come."

Her father gave her a sharp glance. "Aye, but as I told you before, he won't."

Was that a rebuke in his gaze? Did he now regret having given her a choice?

Anna took a deep, ragged breath, trying to still the frantic race of her pulse. A cold sheen of perspiration settled over her icy skin. Her chest squeezed so tightly it was hard to breathe. Every instinct rebelled against what she was about to suggest. But she had no choice. A husband was a small price to pay for the survival of her clan. She would marry the devil himself if she had to. "What if I gave him a reason to reconsider?"

Her father's gaze held hers. From the speculative gleam in his eyes, she knew he'd guessed what she was going to suggest—or maybe had intended her to suggest it all along.

"What if I make a personal appeal to the earl?" She paused, her grasp on the woolen cloak squeezing the blood from her fingers. The frantic sound of her heartbeat pounded in her ears. Her stomach tossed queasily. *It will be all right. I will make it work. He's not that frightening.* Sir Arthur was tall, muscular, and darkly handsome, and she wasn't nervous around him. Perhaps she'd gotten over her unease of warriors.

Sir Arthur. Her heart tugged. An image of his face flashed before her eyes, but she pushed it away. He meant nothing to her. If her heart had momentarily fluttered in his direction, it no longer mattered. Even if it might have been different, he'd made his feelings—or lack of them—painfully clear.

But she'd spend a lifetime trying to forget that kiss.

Her father was waiting for her to continue, but the

words didn't come easily. "What if . . ." She stopped and forced her throat to open. "If Sir Hugh is still willing, I will agree to accept his proposal of marriage. In return, perhaps the earl will see the benefit of joining forces."

Her father didn't say anything for a moment, studying her face with an intensity that made her feel like squirming. "Do you think he will still have you? He wasn't happy when you refused him."

Her cheeks flamed, embarrassed not to have considered the possibility. Her father was right. The young knight had been furious, his nobleman's pride pricked by her refusal. "I don't know, but it is worth a try."

Her pride had taken a beating lately; what was one more blow?

"Your mother won't like it," he said with a glance to the door. "With Bruce and his men on the loose, the roads could be dangerous."

Anna had already considered that. "If Alan is with me, she won't worry. We'll take a large guard."

He nodded, stroking his chin. "Aye," he said. "Your brother will keep you safe." He smiled, and Anna fought the twinge of disappointment. Part of her had hoped he would refuse. He bent over and kissed the top of her head. "You are a good girl, Annie-love."

Normally, Anna would bloom with delight at her father's praise, but instead she felt like crying. Her happiness was a small price to pay, but still it was a price.

He tipped her chin and forced her gaze to his. She blinked through the hot, watery haze. "You know I wouldn't ask this of you if there was another way."

A single tear slid down her cheek. Her mouth trembled, but she managed a smile. "I know."

Right now, this was their only hope. No matter how wrong it felt, she would do what she had to do to secure this alliance.

There wasn't anyone else anyway.

But when Anna left her father's solar, the tears she'd been holding back burst in a storm of extinguished hope—hope that she hadn't realized she'd been harboring.

Arthur's return to the castle—alone—wasn't as difficult to explain as he'd anticipated. Lorn was eager for a report of what his son had discovered of their enemies to the west. The fight for supremacy between the three main branches of Somerled's descendants—the MacDonalds, MacDougalls, and MacRuairis—had dominated West Highland politics for years. The fight had narrowed, with the MacRuairis losing power when the previous chief had died, leaving his daughter Christina of the Isles as his only legitimate heir. Lachlan and his brothers were all bastards born (and in Lachlan's case, it was a title well earned).

Arthur's report from Ewen that the MacDonalds appeared to be mobilizing their forces along the western seaboard could hardly be a surprise, but it nonetheless provoked substantial fury and, though Lorn had tried to hide it, concern. But perhaps not as much as it should have, which made Arthur wonder what the scheming bastard had planned.

And now, thanks to his discovery at the priory, he knew just how to find out.

But, as it was already late in the evening when he'd returned to the castle, his reunion with Lady Anna would have to wait until morning. If he was anxious, he told himself it was only because he needed to find a good reason for what would appear to be a sudden turnaround: instead of avoiding her, he would be looking for reasons to be near her. But he didn't want to give the lass false hope. Despite the mistake he'd made in kissing her—and God, what a mistake that had been—a romantic relationship between them was impossible.

He knew it wasn't going to be easy. The lass had probably been thinking about that kiss for a week. God knows, he'd been unable to think of anything else.

Though he'd seen her across the yard of Ardchattan, when she walked into the Great Hall the next morning his senses fired as if seeing her for the first time. Everything seemed sharper, more intense. Never had he been so aware of anyone as he was at that moment of Lady Anna MacDougall.

He drank her in—every detail, every nuance, from the golden wisps of hair that had escaped the pale blue veil to frame her forehead and temples to the fine silk embroidered cote-hardie that hugged her curvy figure in all the right places.

Don't . . .

His gaze dipped to her breasts. His mouth went dry. He could see (or maybe he just imagined) the faint outline of her nipples beading against the stretch of fabric.

The memories accosted him, sending a flood of heat surging to his groin. His cock swelled as he recalled the lush softness in his hand. How amazing it had felt to cup her and hold the weight of all that perfectly rounded flesh in his palm, as his thumb caressed the taut bead of her nipple. He swore inwardly, the all-too-visceral memories growing uncomfortable.

He was hot. Aroused. Hungry.

How the hell could he look at her and not remember how her body had felt pressed against him? How could he see the sensual pink bow of her mouth and not remember how sweet she'd tasted, how soft her mouth had felt under his, how deeply she'd responded, and how the erotic sensation of her tongue twisting against his had sent him into a whirlpool of desire stronger than anything he'd ever felt before? He'd never be able to look at the pale, baby-soft skin that had felt like velvet under his fingertips and not remember touching her.

Hell, what he wanted to do was toss her down on his

bed, wrap her legs around his hips, and plunge into mind-less oblivion.

Jesus, he needed to stop thinking about it. Stop torturing himself with things that were impossible. He'd always been able to cut himself off before, but with Anna it was differ-ent.

She was different. And it didn't make him happy to ac-knowledge it.

He was aware of his brother's scrutiny, but he couldn't turn away. With every step that brought her closer, his heart pounded harder, every nerve ending standing on edge as he steeled himself for the moment when she noticed him.

But as she drew near, he felt a prickle of unease. Some-thing was wrong.

She wasn't smiling. Her eyes weren't sparkling with mis-chief and joy. And her laugh . . . the light, effervescent sound that he could have listened to for hours was acutely silent. He'd grown so accustomed to her perpetual good cheer, to the lighthearted charm that seemed to brighten the room, the void of its absence seemed darker.

Damn, had he hurt her more than he'd realized? Guilt pricked him.

For a moment he thought she would walk right past him, but then she sensed the weight of his gaze.

Their eyes locked.

Everything went completely still.

He waited for her reaction. Waited to see the color flood her cheeks, her breath hitch, and the pulse in her neck flut-ter. Waited for her awareness.

Instead, she stiffened.

Lady Anna wore her thoughts and feelings on her face. It was one of the things that he found so captivating and irre-sistible about her. The childlike innocence and excitement, the precious vulnerability. But the expression that had al-ways been open to him was closed. He felt her cool regard for only a brief instant before her gaze swept past him.

As if he'd ceased to exist.

As if she'd never melted in his arms.

As if the kiss that *he* couldn't stop thinking about had never happened.

As if she hadn't almost been under him.

Her indifference ate like acid through his chest. Burning. Aching. Filling him with a wild recklessness. The primitive urge to do something crazed, like press her up against the wall and kiss her until she surrendered to him once more.

He was controlled. Restrained. *Different*. He didn't have urges like that. But with one cool glance, Anna MacDougall had brought out every barbaric impulse stirring in his blood.

It seemed he'd achieved his objective. His cruel rejection had worked. Ironically, when he no longer wanted her indifference he had it.

Or maybe she'd never been interested in him at all. Maybe it was only about keeping an eye on him.

His mouth tightened and his muscles tensed, more bothered by the thought than he wanted to admit. Unfortunately, his brother was proving unusually perceptive.

Dugald shivered dramatically. "My, it's feeling a little wintry around here. Seems the lass's infatuation is over, little brother. With all the effort you've gone to to discourage her, I thought you'd be happy." He paused to shake his head. "Could it be a woman has finally gotten to you? I didn't think it possible."

Arthur leaned back against the stone wall behind him, projecting a carelessness he didn't feel. She had gotten to him, but he'd be damned if he'd let Dugald know of his weakness. "She's a sweet girl, nothing more."

"Made even sweeter because you can't have her."

Arthur shrugged, taking a long swig of *cuirm*, emptying his cup. "What I want from her is not something an innocent young noblewoman can give."

Dugald chuckled and slapped him on the upper arm. "I

feel your pain, little brother. I'm experiencing some of it myself. I know a lass whose talented mouth will do much to ease it; I'll send her to you."

Arthur's gaze slid to the dais where Lady Anna had just taken her seat. He was tempted. Damned tempted. But he wasn't interested in one of his brother's women.

One corner of his mouth lifted in a wry half-smile. "Sharing, brother? It isn't like you. But in this case it isn't necessary. I don't think I'll have any trouble finding my own relief." If he wanted, he had a few women to choose from. The problem was that he didn't want. Them, at least.

Dugald shrugged. "Suit yourself." He leaned over and grinned. "But you don't know what you're missing. The lass could milk a cow dry with her mouth, and she does this thing with her tongue . . ."

Dugald's voice faded into the background. The wicked skills proffered by Dugald's jade didn't interest him.

His gaze shifted to the dais.

She interested him, damn it. Though God knows she shouldn't.

But he might as well have been invisible—not once did she look in his direction. He clenched the pewter goblet in his fist, filling it more than once as the meal drew on, his irritation growing with every minute.

His plan to stay close to her side was going to be more difficult than he'd anticipated, but if she thought she could dismiss him so easily, she was bloody well wrong.

He's back.

Anna jerked back the unwelcome tug of yearning in her chest and forced herself not to look at him. Not to think about him.

Sir Arthur wasn't for her. He never had been. Her course was set. She'd made her decision. Her father—her clan—was counting on her. It was too late for regrets or second-guessing, even if seeing him had brought all those unwelcome emotions rushing back.

How could she not have noticed him at first, when now it seemed she could notice no one else? The proud young knight with his dark good looks was the most handsome in the room. And undoubtedly the strongest. Her cheeks heated. One look at his tall, broad-shouldered form and the memories of his naked chest came rushing back. Every sculpted muscle. Every rigid band. Every lean ounce of flesh.

She tried to ignore him, but she could feel his eyes on her as she ate. Or tried to eat. But her mouth was too dry, and the food tasted bland and chalky.

He watched her with a dark intensity that made her want to flee. Which she did at the first opportunity.

Hurrying from the Great Hall with as much ambivalence as she could muster, she ran up the stairs to her tower chamber and started tearing through her ambry, looking for her riding cloak.

She needed to get out of there.

One day. She had to avoid him for only one day, and then she would be gone. They were scheduled to leave for Auldearn Castle, the royal stronghold held by the Earl of Ross in the north, the next morning.

Why couldn't he have stayed away until she was gone? It would have made it so much easier.

She dug frantically through the piles of wool and silk hanging in the ambry, not caring about the mess she was making in her eagerness to escape.

Where was it?

She was about to forget the morning chill and leave anyway, when she realized that her maidservant had probably already packed the cloak in her trunk for her journey. She flipped open the wooden lid and let out a sigh of relief when she saw the gray, blue, and green checked wool folded at the top.

Quickly tossing it around her shoulders, she gathered Squire in her arms—fearing the puppy would run straight for the prodigal knight—and hurried back down the stairs.

She peeked out from behind the door to make sure the *barmkin* was clear before exiting. She didn't want to take any chances of running into him. She knew she was being ridiculous. Sir Arthur had done everything possible to avoid her. But something in the way he was watching her during the meal urged caution.

Crossing the yard, she headed for the stables. Once safely inside, she released the squirming dog from her arms and sent the stable lad to fetch Robby while she readied her horse.

Anna didn't have any destination in mind, just as long as it was outside the castle. The massive stone fortification with its great *barmkin* walls suddenly felt too small.

Having finished, she bent down to scoop up Squire again when the door opened. The puppy burst out into an excited flurry of yips and yelps, and shot out of her grasp like an arrow.

"Damn!" The oath slipped between her lips before she could catch it back.

She didn't need to look to know who it was.

If Squire's reaction hadn't told her, her body's would have. The air shifted. Her skin prickled. Her senses flared. The room suddenly felt hot. And the faint hint of male spice seemed to filter through the pungent, earthy smells of the stable.

She closed her eyes, said a prayer for strength, and then slowly stood to face him.

Their eyes met. The jolt of awareness cracked through her like a whip. The shock never seemed to lessen. Her breath hitched and the sharp flash of tightness wrapped around her chest, squeezing. She felt a poignant moment of longing rise inside her, before she quickly—harshly—tamped it down.

He didn't mean anything to her. Not anymore. Not after what happened in the barracks. Not after he'd left at the first opportunity.

He'd showed her how wrong he was for her. She should believe him.

She schooled her features into an impassive mask, calling on every ounce of royal blood that flowed in her veins. She was the descendant of kings, including great-granddaughter six times over of the mighty Somerled. She gave a short nod of her head, and said coolly, "Sir Arthur, I see you have returned."

Her attempt at imperiousness was somewhat ruined by the soft tremble in her voice. It was one thing to pretend not to be affected by him in a crowded Hall; it was quite another in a small stable. Alone. With him looking at her so . . . intensely. Angrily.

His face was red—except for the lines around his mouth and his throbbing temple. Those, unfortunately, were white.

Her heart fluttered nervously. Where was Iain? The stable boy should be back by now.

He must have read her thoughts. His gaze darkened, which, as it was already forbidding enough, only unnerved her further. He had no reason to be angry at her.

"The lad's not coming. I told him I would take you wherever you need to go."

Good God, no! She didn't want to go anywhere with him. Or be near him, for that matter.

She lifted her chin, refusing to be cowed by the danger she sensed emanating from him. She'd done nothing wrong. But she hoped he couldn't see her hands shaking. "That won't be necessary."

He took a step closer, and she had to force herself to stand still. But her pulse jumped in her throat.

And he saw it. The smile that curved his lips made her feel like a mouse in a cat's eye. "I'm afraid it will. If you leave the castle, I'm going with you." His gaze swept over her in a way that made her skin flush with heat. "I think you've forgotten something."

Thoroughly discombobulated by the heat rushing through her veins, she stammered, "W-what?"

His eyes locked on hers. "Your basket." She froze, her eyes widening. He couldn't possibly know . . .

She nearly sighed with relief when he added, "I don't think I've seen you leave the castle without it."

Too observant—*far* too observant. Sir Arthur Campbell was dangerous in more ways than one. Her father would be furious if someone discovered what she and some of the other women had been up to.

Angry for allowing him to rattle her, Anna quickly composed herself. "I only intended to go for a ride today—not visit any of the villagers."

He held her gaze for a moment too long. Again, she wondered whether he knew something. This time, however, her expression betrayed nothing.

A series of excited barks shifted his attention down to the dog jumping on his leg. "Down," he said, in a voice that brokered no argument. The dog immediately sat and stared at him with an adoring look on his face. "Your pup needs to learn some manners."

Anna's mouth pursed. "He likes you." *God knows why.* Squeezing affection from Arthur Campbell was like trying to get water from a rock—doomed to frustration and failure.

His eyes narrowed as if she'd spoken aloud. "Animals usually have good instincts."

"Usually," she agreed, leaving him no doubt that in this case she thought differently.

The dangerous glint crept back into his eye. "And what about you, Anna? What do your instincts tell you?"

To run. To hide. To get as far away from him as she could so it would stop hurting. It hurt just to look at him, at the square, dented jaw, sensually curved lips, and dark, amber-flecked eyes.

She shifted her gaze, emotion welling in her throat. "I don't listen to my instincts." At least any longer. They were wrong. Her instincts had made her think there was something special between them. That he might need her. That he was lonely. And that he might be different from what he seemed: an ambitious knight, a battle-hard warrior, who lived by—and for—the sword.

Even now, her instincts led her to believe that this simmering tension between them meant something. That if only he would take her in his arms and kiss her again everything would be all right. But it was too late for that. "Instincts only make you do things you regret," she added.

His jaw hardened, and the muscle in his jaw jumped ominously. He stepped closer. Close enough for her to feel the heat radiating off him. To smell the hint of sun and spice on his skin.

Her legs started to melt.

God, she'd forgotten how tall he was. It felt as though the walls were closing in. It was hard to breathe. Hard to think with him looming over her like this.

He was using his fierce masculinity against her with all the subtlety of a battering ram.

"And do you regret it, Anna?"

She did not mistake the deceptive softness of his voice. She could feel the anger radiating off him—almost as if her change of heart mattered to him.

Why was he doing this? Why was he trying to confuse her? He was the one who'd told her to stay away.

"What difference does it make? Especially now. You made yourself brutally clear before you ran off with my brother."

She tried to brush past him, but he blocked her with the implacable shield of his chest. She could tell by the white lines around his mouth that he hadn't missed her taunt.

"So you are done with your spying, is that it?"

Her eyes scanned his face. Is that what he thought? God, what did it matter? She dragged her gaze away and looked past him to the door. "Yes, that's it. Now, if you'll excuse me, I wish to leave."

She pushed against his chest with the heel of her hand, but he was about as yielding as a rocky cliff. A cliff with lots and lots of sharply cut rocks.

"I told you I'm going with you."

"Your *services* are no longer necessary. I've changed my mind; I won't be riding this morning."

She could tell by the way his eyes flared that he didn't appreciate being dismissed. Well, too bad. He was the one who'd appointed himself her knight errant.

The muscles in his shoulders tensed, and she wondered whether she might have pushed him too far. But with a twist of his mouth, he bowed dramatically and stepped aside. "As you wish, my lady. But if you change your mind, you know where to find me."

She swept past him, chin high. "I won't change my mind. I've much to do before I go."

A hand on her arm brought her to a jerking halt. But even the harsh touch made her senses explode.

"Going somewhere, Lady Anna?"

She tried to wrench her arm away, glaring at him when he wouldn't let her go. "It's none of your business."

His eyes flashed, and he drew her near. She could feel the energy pulsing between them, dragging her under. His mouth was so close. "Tell me."

He couldn't kiss her, she thought in a panic. She couldn't let him kiss her. "I'm to be married," she blurted.

Twelve

Arthur dropped her arm as if she'd scalded him.

Married? The word landed like a hammer in his gut. He couldn't seem to move. Every bone, every muscle, every nerve ending had turned to stone.

"Who?" The toneless, vaguely menacing voice didn't belong to him—it sounded like MacRuairi's.

Anna wouldn't meet his gaze. Her hands started to twist nervously in the thick woolen folds of her skirt. "Sir Hugh Ross."

A knife wedged between his ribs would have skewered less sharply. The Earl of Ross's son and heir. Arthur knew of him, of course. The young knight had already made a name for himself. He was a fierce warrior—a tactician on and off the battlefield. The fact that he was worthy of her made it worse.

Arthur didn't understand the rage pouring through him, nor the feeling of betrayal. She didn't belong to him, damn it. Could never belong to him.

But that didn't mean he could forget that not a fortnight past he'd held her in his arms—and come damned close to taking her innocence.

"It seems you had an eventful week, my lady. You work fast."

A hot blush stained her cheeks. "The details have not all been worked out yet."

His eyes narrowed, hearing something in her voice. "What do you mean, details? Are you betrothed or aren't you?"

She lifted her chin. Despite the blush staining her cheeks, he read the defiant glint in her eye. "Sir Hugh proposed to me last year, soon after my betrothed died."

"I thought you refused."

"I did. I've reconsidered."

All of a sudden, Arthur realized what this was about. With no help coming from King Edward, the MacDougalls had decided to turn to Ross for help, offering up Lady Anna to provide added incentive for an alliance.

Whether she'd reconsidered or her father had done it for her didn't matter. He couldn't let them join forces. An alliance between Ross and the MacDougalls would hurt Bruce's chances for victory. It was his job—his duty—to stop it.

Arthur gave her a hard look. "And how do you know that Sir Hugh will be amenable to your sudden change of heart?"

"I don't." She gave him a pointed look. "But I will do what I must to persuade him."

He didn't need to guess what she meant. His reaction was instantaneous. Primitive. For one split second, rage took over and he lost control. His mind went black. She was one hair's breadth from being pinned up against that stable wall with her lips crushed to his, his manhood wedged between her thighs, and his tongue plunging deep inside her mouth. Exactly where she belonged.

But even out of his mind with rage, the urge to protect her was stronger. He didn't trust himself to touch her, not like this.

Anna's eyes widened, and she took a prudent step back.

But he held her in the trap of his piercing gaze. "So you have it all planned out?"

She nodded. "Aye. It will be for the best."

The fact that she sounded as if she were trying to convince herself didn't give him any solace. "There is one problem with your plan."

She looked at him hesitantly. "What's that?"

"Ross is in the north. The roads are too dangerous for you to travel. The risk is too great. Bruce and his men could be on the move at any time. Your father won't sanction this." Lorn was a cold-hearted bastard, but he seemed to genuinely love his daughter.

"He already has. My brother Alan and a score of guardsmen will escort me. King Hood might be a murderous brigand, but he does not make war on women."

Arthur fought to keep his temper under control. Lorn had to be desperate to have agreed to this. The bastard would do anything to win, even put his daughter in jeopardy. "*If* the rebels know you are a woman. In the dark, you will not be so easy to discern. You might be mistaken for couriers."

Had she forgotten already what had nearly happened to her in Ayr? Jesus, when he thought of the danger . . .

His blood chilled. He thought about pressing her up against the stable wall again, this time to shake some sense into her. She could be hurt. Killed.

"My brother will protect me. I'm sure it will be fine."

A vein drummed in his temple. A hundred men could not keep her safe. His struggle for control failed. "Don't be a fool. You can't go. It's too dangerous. Send a messenger instead."

From the way her eyes narrowed and the set of her chin, he knew he'd made a mistake. For such a sweet-looking lass, she had a surprisingly formidable stubborn streak.

"It's already decided. And you, I'm afraid, have nothing to say about it."

Women should be meek and submissive, damn it. But here she stood toe-to-toe with him, not backing down one inch. He'd admire it, if he weren't so furious.

This time when she spun on her heel and flounced through the door, he didn't stop her.

Nothing to say about it. We'll see about that.

If Anna wouldn't see reason, perhaps her father would.

Bruce's men were roaming all over the area—raiding, reiving, interfering with the supply lines—doing whatever they could to cause chaos and spread fear in the heart of the enemy. War took place not just on the battlefield but in the mind.

A party of MacDougall guardsmen would be irresistible. Anna would have an arrow in her chest before they were close enough to realize their mistake.

It was the threat to his mission that was twisting him in knots, he told himself. Preventing this kind of alliance— keeping MacDougall alone—was why he was here.

But it wasn't the messages or alliance he was thinking about. All he could see was Anna lying in a pool of blood.

He had to turn Lorn from this foolish path.

And if he couldn't . . .

There was no way in hell he'd let her go alone. If Anna took one step outside this castle, he was going to be right by her side. Where he could protect her and keep an eye on her.

He knew one thing for damned certain: There was no way in hell she was marrying Hugh Ross.

"Is something wrong, Annie? You seem upset."

Anna gazed over at her brother Alan, who'd come up to ride beside her.

After traveling the first part of the journey by *birlinn* this morning, the rest of the trip would be made on horseback. The sea route from Dunstaffnage to the village of Inverlochy by way of Loch Linnhe had taken less than a half-day, a journey that would have taken days by land.

She wished the rest of the trip would be so easy. Although three lochs and numerous rivers traversed Gleann Mor, the Great Glen, which bisected Scotland from Inverlochy at the head of Loch Linnhe to Inverness and the Moray Firth, the waterways were separated by enough land to make travel by ship infeasible. Instead, they would ride the roughly seventy-five-mile journey from Inverlochy to Nairn. With luck, they would arrive at Auldearn Castle just east of Nairn in four days. She was slowing them down, she knew, although it was a far more punishing pace then the leisurely one she was used to.

Ironically, they would travel along much the same route King Hood had followed last autumn as he cut a swath across the Highlands, taking the four principal castles along the way: the Comyn castles of Inverlochy and Urquhart, and the royal castles garrisoned by the English at Inverness and Nairn.

As the castles were still held by the rebels, they would be forced to find other, less perilous, accommodation on the way. To avoid Bruce's men, Anna suspected she would be seeing quite a bit of the forest.

It would be a welcome reprieve from the blazing sun. They'd been riding for a few hours, and though she wore a thin veil to protect her face, she was hot, sticky, and yes, as her brother had noticed, angry.

Furious, really.

The weather, however, was not to blame for her unusual black mood. That honor belonged to a certain interfering knight.

She'd refused to look at *him* all day. But that didn't mean she wasn't aware of exactly where he was: riding at the head of the party, scouting the road ahead for signs of trouble.

Trouble. That was an understatement. His presence on their journey would be nothing but.

"I'm fine," she assured her brother, managing a wan smile. "Tired and hot, but fine."

Alan gave her a deceptively lazy sidelong glance. "I thought it might have something to do with Campbell. You didn't seem very happy to hear he would be joining us."

Her brother was far too astute. A trait that would make him a good chief someday, but not one valued by a younger sister intent on keeping her thoughts to herself.

Despite her best effort not to react, her teeth gritted together. "It wasn't his place to interfere."

She couldn't believe it when her father told her that Sir Arthur had attempted to change his mind about the journey. Failing in this, he'd asked to accompany them. His skills as a scout would help ensure their safety, he'd argued. Her father had agreed, much to Anna's dismay.

So instead of ignoring him for a single day, she would be forced to endure his constant presence for days, possibly weeks.

Was he purposefully trying to torment her? What she had to do would be difficult enough without him around.

"He's a knight, Anna. A scout. Reporting on the enemy position is exactly what he's supposed to do. And I can't say I'm not glad to have him along. If he's as good as he claims to be, we can use him."

Anna turned to Alan, aghast. "You agree with Father?"

His jaw locked. Alan would never openly criticize their father, even if—like now—he wanted to. "I would have preferred you stay at Dunstaffnage, although I understand why Father insisted you come along. Ross will be more amenable to a direct appeal." He smiled. "You're a minx, Annie-love, but a bewitching one."

Anna's mouth twitched. "And you are annoyingly over-protective, but I love you, too."

He laughed, and Anna couldn't help joining him.

Sir Arthur turned at the sound and caught her unprepared. Their gazes snagged for an instant before she turned brusquely away. But it was long enough to send a fist of pain slamming into her chest. Why did it have to hurt so badly?

Alan didn't miss the exchange. He sobered, his gaze once again intent. "Are you sure that's all, Anna? I know what you said, but I think there is more between you and Sir Arthur than keeping an eye on him for Father. I think you care for him." The throb in her chest told her he was right, even if she wished it otherwise. "We can appeal to Ross without the betrothal," her brother said gently. "You don't need to sacrifice your happiness in the bargain."

A swell of emotion rose inside her. How fortunate she was to have such a brother. She knew not many men would feel the same. Happiness was not usually a consideration in marriage between nobles. Power, alliances, wealth—that was what mattered. But the love Alan had found in his marriage had given her brother a unique perspective.

Yet they would have a much better chance at gaining Ross's support with an alliance. Alan knew that as well as she did.

Besides, helping her family would never be a sacrifice. Especially since there actually had to be something to sacrifice. Arthur had made it painfully clear that there was nothing between them.

"I'm sure," she said firmly.

The certainty in her voice must have convinced him. Alan rode with her awhile longer, recalling previous journeys they'd made in the rare times of peace, but eventually he returned to his men.

They made good progress the first day, reaching as far as Loch Lochy before stopping for the night at an inn near the southern head of the loch. The small stone and thatched building looked ancient, and given its position near an old Roman road, Anna suspected it might be.

She was stiff and achy, feeling every hour of the long day in her legs, bottom, and back, and grateful for the roof and bed, no matter how crude. She washed and managed a few bites of fish stew and brown bread before collapsing into bed, her maidservant, Berta, snoring on a pallet beside her.

The second night, however, they were not so fortunate. Her bed this night would be a pallet in a small tent in the forest just south of Loch Ness.

It had been a long day, made longer by Arthur's steady stream of scouting reports. To avoid potentially dangerous situations, such as open stretches of road or natural places for ambushes, at times they veered well off the road. Which meant that instead of the twenty-five miles they would have been on the road, they'd probably ridden thirty-five through the dense forests and rolling hills of Lochaber.

It seemed an overabundance of caution to her. So far they'd seen nothing out of the ordinary—villagers, fishermen, and an occasional party of travelers. If Bruce's men were patrolling the roads, they hadn't made themselves known.

Perhaps the extra miles were another way Sir Arthur had devised to torment her? As if his presence were not enough.

Not used to the long days riding, Anna's legs shook as she knelt at the banks of the river to wash her hands. She lowered her face, hoping to shock away some of her tiredness, but the cold splash of water did little to refresh her.

She groaned, her bones and joints objecting, as she attempted to stand. Creaking like an old woman, she made it back up to her feet.

In no hurry to return to camp, she took a moment to savor the moment of solitude. Though the rest of the party was only a few dozen yards away, the dense canopy of trees and moss seemed to suck up sound. Occasionally, she could hear the faint sound of voices, but otherwise it was remarkably quiet and the most peace she'd had since arriving in the *barmkin* yesterday morning to find Sir Arthur Campbell ready to ride out with them.

Nearly two days of trying to force herself not to look at him had taken its toll. It was worse than she'd feared. Even though she'd ignored him, avoiding his gaze every time he looked in her direction, she was painfully aware of his every movement. The hole of longing that seemed to be burning in her chest was growing bigger. Heavier. Grinding away at her emotions, leaving her raw and tender.

She didn't know how much more of this she could take. Why did he have to be here?

Heaving a weary sigh, she turned from the soothing stream of water rushing over the rocks. Berta would send her brother after her in a panic if she didn't return in the few minutes that she'd promised. Besides, it was getting dark.

She'd taken only a few steps into the forest when a man stepped out of the shadows to block her path.

Her pulse spiked in panic. She opened her mouth to scream, but it was smothered by recognition.

Her mouth slammed shut. Her pulse, however, remained frantic. "Don't do that," she snapped, gazing up into the handsome face of Sir Arthur. "You scared me to death."

He hadn't made a sound. How such a large man moved with such stealth, she didn't know.

"Good," he snapped back. "You shouldn't be out here alone."

"I wasn't alone," she said with a tight smile. "I had you spying on me."

She took supreme satisfaction from the tightening of his jaw. It was horrible of her to take such delight, but prying any kind of reaction from him seemed like a major achievement.

He gave her a long, penetrating look. "Something I'm sure you know all about."

Now it was her jaw that felt tight.

He was standing too close. Though her brother and the rest of the men were only a shout away, this was far more alone with him than she wanted to be. Being any kind of alone with him was dangerous.

It made her remember things. Like kissing him and the taste of cloves. Or how the thick muscles of his naked chest had rippled in the candlelight. Or how the damp waves of his hair had curled against his neck. Or how he'd smelled. Like soap and—she inhaled—virile man.

He hadn't shaved, and the stubble on his chin gave him a rugged, dangerous edge that—devil take him!—only added to his appeal.

Furious that he was getting to her after all that had happened, she tried to push past him. An exercise in futility if there ever was one. "There is no need for your concern," she said. "I was just about to return."

He grabbed her arm to stop her, as if the impenetrable blockade of his chest weren't enough. "Next time you leave camp, do not do so without a guard—preferably me or your brother."

Her cheeks burned, furious at his tone and his overbearing attitude. Sir Arthur Campbell, knight in her father's service, overstepped his bounds. "You have no right to give me orders. The last time I looked, it was my brother—not you—who was in charge."

His eyes flashed, and his fingers tightened around her arm. His voice was very low and his mouth . . .

She gasped. His mouth was low as well. Perilously so. Achingly close to hers. If she stood up on her tiptoes, she might even be able to reach it with her own.

God, she wanted to. *Desperately* she wanted to. Heat flooded inside her, concentrating in her breasts and between her legs. Her nipples tightened, aching for the heated friction of his hard chest.

Her body's betrayal was humiliating. He had no right to make her feel like this. Not after his cruel rejection. Not after he'd left and proved that he was the man she'd first thought him. Why couldn't he just leave her alone?

"Do not challenge me in this, Anna. If you'd like me to get your brother involved, I will. I was trying to save you from the embarrassment of being treated like a child, but I'll do whatever I have to do to keep you safe."

Something in his voice made her skin prickle with alarm. "What is it? Are the rebels near? Did you see something?"

A shadow crossed over his eyes. He shook his head. "Not so far."

"But you sense something."

His gaze shot to hers, dark with suspicion, as if he thought she was trying to trap him into admitting she'd been right about the abilities he'd displayed before.

He seemed poised to deny it, but then he shrugged, dropping his hand from her arm. "Aye, I feel danger. And you should, too. Don't be fooled into thinking they aren't out there just because we haven't seen them."

Chastened by what she sensed was genuine concern, she nodded. "I will do as you ask."

Both of them knew he hadn't asked, but he seemed satisfied enough by her agreement not to quibble with semantics.

She knew she should walk away, but something made her ask, "Why are you here, Sir Arthur? Why did you insist on joining our party?"

He looked away. Her question had discomfited him. Good.

He squared his jaw. "I thought your brother could use my help."

"And I thought you didn't like scouting."

A wry, enigmatic smile curved his mouth. "It's not as bad as I feared."

Her eyes scanned his face, but she wasn't sure what she was looking for. "And that's the only reason? Because you wanted to help my brother?"

He looked down at her. The intensity of his gaze penetrated with all the subtlety of a bolt of lightning. She could see the tic pulsing below his jaw. He was restraining himself, but from what?

"Since you wouldn't listen to my warning, I had no other choice but to come and ensure you reach your destination safely."

Safely delivered into the arms of another man. "I'm sure Sir Hugh will appreciate your service."

He tensed, his eyes sparking like wildfire. For a moment she thought he was going to push her up against the tree and kiss her.

But he didn't. Instead he clenched his fists and stared down at her angrily.

It wasn't disappointment she felt, it wasn't, she told herself. But it didn't work.

"Don't push me, Anna."

But she was past warnings. "Don't push you? How could I push you when you don't care? You made yourself quite clear that night in the barracks. *You* were the one who told me to stay away, remember? Not the other way around."

"I remember."

The huskiness in his voice told her that wasn't all he remembered. Her skin started to heat and tighten. The memories crackled between them like a breath of air on embers, flaring, ready to catch fire.

Anna didn't understand why he was doing this. Frustration welled up inside her. "Have you changed your mind?"

At another time Arthur would have admired her challenge. Anna's frankness and openness were part of what made her unique. But not right now. He didn't want to think about changing his mind. It was taking everything he had just to keep his hands off her.

Why couldn't she be shy and retiring? That he could handle.

He knew he was acting like an arse, but two days of being near her, of watching her turn away to avoid his gaze, of her acting like he was nothing more than a hired sword, had stretched his restraint to the breaking point. He couldn't take another evening of watching her flit around the campsite, laughing and smiling with the men. Smiles that were conspicuously absent in his direction.

He liked it on the periphery, damn it. But from his familiar position on the edge of the campsite, away from the camaraderie of the fire, he found himself longing for the warmth of one of those smiles. Some of that laughter. Some of that light.

He'd wanted to force her to acknowledge him. But all he'd done was stir up things that didn't need stirring.

Such as the overwhelming desire to push her up against that tree and ravish her. He could almost feel her arms circling his neck, her leg wrapped around his hip, as he sank into her, slow and deep. Her soft little body stretched against his. All those seductive curves melting against him. The erotic bead of her nipples raking his chest.

Hell.

He shifted to adjust himself. But the swell in his braies was hard and unrelenting.

This shouldn't be so bloody difficult. *Focus. Do your job. Stay close enough to watch her, but don't touch. Don't let her get too close.*

Too many people were counting on him. He had to keep his eye on what really mattered: seeing Bruce secure on the throne and vanquishing those who would stand against him. Such as John of Lorn. This was his chance to see his enemy pay for what he'd done to his father.

Justice. Revenge. Righting a wrong. Blood for blood. It was what had driven him for as long as he could remember. He'd devoted his life to becoming the greatest warrior he could be, with one goal in mind: destroying Lorn.

Cold purpose had been his companion for fourteen years. The steely resolve to see a mission through to the end, no matter what the cost. Despite the wide differences in personality—from MacSorley's irrepressible good humor, to Seton's hotheadedness, to MacRuairi's surliness—it was the one thing all the members of the Highland Guard had in common. But he'd never struggled so hard to hold on to it.

He took a step back, trying to clear the haze of desire that gripped him. But his body teemed with unspent lust. Lust that he was finding harder and harder to ignore. Walking around with his cock wedged to his stomach wasn't doing much for his temper. His hand barely took the edge off.

When he didn't answer right away, she said, "Well?"

Had he changed his mind? He shook his head. "Nay."

Nothing had changed. She was still the daughter of the man he'd come to destroy. The only thing the future held for them was betrayal. He wouldn't make it worse.

If she was disappointed by his response, she didn't show it. If anything, she'd seemed to expect it. "Then why are you doing this? Why are you acting as if you care who I marry? You don't want me, but you don't want anyone else to want me either, is that it?"

He muttered a curse, dragging his fingers through his hair. "It's not like that."

Actually, it was exactly like that. She'd nailed his problem squarely on the head. He was jealous, damn it. Even if he had no right to be. Even if he'd discouraged her. Even if there was no chance for them. The thought of her marrying another man sent him into fits of youthful jealousy.

She met his gaze. "Then explain it to me," she said quietly. "How do you feel about me?"

Jesus. That was the last thing he wanted to think about.

Only she would ask such a question. Anna MacDougall didn't have a shy and retiring bone in her body. Straightforward. Direct. No pretense.

God, she was amazing.

All the training in the world couldn't stop him from shifting his feet. Not since his brothers had backed him against a ledge over a cliffside, taunting him to defend against their sword blows, had he felt this cornered. "It's complicated," he hedged.

Her eyes wouldn't leave his face, searching for something that wasn't there. "Complicated isn't good enough." She dropped her gaze. "I don't want you here." Her voice was as stiff as the set of her narrow shoulders.

He didn't want to be there either, but he had no choice.

She lifted her eyes to his once more. The warmth had fled from their brilliant blue depths. "Please, just leave me alone."

The soft plea in her voice tugged at his conscience, but it burned in his chest. She turned and walked away as regally as a queen.

For both their sakes he wished he could. But his mission had to come first. A few more weeks. He could make it through a few more weeks. He'd withstood far more dangerous challenges. All he had to do was shore up his defenses, batten down the hatches, and dig in for the final siege.

Thirteen

Something wasn't right.

Arthur was scouting ahead of the rest of the group with two of MacDougall's men when he felt it. The shift in the air. The cool shiver blowing across the back of his neck. The sudden alertness that set all of his nerve-endings on edge.

Danger.

It was late on the third day of their journey. The day's ride along the west bank of Loch Ness had taken longer than anticipated, due not to avoiding Bruce's men but to a washed-out bridge at Invermoriston. Had Anna not been there, they might have attempted to cross the rushing waters, but instead they'd traveled another five miles out of their way to the next ford.

Thus, it was later than he would have liked as they neared the southern edge of Clunemore wood. From Clunemore they would turn east, leaving the road to steer well clear of the rebel-occupied Urquhart Castle.

For their last night, they planned to camp in the woods along the banks of Loch Meiklie. Tomorrow would be an even more grueling day, when the relatively flat road gave way to hills.

Though Arthur worked better alone, Alan MacDougall

had insisted that two of his men accompany him in case he ran into trouble. He couldn't tell Anna's brother that the men would be more trouble than help without giving away his skills, so reluctantly he'd agreed.

At the first prickle of danger, he held up his hand for the men to stop. He jumped off his horse and knelt, placing his hand flat on the ground. The faint reverberation confirmed what he'd already sensed.

Richard, the larger of the two warriors and MacDougall's usual scout, frowned. "What is it?"

Arthur lowered his voice. "Ride back. Tell your lord to get off the road immediately."

Alex, who was training to be a scout, gave him an odd look from under the steel of his nasal helm. Unlike Arthur, Alan, and the handful of other knights who wore a fully visored helm, heavy mail, and surcoat, the MacDougall clansmen wore lighter armor and the padded leather *cotun* favored by Highlanders. The war coat made it easier to move around. Not for the first time, Arthur wished he could toss off his cumbersome knightly garb and do away with the pretense. The younger man looked around. "Why?"

Arthur's mouth thinned. He stood and quickly remounted his horse. "There's a large party of horsemen heading straight for us."

Richard looked at him as if he were crazy. "I don't hear anything."

The fools were going to get them all killed. With no time for subtlety, Arthur grabbed the big man by the thick scruff of his neck. Lifting him a few inches off his saddle, he brought his face to his. "Do as I say, damn it. In another few minutes it will be too late. Do you want to see the lady killed for your stupidity?"

Shocked by the change that had come over Arthur, the man shook his head. When he started gasping, Arthur released him with a harsh shove.

"I'll circle around and try to distract them." Hopefully

leading them north. "Tell Sir Alan to get off the road right away. To head east and ride as fast as he can. Leave the carts behind if necessary. I'll meet you when I can at the loch."

Suddenly, Richard's thick head jerked to the north. The faint sound of pounding hooves floated toward them. He turned to Arthur, eyes wide with fear and suspicion. Unconsciously, he backed his horse away. "Christ's bones, you're right! I hear them."

Arthur didn't have time to worry about the other man's unease.

"I'll go with you," Alex said.

"Nay," Arthur said, in a voice that brokered no argument. "I go alone."

It would be easier to evade capture. Besides, there was always a chance he would know someone. MacGregor, Gordon, and MacKay were supposed to be in the north.

"Go," he said.

With no further argument, the men did as he bid.

Arthur didn't waste any more time. Horse and man plunged through the trees, as he raced to get behind the approaching riders before they came up on the MacDougall party. Even with the warning, he knew it would take time to maneuver them to safety. Anna was a good rider, but her maidservant wasn't. The carts would slow them down further. If there was one thing about women he knew, they didn't like to leave their fine shoes and gowns behind.

At least she hadn't insisted on bringing that damned pup of hers. He was tired of dodging piss on his toes.

Using the sound of the horses as a guide, he weaved through the trees, riding parallel to the men for a few, all-important seconds before darting toward them.

Now came the tricky part: getting close enough to draw them away, but not so close that he got captured.

He muttered a curse, as a gap in the trees gave him his first look at the riders. A war party, by the looks of it.

There were more of them than he would have liked. At least a score of men armed to the teeth in dark-colored plaids, war coats blackened with pitch, and blackened helms—a means of blending into the night utilized by the Highland Guard, but adopted later by many of Bruce's warriors.

Normally, the sight of such a formidable force wouldn't give him a second thought. He'd been trained for worse. But these men knew the terrain and he didn't. They would have the advantage. One wrong turn and he could end up trapped.

Still, he had advantages they did not: razor-sharp senses, speed, superior strength and training, and the ability to fade into the shadows.

Ahead of him, he saw a break in the trees. This was it. Clenching his jaw, he lowered his head and shot toward the clearing. Pretending he'd just noticed the men, he veered sharply off to the left as if he were trying to avoid being seen.

When he heard the cry go out, he knew they'd sighted him. He didn't dare slow down to look behind him, waiting to see if they'd taken the bait. A fraction of a second's delay could mean the difference between escape and capture.

But a moment later, hearing the thunder of hooves behind him, he smiled.

The hunt was on.

Anna tried not to think about how late it was getting. But as darkness descended and the moon rose high in the sky, it became harder and harder to convince herself that he was all right.

The fear that had been held at bay by the tumult of their effort to evade the enemy soldiers had returned full force once they'd reached safety. And with each hour that passed, and Arthur still hadn't returned, it only grew worse.

He could torment her all he wanted; she didn't care. Just let him come back safely.

She drew her cloak tighter around her shoulders and told herself not to worry. Arthur would lead them on a merry chase, and it would take some time to make his way to them.

But would it take this long?

She bit her lip, trying to slow the rising sense of panic.

He wouldn't get caught.

But there were so many of them and only one of him.

He can't be dead.

She would know it if he was. Her heart clenched. Wouldn't she?

"The stew is delicious, m'lady. Here." Berta held out a spoon to her. "Try a bite. Just a little one," she added, as if Anna were a five-year-old refusing to eat her turnips.

She still didn't like them.

Anna shook her head, managing a small smile for her worried maidservant. "I'm not hungry."

The older woman frowned, her soft brown eyes crinkling into a spray of fine lines at the edges. At barely a hair over five feet and as thin as a whip, Berta didn't look very formidable. But in this case, looks deceived. She could be as stubborn and testy as an old goat. "You have to eat something. You'll make yourself ill."

She already was ill—with worry. The thought of food made her stomach turn. She bit back the bile that rose to the back of her throat. "I will," she lied. "In a little while."

Berta patted her hand, which rested on the mossy log between them. They had gathered around the fire with the rest of the men, but the camp was unusually quiet, the men subdued. They were all aware of the narrow escape they'd made earlier, and she wasn't the only one wondering what had happened to the knight who'd given them the warning to do so.

"Starving yourself won't bring him back any faster," Berta said.

Anna's thoughts were more transparent than she'd realized, but she was too worried to feign ignorance. "Do you think something has happened to him?"

Berta squeezed her hand and gave a sad shake of her head. "I don't know, lassie-mine. I don't know."

Anna's heart gave a sharp tug. It had to be bad if Berta wasn't even going to lie to her.

They fell back into silence, Anna staring blindly into the flames of the fire and Berta finishing her stew.

Anna jumped at the sound of a twig cracking behind her. Heart in her throat, she turned around, expecting to see a mail-clad knight atop his horse.

She did, and for a second she thought it was Arthur.

But then her heart tumbled in disappointment. It was only her brother. Alan hopped down and tied the reins of his horse to a nearby tree. The grim expression on his face as he walked toward her filled her with panic. "Did you find something?" she asked.

He shook his head. "Nay. There's no sign of him."

"Do you think . . ." She couldn't bear to say it.

Alan gave her a long look. "He should have returned by now."

The truth hit like a hammer to the gut. Anguished tears sprang to her eyes. The first one had seeped from the corner of her eye when she heard a whistle pierce the night air.

"It's the night sentry," Alan said, before she could ask. "Someone's approaching."

The alert had caused something of a commotion. Though Anna had shot to her feet at once, so had everyone else. She heard the raucous cheer of excitement and relief go up before she caught sight of him.

A moment later, her heart leapt high in her chest when

Arthur strode into the circle of light provided by the camp-fire. Her eyes raked over him for any sign of injury. But other than the weariness on his handsome face and the dirt and dust staining his mail, he looked hale. Perfectly hale.

The swell of emotion overwhelmed her. She took a step forward before she caught herself.

She fought the urge to go to him. To run into his arms, throw her arms around his neck, and sob out her relief on his dirty, grimy, mail-clad chest.

She had no right. No cause. They were not courting or betrothed. They were nothing to each other. Soon, she'd belong to another man.

He saw her then.

For one foolish moment she told herself he'd been look-ing for her.

Their eyes met. She felt the force of it in her chest. Rever-berating. Pounding. Squeezing with longing.

If he'd turned away from her then, coldly dismissing her, she might have been able to face her future with a steady heart. But instead, sensing her desperation, he gave her a short nod. *I'm fine.*

It was a small chip, but a chip nonetheless, and an ac-knowledgment of the connection between them. There was something special between them; he could no longer deny it. She mattered.

With one last look, he turned away and strode forward to meet her brother.

Anna's emotions were reeling. She listened with half an ear while he gave his report, too caught up in what had just happened to focus on anything else.

Bruce's men. A large war party. The number drew her at-tention. She gasped. Twenty-five men? He should be dead.

Arthur had led them a few miles north of Urquhart Cas-tle before attempting to head east. The outlaws proved hard to lose, however, and he'd been forced to abandon his horse and make his way to them on foot. Anna suspected there was much he was leaving out.

Alan thanked him for the service he'd done them all, before sitting him down and ordering food and drink.

Her brother spoke with him awhile longer, in low tones that she could not hear, before leaving Arthur to his meal—alone.

Anna nibbled on an oatcake and piece of dried beef, lingering as most of the men had done.

As the night drew on, however, something began to trouble her. The camp had livened with his return—the men were clearly relieved that he'd evaded capture—but there wasn't the celebration that she'd expected. She frowned. And there was something strange going on. Other than her brother, no one else had gone near him. Instead of the backslaps, crude jests, and toasts that would usually be called for, she noticed more than one of the men casting him uneasy glances.

Arthur didn't seem to notice. He finished his food, finished the skin of ale that had been brought him, and retreated to the solitude of the forest.

She watched him go, feeling the overwhelming urge to do something. She looked around at her clansmen. What was wrong with them? Why were they acting like this?

When she couldn't stand it any longer, she excused herself and went to find her brother. He was speaking with some of his men, but seeing her approach, he dismissed them.

"I thought you'd be relieved," Alan said.

She didn't pretend to misunderstand what he was talking about. "I am."

"Then why the frown, little one?"

"Why are the men acting like this? Why don't they thank him? Why are they avoiding him?"

A wry smile turned his mouth. "Are you sure it's not the

other way around, sister? Campbell isn't exactly known for his sociability. He likes to keep to himself."

He was right, but there was something more this time. The men were uneasy—almost fearful. When she said as much to her brother, he sighed and shook his head. "Something happened today when the men were scouting. Richard told me about it and probably some of the other men as well. Apparently, Campbell heard the riders well before there was any sign of them. Richard said it was unnatural."

Any delight she might have felt in having her own suspicions confirmed after what had happened with the wolves paled in comparison to the fury that stormed through her.

Outrage flooded her cheeks with heat. "That's ridiculous. Don't they realize that he saved us all? They should be grateful, not casting wild aspersions."

"I agree, but you know how superstitious Highlanders can be."

"That doesn't excuse it."

"Nay, it doesn't. I'll speak with Richard and try to put an end to it."

Anna drew herself up to her full hand over five feet. "See that you do or I will speak to him myself. I won't see Sir Arthur shunned for helping us. God's wounds, Alan! Without that 'unnatural' ability we might all be dead."

Alan gave her a long look, and what he saw there seemed to worry him. He frowned, and rather than admonish her coarse language, he simply nodded his head.

She started to walk away, intent on finding Arthur. Her brother must have guessed her destination.

He called out. "We'll arrive at Auldearn tomorrow evening, Anna."

She turned and gave him a quizzical look, puzzled by the non sequitur. "Aye."

"If you mean to go through with the betrothal, perhaps it would be best if you left him alone."

She hesitated, hearing the truth in her brother's words. But she couldn't. The men's actions had raised every protective instinct in her body. She had to thank him, even if they would not.

She found him by the loch, seated on a low boulder. He'd bathed. His hair was damp and he wore a simple linen shirt and tunic with his leather chausses. He was bent over, oiling his mail with a cloth, and his expression in profile seemed unusually somber.

She knew he'd heard her, but he didn't turn around. As she moved closer, she could see what he was cleaning.

Her stomach dropped to her feet. *Blood.*

Without thinking, she rushed forward, kneeled beside him, and put her hand on his arm. "You're hurt."

His gaze lifted to hers, catching in the moonlight. "It's not mine," he said.

Relief crashed through her. She exhaled deeply. Though his expression betrayed nothing, she heard a strange emotion in his voice. He almost sounded as if he regretted it. That the death of one of their enemies might have bothered him.

Perhaps it wasn't as easy for warriors to kill as she'd assumed. At least it wasn't for him. The realization made him seem somehow more human. More vulnerable.

Sir Arthur Campbell vulnerable? The thought would have made her laugh a few weeks ago.

"You had no choice," she said softly.

He held her gaze for a moment longer before dropping it to the hand that rested on his arm.

Immediately she became conscious of the intimacy of the warm, hard skin flexing beneath her palm, and she hastily snatched it away. But it didn't stop the urge to curl up against him and rest her cheek on that broad shield.

He resumed his task in removing the bloodstains from the small, interlocking pieces of steel.

She sat beside him on a lower rock, watching him for a few minutes in silence.

"Why are you here, Anna?"

"I wanted to thank you for what you did today."

He gave a short shrug, not lifting his gaze from his task. "I was only doing my job. It's why I'm here."

She bit her lip, recalling her anger at his interference and skepticism at his motives. "It seems you were right," she admitted. "I'm grateful for your presence on our journey. We all are." Her mouth thinned with annoyance. "Though some of the men might have an odd way of showing it."

His shoulders tensed almost imperceptibly. "What are they saying?"

"That you sensed the riders coming before it was possible to do so."

He cocked a brow, amused by her attempt to soften the blow. "I'm sure that's not all they said."

Her cheeks burned, ashamed for the superstitions of her clansmen. "It's true, isn't it? It's like what happened with the wolves, and when I stumbled off the cliff. You know things before they are going to happen."

She pleaded with her eyes for him not to lie to her. Not again. He was quiet for so long, she thought he wasn't going to answer.

"It's not like that," he said finally. "It's more a feeling. My senses are sharper than normal, that's all."

"Sharper?" she repeated. "They're extraordinary." Her praise only seemed to make him more uncomfortable. "I don't understand why the men don't see it. You saved us all."

He gazed up at her sharply. "Leave it be, Anna. It means nothing."

The fact that he actually seemed to mean it made it that much worse. "How can you say that? Doesn't it bother you? They should be thanking you for what you've done and praising your extraordinary abilities, not acting like children afeared of goblins under the bed or ghosts in the ambry."

Her outrage on his behalf didn't seem to be appreciated. Once again she sensed that the conversation made him uncomfortable. He gave her a hard look. "It doesn't bother me, and I don't need you making things more difficult by championing my cause. I don't want you saying anything about whatever it is they thought they saw. Let it go and it will die a natural death. Prolong it and you will only make it worse."

He spoke from experience.

Anna pressed her lips together, fighting the urge to argue. It wasn't right, and the injustice of it raised every protective bone in her body.

It bothered him. It had to, no matter how nonchalant he seemed. The fact that he'd grown so accustomed to people's subtle cruelty—that he expected it—only made it worse.

Her heart squeezed. How many times had he been rejected or shunned to become so callous and indifferent?

Was that why he pushed people away?

Suddenly, his remoteness and separateness seemed more a cloak to loneliness. He'd been doing it so long, he'd actually convinced himself he liked to be alone.

Her heart went out to him. She was so lucky to have her family; she hated to think of anyone alone.

"Anna?" he said, his gaze leveling on her in the moonlight. Had he guessed the direction of her thoughts? "Promise me you won't say anything."

She scowled, but nodded.

He stood up. After dropping the slinky mail over his head, he donned a clean tabard and started to strap on his numerous weapons. Though there was something intimate about watching him dress, she didn't feel embarrassed. Rather, it felt natural. As if she could watch him ready himself for war forever.

The thought should have horrified her. Instead it filled her with a strong sense of yearning, of longing for something hovering just beyond her reach. His quiet solidness called to her. It made her think of a future. That maybe he wasn't wrong, but exactly right.

A stable warrior. It seemed contradictory. But maybe she'd gotten it all wrong.

"What will you do when the war is over?" she asked.

She wondered if he'd ever given a thought to doing something with his drawing, perhaps? Or would he just be looking for the next battle to fight?

The question took him aback. Arthur paused in the middle of fastening his sword belt. In truth, he hadn't given it much thought. War had consumed his life for so long. All he knew how to do was fight. First alongside his brother Neil, and later as a member of the Highland Guard. He was a professional soldier. One of the best in the world. It was all he knew how to do.

But was it what he wanted? Was it what he would do if given a choice?

Once his father had justice, once Bruce was secure on the throne, once he'd achieved his goals, what would he do then?

Land and a rich bride were to be his reward. It should be enough.

But as he stared at the woman who'd so staunchly defended him moments ago, who thought him extraordinary, not eerie, whose heart was too big for her own good, he wondered whether it would be.

He felt a strange heaviness in his chest, looking at her tiny upturned face bathed in soft shadows and moonlight. Knowing it was impossible didn't stop him from wanting her.

But he'd already revealed too much. He'd grown so accustomed to lying about his abilities, it had been strange to admit the truth out loud. Strange, but also a relief. He'd kept himself apart for so long, he'd forgotten what it was like to feel close to someone.

He was a damned fool.

His only excuse was that she'd caught him in a moment of weakness. The blood he'd been cleaning from his mail was that of the two men he'd been forced to kill to defend himself.

Protect your cover at all costs. Protect the mission.

God, sometimes he hated what he had to do.

He finished securing his weaponry before he answered. "I would think that depends on the outcome."

Even in the semidarkness he could see her pale, but she recovered quickly. "There is only one possible outcome. You don't know my father—he will not lose."

Arthur stiffened. He knew that better than anyone. That was why he was here.

"King Hood and the rebels will be subdued and brought to justice."

Though she sounded like a good, loyal MacDougall soldier, beneath the bravado he sensed her fragility. Anna was holding on tightly to illusions that were beginning to show cracks. But she had to know the direness of the situation or they wouldn't be here.

"And yet you go to Ross to barter yourself for additional men."

Her back straightened, her eyes flashing bright in the moonlight. "It's not like that."

It was exactly like that. And it was his job to ensure it didn't happen.

He didn't want to be cruel, but she needed to face reality. The pendulum had swung away from the MacDougalls; Bruce was winning this war. "What if you fail, Anna? What if Ross won't agree to send men? What then?"

"My father will think of something." She sounded so desperate, he almost reached out to comfort her before he caught himself. "Why are you talking like this?" she demanded. "You sound like a rebel. Why are you here if you don't believe we will win?"

He swore silently. She was right. And soon she would know just how right.

His stomach twisted; he thought of what she would think when she learned the truth. He wished he could somehow soften the blow. "That's exactly why I am here, Anna. Belief in a cause. Belief that the right side will win. But it doesn't always turn out the way you think it will. I don't want to see you hurt." He paused, going back to her original question. "When the war is over, I've been promised lands and other rewards. That should keep me busy enough."

She tilted her head, tiny lines appearing between her brows. "Other rewards? What kind of other rewards?"

He didn't say anything, but all of a sudden the answer seemed to come to her. She gasped, the stricken expression on her face giving away too much. "A bride? You've been promised a bride?"

He gave a short nod of acknowledgment.

"Who?"

One of the greatest heiresses in the Western Highlands—Lachlan MacRuairi's half sister, the Lady Christina of the Isles. "I don't know," he lied. "Someone suitable will be found after the war is over."

Not for the first time, he wished she would hide her emotions better. The pained look on her face made him want to do something rash, like take her in his arms and make promises that he could never keep.

"I see," she said in a small voice. "Why didn't you tell me?"

He gave her a long look. "Like you told me?"

She flinched. Apparently she'd forgotten where they were going. But he hadn't. With every mile that brought them closer to Auldearn and Ross, Arthur felt the restlessness teeming inside him building and building. He knew he had to do something to prevent this alliance—for his mission, he told himself—but what?

Perhaps he wouldn't need to do anything at all. Perhaps Ross would refuse the renewed talks of a betrothal.

But one look at her sweet face and Arthur knew he was dreaming. Sir Hugh would snatch her up in an instant.

His jaw hardened, and he held out his hand. "Come, we should return. It's getting late, and we have a long day tomorrow."

She slipped her hand in his and warmth spread through him. He felt . . . content. As if there was nothing more natural than her small hand in his. Every instinct clamored to hold on and not let go.

Instead, he let her fingers slide from his. They walked back to camp in silence.

They'd said enough already. Perhaps they'd said too much.

Fourteen

"Is something wrong with your meal?"

The sound of Sir Hugh's voice startled Anna out of her reverie. How long had she been staring absently into her trencher, flaking tiny chips of crust off her bread without saying anything?

An embarrassed flush rose to her cheeks as she tried to cover her gaffe with a smile. "Nay, it's delicious." To prove it, she popped a bit of beef in her mouth, feigning enjoyment she did not feel. When she finished chewing, she apologized. "I fear I am still tired from our journey, and poor company this evening."

They'd arrived at Auldearn two nights ago. The final day of their journey had been exhausting, but—thankfully—uneventful. If she'd secretly hoped for another chance to speak with Sir Arthur alone before they arrived, she was to be disappointed. He hadn't avoided her, but neither had he sought her out.

Something had changed that night at the loch; at least it had for her. He'd let her see a part of him that she sensed he didn't often reveal. A part of him that might need her. And most importantly, he hadn't pushed her away.

Oh, why hadn't he pushed her away? It would have

made it so much easier. Misery rose inside her; she fought the hot swell to her eyes and throat.

That was all she needed to do, start crying in the middle of the meal like an unstable, lovesick maid. That would be sure to impress Sir Hugh.

Though young, only a year past her two and twenty, Sir Hugh Ross was big, imposing, and rakishly handsome, from the bridge of his finely shaped patrician nose to the tip of his short, pointed beard. But the proud knight seemed far older than his years. Self-possessed and confident, with the arrogance of a prince—which, given his rank among Scotland's noblemen, wasn't that far off—he seemed almost *too* controlled. Stiff. Humorless. With that cold, ruthless look particular to men of his station.

He gave her an understanding smile, but it did little to soften his hard-edged countenance. "Of course, it is to be expected after such an exhausting pace and nearly coming face-to-face with a party of rebels." His face darkened. "Bruce should be stripped of his spurs for becoming leader to such a band of cateran pirates." His steely-eyed gaze shifted to her. "You were very fortunate you were warned in time to get away." He stroked his beard, watching her. She couldn't take her eyes from his big, thick-boned hands. Hands that could crush or kill as easily as she snapped a twig. "It was Sir Arthur Campbell, was it not? The rebel Neil Campbell's youngest brother?"

Anna nodded, feeling uncomfortably self-conscious. The nervousness she experienced in Sir Hugh's presence that had initially caused her to refuse the betrothal had only grown worse since they'd arrived. Smiling and responding to his polite attempts at conversation was a struggle.

He had a way of looking at her as though he could read her thoughts. Had she given something away? She hadn't looked in Sir Arthur's direction since they'd arrived. At least she thought she hadn't. But she was keenly aware that he'd been watching her. Which probably explained some of her jumpiness. Wooing one man under the fierce glare of another wasn't easy. But it had to be done. Even if she wished it differently.

And she did wish it differently. The past few days had told her how much. She was scared to put a name on her feelings for Arthur for fear of what she would discover.

"We were very fortunate," she said, sensing that Sir Hugh was waiting for her to say something.

Anna didn't know what was wrong with her. She'd never had this kind of problem talking to anyone.

She tried to control the shaking of her hands, but the intensity of his stare made her drop the piece of bread she'd been holding. It fell on the table beside her goblet. She reached for it at the same time he did, and their hands touched. Before she could jerk it away, he covered her fingers with his own.

Her pulse spiked with something akin to panic. Like a bird caught in a cage, her heart fluttered wildly in her chest.

"You're nervous," he said, releasing her fingers and handing her back her bread.

Her cheeks burned.

"You've nothing to fear, Lady Anna," he said, amused. "I'm quite harmless."

The expression on her face must have registered her utter disbelief. He took one look at her and chuckled mildly. "Well, maybe not completely harmless."

The unexpected show of humor made her smile, and for the first time, Anna felt herself begin to relax. She gave him a sidelong glance from under her lashes. "You are rather . . . imposing, my lord."

He laughed. "I'll take that as a compliment even though I don't think you meant it as one." He leaned closer to whisper. "How about if I endeavor to be imposing to everyone but you? With you I will be quite harmless. It will be our secret."

She dimpled, unable to resist his charm. Sir Hugh Ross

charming? She wouldn't have believed it. Was there more to the humorless nobleman than she'd realized?

"I believe I should like that, my lord." She felt a smidgen of her boldness return. "Perhaps it would help if you smiled more." She glanced up at him then. Yes, when he smiled he didn't seem quite so intimidating.

He grinned, his gaze seeking hers out. "I shall do that." He paused. She watched his fingers trace the carved stem of his goblet in a soft, lazy way that was almost sensual. Some of her discomfort returned.

"I'm very happy that you decided to journey north, Lady Anna."

Her blush intensified; she hadn't missed his meaning. He was amenable to the renewed talk of a betrothal. She knew she should be relieved. It was what she'd come for. It might help save her family.

Then why did it feel like something hard had just lodged in her chest?

She nodded shyly, suddenly unable to meet his gaze, fearing that he would see too much. Her chest squeezed, feeling the noose of her future pulling tighter and tighter.

Her personal feelings didn't matter. She should be happy knowing she'd done her part to help her family. That would be reward enough. Wouldn't it?

When he turned to motion a passing serving girl to refill their goblets with wine, her gaze unconsciously slipped to Arthur's.

She knew where he was without looking. The heat of his anger seemed to penetrate across the room.

Their eyes caught for only an instant, but it was long enough to feel the force of his rage like a smith's bellows. He usually kept his emotions so tightly wrapped that she'd wondered if they were even there. No more. She'd never seen him so raw and fierce. He looked like a man holding himself by a very tight rein.

She turned away, shaken by the intensity of the emotions that came over her.

Unfortunately, she hadn't looked away fast enough, and Sir Hugh observed something of the exchange. She felt him stiffen beside her, his gaze narrowing on Sir Arthur. "Campbell doesn't look too happy with our arrangement. I don't like the way he watches you." His gaze shifted back to her, one brow cocked in a way that was anything but lazy. "Is there something I should know, Lady Anna?"

She cursed Arthur for his recklessness. He was going to ruin everything. And for what? He'd had more than enough time to make his feelings—if he had any—known. And now she didn't have a choice. Her father was counting on her.

Still, she hesitated. If there was a time to change her mind, it was now. Her heart tugged in one direction and her duty and love for her family tugged in another. The conversation with Sir Arthur came back to her. Hearing him speak of losing the war had shaken her. She took a deep breath and forced away all her doubts. Her personal feelings didn't matter. She had to do this. When Bruce came, they would have a better chance with Ross and his men by their side.

She shook her head. "Nay, there is nothing you should know."

The certainty in her voice must have convinced him. He nodded. "Good." He held out his hand for hers. "Come, there is something I should like to show you. And I believe there are some things we should discuss."

Anna ignored the pain twisting in her chest and smiled—albeit tremulously. Without another glance, she slid her hand into his and allowed him to lead her from the Great Hall, her future all but decided.

This was how it felt to lose control.

This was how it felt to want something so badly he'd be

willing to kill for it. Not for right or wrong or on a battle-field, but for the pure satisfaction of seeing another man at the end of his blade.

Arthur wanted to kill Hugh Ross. He wanted to kill him for looking at her. For touching her. For the lustful thoughts that were surely running through the bastard's mind. If Ross's gaze dropped to her chest one more time, Arthur didn't think he'd be able to stop himself. A spear right between the eyes from across the room. He could do it blindfolded.

Standing aside the past two days, being forced to watch as another man wooed the woman who wasn't supposed to mean anything to him, was like a slow, agonizing descent into madness.

Arthur was waging a losing war. His attempt to remain indifferent—to focus on his mission—wasn't working. All his training and years of battle experience hadn't prepared him for this. Watching Anna with Hugh Ross was tearing him apart.

But tonight had pushed him over the edge. When he'd seen Ross cover her hand with his, Arthur had been inches away from storming over there and punching his fist through the other man's teeth. To hell with subterfuge.

They'd been laughing together, damn it. *Laughing*.

Arthur had half-convinced himself she wouldn't be able to go through with it. Her wariness of the heralded knight hadn't exactly been hard to see the past two days. But he'd underestimated her resolve—and Sir Hugh's charm.

When Ross leaned closer to whisper in her ear, Arthur's fists clenched. It wasn't until he looked down and noticed his bloodless knuckles that he realized how hard he'd been squeezing his cup. Good thing it was made of wood or he might have crushed it.

He cursed, knowing he had to do something. He had to think of his mission. Sir Hugh wasn't wasting any time—

not that Arthur blamed him. If Arthur didn't do something to prevent the alliance, it would be too late.

He tossed back the contents of his drink. The amber-colored *uisge-beatha* burned its way down his throat, but it did nothing to calm the restlessness raging inside him.

"What the hell is the matter with you, Campbell? You look like you want to kill someone." Alan MacDougall's gaze slid meaningfully to the dais. He knew exactly who Arthur wanted to kill. He leaned across the table. "Have care. I think our host has noticed your interest in my sister."

Arthur didn't embarrass himself by trying to deny it. Alan MacDougall might be the son of a cold-hearted despot, but he was no fool. "And you are here to order me to stand down?"

Too experienced to give anything away in his expression, the older warrior gave him a blank stare. "Do you want me to?"

Arthur's jaw locked, his teeth clenching together. "You should," he said in a rare moment of frankness. He would only bring her misery. If he were her brother, he would order him to Hades—and then send him there himself.

But if Anna's brother thought there was anything odd about his reply, he didn't let on. Instead, he smiled wryly. "I think it's too late for that."

Arthur took his eyes off Anna and Sir Hugh long enough to gaze at Alan sharply. He didn't know what the hell Alan thought he knew, but he was wrong.

Wasn't he?

Hell, he didn't know anymore. His mission. Jealousy. His intense attraction to the lass. They'd all tangled together in a confusing mess. He tossed his cup back again.

Alan eyed his drink with amusement. "I thought you didn't drink whisky."

"I don't," Arthur said, motioning for the serving lass to refill his cup.

Alan had been watching him closer than he realized. It might have concerned him, if he hadn't sensed something that shifted his attention back to the dais.

Every muscle went rigid as he watched Anna slip her hand into Ross's. Rage surged through him as the other man leaned over to speak briefly to his father before leading her from the Hall.

Right before Hugh passed through the door, he glanced at Arthur. The taunting look in his eye made Arthur's blood run cold.

Something akin to panic rose in his chest—which was ridiculous. He was an elite warrior. Detached. Controlled. His heart might be beating too fast, and he might not be able to think straight, but it damn well wasn't panic.

But where the hell did she think she was going?

Ross—the lecherous whoreson—was obviously eager for the betrothal. Who knew what he would do to secure it? Didn't Anna realize what could happen when she was alone with him? Arthur's mind immediately went back to the barracks.

Ah, hell.

He managed to hold himself back for about thirty seconds before he couldn't take it anymore. He stood to leave, but Alan stopped him by moving his leg around the edge of the table to block his exit. It wasn't an accident.

At first Arthur thought he meant to stop him, but to his surprise the older warrior slowly adjusted his leg to allow him to pass. But not before giving him a warning. "If you do anything to hurt my sister, Campbell, I'll have to kill you."

Though he said it as calmly as if he were reporting on the weather, Arthur knew he meant every word.

Hell, if Alan MacDougall wasn't his enemy and the son of a despot, he might actually like him.

He met the other man's eyes and nodded, suspecting it was a promise he wasn't going to be able to keep. To put an

end to the betrothal and stop the alliance, hurting Anna
had become inevitable.

Anna had expected Sir Hugh to take her outside to stroll
around the *barmkin,* but instead he led her through the
passageway to the donjon tower.

The Royal Castle of Auldearn had been built by William
the Lion over a hundred years earlier. The donjon and adjoining Great Hall stood atop a large circular motte, surrounded by a wooden rampart. The stone wall around the
bailey below provided an additional level of defense.

Compared to the noise of the Great Hall, quiet punctuated the torchlit corridor. Anna was uncomfortably conscious of how alone they were. Although the last echoes of
daylight still sounded on the horizon, the stone tower was
already dark. The flickering flames from the torchieres that
lined the walls provided little reassurance.

"W-where are we going?" she asked, ashamed of the
trembling in her voice.

Sir Hugh gave her an enigmatic smile that made her
wonder whether he was aware of his effect on her. "We're
almost there."

He stopped before the door to the earl's private solar.
Opening the door, Anna was relieved to see it well lit by
candles from a circular iron chandelier above.

Unfortunately, when Hugh led her across the room to
another door, she realized this was not their final destination. The second room was bathed in darkness. Anna stood
safely in the solar until Sir Hugh lit a few candles.

Then she gasped.

Nervousness forgotten, she rushed into the tiny room—
not much larger than an ambry—and spun around in
amazement. A lone table and bench stood sentry in the
middle of the floor, but it was what lined the walls that
filled her with awe. Shelves and shelves stacked with thick
leather folios—some encrusted with gold, some with jew-

els. It was a treasure trove. More books than she'd ever seen in one place in her life.

Sir Hugh watched the incredulity and wonder transform her features. "I thought this might interest you."

Anna clapped her hands in delight, her fingers practically itching to explore the titles. Dear Lord, that looked to be four volumes of Chrétien de Troyes!

"It's magnificent." She turned to him. "How did you know?"

He shrugged. "You mentioned something about enjoying reading once."

She tilted her head, looking up at him. Again, she felt as if she'd misjudged him. "And you remembered?"

He didn't respond, but the way he was looking at her sent a flicker of unease whispering down her spine.

He wanted her.

Suddenly the tiny room felt like a trap. She looked to the door, but whether intentionally or not, he'd moved around to block it.

"Why did you bring me here?" she asked.

He took a step closer, his eyes glinting dangerously in the semidarkness. He took her chin in his hand and tilted her face to his.

Her pulse spiked with panic. He was shorter than Sir Arthur—perhaps by an inch or two—but somehow his size seemed threatening. It took everything she had not to shirk away.

"I wanted to show you what you would have as my wife. This room would be at your disposal. You will be one of the most important ladies in the kingdom. That is why you are here, Lady Anna, is it not? To renew talks of our betrothal?"

"Aye," she whispered, trying to control the shakiness in her voice.

His eyes bored into her, challenging. "Is that what you really want?"

Her heart pounded furiously. She forced herself to nod. "Aye."

"Then prove it," he demanded. She blinked questioningly. "Kiss me."

Her eyes widened with shock. "I . . . I . . ."

She struggled with what to say. Oh God, she couldn't.

And he knew it. His gaze hardened. "Are you playing games with me, Lady Anna? I assure you I've no wish to be cuckold to another man. Recall that it is *you* who came to *me* this time." His thumb slid over her bottom lip and she sucked in her breath, frozen in fear. "Decide what you want before you do something that cannot be undone. Once we are betrothed, I assure you I will not tolerate this foolishness."

Anna's cheeks flooded with heat, shamed by the truth of his accusations.

She pushed aside her fear, trying to remember why she was here. Trying to remember how important it was for her to succeed in forming this alliance. This was their chance. Why was she being so foolish? It was only a kiss.

"My lord, I'm sor—"

He dropped his hand from her face. She exhaled with too much relief.

"We should return to the Hall," he said stiffly, coldly. "Your brother will wonder where I've taken you."

She nodded, feeling helpless, knowing what she should do but unable to get the words out.

Damn Arthur Campbell to Hades for doing this to her! For confusing her. She'd been prepared to do this before he'd returned.

"If you don't mind, my lord, I'm tired and would rather retire to my chamber."

He nodded. "Take your time. Perhaps you might wish to borrow a book?" Her gaze shot to his, knowing he was trying to tempt her. "We can discuss this in the morning."

He turned to leave. But then he seemed to change his

mind. Before she realized what he was about to do, he'd pulled her in his arms and brushed his mouth over hers. Anna froze, too startled to resist.

His lips were cool and hard, not unlike the man. She caught the faint scent of wine, but it was over before she could process anything else.

He smiled, looking down at her stunned expression. "You have the night to decide. But if you want this betrothal to go forward, I'll expect a response tomorrow. One a bit more enthusiastic than that."

Ross had no idea how close he was to death.

Arthur gripped his dirk in his hand, every muscle straining against the bloodlust pounding through him. All he had to do was take a few steps, slipping out from his hiding place in the shadows behind the door, and plunge his blade deep in the bastard's gut.

He'd kissed her.

He'd taken her in his arms and put his mouth to hers.

Something inside Arthur snapped. Every instinct urged him to strike out and kill the man who'd dared to touch what belonged to him.

But at the last minute, something stayed his hand. Killing Ross would put an end to his mission. He'd be forced to flee, and his opportunity to destroy Lorn would be lost.

It took every shred of control he had left not to move. But he let Ross walk out of the room. He let him live. This time.

Anna, however, would not escape his wrath so easily. He was going to make damned sure she had only one answer to give Ross in the morning. This planned betrothal of hers was about to come to a decisive end.

Ross's footsteps had barely faded before Anna started to follow him. As she reached the door, Arthur slid out of the shadows to block her path.

She gasped. Any fear she might have felt quickly faded in

the sudden flash of anger that set her eyes blazing. "How dare you spy on me!" She tried to push him out of the way, but he clasped her wrists in his hand. "Let go of me, you have no right."

He spun her into the room and shut the door behind him. "I have every right," he seethed. "You aren't going to marry him."

He could see her cheeks flush in the candlelight. Her chest—her incredible, too-ample chest that he couldn't stop dreaming about—heaved with righteous indignation. That sweet face with its adorable, stubborn chin lifted to his. "Yes. I. Am."

He didn't like her tone at all. Not one bit. His eyes narrowed. "You couldn't even kiss him." He leaned closer, inhaling the sultry warmth of her fury. "How will it be, do you think, to bed him?"

She made a sharp sound of outrage. If she'd a dagger in her hand, Arthur had no doubt it would now be stuck between his ribs. But her tongue eviscerated just as painfully. "I suspect I will get used to it. Perhaps even come to enjoy it. Sir Hugh is a very handsome man. And he seems quite determined, don't you think?" Her eyes taunted. Challenged. Driving him insane. "Yes, if it's anything like that kiss, I imagine I'll come to enjoy it quite a lot."

He grabbed her arm. "Stop." He shook her to him. "Stop." He felt as if he were going to explode. Feelings he'd kept so long contained had been whipped to a frenzy by her taunting words. Feelings he didn't want to acknowledge. Feelings he couldn't let out. His head spun. His chest burned. God, it hurt. He had to make her stop.

"Why?" she demanded, leaning closer to him. The tips of her breasts grazed his chest, and he shook—he actually shook, every inch of his body poised on the knife-edge of restraint. Heat pulled him down a dark vortex of lust and desire. He wanted to crush her to him. To kiss her. To ravish her senseless. To make her scream his name and his alone.

"Why should I stop? It's the truth. Sir Hugh strikes me as a man who sees what he wants and won't let anything stand in the way until he gets it."

He knew she was goading him, but he didn't care. Arthur knew exactly what he wanted, damn it. *Her.*

He swore, knowing the battle was lost. He took her into his arms and crushed his mouth to hers, giving in to the powerful feelings that had been waging war inside him.

He kissed her like he'd never kissed another woman before. He kissed her with all the passion that had been building inside from the first. He kissed her to make her stop. He kissed her to wipe away the hateful images she'd branded in his mind. He kissed her so she would never think about another man again.

But when she melted against him in silent surrender and opened her sweet little mouth to his with a sigh and a moan, he wasn't thinking about missions or alliances, enemy clans or revenge. Nay, all he was thinking about was making her his.

Fifteen

Anna knew she was being rash, knew she was provoking him, but she didn't care. Anger blinded her to anything but the need to lash out.

She hated him for interfering. For making her hesitate. For getting in the way of her plans.

All she'd ever wanted to do was protect her family and keep the people she loved safe. And now, when she had the chance, Arthur Campbell stood in her way.

He confused her. Confounded her. Made her care about him and then pushed her away. He saved her and protected her one moment, and then ignored her the next. He was an outsider, a man who kept himself apart and seemed as if he didn't need anyone. But he was also lonely, a man who'd been forced to the periphery by gifts that set him apart.

Did he want her? Did he need her?

One way or another, he would have to decide. Time had run out for them both. So she pushed. Knowing he was jealous. Knowing he'd seen the kiss Sir Hugh had given her. Knowing he was struggling for control.

She wanted him so badly. Standing so close to him, all she could think about was how good he smelled. How the dark shadow of his beard made him look even more ruggedly handsome. How tall he was. How broad his chest was. How soft his mouth looked even when white with anger. How she would give anything if he would take her in his arms and never let go.

Pain stabbed her chest. Why didn't he want her? Why was he holding back?

So recklessly—desperately—she taunted him, wanting to hurt him as he'd hurt her. So what if it was a lie? So what if the thought of herself in bed with another man made her blood run cold? Enjoy? She could barely stop herself from trembling in fear in Sir Hugh's presence.

When he snapped, she had her reward. Anna found herself in his arms with his mouth on hers, and he was kissing her with all the passion and emotion of which she'd dreamed.

He devoured her with his mouth and tongue. She moaned, sinking deeper into the kiss, wanting to feel every inch of his body against hers.

His big hands slid possessively over her, down her back, over her hips, slipping down to cup her bottom. He groaned in her mouth, kissing her deeper and harder as he molded her more firmly against him.

Sensation exploded inside her in a shimmering wave of heat.

Oh God, it was perfect! Chest to chest. Hip to hip. The hard evidence of his desire wedged intimately between her legs. She knew she should be shocked by the size and feel of him, but all she felt was excitement. Excitement that made her heart race, her skin flush, and her body tingle.

They were plastered together, but it wasn't close enough. Restlessness built inside her with each delicious stroke of his tongue and each possessive caress of his hands.

She matched his boldness with her own. Her hands gripping the hard muscles of his arms, his shoulders, his back. She wanted to feel every inch of him under her fingertips, to sculpt every muscle with her palms. To hold his strength under her hands.

It made her feel . . . wild—heady with desire.

She'd never experienced anything like this. Her body had seemed to come alive. Her responses came naturally, as if she knew what she was doing. It was happening too fast to think. Desire had grabbed hold and would not let go.

He was pressing against her more insistently, rubbing his manhood against the most feminine part of her. It made her feel strange and tingly—warm and achy. But it wasn't enough. She circled her hips harder against the thick column of flesh, craving the friction. Craving a deeper connection.

His mouth dipped down her throat, kissing, devouring. The scruff of his beard singeing a path across her flaming skin. The small room blazed hot and sultry with passion.

His hands slid around her waist, moving up to cup her breasts. She gasped, pressing harder and harder against his manhood as her back arched into his hands. He muttered something that sounded like a curse and rubbed his thumbs over her turgid, aching nipples, as his mouth feasted on the tender skin just above the edge of her bodice.

She felt so hot. So weak. Languid and heavy. Her legs seemed to have lost the strength to hold her up. She collapsed against him, and he pushed her back on the table to steady her—and maybe himself as well. The fiercely controlled knight seemed just as wild and frantic in his need as she.

His dark, silky hair spilled against her chest. Unable to resist, she threaded her fingers through the soft waves, gently pressing him harder against her. She could feel his mouth on her nipple through the fabric of her gown as his hands cupped and squeezed.

Not enough . . .

Seeming to sense her frustration, his tongue darted below her bodice.

She cried out at the wickedness, at the exquisite pleasure that rocked her. His mouth was so warm. His tongue circled and circled until she didn't think she could stand any more. She was writhing against him, begging him to unleash the strange maelstrom building inside.

Finally, he pushed aside her gown—stretching the fabric to the ripping point—to release her breast. The cool air blew over her skin, prickling where he'd kissed her.

"Christ," he groaned, sounding as if he were in pain. "You're so damned beautiful."

The sound of his voice might have broken through her trance, but before she could hold on to the moment of clarity, he covered her aching nipple with his mouth and sucked.

The sweet needle of sensation made her cry out.

Pleasure so acute it was nearly pain. He plied her with his teeth, flicked her with his tongue, and sucked her deeper and deeper into the warm suction of his mouth.

Heat spread between her legs in a rush of dampness. The tender flesh felt swollen and tingly.

The table was hard against her back. He'd wrapped her leg around his hip as he'd bent over her breast.

She could feel the pounding of his heart against hers. Feel his muscles straining with his desire for her. His weight covering her. She was hot. So incredibly hot. Aroused to the point of no return.

His hand slid under the edge of her gown, connecting with skin. He smothered her shock with a long drag of her nipple between his teeth.

Then his mouth was on hers again and his hands—dear Lord!—his hands were sliding between her thighs.

Embarrassed, she tried to close her legs. But he wouldn't let her. His mouth distracted with long, languid strokes of his tongue, as his finger swept over her dampness.

Her body trembled at his touch. Her protests dissolved in a wave of shuddering relief. It felt so good. So amazingly good.

"Jesus, you're so wet."

He stopped kissing her and she wondered if she'd done something wrong, until she realized he was struggling, holding himself still as if fighting for control. As if touching her had taken his last bit of reserve. As if he was close to the breaking point.

His eyes met hers, holding her gaze as his finger slid inside her with a firm little push. It was the most wickedly erotic moment of her life.

She sucked in her breath, trying to still the sensations, but they were rushing by her so quickly in wave after quickening wave. He stroked her. First in soft little circles and then harder and faster in deep, frantic thrusts that mimicked the way he'd kissed her.

The sensations building inside her were too intense. Too powerful to contain. Tightening and coiling in a wicked whirlpool of need.

His face was a mask of pain. Sweat had gathered on his brow. His gaze held hers, dark and penetrating, holding her to him in a way that made her heart clench with happiness. In his eyes she read the truth—what she'd known all along. This connection between them was special. And he felt it, too.

She didn't know what was happening to her, but it was perfect. Each stroke of his hand brought her closer to a peak she didn't understand. She writhed in frustration, her body aching for . . .

"Let go, love," he whispered. "I want to see you shatter."

The husky sound of his voice broke through the last vestiges of maidenly repression. Her breath caught, and then released in a shuddering cry as her body seemed to come apart in sharp spasms of intense pleasure.

It was the most wondrous moment of her life, but as she stared into the dark depth of his gold-flecked eyes, Anna knew it wasn't enough. Her passion had been satisfied, but her heart still throbbed with the need for fulfillment. She wanted a deeper connection. She wanted to feel him inside her. She wanted all of him. Forever.

I love him. Of course. It was so clear—so certain—she wondered how it could ever have been otherwise.

Warrior. Knight. It didn't matter. For in her heart, Anna knew she'd found the man she was meant to share her life with.

Arthur couldn't wait any longer. The pressure had gathered like a hot fist at the base of his spine, building toward the throbbing tip of his cock, demanding release.

Touching her.

Hearing her cry out in sharp gasps of pleasure.

Feeling her body weep and shudder around his hand.

He clenched his teeth, holding it back, knowing he was about to come like he'd never come before.

Jesus, she was so damned beautiful. Honey-gold hair spread out behind her head, shimmering in the candlelight. Cheeks flushed. Lips parted. Eyes dazed and heavy with passion. One perfectly formed breast heaving out of her bodice, big and soft, the tight little nipple red from his mouth.

She looked like a wanton who couldn't wait to get tupped. *My wanton. All mine.*

Jesus, he repeated, half prayer, half oath. He'd never felt like this before. Desire had consumed him.

"Arthur," she whimpered. "Please . . ."

The raw desperation in her voice was the last thread. He couldn't wait another moment to be inside her.

He practically ripped open the buckles and ties of his chausses and braies to release his engorged cock. But the freedom from confinement and breath of fresh air provided little relief. The only thing that was going to ease his pain right now was being inside her.

He lifted one lithe, long, and flawlessly creamy leg around his hip and positioned himself at her warm and deliciously wet entry. Next time he'd take the time to taste her. To slide his tongue inside and make her come against his mouth.

He held her gaze the entire time, not daring to look away for fear of breaking the powerful connection that had risen between them.

He should have felt a flicker of hesitation. A feeling that what he was about to do was wrong. Honor was important to him, even if the knightly code was not.

But he didn't.

All he could think about was that he couldn't lose her. That he had to make her his. That if he could only do so, everything would be all right.

When the sensitive head of his cock met the damp heat of her entry, a deep, guttural groan of pure pleasure tore from him.

He rubbed himself in her creamy dampness, lingering, wanting to prolong the pleasure. He knew that when he was inside her, it would be too late.

His body was on fire. Every muscle tense, poised for entry. Blood pounded in his veins. In his ears. In his bones. His skin felt tight and hot.

Thrust. God, he wanted to thrust. He'd never wanted to thrust into someone so badly.

He knew it would be incredible. Her body would grip him like a hot glove. Milking him in long, hard pulls. Sending him deeper and deeper into mindless oblivion. He wanted to see her moving under him with the power of his thrusts. Lifting her hips to meet each deep stroke. He wanted to watch his cock sliding in and out of her.

He clenched, the urge to plunge inside almost overpowering.

But he couldn't hurt her.

So, he forced himself to go slow, teasing her with his thickness, getting her used to the size and strength of him, slicking the head of his cock with her dampness to ease his entry.

It felt too good. The pressure was coiling at the base of his spine, cinching tighter and tighter.

She was moaning again, her breath coming hard and heavy. Desire flushed her beautiful face. Her leg tightened around his hip, trying to draw him inside her.

It was all he could take. He started to push.

She cried out in surprise.

Jesus. He gritted his teeth. Sweat gathered on his brow. Blood drummed through his veins. Tight. So incredibly tight. He had to go slow and easy. God, he wanted to come.

Almost there . . .

A faint sound penetrated the haze.

He froze, a flicker of premonition brushing the back of his neck. The air shifted.

He swore and pulled away, his body throbbing in protest. "Cover yourself," he said, yanking up her gown while simultaneously fumbling with the ties of his braies.

But it was too late—or too soon, if the frustration burning in his bollocks right now meant anything.

The door opened with a crash.

Sir Hugh Ross stood in the doorway, his steely gaze taking in every detail.

Though they'd managed to cover themselves, nothing could hide what they'd just been doing. Anna was still leaned back on the table—cheeks flushed and eyes hazy— Arthur was still positioned between her legs, and the small room was hot and heavy with the musky scent of mating— or near mating.

She gasped. Horror draining the blush of pleasure from her face.

Instinctively, Arthur moved in front of her, trying to block her from view, as if he could protect her from the venom shooting from the other man with the shield of his body.

The dead silence—punctuated only by the flicker of flames—extended to well past uncomfortable.

Sir Hugh stood stone still. Too still. As if he were waiting to pounce. Arthur watched him like a hawk, waiting for the first sign of movement. Hell, he hoped for it, wanting the excuse.

"I heard a cry," Sir Hugh finally said. "I thought you might be hurt." The proud knight's face twisted with disgust, contempt dripping from his voice. "But I guess you didn't need rescue."

Anna made a sound of pain that tore at Arthur's heart. Knowing he had to protect her from Sir Hugh's anger, he turned and took her by the shoulders. "Go to your chamber," he said roughly. She tried to protest, but he stopped her. "We will talk about this later. Right now I need to speak with Sir Hugh. Let me handle this."

He looked into her eyes. She looked confused, horrified, and frightened at the same time, ready to burst into tears at any moment. It was hard for him to breathe. A knife of pain twisted in his heart. He'd done this to her. This was his fault.

He shook her gently, trying to get her to focus. "Anna, do you understand?"

She looked at him then, seeming so lost he almost dragged her into his arms again.

"It will be all right," he promised, knowing that it wasn't true. How could it ever be all right? Not only was he lying to her, but he'd just destroyed her chances of an alliance with Ross, and he knew how much that meant to her. She loved her family. Failing them . . . it would shatter her.

She nodded, and the look of utter trust she gave him lodged like a giant albatross in his chest. He was a bastard. A cold-hearted bastard. He'd never forgive himself for what he was doing to her. Anna didn't deserve this. She deserved to be safe and protected, to have a happy home, a husband who loved her, and a half-dozen children clinging to her skirts.

He could never give that to her. All he would leave her with was a broken heart. He might not have taken her maidenhood, but when she learned the truth about him, he would have taken her innocence all the same.

Where desire had burned a moment ago, now there was only sorrow and pain.

Sir Hugh had not moved from his position in the doorway, but as Arthur ushered her out, he stepped to the side to let her pass. Feeling cornered in the small room himself, Arthur followed her out and into the solar. It wasn't much larger, but at least he would have room to maneuver if necessary. Sir Hugh seemed eager for a fight, and Arthur was just as eager to give him one.

She glanced at him uncertainly once more before she left.

"Go," he said gently, trying to reassure her. Her gaze flickered to Sir Hugh, and her face crumpled. The knight wouldn't meet her eye, but animosity radiated from every proud, noble inch of him.

Arthur's mouth thinned, wanting to kill the man for hurting her. Anna wasn't to blame. This was his doing.

Jesus. The realization struck him. Had he wanted this? Had this been his intention all along?

He'd wanted to ruin her chance for an alliance.

Nay. Not this way. He hadn't meant to push it so far.

But he'd overestimated his control and underestimated the intensity of his desire for her. Arthur was in too deep. He'd gotten too close, and it was only going to hurt them both.

"I should kill you," Ross said when the door had closed behind her.

The knight was trying to stare him down, but Arthur met the challenge with his own. "Why don't you?"

Ross's gaze hardened. "Because then I would have to explain why."

The certainty in his voice made Arthur smile. They were near the same age and evenly matched in height and muscle. But not in skill. Arthur would not be the one to die. Sir Hugh, however, didn't know that. Then why . . .

Suddenly the reason came to him. "And you don't want anyone to know that the lass humiliated you—twice. First in refusing your offer and then in being caught with another man right under your nose."

The truth of his accusation was revealed on Ross's face. It turned florid with anger, the white lines around his mouth sharp in contrast. "Did you defile her?"

Arthur's jaw clenched. It was none of his damned business. He wanted to lie—to claim her as his own—but to salvage what he could of her reputation, he spoke the truth. "Nay."

Sir Hugh's eyes were cold. "But you would have had I not interrupted."

Arthur shrugged as if the answer didn't matter to him.

Ross took a step toward him, hand on his sword. "You bastard! You're a knight. Have you no honor? She was betrothed—"

Arthur moved quickly. Using a maneuver he'd learned from Boyd, he knocked Ross's arm, forcing him to release the grip of his sword, and then twisted the same arm behind his back, leveraging his own body weight against him. "Nay. *Not* betrothed."

Ross instinctively tried to free himself, but his movements only increased the twisting—and thus the pain—in his arm.

"Close enough," he bit out, his voice tight with pain. "I'll kill you for this! Let go of me."

"Not until we reach an understanding about what happened here. I don't want the lass hurt. She is not to blame."

Wisely, Ross chose not to argue, but Arthur could see the rage in his eyes. He twisted harder, eliciting a grunt of pain from the spitting-angry knight.

"Why did you come back here?" Arthur asked.

"I heard a cry—"

"Bollocks," Arthur cut him off. Unless Ross possessed senses akin to his, he hadn't heard anything.

Ross eyed him murderously. Pained sweat seeped from his brow. "I saw you staring at her, and her trying too hard not to look back. I knew you'd follow us."

Arthur swore. "So this was some kind of test?"

"I wasn't going to be made a fool of. I'll not marry a woman in love with another man. No matter how much I want to fu—"

Arthur twisted his arm harder. "Don't," he warned. "Don't say it."

Knowing he was damned close to breaking Ross's arm, he pushed him harshly away. Ross was right about one thing—the less they had to explain, the better.

Ross exhaled, massaging the top of his arm and shoulder. But something in his eyes made Arthur wonder whether he'd just been tested again. Whether Ross's crude remark had been uttered to elicit a reaction. If so, it had worked.

"You care for her," Arthur said, realizing the truth. "This wasn't just a political alliance to you."

Ross didn't respond by word or expression, but Arthur knew he was right. Hell, he almost felt sorry for the bastard. "But you know what brought her here?"

Having restored the feeling to his arm, Ross had turned to watching him suspiciously. "Aye. For support against Bruce. I hoped to win her hand without it."

Arthur's gaze shot to his, comprehension dawning. "Your father has no intention of sending men with or without the betrothal, does he?" Ross didn't need to respond. *Damn.* Arthur felt like killing him all over. "You let her believe . . ."

Ross shrugged.

Devious bastard. Hell, Arthur might have admired his determination if it wasn't Anna he'd been manipulating.

"We'll leave as soon as it can be arranged. After you inform Anna and Sir Alan of what you just told me."

The other man scoffed. "And why in Hades would I do that?"

Arthur took a threatening step toward him. To Ross's credit, he didn't move. But Arthur could see the wariness in his eyes. "Because I don't want to see her hurting any more than she already is. And despite what happened here, I don't think you want that either."

They looked at each other a moment, and then Ross nodded. Arthur started to leave.

"Campbell." He turned, seeing Ross gripping his injured shoulder again. "Where did you learn how to do that?"

Arthur's mouth curved wryly. "Do this right, and maybe one day I'll tell you."

Anna wiped her hands on her skirts and tried to calm the nausea threatening to rise in her stomach as she scanned the crowd of clansmen who'd gathered in the Great Hall to break their fast.

Unconsciously, she found herself looking for Arthur, as if seeing his face would give her some much-needed courage. When she didn't find him seated among her brother's men, she told herself not to worry. It was still early. He'd sent a serving lad to her room last night to tell her everything had been taken care of and not to worry.

Not to worry. As if such a thing were possible after what had happened. His thoughtful message might not have eased her restless night, but it was appreciated. At least she didn't need to fear one of them dead or lying in a pit prison somewhere.

She took a deep breath, forced her shoulders back, her chin up, and stepped into the Hall.

Her leg buckled it was shaking so hard, and her heart

fluttered like the wings of a bird against the cage of her ribs. Every instinct screamed to flee, but she forced her feet forward.

The blood of kings ran through her blood. She was a MacDougall, not a coward.

Though she'd wanted nothing more than to hide in her chamber, curled up in a ball, and pretend none of this had ever happened, it had. At the very least, she owed Sir Hugh an apology.

When she thought of what she'd done . . .

Her stomach twisted. Shame washed over her. Not for succumbing to Arthur—she wasn't ashamed of the passion that lay between them—but for failing her family and horribly misusing Sir Hugh in the process. He hadn't deserved that. The proud knight had treated her with nothing but kindness. It wasn't his fault she was in love with another.

Love. Even as she weighed the enormous gravity of what she'd done, a tiny ray of happiness peeked out from behind the clouds of despair. She loved him. And he cared for her—he must.

But that spot of joy in her heart only made her feel guiltier. In finding love, she'd failed her family. How could she ever forgive herself? She'd ruined everything. Her father and clan would stand alone against Robert Bruce. There would be no alliance after what Sir Hugh had witnessed last night.

Her cheeks heated at the memory—at what he must think of her.

Harlot. Whore.

She half-expected to hear the jeers as she crossed the Hall to her seat on the dais beside the man she'd wronged. But her entrance caused no unusual comment. The earl and countess greeted her with their normal pleasantries—as did their son, when she took her seat beside him.

She forced herself to eat, though each mouthful of food

added to the queasiness tumbling around in her stomach. As the meal stretched on, her anxiety only grew worse.

The brief good humor she'd glimpsed in Sir Hugh yesterday was—not surprisingly—gone. He sat stiffly beside her, too proud and engrained with knightly chivalry to completely ignore her, but coming close. She was grateful for the presence of Hugh's sister on his other side, and Ross's henchman beside her, to break up the awkward periods of silence.

Anna knew she had to say something but didn't know how to broach the subject in so public a setting. She was still waiting for the right opportunity, when Sir Hugh rose from the table and excused himself.

"Wait!" She flushed, feeling a few eyes turn in her direction and realizing she'd spoken a touch too loudly.

Sir Hugh glanced down at her, giving her his full attention for the first time. He waited for her to finish while she tried not to squirm.

"I . . ." She said the first thing that came to her, wishing she'd done this earlier, when other people weren't so obviously listening. "It's a lovely morning. If you aren't too busy, I thought you might show me around the castle as you promised."

He'd made no such promise, and it would serve her right if he said as much, showing her pretense to get him alone as exactly that.

His eyes held her, and for a moment, she thought he meant to deny her. But his knightly sensibilities apparently won out. He bowed and extended his hand. "It would be my pleasure, my lady."

As she'd done a few short but significant hours before, she allowed him to lead her out of the hall. If he was aware of the speculative whispers that followed them, he didn't show it.

This time when they reached the end of the corridor, he led her outside into the yard. There were plenty of people bustling about—soldiers practicing and guarding the gates, servants attending to their duties, and a steady stream of clansmen passing through the gate—but no one paid them too much attention.

"Is there anything in particular you would like to see?" he asked.

She gave him a sidelong glance from under the veil of her lashes, hearing the dryness in his voice. He knew it had been an excuse—and a weak one at that. She shook her head. "I'm sorry, I needed to talk to you." She stopped and looked at him fully. "I must apologize for what happened last night."

His mouth hardened, and her nerve faltered.

But she had to do this. Her clenched fingers bit into her palms. She couldn't manage a deep breath, so she burst out, "I can offer no excuses, other than to say how dreadfully sorry I am."

He held her gaze for a moment, and then nodded. She thought he would turn and leave her there, but surprisingly he led her to a quiet spot along the rampart, overlooking the bailey and the town of Nairn beyond.

It was windy, and she had to tuck an errant lock of hair behind her ear. But after the long night of darkness, the bright sunshine on her face was rejuvenating.

"Do you love him?"

Anna startled. She didn't know what she'd expected him to say, but it certainly wasn't that. Sir Hugh didn't seem like a man to hold much value or give much credence to romantic love. He seemed far too cold and practical for that.

But he deserved the truth. "Aye," she said softly.

"But you would have married me to secure additional men for your father?"

When he put it like that it suddenly seemed wrong, though marriage and duty went hand in hand—it was love that didn't matter. "Aye." The desperateness of the situation rose in her chest. She pleaded with him, trying to make him understand. "Don't you see? The only way to fight the rebels is for us to stand together. If our clans join forces, we can defeat the usurper. Alone we risk defeat."

If her words held any sway, he did not show it. His expression remained stern and implacable, as he studied her face.

It was strange. Now that there was no hope of a betrothal between them, her fear and nervousness seemed to have vanished.

"You can absolve yourself of guilt, Lady Anna."

She blinked at him questioningly, shielding the sun with her hand to see him more clearly.

His mouth twisted in an odd grimace. "My father had no intention of sending men to Lorn."

She gasped in surprise. "But the betrothal. You let me believe . . ."

He shrugged unrepentantly.

A spike of anger cut through her guilt. "And when did you plan to tell me this?"

"You would have found out soon enough."

"*After* we announced our betrothal?"

He met the accusation in her eyes without flinching. "Perhaps."

"But why?"

He seemed to purposefully misunderstand her question. "We don't have men to spare. Bruce will be coming after us as well, and when he does . . ." His voice drifted off in the wind. "King Robert has grown too powerful. Our allies have deserted us. The Comyns, the MacDowells, the English. My father has much too much to lose."

He gazed back over the wall to the mini-kingdom below.

It was a telling movement, and she sucked in her breath at the significance. Too much to lose. His father wouldn't risk it. "Nay," she said, stepping back. "You can't! Your father can't submit. Bruce will kill him for what your father did to his wife and daughter."

She spoke without thought, and she could tell that the reminder of what his father had done in violating sanctuary and turning Bruce's womenfolk over to the English was not something Sir Hugh wanted to be reminded of. For the first time, she caught something resembling shame on his proud features.

"Bruce has vowed to forgive all the nobles who were against him, if they submit."

"And you believe the word of a traitor? Surely, you cannot think King Hood will forgive your father and the rebellious men of Ross and Moray? The fires have barely died from the 'harrying of Buchan.' "

He did not argue with her. But his jaw was clenched tight as he said, "What choice do we have? The tide has turned toward Bruce. The people think he is a hero—a warrior king who defeated the English. Submitting may be the only way to survive. My father is willing to die if it means our clan will continue."

Anna's mind spun. Never, in all her imaginings, had she expected Ross to submit.

What did this mean for her clan? Would her father do the same?

Nay. Her father would never submit. And for the first time, Anna realized what that might cost them.

Sobered by what Sir Hugh had confided, Anna felt little relief in knowing that her conduct had not been to blame. "Thank you for telling me," she said.

He gave her a long look. "What will you do?"

"Fight," she answered. Even alone. What else could they do?

"You will marry Campbell?"

Her cheeks heated. After what had happened last night it was natural to assume . . . But there hadn't been much of a chance to discuss the future.

He seemed to understand her silence. "How well do you know him?"

The hint of warning in his voice roused the little voice in the back of her head that she'd sought to quiet. "Sir Arthur arrived at Dunstaffnage last month with his brother to answer my father's call for knights and men-at-arms."

It seemed to confirm something for him. "There's something strange about him. Something off. He's not what he appears."

Anna sprang immediately to his defense, thinking Sir Hugh must be picking up on Arthur's unusual abilities. "He's just quiet," she said. "He likes to keep to himself."

Sir Hugh looked at her appraisingly, as if he wanted to say more, but instead he nodded.

She was relieved when he told her he would explain things to her brother and parents, making no mention of the compromising situation in which he'd found her, agreeing simply that they didn't suit.

By the time he'd led her back to the tower, Anna was feeling much relieved. With some of her guilt assuaged, she allowed a little bit of the happiness she'd felt in discovering that the man she loved cared about her to return. She couldn't wait to see him—and talk to him.

Surprisingly, given the intimacies they'd shared, she wasn't embarrassed. Even now, after all that had happened, it seemed *right*.

She was just about to take her first step up the stairs that led from the yard to the tower, when she glanced to the left and glimpsed Sir Arthur coming out of the barracks.

Her heart jumped. She smiled and instinctively took a step toward him, but then stopped in her tracks. He wore his armor and it was obvious he was getting ready for practice, but she could make out enough of his face beneath the visor of his helm.

It wasn't as if she expected him to race across the yard to her—at least, not with Sir Hugh still at her side. But a look of tenderness would have been nice. Anything would have been nice compared to the look of regret—aye, and even shame—that swept across his handsome features.

The joy that had made her heart leap fizzled, bringing it crashing to the ground.

She felt Sir Hugh stiffen beside her, as he noticed what had caught her eye.

Arthur's gaze shifted to the other knight. She could feel the animosity sparking between the two men. It was Arthur who retreated first. He nodded to them both, and then moved away to join the other warriors.

Anna told herself not to be disappointed. Not to overreact. They would talk later. In private. She'd probably imagined what she thought she'd read in his eyes.

But Sir Hugh's next words told her she hadn't. "If it doesn't work out the way you plan, Lady Anna, I'll be here." A man to count on.

She prayed Arthur was as well.

Sixteen

It had taken them longer to leave Auldearn Castle than Arthur had anticipated. Alan MacDougall had been locked away with the earl, his council, and Sir Hugh in the solar for three more days, attempting, Arthur assumed, to persuade Ross to join forces even absent a betrothal. Thankfully, Alan's efforts had been to no avail.

As Arthur had not been privy to the meetings, he could not be certain of the earl's reasons, but the refusal boded well for King Robert. He would pass on the information as soon as he had the opportunity. He didn't think any messages had been passed, but he would check Anna and Alan's belongings at the first opportunity to make sure.

They'd left Auldearn at dawn, reversing the journey that ended only a week ago, pushing hard to make it safely past Urquhart Castle on the first day. The men, taking a cue from their lord and lady, seemed to sense that all had not gone as hoped, and the cloud of failure weighed heavily on the travelers. The mood was somber, if not outright morose.

Arthur knew he should be relieved and pleased that his mission had been a success. Ross and Lorn would not be joining forces. The MacDougalls' failure would help bring Bruce one step closer to victory and Arthur one step closer to seeing his enemy destroyed. Seeing John of Lorn pay for what he'd done to his father was what he wanted most in the world.

Wasn't it?

It should be, damn it. But he'd feared it was going to cost him far more than he'd ever anticipated.

Behind the mask of his helm he could give in to the urge to look at her. He felt it again, sharp and burning. It wasn't just his conscience eating at him but something else. The twinges of pain in his chest when he looked at her had become almost unbearable. But it hurt even more not to look at her.

She rode ahead of him, beside her brother and serving maid, allowing him only the occasional glimpse of her profile. He didn't need to see her face to know his silence on what had happened between them was hurting her. Badly.

God, what had he done? And more importantly, what the hell was he going to do about it?

Now that they were away from the castle, he couldn't avoid it—or her—any longer.

He knew what he *should* do. He didn't need to be a knight to know that after coming within inches (literally) of taking her virginity, he should offer for her. No doubt it was what she was expecting—and should be expecting, damn it. If he had any honor, he would. But those inches gave him just enough of an excuse not to.

The battle within him was intensifying. Every instinct urged him to go to her, to give in to the feelings—damn it, the emotions—tossing around inside him, but the other part of him, the rational part, held him back from doing something even more damaging.

Even if at times he wanted to forget it, he was lying to her. And he sure as hell couldn't tell her the truth. His duty and loyalty belonged to Bruce. Whatever feelings he had for her didn't change that. They were on opposite sides of a brewing storm. Eventually she would discover his true allegiance and learn that the only reason he was at Dunstaffnage was to spy on and help destroy her family. Offering for her, he knew, would only make his ultimate betrayal that much worse.

It was an impossible situation, and one, he knew, of his own making. He should have stayed away from her. But her smile, her vitality, her sweetness and kindness, had chipped away at his good intentions. When he looked into those big blue eyes, it made him long for something that he hadn't even known he'd wanted.

He liked being alone, damn it! It was easier and a hell of a lot less complicated.

But she made him yearn for something he couldn't afford to give in view of what was to come. And hurting her like this—and not being able to do anything to change it—was tearing him apart. He was finding it difficult to focus on anything else.

Though she hadn't turned to look at him, he knew she was as aware of him as he was of her. He'd seen the way her shoulders had stiffened as he'd ridden up behind them.

With Richard and Alex scouting ahead, Arthur had circled behind them to make sure they weren't being followed. They were nearing the day's end of their journey, and as they drew closer Urquhart Castle—where Bruce's men had come upon them before—they had to be especially careful. Again, they would skirt well west of the road to avoid patrols from the "enemy" fortress.

"Here, my lady," he heard her maid say. "Lady Euphemia had the cook make these especially for you, seeing how much you loved them."

The older woman tried to ply her with the sugary confection, but Anna shook her head, the wan attempt at a smile tearing another shred in his heart. "Nay, thank you. I'm not hungry."

The servant huffed, pursed her mouth, and chomped down on the almond treat with little enthusiasm. She had barely finished chewing before she tried again. Drawing what looked to be a small meat pie from her bag, she said, "How about a bit of mutton and barley." She sniffed dramatically. "It smells delicious, and it's still warm."

Anna shook her head again. "You go ahead. I'll have something when we stop."

The maid murmured something under her breath. "You must eat something, my lady," she whispered urgently, shooting Arthur an angry glare.

His jaw clenched, guessing who the maid blamed for her mistress's lack of appetite.

"I will," Anna said placatingly. She called out to her brother, who'd ridden slightly ahead. "When will we stop for the night, brother?"

"Soon, I hope." Alan looked around, and seeing Arthur had returned, he motioned him forward.

Steeling himself, Arthur did as the other man bid, lifting the visor of his helm as he swung around the handful of riders between them.

"Anything suspicious?" Alan said.

He shook his head. "Not so far. When Richard and Alex return we can make sure, but if nothing looks out of the ordinary we can stop at the falls as planned."

"We aren't returning to the loch where we made camp last time?"

She was talking to him. Unable to avoid it any longer, he turned his gaze to hers—slowly. He wasn't prepared for the searing heat that cut through him when their eyes met. He—who had barely moved when an arrow had sunk deep into his shoulder, when a sword blade had sliced open his gut, or the numerous times he hadn't been fast enough to catch his brother's dagger—flinched, seeing the sadness and unspoken question in her eyes.

She looked tired and unbearably fragile. Tiny lines were etched around her eyes, and her skin seemed paler than usual.

He gritted his teeth, fighting the desperate urge that rose inside him to give her what she wanted.

Offer for her.

Damn it, he couldn't. It would only make it worse.

"Nay, my lady," he answered evenly. "It's safer if we don't retrace our steps too closely. We'll camp at different places each night. There's a waterfall in the forest near Dhivach, at the head of the glen, southeast of the castle. We'll stop there tonight."

She nodded, looking as if she wanted to say more, but conscious that they were not alone. "Is it much farther?"

"Three or four miles. We should be there before dark."

"I—" She stopped herself, but the way she was looking at him tore at his insides. "Thank you."

When he finally dragged his eyes away, he was surprised to see that one of Alan's men had come up behind him.

He frowned, but was too caught up in his own turmoil to heed the warning.

Apparently, one of Anna's trunks had not been well secured and had fallen out of the cart. When Anna and her maidservant went back to check to make sure nothing had been lost, Arthur was grateful for the interruption. But he knew he could not put off the inevitable discussion for much longer.

Indeed, Alan's parting words before he rode ahead to check on Richard and Alex ensured it. "I don't know what the hell happened at Auldearn, Campbell, but my sister is unhappy." The older knight's gaze leveled on him, his blue eyes wintry and utterly ruthless. His father's son after all. "Fix it. Or I will."

Arthur's mouth fell in a grim line. He didn't pretend to misunderstand his meaning. The threat didn't bother him. What bothered him was that he couldn't do as her brother asked. Nothing could fix it.

*   *   *

"Why are you avoiding me?"

Startled, Arthur jumped to his feet, causing the snare he'd been setting to snap.

She'd surprised him. Something Anna would wager didn't happen very often. Perhaps she hadn't imagined the turmoil in his eyes earlier. He'd looked at her with barely repressed longing. But something was holding him back.

The disappointment she'd felt that first morning had only worsened with each day that passed, and he still hadn't sought her out—let alone offered for her. She'd tried to convince herself that he was simply waiting to speak to her father, but it didn't explain why he was avoiding her.

"Are you following me again, Anna?"

If he was trying to distract her by putting her on the defensive, it wasn't going to work. "It's hardly following when camp is but a few yards away." She motioned to the twine and sticks. "I saw you take the snare from your bag and figured you wouldn't be going far."

She searched his face, half-hidden in the shadows. At least an hour of daylight remained, but under the dense canopy of trees in the forest, night seemed much closer. She took a step toward him, narrowing the gap between them. His jaw tightened and his entire body drew up stiffly. She could see the slight flare of his nostrils—as if her closeness bothered him.

Tears gathered behind her eyes. Why was he acting like this? Was she so offensive?

"Are you going to answer me?" Her voice broke, the emotion and uncertainty of the past few days catching up to her. She wanted to put her hand on his chest to steady herself, but she feared she would fall apart completely if he jerked away. "Do I not deserve an explanation?"

He sighed and stepped away from her, ostensibly to drag his fingers through his hair. Though he still wore his armor, he'd removed his helm. His dark brown hair fell in soft waves to the edge of his habergeon of mail. "Aye, lass, you do. I intended to speak to you once I'd seen to our meal."

She didn't know whether to believe him, but she waited for him to continue. She'd said enough. It was his turn to speak.

"What happened was . . ."

Beautiful? Amazing? Perfect?

". . . unfortunate."

Her heart plummeted—not the word she was hoping for.

"I'm ashamed of my conduct," he said, sounding every inch the stiff, courtly knight. "I never should have let it go so far—"

Unable to stand the regret and distance in his voice any longer, she cut him off. "Why are you talking like this? Why are you acting as if it didn't mean anything?"

His jaw hardened and the pulse in his neck began to tic ominously.

He tried to turn away, but she grabbed his arm. Her chest burned. "Did it mean anything, Arthur?" His gaze bit into her, scorching in its intensity. She drew a deep, ragged breath through her tight throat. "It did to me."

"Anna . . ." He seemed to be waging some kind of internal war. The muscles in his arm were rigid under her fingertips; his powerful body seemed to radiate tension. "Why are you making this so difficult?"

"*Me? You* are the one making it difficult. It's a simple enough question. It either meant something to you or it didn't."

She held his gaze, refusing to let him turn away, waiting for him to say something. His face was strained taut, as if she were torturing him.

"You don't understand."

"You're right, I don't. Why don't you explain it to me."

"I can't." He gave her a hard look. "Don't you see, it would never work."

My God. Her heart felt lodged in her throat as the realization struck: *He's not going to ask for me.* How could she have so completely misread the situation?

No! She hadn't. Something else was at work here. "Why not?"

"We're completely wrong for each other. Family is everything to you. But for me? My parents died when I was young. My brothers have been fighting on opposite sides of the war for years. I know nothing about family."

"I can show you—"

He cut her off angrily. "I don't want you to show me. I like to be alone. And you . . ." He waved his hand. "I'd wager you've never been alone a day in your life. You deserve to be surrounded by family and friends, with a husband who adores you and a handful of children tugging at your skirts. Don't tell me that you don't want that, because I know you do."

She did want that—with him. "Don't you want children?"

His mouth turned white, as if the question—the thought—caused him pain. "You're missing the point."

"Am I? Have you ever thought that maybe it's not that you *like* to be alone, but that you have not been around the right people?" She paused, letting her words sink in. She understood why he kept himself apart, but Anna suspected that he would feel differently with a family who loved him—who accepted him. "If you care for me, none of the rest matters." His face was about as yielding as granite, but she pressed on. "Do you care for me, Arthur?"

She held his gaze, daring him to lie to her. He looked as if he wanted to. Eventually he admitted, "Aye. But it doesn't matter."

He did care for her. She hadn't been wrong. She shook her head. "It's *all* that matters."

"It's no use, Anna. Trust me when I say it won't work. I could never give you what you want. I can never make you happy."

Frustration and anger rose inside her. "How dare you presume to know my mind better than I do! I know exactly what I want. After what happened, how can you not know that you are the only man who can make me happy? Don't you realize that I love you?"

Her declaration was as unexpected to her as apparently it was to him. She snapped her mouth shut, but it was too late. Her words seemed to echo in the sudden blast of silence.

He went utterly still, his expression not unlike that of someone who'd taken an arrow to the chest. Hardly the re-action she'd hoped for. She hadn't expected a return decla-ration. Really, she hadn't. Not yet at least. But neither had she expected the silence. Silence that slowly—cruelly—broke her heart.

I love you. The words reverberated in his ears. Pound-ing. Ringing. Tempting, damn it, tempting.

Arthur stood stone still, not daring to allow himself to believe her. He *couldn't* believe her. Because if he did, it might make him happy. Happier than he'd ever been in his life.

She didn't mean it. She was confused. Anna MacDougall gave her heart to everyone. It was part of what made her so damned irresistible.

He shook his head, as if trying to convince himself. "You don't know what you're saying. You can't love me. You don't even know me."

"How can you say that? Of course I know you."

"There are things about me, if you knew . . ." He couldn't say any more. He'd said too much already. She was too damned perceptive.

Her mouth pursed, and he recognized the stubborn glint in her eye. "I thought we'd been over that. Your abilities are a gift—one that has proved extraordinarily useful more than once."

He hadn't been talking about his skills, but about the fact that he was with Bruce and a spy. About the fact that there was no one he hated more in the world than her father, and that he'd been waiting fourteen years to destroy him. But he could hardly tell her the truth.

"I know all about you that matters," she continued. "I know you like to watch and listen rather than speak. I know that you don't like drawing attention to yourself and try to blend into the background. I know you have valuable skills that you try to hide because you think they make you different. I know you've convinced yourself that you *are* different and that therefore you don't need anyone, and so you try to push people away before they get too close because of it. I know that you've spent most of your life on the battlefield, but that you can wield a quill as effectively as you can a blade."

She stopped long enough to take a breath. He should have cut her off, but he was too unsettled to speak.

"I know that you are smart, and as strong of character as you are of body. I know that when I'm with you I feel safe. I know that you pretend not to care about anything but would protect me to your dying breath. I know that a man who can hold a child in his arms with gentleness, and show patience to a puppy who's given him nothing but trouble, has a kind heart." Her voice lowered to almost a whisper, the anger drained out of her. "I know that since the first time you kissed me there would never be another man for me. I know that when I look up into your face, it's the one I want to see for the rest of my life." Her eyes, bright with unshed tears, met his. "I know you are loyal and honorable and care for me but something is holding you back."

Jesus. He felt as if he'd been poleaxed. No one had ever said anything like that to him before.

It humbled him.

It moved him.

It scared the hell out of him.

She'd seen too much. She wasn't just a threat to his mission but to him in ways he'd never imagined.

He hardened his jaw, and his heart. "You see what you want to see, Anna—not reality." The war. Her father. Him. She was blind to the faults of those she professed to love. "But little girls who believe in faerie tales only grow up disappointed."

"Don't do this," she whispered. "Don't try to push me away."

It's what he did. What he always did. Even if for the first time he didn't want to, it was what he needed to do. For her own good.

He grabbed her arm, intending to shake some damned sense into her, but it was a mistake. Touching her only made the emotions firing inside him hotter. Louder. More twisted and out of control.

"Then don't act like a naive postulate. We're in the middle of a damned war. Bruce is about to bring the full force of his army down on top of you, but you want to plan for the future. There is no future, Anna. Only today. Hell, you might not have a home next month."

She flinched as if he'd struck her. "Do you think I don't know that?" A sob strangled in her throat. Her beautiful blue eyes blurred with tears, stoking the fires burning in his chest. "Why do you think I went to Ross? I know what's at stake. But I couldn't do it. Because of *you*."

"Your father should never have asked it of you," he snapped.

Her stricken expression made him wish to call his words back. She had a girl's vision of her father—the perfect knight who could do no wrong. One more illusion he would help destroy.

"He didn't ask it of me. It was my idea. You talk of war and uncertainty, but I can tell you one thing that's certain. If you never take a risk, if you always push people away, you'll be guaranteed to be alone. Is that what you want?"

His jaw was clenched so tight his teeth hurt. "Yes." *Damn her.*

"Good, because that's exactly what you'll be." The tears fell on her cheeks. "I don't know why you're doing this, but you're a coward, Arthur Campbell."

Anger rushed through him in a fiery blast. He wasn't a coward. He was trying to do the right thing. But she wouldn't let him. She kept pushing and pulling him, making him crazy with feelings that didn't belong to him. He couldn't think straight. All he wanted to do was drag her into his arms and kiss her until the hammering in his head—in his chest—stopped.

He might have done just that, but he didn't have the chance.

"What the hell is going on here?"

Arthur jerked around, his head still spinning, as Alan MacDougall strode into the clearing.

Arthur swore. He'd been too wrapped up in Anna and hadn't heard a damned thing.

What the hell was the matter with him? He was out of control. He needed to get a rein on his emotions. His senses were dull and fuzzy. He was too distracted. Too twisted up in knots. He'd felt like this only once before—the day his father died. He was losing his edge.

So much so that he wasn't ready for what came next.

"Let go of her," Alan boomed, tearing Anna out of his arms at the same time his fist came slamming toward his jaw.

Arthur's head snapped back as he took the full force of the blow. His head exploded in pain. A white flash blinded him.

Anna cried out in horror. "Alan, please, it's not what you think!"

But her brother wasn't listening. Proving his efficiency with both fists, another blow caught Arthur from the other side. Then the stomach. Then his ribs.

"I told you to fix it, damn it. Not make her cry. What the hell did you do to her?"

Arthur didn't try to defend himself. Not because he couldn't—MacDougall might have a smith's hammer for an arm, but Arthur had learned enough tricks from the best hand-to-hand warrior in the Highlands to have him on his back in a few seconds. He didn't fight back because he deserved it. Hell, he deserved far worse for what he would do.

"Stop! Stop!" Anna sobbed, her voice teetering on hysteria. "You're hurting him."

Alan dragged him up by the collar, shoving him hard against a tree. "What did you do?" His gaze shot to his sister's. "One of you had better tell me what the hell is going on."

Neither of them responded.

Alan looked back and forth between them, his face fired hot with anger. "Don't take me for a bloody fool! Don't think I believe for one minute that Ross suddenly decided to cry off!" He looked at Anna, his hand still grasped tight around Arthur's throat. "What happened at Auldearn? Did this bastard touch you, Anna?" His hand squeezed. "Did he touch you?" He jammed Arthur harder. "Did he?"

Arthur felt the noose tightening around his throat, and it wasn't MacDougall's hand. Nay, he knew that he was going to be called to answer for what had happened—or nearly happened—at Auldearn.

"Let go of him!" He heard the panic in Anna's voice. She tried to pull on her brother's arm to no avail. "Yes, but it's not what you think."

Actually, it was probably exactly what he thought.

"You bloody bastard," MacDougall said, jamming his head farther into the tree. "I'll kill you for this."

Arthur did not doubt his intent—or his ability. But he couldn't let him do that. He was just about to free himself, when he heard a small pop followed by a soft whirling sound.

Arrow.

His senses exploded in a burst of sharp clarity. His gaze shot over MacDougall's shoulder, seeing the iron tip spinning through the air. A split second away from impact into the back of MacDougall's head.

Arthur didn't think; he reacted. In one seamless movement, he used an upward jam of his forearm to break MacDougall's grip around his throat and then twisted his leg around the other man's ankle to knock him off balance. MacDougall fell to the ground right as the arrow hit the tree with a thud, followed swiftly by the piercing cries of an attack.

He heard Anna's terrified gasp but couldn't turn around to calm her. The first man had already plunged from the trees, sword raised. Again, Arthur's reaction was instantaneous. He found the grip of his dirk, jerked it from its scabbard, and threw. The attacker grunted as the blade found the few inches of unprotected skin on his neck. He staggered, then fell.

By the time the next man was on them, MacDougall's head had cleared for long enough to realize what was happening and had gotten to his feet. He pulled out his sword, whirled around, and got his blade up just in time to fend off a blow that would have taken off his head.

Anna. Arthur turned his gaze from the oncoming assault just long enough to make sure she was all right. He found her huddled behind the tree, eyes wide with fright. His heart rose in his chest when he saw how vulnerable she was, and then it froze when he realized how vulnerable that made him.

He couldn't let anything happen to her. He had to protect her. He would kill them all if he had to.

Their eyes met for only a second. But the look that passed between them was fast and fierce in its intensity.

"Stay down," he said, his voice calm despite the rush of blood pounding through his veins.

Positioning himself in front of Anna—and shoulder-to-shoulder with MacDougall, who was still battling his opponent—Arthur swung his sword around to meet the onslaught of attackers pouring through the trees. A score of men. Maybe more.

He didn't have long to wait before the next attacker reached him. For the first time in over two years—since he'd been forced from the Highland Guard and inserted into the enemy's camp—Arthur let himself go, fighting with all the skill and frenzy he'd kept so carefully hidden. He took down the first man with one vicious swing of his sword, spun, and using the momentum of the first, took down the next.

They came at him harder. But it didn't matter. He was like a siege engine, cutting down all who came in his path. Three. Four.

The crash of steel on steel pierced the dusky night air, mingling with the grunts and battle cries. The sounds had alerted the camp—thankfully only a few steps away—and MacDougall's men started to pour into the small clearing, now shrouded in almost complete darkness.

But the attackers had expected the men to race to their aid. Indeed, they'd planned for it and were lying in wait. More attackers dropped from the trees onto the unsuspecting MacDougall clansmen as they funneled through the trees.

"Look up," Arthur shouted, trying to warn them. "Spread out."

If they didn't, they'd be cut down as easily as herring in a barrel.

But it was all the warning he could give before his next opponents diverted his attention. Two men were on him. Two men in nasal helms, darkened plaids, and the distinctive black ash smeared over their faces.

Dread sank like a stone in his gut.

The attackers were Bruce's men. Of course they were. He saw the bodies littered on the ground before him—men he'd killed—and bile rose in his throat.

Jesus, what had he been thinking? He hadn't been. The instinct to protect Anna had overridden everything else.

But it was worse than he'd realized.

While he attempted to incapacitate the two men attacking him without actually killing them, a third man joined the fray.

A third man who wielded two swords.

He moved like lightning, coming at Arthur with a fierceness unmatched by even those among their elite Highland Guard brethren.

Arthur swore under his breath, finding himself face-to-face in the darkness with Lachlan MacRuairi.

Seventeen

It all happened so fast. One minute Anna was trying to prevent her brother from killing the man she loved, and the next they were under attack.

To say the situation was dire was an understatement. From her place huddled in the darkness, she forced shallow breaths from her lungs between the hard pounding of her heart, watching in horror as the men descended on them like a plague of locusts. It seemed as if there were hundreds of them—against only two.

Arthur cut down the first man so easily, she thought it was an aberration. But then came the next. And the next.

She gazed in stunned amazement as he effortlessly dispatched all who came before him. His skill was so extraordinary—so dominating—it seemed she was watching another man. She'd spied him at practice enough times to recognize the difference. He made her brother, who was known as one of the most skilled knights in the Highlands, look like a squire.

He was quicker. More agile in movement and technique. And most significantly, stronger. She could feel the ground reverberate with the force of his blows. When one of his opponents managed to get in a swing of his blade, Arthur's arm barely moved when he blocked it, absorbing the force as if it were nothing.

His arm . . .

Her eyes widened. His *right* arm.

She didn't understand. Arthur was left-handed. At least he was supposed to be, but watching him now, she knew he'd only pretended.

Why would he hide such a thing?

And why had she never seen him fight like this before? It didn't make sense. She could understand his reasons for hiding his unusually keen senses, but there was nothing off-putting about swordsmanship. God, he could be one of the most revered knights in the kingdom if he wanted to be. So why didn't he want to be?

But her questions fell by the wayside when she saw the next wave of attackers drop from the trees. No doubt seeing the fallen bodies of their compatriots, they identified the threat and were converging on Arthur.

She forced back the cry of warning, knowing it would only distract him. But her heart clenched in her throat. Two men. And a third not far behind them.

Suddenly, something seemed to change with Arthur. Instead of the cold, ruthless death strokes, he wielded his sword with less deliberateness. It was almost as if his purpose had changed from killing them to fending them off.

But that didn't make any sense. She shook off the strange thought. These warriors were simply better trained, that was all.

And they were. It was hard to see in the near-darkness; they wore dark clothing and seemed to have blackened their skin with something . . .

Her blood chilled. Recalling the attack of the year before. Those men had darkened their skin as well. Could these be the wraiths of Bruce's phantom army of marauders? The men who'd struck fear in the heart of Scotland and England alike?

Her worst fears seemed confirmed when a third man descended on Arthur like a hound of hell. Rather than the long, two-handed broadsword used by the Highlanders, he wielded two shorter swords. One for each hand.

But it was his clothing that sent tremors of terror sliding through her bones. Like the other attackers he wore a darkened nasal helm and his skin had been blackened with mud or ash, but it was what else he wore that struck the chilling chord of memory. Dressed head-to-toe in black, instead of mail he wore a leather war coat studded with metal, leather chausses, and an oddly wrapped dark plaid. Just like the man—the ridiculously handsome rebel—who'd attacked her last year.

This man was one of them. She knew it. Fear turned to terror. They were reputed to have extraordinary abilities. To fight like demons possessed. *Oh God, Arthur!*

Her breath caught high in her chest as the attacker flew at him, swords raised on either side of his head. Time seemed to slow. Still engaged with one of the other attackers, Arthur wasn't going to be able to defend himself.

Ice lodged in her chest. In her blood. He was going to die.

She opened her mouth to scream, but at the last minute, Arthur jammed the pommel of his sword in the nose of one of the men attacking him, enabling him to get his sword up to block the two blades before they crossed at his neck.

He and the hellish attacker met face-to-face, blades caught in a tangle above their heads. The attacker, coming down, had momentum on his side, but with both hands on his sword, Arthur managed to hold him off.

Arthur had his back to her, but she could just make out the attacker's face in a beam of moonlight. He had the eeriest eyes she'd ever seen. She shivered. They seemed to glow in the darkness. Dark features twisted in rage, he looked like a demon from hell—or Lucifer himself.

She felt a prickle of recognition tease the edges of her memory. My God! Could it be . . .

Her eyes widened. He looked like Lachlan MacRuairi—her deceased Aunt Juliana's husband. She hadn't seen him in years, but she heard he'd joined the rebels. Her Aunt Juliana, whom her sister was named after, had been much younger than her father—nearly twenty years. MacRuairi was probably of age with her brother Alan.

He drew closer to Arthur and suddenly his expression changed. If she hadn't been watching so carefully she wouldn't have seen it. Surprise. Recognition?

The man she thought to be her uncle dropped back. Or was she just imagining it? It was dark, and so hard to tell. The men exchanged a few more blows, but the fierceness and intensity seemed to be gone. Compared to what had come before, it seemed more practice than all-out battle.

She peered into the darkness, trying to make sense of it. Then, out of the corner of her eye, she saw her brother stagger back, his sword dropped as both hands went to his head. He fell to his knees, swaying . . .

She cried out, unable to stop herself. She would have rushed toward him, but Arthur moved back to block her. "Stay back, damn it. Stay back."

Helplessly, she watched as the attacker her brother had been fighting lifted his sword to finish him off.

Her bloodcurdling scream tore through the night.

Arthur seemed to hesitate, but only for an instant. Somehow he managed to block a blow from the man who looked like her uncle, then spin around in time to block the swing intended for her brother. Not prepared for Arthur's defense, her brother's attacker's arm collapsed and he fell forward onto Arthur's sword. His eyes widened in surprise before freezing for all time.

Even in the midst of this horrible nightmare, the gruesome sight was too much. With a sob, she turned away.

The next instant a sharp whistle pierced the dark night

air. She turned back to the melee, stunned to see the attackers falling back in retreat. MacRuairi—or a man who looked just like him—had apparently called them off.

Her brother's men now filled the clearing. Before the last rebel had faded into the forest, she rushed forward to Alan's side.

He'd managed to get to his feet, but he still appeared unsteady.

"Oh God, Alan. Are you all right?"

Even in the darkness, she could see from the way he was looking at her that it was hard for him to focus. He shook his head as if trying to clear the haze.

"A knock on the pate," he said. "I'll be fine." He cupped her cheek and gave her a fond smile. "No need for tears."

Anna nodded and wiped her cheeks with the back of her hand, not even realizing she'd been crying.

She turned, instinctively seeking him out. Arthur stood a few feet away, watching her. She wanted to run to him. To throw herself into his arms, bury her face into his chest, and fall apart. He would take away the horror. But her brother was standing there.

And Arthur's face was too grim. "You are unhurt?" he asked.

She nodded. Her eyes scanned him, lingering on his jaw and cheek—bruised from where her brother had struck him. "And you?"

He returned the nod.

Alan stiffened beside her. He strode toward Arthur and Anna froze, fearing what he would do. He stopped a few feet in front of him. The two men faced off silently in the darkness.

Finally, her brother said, "It seems I am in your debt—not once, but twice."

Arthur stilled, and then gave a short shrug.

"I don't like to see my sister upset," Alan added.

Anna assumed that was meant to be an apology.

"Neither do I," Arthur said.

Alan studied him for a moment and then nodded, as if he'd come to some sort of decision. "You fought well," he said, changing the subject, but not the intensity of his scrutiny.

Apparently, she had not been the only one to notice his improved skills. "The rush of battle," Arthur explained.

Anna almost mentioned the change of hand, but something stopped her. If her brother had noticed too, he didn't let on.

Alan was still watching him. "Aye, for some men it is like that." From his tone, Anna couldn't tell whether he believed Arthur's explanation. When Arthur didn't respond, Alan added, "The rebels are better trained than I expected."

Anna stepped forward. "Not just any rebels, brother."

Both men looked at her, but it was Alan who asked the question. "What do you mean?"

"I think one of them—maybe more—was one of Bruce's phantom guard." She explained the similar clothing to the man who'd led that attack at the church the year before.

Alan stroked his chin. "It makes sense. I think you might be right."

"There's more. I can't be sure, but I think I recognized him. The man with two swords."

"What?" Both men reacted. Her brother with excitement and Arthur with . . . something else.

"Our uncle—former uncle."

Alan swore. "MacRuairi?"

She nodded.

Alan's mouth fell in a grim line. "Father will not be pleased."

Anna did not know the source of the enmity between her father and his former brother by marriage, but she knew the hatred ran fiercely on both sides.

Alan let out a bark of laughter. "Though perhaps he

should be. Let Bruce have that traitorous, opportunistic bastard in his camp. The only thing that Lachlan MacRuairi is loyal to is himself. If he is the kind of man recruited for this band of phantoms, we have nothing to worry about."

Arthur had fallen strangely silent. She wanted to ask him about what she'd seen between him and the man she thought was her uncle, but like before, something held her back. Instead she asked, "What made them leave?"

Her brother frowned. "I'm not sure. My head was ringing; I didn't see much of anything."

"Your men had broken through," Arthur explained. "They were outnumbered."

It hadn't seemed that way to her, but she'd been too focused on her brother to pay attention to the rest of the battle. "You should return to camp," he said.

"Aye," Alan said. "One of my men will take you. We must see to—"

He stopped.

She filled in the rest. *The dead.*

The horror of the attack—of what they'd barely escaped—hit her full force. The dam had given way, and all the emotion kept carefully at bay rose inside her, threatening to flood in a sea of tears.

She turned, realizing that Arthur had come to stand beside her. Heedless of her brother's presence, he reached down to tuck a stray lock of hair behind her ear. His fingers swept the side of her cheek, lingering.

The tenderness of the gesture brought tears to her eyes. She gazed up at him. Beneath his grim expression, she read his concern. His solid presence, his strength, nearly shattered her. If he took her in his arms, she would fall apart.

Guessing as much, he didn't. "It will be all right," he said gently. "Do as your brother says."

"But—"

He cut her off with a shake of his head, his expression

firm. He had to have guessed that she had questions. "Not now," he said, his gaze shifting to the fallen men at their feet. "Later."

Anna kept her eyes on his face, careful not to follow the direction of his gaze. She'd seen enough bloodshed tonight to last a lifetime. The memories of this night would haunt her.

Her reaction was understandable. She was a woman, not used to the blood and gore of battlefields. Arthur, however, was used to it. Or he should be.

But something in his expression—the tightness of his jaw, the whiteness of his mouth, the starkness in his eyes— made her think the attack had affected him deeply.

As two of her brother's men led her away, Anna suspected that she would not be the only one haunted by the night's events.

The question was why.

Arthur didn't sleep. He half-expected MacRuairi to slither through the darkness and slit his throat or stick a dirk in his back for what had happened. It wouldn't be the first time. MacRuairi hadn't earned his war name "Viper" for his venomous personality alone, but also for his deadly, silent strike.

Not that Arthur would blame him.

As he'd done most of the night, he stared at the pile of bodies moved off to one side of the clearing, left for the "attackers" to collect.

Nine of Bruce's men killed. More than half at the end of Arthur's sword.

He'd erred. Badly. On too many levels to count. It was bad enough that his senses had failed him—that he'd missed the signs of the attack—but he'd also seemed to have forgotten what side he was on. He'd been entrenched in the enemy camp for so long, he'd started to believe his own lies.

Christ. He closed his eyes, trying to block it out. He'd been forced to kill his own men before, but not like this. He hadn't been just defending himself. He'd been in a frenzy. So focused on protecting Anna and killing anyone that threatened her that he hadn't thought about anything else.

Even when he had realized what was happening, he hadn't stopped. He'd saved MacDougall's life at the expense of one of his compatriots.

He couldn't forget the look on MacRuairi's face when Arthur stabbed the man trying to kill MacDougall. That he hadn't meant to kill him didn't matter. He shouldn't have interfered. Anna's heart-rending cry wasn't an excuse—or at least one that would matter to his brethren.

When the first orange rays of dawn flickered through the forest, he stood from his solitary post leaning against a tree. They weren't coming. MacRuairi—and unless he'd erred in identifying three other members of the Highland Guard as they retreated, Gordon, MacGregor, and MacKay. He hadn't expected them to, even if he'd hoped for the chance to explain. They wouldn't further risk his cover. He'd done that enough himself.

He knew how close he'd come to blowing his cover and putting his entire mission in jeopardy. As her questions had proved, Anna—even terrified—was too observant. And she wasn't the only one. Alan, too, was suspicious of his suddenly improved fighting ability and of how quickly the attackers had fled. He'd put them off for now, but he knew she had more questions and didn't dare think about what else she'd noticed.

Recognizing MacRuairi was bad enough, but to have connected him with the Highland Guard was a disaster. Keeping their identities secret not only added to the mystique and fear surrounding the "phantom" guard, but also helped to keep them safe. If their enemies learned their identities, not only would they have a price on their heads, but their families could be at risk. It was the reason they'd decided to use war names when they were on missions.

There would be hell to pay when Bruce learned MacRuairi had been unmasked.

It shouldn't have happened, damn it. Anger and guilt coiled mercilessly inside him. If he hadn't been so wrapped up in Anna, so twisted with emotion, he would have sensed the attack. Those men wouldn't have been killed, and Anna wouldn't have been put in danger. Christ, she could have been killed. All because he'd failed to control his emotions and had gotten too close.

He walked back into camp just as the men not on guard were starting to stir. He glanced at Anna's tent, seeing the coated linen flaps still closed. *Good. Let her sleep.* She'd earned it. He'd checked on her often during the night, assuring himself that she was all right. He knew how shaken she'd been by the attack, but he'd been battling his own demons and in no condition to comfort her—even if it had been his place to do so.

By the time he'd returned from seeing to the horses, however, he noticed the flap was opened. A quick scan around the camp made him frown. A moment later, however, he spied her speaking with her brother, who was engaged with some of her men. The exasperated look on her face was so normal, he heaved a sigh of relief, not wanting to acknowledge how worried he'd been.

Her gaze landed on him. She hesitated, but then started to march across the leaf- and moss-strewn ground toward him. He noticed she carried a bundle of cloth in her arms.

She stopped before him, tilting her pale face to his. His chest squeezed. Sleep, it seemed, had eluded her as well.

"Since it is your rule, and my brother is busy, I'm afraid you will have to accompany me."

He gave her a quizzical look.

"Did you not make me promise not to leave camp without you or my brother?"

His mouth twitched, the first smile in what felt like years. "Aye."

"I need to go to the burn to wash."

The river was within easy sight of the camp, but he didn't argue, realizing how much the attack must have unsettled her. He bowed with a mocking flourish of his hand. "After you."

She didn't appear anxious to talk, which was fine by him. He waited by a tree, pretending not to watch, while she went through her morning ablutions.

After tidying her hair with a damp comb and cleaning her teeth with powder from a vial that she rubbed on a small square of linen, she dipped a fresh linen cloth in the river. She'd brought a sliver of soap, which she rubbed on the cloth, and then proceeded to wash her face, chest, hands, and arms.

It was one of the most erotic sights he'd ever beheld.

When she dipped the cloth between her breasts, it was too much. He turned away, furious that something so mundane could arouse him. But with the sun streaming through the trees, catching the golden strands of hair, and the rivulets of water cascading down her face and chest, she looked beautiful, sweet, and utterly entrancing. A ray of light in the darkness. And all he could think about was how close he'd come to heaven—and how badly he wanted to touch her again.

God, had he learned nothing from what happened last night?

He focused on their surroundings with almost exaggerated intensity, keening his senses toward anything out of the ordinary.

But his gaze drifted back. She'd finished and walked toward him, the sun illuminating her from behind. He sucked in his breath. But that didn't prevent him from getting a mind-numbing whiff of her sweet feminine fragrance: freshly washed skin tinged with rose petals.

"What's wrong?" she asked.

"Nothing," he said tightly.

"You look as if you are in pain." Her eyes flew to his. "Is it your face?" She reached up to cup his bruised chin. Every muscle in his body jumped at the contact. "Did my foolish brother break something?" Jesus, her hands were soft. Velvety fingers caressed the hard line of his flexed jaw. "Look at all those bruises. It must hurt." Her thumb slid toward his mouth. "Your lip is split."

It did hurt. The innocently erotic gesture sent a rush of blood low in his groin and fired his blood with heat. He had to force himself not to take her finger in his mouth and suck.

She had no idea what she was doing to him. Or how hard it was for him to keep his hands off her.

She gazed up at him with wide-eyed concern. A little kitten in the jaws of a wolf. "Does it hurt very badly?"

"It's not my face." He gave her a hot look that told her exactly the source of his pain. He was as hard as a spike.

A soft pink stained her cheeks. If that wasn't bad enough, she proceeded to nibble on her soft bottom lip. "Oh. I didn't realize—"

"We should get back. Your brother will wish to leave soon."

She nodded, and he thought he saw her shiver. "I shall not be sad to leave this place."

He couldn't stop himself. He tipped her chin, looking deep into her big, blue eyes. "You are all right?"

She tried to smile, but her mouth wobbled. "Nay, but I will manage."

He dropped his hand; his mouth fell in a straight line. "What happened last night will not be repeated."

Her delicately arched brows furrowed. "How can you be so certain?"

"Because I won't let it."

Her eyes searched his face, and then widened with understanding. "Good God, that's why you are upset. You blame yourself for what happened. But that's ridiculous. You couldn't have known—"

"Yes, I should have. Had I not been so distracted, I would have."

"So I'm to blame?"

"Of course not."

"You aren't perfect, Arthur. You're human; you make mistakes."

He didn't respond, his jaw clenching so tightly his teeth hurt.

"Is that what you think?" she asked softly. "Have your senses never failed you before?"

Once. He pushed aside the memory. "We should get back."

He started to turn away, but she grabbed his arm to stop him. "Won't you tell me?"

"There's nothing to tell."

"Does it have something to do with your father?"

He glanced at her sharply. How in Hades had she figured that out?

She read his surprise. "When you spoke of his death before, I sensed there was something you were leaving out."

There was a hell of a lot he'd left out. Namely her father's part in the foul deed.

She was waiting for him to respond. He wasn't much for discussing the past, but if the look on her face was any indication, it meant a lot to her. "There isn't much to tell. It was my first battle. My father had brought me alone to prove myself. I was so worried about impressing him that I missed the signs of the attack." But that wasn't the worst part. "I watched him die."

Her face filled with sympathy. "God, I'm so sorry. That must have been horrible. But you were only a lad; you couldn't have done anything to help him."

"I should have warned him." Had he not been so upset, so scared, he would have seen the signs. Then, just as last night, emotion had gotten in the way. "I was distracted."

Her frown barely had time to form before her eyes lit with sudden comprehension. "You loved him."

He shrugged, the subject making him uneasy. "It didn't do him any good."

"Even Achilles had a weak spot, Arthur."

His brows gathered together in a frown. What was she talking about?

"It's hard to remain detached and observant with people you care about." She gave him an understanding smile. "You can't blame yourself for caring."

But he did. What use were his vaunted skills if he couldn't protect the people he cared about?

"Thank you for telling me," she said.

Why again did he feel as if she'd seen too much? "I didn't want you to worry about another surprise attack."

"I'm not," she said. "I trust you."

Arthur's chest tightened to a burn. He wanted to warn her not to—that he didn't deserve it, that he would only hurt her, that she gave her heart too easily, too blindly—but instead he nodded, and they started back toward camp.

He led her up the path from the burn. When they reached the edge of camp, she gave him a sidelong look out of the corner of her eye. "My uncle looked as if he recognized you."

The observation caught him completely off guard. Something for which she seemed to have a particular talent. His step faltered. Not much, but he feared she'd noticed.

"Are you sure it was your uncle? It was dark. I couldn't see him clearly behind the nasal helm, and he was much closer to me."

Her nose wrinkled, the adorableness of the movement at odds with the threat she posed.

"I haven't seen him in a number of years, but I'm

fairly certain it was him. His eyes are"—she shivered—"unforgettable." If he'd hoped to distract her from her original question, it didn't work. "But he seemed to recognize you."

"Did he?" he shrugged. "We may have crossed paths once before."

She didn't say anything for a moment. But unfortunately, she did not allow the subject to drop. "So you don't know him?"

He fought the instinctive flare of alarm. "Not personally."

"He seemed upset to see you."

The rapid fire of his heartbeat belied his outward calm. She was dangerously perceptive and treading too damned close to the truth.

"Upset? From what I know of Lachlan MacRuairi he's an evil, foul-tempered bast—" He stopped himself, remembering his audience. "He was probably angry that I'd killed so many of his men."

She seemed to accept his explanation, but her next question told him she was not satisfied. "Why did they retreat?"

He swore to himself, the flare of alarm growing louder. "As I said, your brother's men had broken through. They were outnumbered."

She frowned. "It didn't seem that way. It seemed like they were winning."

He forced a wry smile to his mouth. "Your brother was in danger," he reminded her. "I think you were distracted."

She looked up at him and gave him a half-smile. "Perhaps you are right. I was focused on my brother. I've yet to thank you for what you did." A shadow crossed her face. "If you hadn't stopped that man—"

"Don't think about it, Anna; it's over."

She nodded and gave him another sidelong glance.

"Nevertheless I am grateful. Alan is, too, even if he has an odd way of showing it."

MacDougall was making no secret of his interest. Arthur had felt his eyes on them the entire time. He met his gaze and knew the "discussion" of the day before was not finished. "He has a right to his anger, Anna. What I did was wrong. All I can do is promise that it will never happen again."

Her sharp intake of breath was like a stab to his chest. She looked shocked. Bewildered. As if she'd been expecting something else. "But—"

"They're waiting for us," he said to cut her off, indicating the men readying the horses. He couldn't take another conversation like yesterday's. "It's time to go."

He spoke the words to himself as much as to her.

Blind spot. Weak spot. No matter what he called it, his feelings where Anna was concerned had become a liability.

He'd let her get too close, and now his cover and his mission were hanging by a thread. Time was running out.

Eighteen

Two uneventful days later Anna rode through the gate of Dunstaffnage Castle. One of the guardsmen had ridden ahead, so they were expected. She could tell by the barely concealed anger on her father's face that he knew their journey had ended in failure.

She'd hoped for a good night of sleep before having to face her father's questions, but the lateness of the hour did not forestall their report. She and Alan barely had time to wash the dirt from their hands and eat a small meal before they were ushered into the lord's solar.

He stood in the middle of the room with his hands clasped behind his back, the important members of his *meinie* flanked behind him. From their universally grim expressions, Anna felt as if she'd just walked into a burial cairn. As no one was seated, she and Alan came to an awkward stop before him. She felt not unlike a child called to answer for some egregious prank gone wrong.

The door had barely closed behind them before her father spoke. Attacked, really. "Ross refused."

It wasn't a question. Hearing the accusation in his voice, she wanted to explain, but it was not her place.

Alan answered for them. "Aye. Ross's response to our request for an alliance was the same as before. He said Bruce would be marching toward him as well, and he couldn't spare any more men."

"But what about the betrothal? Did that not change his mind?"

Anna felt the men's eyes on her, sending a flood of heat to her cheeks. She kept her eyes downcast, not wanting her father to see her shame. Whether it would have made a difference or not, she'd failed in the task he'd set before her. She couldn't bear to see his disappointment.

"There is no betrothal," Alan explained. "It was agreed they did not suit."

She hoped she was the only one to detect Alan's carefully worded response.

"You mean he did not forgive you for refusing him the first time," her father snapped at her.

She ventured a glance in his direction, seeing the fury on his face. Her heart lurched. It wasn't good for him to be so upset. She wanted to say something but knew he'd be even more furious to be treated like an invalid before his men.

Anna didn't know what to say. She didn't want to lie to him, but neither could she tell him the truth.

"I . . ." she stumbled.

"Well," her father said impatiently. "I thought you were going to persuade him."

Her cheeks burned with shame. "I tried, but I'm afraid he, um, sensed that my feelings might have been engaged elsewhere."

"What do you mean, 'engaged elsewhere'?" Her father's eyes narrowed, piercing like arrows. He knew there was something she wasn't telling him. "Campbell," he said flatly, answering his own question. He swore, his gaze unrelenting. "And how would he sense this? What did you do?"

She'd never seen her father so angry with her. For the first time, Anna was frightened by his rage. That she deserved it made it no less devastating.

What could she say?

Thankfully, Alan took pity on her. "The betrothal would not have mattered. Ross had already made up his mind. I'm afraid you have not heard the worst of it."

Anna braced herself for her father's reaction. She feared it could throw him into another fit of apoplexy.

Alan apparently decided that the truth was better not measured, but given in one unpleasant dose. "Ross is considering submission."

Her father didn't say a word. But like a slow-moving wave on the horizon careening toward shore, she watched the anger build to a frightening crescendo ready to crash. His fists clenched at his side, his face turned beet red, veins bulging at his brow, and his eyes blazed like the pits of hellfire.

She took a step toward him, but Alan put his hand out to stop her. He shook his head in warning.

When her father finally spoke, it was to utter a string of curses that would have put her mother on her knees doing penance for his blasphemous soul for weeks. He stormed around the small solar like a lion in a cage—even his men stood back and gave him plenty of room to rampage.

"Ross is a bloody fool," he blasted angrily. "Bruce will never forgive him for what he's done to the women. His sister and the countess were hung in a cage, for God's sake. If he submits, he is signing his own writ of execution." He paused long enough to bang the side of his fist on the table. "How can he think of bowing to that traitorous murderer? He cut down my kinsman before an altar."

Anna didn't dare point out that the sanctity of the church hardly seemed to matter to Ross. After all, he'd violated sanctuary to capture Bruce's womenfolk.

Alan tried to calm him down. "The people are behind Bruce. He's incited a patriotic fervor in the countryside not seen since Wallace. They think he is the savior, the second coming of King Arthur, who has freed them from the yoke of English tyranny. Ross is thinking of his people and the future of his clan. He is thinking of what's best for Scotland."

Anna tried to hide her shock. Fortunately her father was too angry to hear what he'd really said. But she'd heard the admonition in her brother's voice, even if her father had not.

Did Alan agree with Ross? Did he believe Bruce was the best choice for Scotland? Dear Lord, what if her father was *wrong*?

Anna couldn't believe she'd allowed the disloyal thought to take form. But the MacDougalls, once fervent patriots, had turned to the English rather than see Bruce take the throne. Was that what was best for Scotland?

"I will die before I see that murderer on the throne," her father said, the rage in his eyes no longer burning, but cold as ice.

Anna felt much relief when she heard the unanimous murmurs of hearty agreement by his men. Her father knew what he was doing. He was one of the greatest men in Scotland. He had his faults, of course—what great man did not? But he would see them through.

Having reported on the most important part of their journey, Alan began to tell her father the rest, giving a short account of the trouble that had befallen them on the road.

He listened with growing concern, visibly paling when he heard of his heir's near escape from death—twice. His eyes narrowed when Alan reported Anna's suspicion of MacRuairi's involvement, and then gleamed with excitement when he realized the connection with Bruce's mysterious phantom guard.

"Good work," he said to Anna, who beamed under the praise.

Alan gave Arthur's version of the retreat, but it seemed to cause her father some trouble as well.

Finally, he came forward and took her hand. "You were not harmed, daughter?"

She shook her head, and he folded her in his big, bearish embrace, his anger seemingly forgotten.

For a moment, Anna felt like a child again, and the urge to cry out her sorrow all over the front of his finely embroidered tunic took hold. Arthur was still set against her. The attack had changed nothing. If anything, it had made it worse. She'd hoped that after their talk he might have changed his mind. He cared for her, but something was holding him back.

Two days on the road had given her no new insights. She couldn't shake the feeling that something about the attack wasn't right. Nor could she shake the niggle of unease that he was hiding something.

Her father pulled back to look at her. "You're tired. I will hear the rest in the morning."

She nodded, relieved that the worst was over.

Or so she thought.

"And Alan," he said to her brother. "Have Campbell and his brother join us." He gave her a look that sent a shiver of trepidation slithering down her spine. "It seems Sir Arthur has much to answer for."

Arthur was prepared for the summons when it came. He wasn't, however, expecting it to include his brother.

"What the hell did you do?" Dugald asked suspiciously, as they made their way across the *barmkin* to the donjon tower. "Why is Lorn so anxious to see you?"

Arthur climbed up the stairs beside his brother, the steel of their mail and weaponry clanking as they walked. "I suspect he has questions about the men who attacked us."

"And what would you know about them?"

"Nothing," he said, pulling open the large wooden entry door to the tower.

"What do I have to do with any of this?"

Arthur glanced at Dugald. His brother's expression showed the bitterness they both were feeling. Dugald didn't like being called to Lorn's presence any more than he did. Even if he and his brother were on opposite sides of the war, at least they could agree on their hatred of Lorn.

"Hell if I know," Arthur said, the uncertainty giving him a prickle of unease. A guard knocked on the door to announce their arrival. When they were bid to enter, Arthur turned and said, "But we're about to find out."

He quickly scanned the occupants of the room: Lorn, sitting like a king in a big thronelike chair, his expression unreadable; Alan MacDougall standing to the side against the wall, looking mildly puzzled; and Anna sitting on a bench before the fire, looking extremely anxious. Except for the solitary guard who'd admitted them and then left at Lorn's order, no other members of his *meinie* were present.

Whatever this was about, it was personal.

The prickle of unease turned to a full-fledged stab.

Lorn, the imperious bastard, didn't invite them to sit, so they stood opposite him. The black hatred that gripped Arthur whenever he came face-to-face with the man who'd murdered his father had not lessened with repetition. He schooled his features into blank repose, but the fire burning in his chest and the urge to stick a dirk in Lorn's black heart were far more difficult to control.

"You wished to see us, my lord," Dugald said, his tone in no way deferential.

Lorn took his time lowering the quill in his hand, and then eased back in his chair to look at them. He drummed his fingertips together on the table. When he replied, it wasn't to Dugald but to Arthur. "I hear you had an eventful journey."

Something in his tone set off warning bells in the back of Arthur's head. He had to fight the urge to look at Anna. What had she told him?

"Aye," Arthur said. "We were fortunate to evade the

first band of brigands, but not the second. We sent them scurrying soon enough."

Lorn gave him a long stare that set every nerve ending on edge. "So I hear. My son has had nothing to say but praise for your fighting prowess. He said he's never seen the like." Dugald turned sharply to Arthur, a frown on his face. "I must admit," Lorn added, "I was surprised to hear him describe it." He smiled, but there was no amusement in his cold, assessing gaze. "I wonder that we've not seen this from you before."

Lorn's gaze flickered to Dugald, gauging his reaction. His brother's frown, unfortunately, had only deepened.

"Sir Alan is most generous with his praise, my lord."

Alan stepped forward, clearly objecting to his father's line of questioning. "Sir Arthur was instrumental in defeating the rebels, Father, and in saving my life. We owe him a debt of gratitude."

"Yes, of course," Lorn said. "I am most grateful. But I wonder," he paused, tapping one finger on the table. "I wonder if you could shed some light on the rest of the attack."

"Of course," Arthur said, not liking where this was going. Lorn was a devious bastard, a man who liked to keep those around him on edge. But was he suspicious? It was hard to tell.

"My daughter believes she identified my former brother-in-law, Lachlan MacRuairi, as one of the scourge, and that he might be one of these secret warriors that we've heard so much about."

"I've crossed paths with the man once or twice, but don't know him well enough to say one way or the other. If Lady Anna has doubts, I'm afraid I can't help."

Arthur was walking a fine line. Too adamant a denial would rouse suspicion, but he wanted to keep the seed of doubt planted in Lorn's mind.

Lorn's face hardened, his hatred of his former brother by

marriage evident. "MacRuairi is a treacherous snake—
a cold-blooded killer who'd sell his mother for a piece of
silver, but there is one thing he doesn't do, and that is give
up. I've never seen him retreat from a battle."

Bàs roimh Gèill. Death before Surrender. Part of the
Highland Guard creed. But it was damned unfortunate
that it had given Lorn something to sink his teeth into.

That thin line Arthur was treading had just become nar-
rower.

He shrugged noncommittally. "Then perhaps it was not
him?"

Lorn's gaze landed back on his daughter. Anna's eyes
darted to him before she answered. "I can't be sure, Father.
It was very dark. I only saw his face clearly for an instant,
and I haven't seen him in years."

Arthur felt his chest tighten. She was trying to protect
him. Had Lorn realized it as well?

Dugald had grown impatient. "Was there something you
needed from me, my lord?"

In other words, why the hell was he here? A question
Arthur was interested in as well.

"I'm getting to that."

Lorn was tapping his fingers again, and Arthur had vi-
sions of taking his war hammer and putting an end to the
annoyance.

"I'm not sure whether you were aware of the purpose
of the journey north to Ross," he said to Dugald. "It was
to renew discussions of a betrothal between my daughter
and Sir Hugh Ross, in the hopes that an alliance between
us would encourage the earl to send troops to aid in the
war against Bruce. Unfortunately, it didn't quite go as
planned."

Dugald shot Arthur a sideways glare. "It didn't?"

"Nay." Lorn's gaze fell back on him. "It seems Sir Hugh
became aware that my daughter's affections lay elsewhere.
Do you have any knowledge of this, Sir Arthur?"

Out of the corner of his eye, Arthur could see Anna pale, her hands clenched tightly in her lap.

What the hell had she told him?

He gritted his teeth together, feeling backed into a corner with little room to maneuver. "Aye."

"I thought you might," Lorn said.

The flash of anger in his gaze told Arthur that he'd probably guessed some of what had happened. He waited tensely, bracing himself for what was to come. The noose drew tighter.

Lorn turned back to Dugald. His brother's reason for being here had become clear. "With all that has happened, I would like to propose a different alliance. One that would solidify the bond between our families and show my gratitude to Sir Arthur for the service he has done my son, as well as see to my daughter's happiness."

Every bone in his body tensed as he waited for what was to come. He wondered if she'd had something to do with this, but Anna's wide eyes showed her surprise when her father said, "I should like to propose a betrothal between Sir Arthur and my daughter."

Dugald choked. "A betrothal?"

Lorn's mouth thinned in a straight line. "I believe that's what I said. We can work out the terms later, but be assured that my daughter's tocher is more than generous. It includes a certain castle that I believe might be of interest to you."

Both Arthur and his brother went completely still. It was Dugald who finally spit out, "Innis Chonnel?"

A devious smile played upon Lorn's mouth. "Aye."

Arthur couldn't believe it. The Campbell stronghold on Loch Awe that had been stolen from his clan years ago, returned for marrying the woman he wanted more than any other. A true devil's bargain.

For a moment he hesitated, more tempted than he

wanted to admit. Switching sides in this war was far too common.

But he couldn't do it. Even if he could get past allying himself with the man who killed his father, too many people were counting on him. Neil, King Robert, MacLeod and the other members of the Highland Guard. Nor could he ignore his conscience. He believed in what they were doing.

The return of the castle to the Campbells—even to a younger son—was enough to convince Dugald. He turned to Arthur. "I have no objection. Arthur . . . ?"

All eyes turned to him, but he was conscious of only two sets: those of Anna, who watched him with her heart in hers, and Lorn, who watched him with his suspicions in his.

Even if he had no intention of going through with it, Arthur knew he had to agree in order to defray any suspicion. This betrothal was a test of his loyalty. It was just as much about Anna's happiness as it was about proving his allegiance.

His conscience warred with his duty, but it was a short battle. He had no choice. The stakes were too high. He couldn't think about how much she was going to hate him when she found out the truth.

"I would be honored to have Lady Anna as my wife."

Perhaps the worst part was that he actually meant it.

Nineteen

❧

Anna had everything she wanted. Then why was she so miserable?

It was a week after her father's surprise betrothal announcement in his solar. Once she'd gotten over the shock, she'd been elated. To marry the man she loved . . . Nothing could have made her happier—except maybe news that Bruce had decided the crown really didn't belong to him and had disappeared in the Western Isles as he'd done before. But that dream had yet to come true.

While she'd been overjoyed, Arthur had looked as if he'd swallowed a fistful of nails.

In the days since, he'd been unfailingly polite. Attentive at meals and the few times their paths crossed during the day. He'd even allowed Squire to follow him around without complaint.

On the surface he was the perfect fiancé. But that was the problem: it was all on the surface. His formality—his increasing distance—dimmed the happiness inside her to a flicker. Every "Did you have a pleasant day today, Lady Anna?" or "Would you like another cup of wine, Lady Anna?" put a tiny fissure in her heart.

She didn't understand. He cared about her—he'd admitted as much—so why couldn't he see how perfect this could be?

But as the days went on, it became harder to convince herself that he wanted this. He was pulling farther and farther away from her. Something was troubling him. Though the week had brought them closer to the end of the truce— the Ides of August was fast approaching—the increased anxiety could be felt everywhere, and she didn't think it was the looming battle.

She wished he would confide in her, but he'd rebuffed her attempts to speak with him. Not that there had been many opportunities. Other than their brief exchanges at meals, the only time he'd sought out her company was a few days ago, when he'd insisted on accompanying her to Ardchattan Priory. With no messages waiting for her, she didn't have to hide anything from him.

But perhaps her father wouldn't have minded him knowing about her role in passing messages. Their betrothal seemed to have eliminated any lingering suspicions her father had of the Campbells. As war moved closer and preparations for battle intensified, the Campbells had been spending more time with her father and brother, which she hoped was a sign of the thawing of any lingering coolness from the old feud.

She sighed, allowing her gaze to wander around the room as her maidservant finished arranging her hair. It was the sixth day of August. One day closer to the expiration of the truce.

Glancing out the window of her tower chamber, she saw a *birlinn* sail into the bay, the main anchorage for the castle. It was an ordinary occurrence, and one that would not have caught her attention but for the speed at which it traveled. The sleek wooden ship had barely pulled onto the sand bank when men started jumping out and racing toward the castle gate.

Her heart jumped, knowing something was happening.

Not bothering with a veil, she raced down the tower stairs and entered the *barmkin* at the same time her father was greeting the troop of men from the *birlinn*.

MacNabs.

"What news have you?" her father asked.

The MacNab captain's face was grim. "It's King Hood, my lord. He's on the move."

She gasped, fear turning her blood to ice. It was here. The day she'd dreaded yet anticipated at the same time. The battle that could be an end to the war.

The castle was in an uproar. The warriors in the crowd seemed to bristle with excitement, eager for the chance to destroy their enemies. The few women who were about, however, had far different reactions—concern and, like Anna, fear.

Instinctively, her gaze sought out Arthur's. The news had affected him as well. He was watching her with a burning intensity that she hadn't seen since the attack. Their eyes held for a moment before he turned back to the MacNabs.

Her father ushered the newcomers into the Great Hall. Anna followed, anxious to find out all that she could.

Unfortunately, the MacNabs had little more information. One of their scouts had alerted them that Bruce had left the Earl of Garioch's castle in Inverurie with a force of at least three thousand—three thousand, to her father's eight hundred!—and started to march west. Whether he intended to head for Lorn or Ross first, however, they did not know.

Bruce was wasting no time. He would be ready to attack right when the truce expired. Dear God, the barbarians could be knocking at their gate by the next week.

Her sisters and mother had heard the commotion and hurried down to the Hall. Finding Anna at the back of the crowd, they asked her what was happening. She quickly filled them in, seeing her fear mirrored in their anxious faces. It was a day they all knew was coming, but now the bell had begun to toll.

"So soon?" her mother said fretfully. "But he's only just recovered."

"He'll be fine, Mother," she said, trying to convince them both. But it wasn't just her father Anna was worried about. What if . . .

Nay. She couldn't think about it. Arthur would come back. They would all come back.

But the uncertainty. The capriciousness of war was exactly what she'd sought to avoid. Why did she have to fall in love with a knight?

The men conversed for a while longer. She'd lost sight of Arthur and his brothers when they'd moved to the Hall, but when the talk turned to a scouting mission she saw him ease forward toward the dais, where her father was seated at a trestle table with some of his men and the MacNab captain.

Her heart froze, guessing what he was about to do. She wanted to call him back, to tell him not to do it, but she knew she could not. It was what he did.

"I'll go, my lord," Arthur said.

Her father looked at him and nodded, obviously pleased that he'd volunteered. Alan offered to go as well, but her father refused, saying he needed him at the castle. Eventually, it was decided that her brother Ewen would lead the small scouting party, which also included Arthur's brothers.

The men wasted no time. Less than an hour later, the team had gathered in the *barmkin* to leave. Anna stood silently beside her mother, feeling as if she were spinning in a whirlpool with nothing to hold on to.

She watched Arthur ready to leave with her heart in her throat. He finished securing his belongings to his horse, took the reins in his hand, and positioned himself as if preparing to mount.

Her heart lurched. Did he mean to ride out without saying goodbye?

If he did, he changed his mind. After handing the reins to one of the stable lads, he turned and strode toward her.

His jaw was squared as hard as his shoulders, as if he expected to confront something unpleasant.

Me, she realized, feeling a sharp stab in her chest.

"Lady Anna," he said with a curt bow.

Her mother and sisters had not so subtly turned their backs, shielding them somewhat from the rest of the crowd to afford them some semblance of privacy. But she was still deeply conscious that they were not alone.

"You must go?" She hated herself for asking but couldn't help it. She knew it was his job, but she didn't want him to leave. Was this how it would always be?

"Aye."

There was a long pause. It sounded so final. "How long will you be gone?"

Something flickered in his eyes, but it was gone before she could put a name to it.

"It depends on how fast the army is marching. A few days, maybe more."

She stared at his handsome face, trying to memorize the hard lines of his features, the scars, the strange golden amber of his eyes.

"You will be careful?" It was a silly thing to say, but she had to say it all the same.

A smile hovered at the corner of his mouth. "Aye."

He held her gaze for a moment longer, as if he, too, were trying to put it to memory. There was a bleakness to his expression that she'd never seen before.

A shiver of trepidation blew across the back of her neck. *It's just the war,* she told herself. *He's focused on the battle ahead.*

He took her hand and raised it to his mouth, the warm

imprint of his lips radiating over her skin. "Goodbye, Lady Anna."

Something in his tone made her heart clench. He turned to go, and she wanted desperately to call him back.

The type of man who was always looking at the door . . .

Nay. She told herself she was being silly. He wasn't leaving her. It was only for a few days.

But why did it seem like goodbye?

Then, as if he couldn't stop himself, he spun back around, cupped her chin in his hand, and lowered his mouth to hers.

His lips brushed over hers in a soft, tender kiss that made her heart lurch. It tasted of longing. Of pain. And of regret. But most of all it tasted of goodbye. She wanted to hold on, to make it last, but she barely had time to gasp before it was over.

He dropped his hand, held her gaze for one soul-piercing moment, and left. He didn't look back. Not once.

Anna stared after him—stunned—not sure what had just happened.

She pressed her fingers to her lips, wanting to hold on to the heat and his taste for as long as she could. But before the last man had ridden through the gate, it was gone.

Arthur had been looking for a way out, and he'd found it. The scouting trip east gave him a chance to do something that months ago would have seemed unthinkable: back out of his mission.

He had to *do* something. He couldn't stand by and let the situation get worse. The days following their betrothal had been impossible. The pretense was killing him. Anna was so damned happy. So pleased to be marrying the man who was going to betray her. Each tentative smile, each glance seeking reassurance he could not give, was like a drop of acid eating at his conscience.

He couldn't do this to her. Even if it meant sacrificing his mission. The irony was that he couldn't have chosen a more effective means of infiltrating the MacDougalls than becoming engaged to the lord's daughter. The betrothal, coupled with the fact that he'd saved Alan's life, had given him access to the very center of power: the lord's council.

He wasn't sacrificing his mission, he told himself. He'd done enough already in identifying the source of the messages as the women, passing intelligence of the MacDougalls' numbers and readiness, and providing a map of the terrain, as well as preventing an alliance with Ross—even if that hadn't happened exactly has he'd wanted it to.

They were on the eve of battle. King Robert would understand.

It was the middle of the night, three days after his disastrous parting with Anna. He hadn't expected saying goodbye to be so hard. But riding away from her, knowing he might never see her again, had taken every ounce of his resolve. He shouldn't have kissed her. But looking into her eyes, seeing her fear and worry for him, had been more than he could take. He'd needed that feeling of utter connection one more time, knowing that he'd never have it again.

He glanced over his shoulder, assuring himself he hadn't been followed, before tethering his horse to a tree. He was about a mile away from where Bruce's army had camped for the night. He would travel the rest of the way on foot. The sentries were liable to shoot at anything approaching camp at this time of night without stopping to ask questions, and the horse could give him away.

His senses sharpened as he drew closer to the king's camp, anticipating the first sign of the perimeter guard. He was taking a chance, coming unannounced like this, but he had no choice. There hadn't been time to arrange to meet or get a message to the Guard, and the MacDougall scouting party was readying to return to Dunstaffnage castle with their report tomorrow. He'd volunteered for night patrol, knowing this would be his only chance.

He knew Chief would have one of the members of the Highland Guard on post as he did every night. Arthur would attempt to make contact with one of his fellow guardsmen first.

Suddenly, the back of his neck prickled. He stopped, sensing the strange shift in the air that occurred when someone else was near. He waited, blending into the darkness of the forest, knowing that he would hear whoever was approaching first.

But after a few minutes, he knew something was wrong. He hadn't heard anything. Either the man hadn't moved or Arthur's skills were failing him.

Again.

But when a dark figure emerged from behind a tree about twenty feet away, he knew there was a third answer: The man's skill at stealth matched Arthur's skill at hearing.

Damn. This wasn't what he needed. He let out the hoot that should identify him as a friend. Although he suspected that the man who approached might disagree.

Apparently, Lachlan MacRuairi was no longer harassing Ross in the north, and he had picked this night for guard duty.

MacRuairi stilled, readying his bow in Arthur's direction, despite the secret call. "Who's there?"

"Ranger," Arthur replied, flipping back the steel visor from his helm and stepping out from behind the tree that had shielded him.

Even in the darkness he could see MacRuairi's eyes narrow, the unnatural glow slitted. He shifted his arm to the left, aiming the point of the arrow right between Arthur's eyes. MacRuairi had an uncanny ability to see in the dark—a hell of a thing to remember now.

"Are you going to use that?" Arthur said.

"I haven't decided. One death doesn't seem like much

when compared to nine. I could claim I thought it was a traitor—which wouldn't be that far off."

Arthur swallowed the crude retort that sprang to his tongue. Knowing he deserved the other man's scorn didn't make it any easier to hear. He ignored the arrow pointed at him and strode forward. "Do you think I don't regret what happened?"

"Do you? I sure as hell couldn't tell. You looked like you were having too much fun fighting alongside Alan MacDougall, not to mention saving his bloody life."

They were separated by only a few feet, but MacRuairi wouldn't have missed at a hundred. "I will answer to the king, Viper, not to you. I need to speak with him."

"He's abed."

Arthur gritted his teeth, clenching his fists at his side. It wouldn't help anything to come to blows with MacRuairi, but he didn't have time for his shite. "Then you'll have to wake him. And my brother as well."

Finally, MacRuairi lowered his bow. "You sure as hell better have something good to report." He gave him a hard stare. "And it better have been worth it."

Had it been? Arthur hadn't been thinking in terms of worth at the time. He hadn't had time to make that kind of analysis; he'd been too busy defending himself and protecting Anna.

Less than fifteen minutes later, he was ushered into the king's tent. If Bruce had been asleep, his appearance gave no indication that he'd just wakened. His dark hair had been combed, his eyes were as clear and sharp as ever, and he was dressed in a richly embroidered dark surcoat and chausses.

He was seated on a trunk. The lack of furniture attested to the lightness and speed with which the army was moving. King Edward would never have dreamed of leaving on campaign without carts full of his household goods and plate. But living as an outlaw for over a year with his headquarters in the heather, Robert the Bruce had grown accustomed to far less.

Neil, looking slightly more disheveled, stood to his left and Tor MacLeod, leader of the Highland Guard, to his right. Like the king's, MacLeod's expression was grim.

The question in his brother's gaze cut like a knife. Surely Neil couldn't be questioning his loyalty.

"What the hell happened out there, Ranger?" the king asked.

As succinctly as possible, Arthur gave his account of the events leading up to his unexpected trip north, the planned betrothal between Lorn's daughter and Sir Hugh Ross, Lorn's hope to join forces, and Arthur's intention to prevent the alliance from happening.

"You were successful?" Bruce asked.

Arthur kept his expression neutral. "Aye, your grace."

The king nodded, pleased. If any of the men wondered how this had been accomplished they did not ask.

Arthur went on to explain how he'd led the patrol away from the MacDougall party on the way north but had been forced to defend himself to protect his cover.

"That was you?" MacLeod said. "Our men at Urquhart Castle were furious that a solitary rider managed to elude them."

"Not completely. I wish I had. But the men had me pinned near a cliff. I couldn't tell them who I was."

None of the men said anything. Like him, they knew such situations were necessary to preserve his cover, but none of them liked it.

He continued, explaining that he'd been surprised by MacRuairi and his men on the way back to Dunstaffnage.

Neil drew in his brows. "You didn't hear them?"

Arthur shook his head, offering no further explanation. He explained how at first he'd simply reacted, then, when he'd realized who the attackers were, he'd retreated to defensive maneuvering. When it came to the point where he'd saved Alan MacDougall's life, he offered no excuse other than the truth. He'd only meant to block the blow; killing the man had been an accident.

Neil asked the question no doubt all of them were thinking. "But why save him at all? Protecting Lorn's heir is not part of your mission. Killing him would almost be as good as killing Lorn himself."

Arthur met his brother's gaze, not shirking from the truth. "I wasn't trying to protect him."

"It's the lass," MacLeod said, putting it together. "You care for her."

Arthur turned to his captain, not denying it. "Aye."

"Lorn's daughter!" Neil exclaimed, not holding back his outrage. "Jesu, brother, what could you be thinking?"

Arthur didn't have an answer. There wasn't one.

"What are you saying, Ranger?" the king said, his dark eyes hard as ebony. "Has a lass made you forget what side you are on?"

"My loyalty is to you, sire," he said stiffly, but the king's barb stung.

Neil stared at him. "Have you changed your mind about Lorn? Have you forgotten what he did to our father?"

Arthur's mouth thinned in a flat line. "Of course not. But my wish to see John of Lorn destroyed does not extend to his daughter. That's why I'm here. I need to leave Dunstaffnage."

The room was dead silent. He could feel his brother's stare burning into him, but he didn't dare look in his direction. He'd let him down. The man who'd been like a father to him. He didn't want to see the disappointment on his face.

"Have you been compromised?" the king asked. "Are you in danger of discovery?"

He shook his head. "The lass knows I'm hiding something, but I do not think she suspects."

"Then the reason you wish to leave your mission before it is completed is because of the lass?"

"It's gotten complicated." Knowing it sounded insufficient, even to himself, he explained how Lorn had questioned him about the attack, how he'd feared Lorn might be suspicious, and how he'd been forced into a betrothal.

"But that's fantastic news," the king said, looking happy for the first time since he'd entered the tent. "You've gotten closer to Lorn than I ever dreamed possible. I'm sorry the lass is involved, but no harm will truly come to her. A young girl's heart is quick to mend."

Admittedly, the king, who was known for his way with the lasses, had far more experience than he did, but in this case Arthur didn't think so. Anna loved too fiercely. Too blindly.

"I can't let you leave," the king finished. "Not yet. Not with battle so near. I need you inside to see what they intend. The information you've been providing is too valuable. Victory is too close to let it be snatched away at the last minute. John of Lorn is a black-hearted devil, but I do not underestimate his strategy in warfare, or his ability to surprise."

Arthur knew the king would not be dissuaded. Robert Bruce burned for retribution. Lorn had defeated him before; he wouldn't let anything stand in his way this time. One woman's heart was a small price to pay.

"We will attack the castle at dawn on the sixteenth," MacLeod said, seeming to sense his frustration. "It will only be a few more days."

But he didn't know Anna MacDougall. Arthur would rather face the first King Edward's war-wolf siege engine than try to resist Anna for "a few more days."

Twenty

"They're back!"

Mary's excited voice sent Anna rushing to their bower window. Frantically, she searched the mail-clad forms streaming through the castle gate. When she finally saw the familiar broad shoulders, she exhaled the breath it seemed she'd been holding for four days.

He'd come back. He hadn't left her. She felt foolish even thinking it of him. But she didn't want to admit to herself how worried she'd been.

Anna tossed down her embroidery and ran out of the room on the heels of her sister, who seemed just as excited as she was by the scouting party's return. Her brow furrowed. Did her sister care for Arthur's brother more than she let on?

They arrived in the Hall just as the men were being ushered into her father's solar to give their report. The evening meal had finished some time ago, but she and Mary ordered food and drink to be prepared for the scouting party while they waited. A wait that seemed interminable. Finally the men emerged from her father's solar and came into the Hall. First her brothers, then Sir Dugald, and then, at last, Arthur.

He was caked with dirt and dust, his face weathered by

the sun, his jaw bearing four days of a beard, and he smelled of horse and sun, but he'd never looked more wonderful to her. If a hall full of clansmen weren't surrounding them, she would have catapulted herself into his arms.

They stood off to the side for a moment, while the servants readied the tables. This time he couldn't avoid her.

"You are well?" she asked, not trusting her eyes.

His gaze softened, sensing her concern. "Aye, lass, I am well. In need of a good long dunking, but otherwise perfectly hale."

"I'm glad to hear that." She bit her lip, gazing up at him hesitantly. "I-I missed you."

His face shuttered, the pulse below his jaw ticking. "Anna . . ."

She swallowed hard, her throat suddenly tight. "Did you think of me at all?"

"I had much on my mind." But seeing her expression, he sighed. "Aye, lass, I thought of you."

The admission might have made her happy had it not been so reluctantly given.

The trestle tables had been set out, and the servants had started to bring out the platters of food. The rest of the men began to filter over to the benches. From their place near the door of her father's solar, he looked over her shoulder as if he were anxious to join them.

She couldn't fool herself any longer. "You don't want this betrothal." The truth stung. She stared at him, the burning in her chest excruciating. "Is there . . ." She could barely get the words out. He'd spoken of a bride as a reward. "Is there someone else you were hoping to marry?"

He gave her a harsh look. "What are you talking about? I told you there was no one else."

"Then it's just me you don't want."

His face looked pained. "Anna . . ." He cleared his throat. "This isn't the time."

Some of her frustration gave way, despite the people

around them. "It's never the time. You are either gone, locked away in meetings, or busy practicing. When, pray tell, *is* the time?"

Clearly frustrated, he raked his helm-crimped hair back with his hand. It fell in soft waves past his ear, and she almost reached out to tuck it behind his ear before she stopped herself.

"I don't know, but right now all I want to do is get something to eat, wash the filth from me, and sleep for more than a few hours."

He had to be exhausted. She felt a prickle of guilt but pushed it aside. She wouldn't let him keep putting her off. "Then tomorrow. We will talk tomorrow." She gave him a meaningful look. "In private."

He actually looked alarmed. She'd not thought him capable, but apparently being alone with her did what dozens of armed men could not. She didn't know whether to laugh or cry.

"I can't. I'm supposed to ride out—"

"When you get back." He seemed poised to find another excuse, but she cut him off. "I know you are busy with the preparations for war, but do I not warrant a few minutes of your time?"

He held her gaze for a long time. "Aye, lass, you do."

"Good. Then get some food." She waved him toward one of the tables. "Your brothers are waiting for you."

He gave her a short nod and went to join his family. She turned to find her sister Mary standing closer to her than she'd realized. She was watching Anna with a pitying look on her face.

"It's nothing," Anna said, embarrassed by what her sister might have heard. "He's tired, that's all."

Mary took her hand and gave it a squeeze. "Have care, Annie-love. Some men don't want to be loved."

She frowned. "That's not true, Mary. Everyone wants to be loved."

A wistful smile turned her sister's perfect mouth. "You love too much, little sister. But some people don't want that kind of closeness. Some people are better off alone."

Anna didn't want to believe it. But her sister's words haunted her throughout the next day as she waited for her opportunity to speak with him.

He rode out early in the morning, returned in time for the midday meal, and afterward joined his brothers and the rest of the men for their afternoon training in the yard. With battle drawing near, training had intensified. Taking advantage of the long daylight hours of midsummer, the warriors didn't finish until past eight o'clock. The evening meal was brief, as were the evening prayers.

She was tempted to follow him when she saw him heading for the loch, but her mother pulled her aside to help her sort out a discrepancy in the household accounts, and by the time she'd finished, he'd already returned and was locked away in a meeting with the high-ranking knights and warriors of her father's *meinie* in what had become the nightly war council.

She waited for him in a small mural chamber built into the wall of the stairwell, knowing he would have to walk by on his way to the barracks. It was usually a place she sat to read a book, but hidden from view by a velvet hanging, it was slightly more private than waiting in the Hall crowded with sleeping clansmen. She'd brought a candle to read by, but as the night drew on, her eyes grew tired, and she put it aside.

When the men finally started to emerge from her father's solar, it must have been close to midnight. Arthur was one of the last to leave, but eventually she saw him coming down the corridor with his brothers. She pushed back the curtain as he drew near and trod down the few steps to wait for him.

His brother said something, and Arthur glanced over and saw her, his expression more resolved than surprised.

He walked toward her as his brothers pushed open the door to the *barmkin*.

"You shouldn't have waited up," he said.

She frowned. "Did you forget that we'd arranged to meet?"

"Nay." He sighed. "I did not forget."

More men were starting down the corridor. "Come," she said, ducking into a small room used to store the lord's wine. They wouldn't be disturbed in there.

The rich, fruity aroma hit her as soon as she opened the door, intensifying when she closed it behind them. After placing her candle on one of the barrels, she turned around to face him. The stone storeroom was small, and—she realized with a flush—intimate. Very intimate.

He stood stone still by the doorway, his expression hard and tight in the flickering candlelight. She glanced down to his side, surprised to see his fists clenched.

"This isn't a good idea," he said tightly.

"Why not?"

He gave her a hard look. "Do you remember what happened last time we were alone in a small room?"

She flushed; being this close to him she remembered quite well. His warmth surrounded her, and her skin tingled with awareness of the intimacies they'd shared.

But that wasn't why she'd brought him here. "This will only take a few minutes. I need to know . . ." She looked up at him, searching his taut, handsome face. "I need you to tell me if you want this betrothal."

Her frankness no longer surprised him. "Anna," he hedged. "It's complicated."

"So you've said before. What are you hiding, Arthur? What is it that you won't tell me?"

"There are things—" He stopped and gave her a harsh look. "I am not the man you think I am."

"I know exactly the type of man you are."

"You don't know everything."

She heard the warning. "Then tell me." When he didn't respond, she said, "I know what's important. And I know that I love you."

Her words seemed to pain him. He reached down to cradle her cheek in his hand. The sadness in his expression clutched at her heart. "You might think that now, but soon you will change your mind."

His patronizing tone and cryptic warnings infuriated her. "I won't," she said fiercely, clenching her fists against the urge to shout—or burst into tears. She took a deep, calming breath and said, "It's really very simple, Arthur. Do you want to marry me or not?"

"What I want isn't the issue. I'm thinking of *you*, Anna. You might not believe me right now, but trust me when I tell you I'm trying to do the right thing. I don't want to hurt you. A lot can change over the next few days. The war will change everything."

He was right. It seemed as if all her dreams were hanging by a thread. War was upon them and everything she'd known could change in the blink of an eye. The MacDougalls' power in the Highlands was balanced on a sword's edge. But there was one thing she could hold on to. "It won't change my feelings for you. It's yours that are in question." She paused. "You haven't answered my question."

He cursed and took a few steps away from the door, trying to pace but unable to find the room. His head nearly touched the ceiling. He looked like a lion stalking in a too-small cage. He was drawn up tight, tension radiating from every inch of his powerfully built form. Finally he jerked around and grabbed her by the arm, his expression furious. "Yes, damn it. Yes, I want to marry you."

The dark cloud that had descended over her lifted. It wasn't the most romantic declaration she'd ever heard, but it was enough. Warmth spread through her, and she smiled. "Then that is all that matters."

She leaned closer to him, instinctively seeking the connection of his body pressed to hers. He flinched at the contact, but this time she did not mistake the reason. He wanted her. Badly. Though he was struggling to resist. She could feel the tension reverberating off him like a drum.

His eyes fell to her mouth, darkening with desire. But still he tried to fight against it. "What if I don't come back, Anna? What then?"

Her blood stopped cold. Was that what this was about? Was he trying to prepare her for the possibility that he could die on the battlefield?

She couldn't bear to think of it, but she knew it was a possibility. He could die. She clutched him closer to her, gripping the hard muscles of his upper arms in her hands as if she would never let go.

God couldn't be cruel enough to take him from her. Her heart squeezed. But if he did . . .

She knew what she wanted. She couldn't control what happened tomorrow, but she could control right now.

Perhaps she had brought him here for a reason.

Arthur knew this was a bad idea, but as he'd already proved more times than he cared to think about, he was a damned fool when it came to Anna MacDougall.

A sheen of perspiration gathered on his brow as his blood pounded hot through his veins. The heavy scent of the wine, the musky earthiness of the small room, and the faint floral fragrance of her skin wrapped around him, intoxicated his senses with desire.

She was too close. His need too raw. His mind was half-crazed with images of what he wanted to do to her.

They were alone, damn it. This was too dangerous.

But if he'd hoped to discourage her with talk of an uncertain future, he'd miscalculated.

"I don't want to think about war and tomorrow. I want

to think about right now. If today was the last day we had together, what would you want?"

You. He felt the pull. He wanted what she offered more than anything in the world.

Her words. Her certainty. She made him dream. He wanted to believe a future could be possible. Just for a moment, he wanted to believe she could be his.

His heart pounded like a drum as she lifted up on her toes and pressed her mouth to his.

He groaned, fighting the urge to sink into her. He knew if he did, he wouldn't stop.

Her mouth was so warm and silky soft. So sweet. She tasted like honey and smelled . . .

God, she smelled like a fresh summer garden steaming in the sun.

She slid her mouth to his jaw, his neck. His body started to shake. He couldn't hold back much longer. He stood powerless to resist. Praying for her torture to stop.

Instead it grew worse. She nudged her hips to his, rubbing against the neediest part of him. The part of him that was hard, throbbing, and incapable of thought.

"We came so close before," she whispered against his neck, the warmth of his breath sending shivers over his burning skin. "I want to know the rest."

A bead of sweat slid down his temple. The cool room was fast growing warm and sultry.

She stretched against him, wrapping her arms around his neck. Her eyes found his. "Show me, Arthur."

The bold request snapped the last thread of his reserve. With a growl, he pushed her up against the door, pinning her hands back on either side of her head, and kissed her. Nay, devoured her. He feasted on her mouth with his lips and tongue, kissing her as if he'd never be able to get enough.

She met his fervor with her own, sliding her tongue against his, mimicking his erotic movements with her own.

The roaring in his head got louder.

His body got harder.

It wasn't enough. He leaned into her, fitting his body to hers, and rocked. Gently, and then more insistently as she started to writhe and whimper in innocent frustration.

He wanted to lift up her skirts and sink into her. Feel her shatter around him as he drove into her hard and deep. Over and over. Claiming her as his.

But she was so responsive—so pure in her pleasure— a swell of tenderness rose up inside him, and he pulled away.

She blinked up at him, her eyes swimming with passion, her lips softly parted and swollen from his kiss. "Please, don't—"

"Shhh." He stopped her protest with a soft kiss. "I'm not stopping." It was too late for that. He was a man, not a bloody saint. He wanted her too badly, and she'd pushed him too far. Recriminations would come later. Right now, she was his.

But he wouldn't take her like a rutting beast against a door.

He unfastened the Campbell brooch that he wore to secure his plaid and spread it out on the stone floor. After sitting, he held out his hand.

She didn't hesitate, but slid her hand into his with a smile that tore at his heart and allowed him to lower her down beside him. There was just enough room to stretch out between the barrels of wine.

He slid his hand in her hair and drew her face to his, kissing her with all the passion and emotion teeming inside him. Kissing her as if she meant everything to him.

Anna gave herself over to the sweet possessiveness of his kiss. She curled against him, feeling warm, protected, and sheltered from the events taking place outside the magical bower of his embrace. She felt . . .

Peace. In his arms she felt the sense of peace and contentment that had always eluded her.

He slid his hand through her hair, cradling the back of her head in his big, callused palm. His thumb caressed soft little circles at the back of her neck.

She could kiss him like this forever. Lying beside him, molded together, feeling the hard strength of his body pressed against her. His warmth a protective cocoon around them. The long, languid strokes of his tongue making her hot and boneless. It was perfect.

But when the long, languid strokes grew more demanding, when his kiss became harder and deeper, when his hold around her tightened and she became aware of the hard column of steel wedged against her stomach, kissing wasn't enough.

She felt that strange sensation building inside her again. The awakening. The stirring. The restless energy that pulsed between her legs, making her feel anxious and desperate for pressure.

But this time she knew what would happen. She remembered his hand between her legs. His fingers inside her. The sharp spasms of release. She remembered the plump round head of his manhood pressing intimately inside her.

She moaned, circling her hips against him, wanting the relief that only friction could bring. Her body was on fire, her nipples tight and achy as they raked his chest.

Her hands roamed over the broad span of his shoulders, the hard muscles of his arms and back, trying to draw him closer. Though beneath his plaid he wore only a tunic, chausses, and braies, the thin layers of wool and linen had become a maddening barrier. She wanted to touch him. She wanted to feel the heat of his skin pulsing under her fingertips.

He must have sensed her frustration. Wrenching his mouth away, he unbuckled his belt and jerked the tunic over his head, tossing it to the side.

His chest was as incredible as she remembered. Broad shoulders, heavily muscled arms, flat stomach bisected by rigid bands of steel, the smooth plane of tanned skin marked by various-sized scars. The worst was the star-shaped scar on his upper arm near his shoulder—the type of mark left by an arrow. And she could see the marking on his arm clearer now: the Lion Rampant, the symbol of Scotland's kingship.

She couldn't tear her eyes away. Lord, he was beautiful.

"Keep looking at me like that, lass, and this won't last that long."

The huskiness of his voice sent a shiver of desire running down her spine. She blushed. "I like looking at you." His eyes darkened. "You're magnificent."

Unable to wait a moment longer, she flattened her palms over his chest, gasping at the sharp sizzle of contact.

He made a deep, guttural sound and drew her into his arms again. This time there was no holding back. She could taste his desire. Feel his need in the erotic thrusts of his tongue.

It was all happening fast now, but each moment burned sharply in her mind. She wanted to remember everything about this. The way he tasted. The way his mouth felt on hers. The rough scrape of his beard on her chin. The heat of his skin. The power of his muscles flexing under her palms. The hard pounding of his heart against hers. She wanted to remember every sensation. Every smell. Every touch.

She was so hot and achy, her skin fevered and flushed. Vaguely she was aware of his hands loosening the ties of her sleeveless surcoat and easing it past her shoulders. Then he was cupping her breasts, kneading them through the wool of her cotte and linen of her chemise as his mouth traveled down her throat. His thumb moved over the hard nub of her nipple. Circling. Caressing. Pinching gently between his fingertips.

Her hands skimmed wildly over his back, clutching his shoulders, her fingers digging into his skin with every teasing stroke. She moaned, wanting to strip away the fabric, to feel his hands—his mouth—on her skin.

And then they were. First her cotte, then her chemise, were eased up her legs, past her waist, and then over her head.

She might not have noticed if he hadn't stopped to look at her. He lifted his head from her throat and slid his gaze over her nakedness.

She blushed and tried to cover herself, but he wouldn't let her.

He grabbed her wrists and shook his head. "Don't," he said roughly, something thick and raw in his voice. "You're beautiful." He lay on his side and trailed his finger down her arm as if she were so delicate she might break from his touch. His eyes caressed her breasts, making her nipples tighten even more. He slid a finger over the tip, then around the heavy curve. "Jesu," he breathed raggedly. "Your breasts are unreal." He groaned and eased down to cup them in his hands, lifting them to his mouth.

He kissed one throbbing tip, then the other, leaving her trembling with need. When he finally closed his lips over her and sucked one nipple deep in his mouth, she cried out.

Arthur had never seen anything more beautiful. He knew he should slow down to take in every inch of creamy, baby-soft skin, but one glance had been enough to nearly send him over the edge.

Slim and delicately formed from the top of her head to the tiny arches on her feet, she looked like an angel. He might have thought he'd died and gone to heaven, if it weren't for her breasts. Her breasts were pure sin. A male fantasy come to life. A little too big, round and high with youthful pertness, the soft, creamy flesh was tipped by berry-pink nipples that made his mouth water. And they tasted . . .

He groaned and drew her in his mouth again, circling the warm, taut peak with his tongue. They tasted of sweet carnal desires and dark honey pleasures.

He wanted to go slow, to draw out every moment of pleasure, but their need was too hot. Too desperate. And too long denied.

He eased his hand between her legs, testing her with his fingers.

He was hard as a spike, but feeling her dampness—knowing she was already wet for him—made him swell even harder. He sucked her breasts and stroked her with his fingers until her hips lifted against his hand and her breath started to hitch erratically.

When he knew she was close, he quickly rid himself of his chausses and braies and moved over her, positioning himself between her legs.

Their eyes met.

He wished he could say he hesitated, but he didn't. All he could think about was that he needed to make her his. That he had to hold on to her. That in her eyes he'd seen the acceptance and love he'd never thought would be for him. Love that God knew he didn't deserve but wanted more than anything in the world.

"Please," she whimpered.

It was all the invitation he needed.

Gritting his teeth against the urge to thrust hard and deep, he lifted one of her legs around his waist and started to ease inside. Although "ease" was probably the wrong word. She was tight, and he was big—very big.

Sweat gathered on his brow.

Tight. God, so incredibly tight.

He clenched against the hard pull in his groin. His bollocks tightened as the pressure built at the base of his spine.

Her body fought against the invasion, but he wouldn't be denied. He pushed a little deeper.

She flinched and made a sharp sound of distress.

Blood pounded through his veins. He felt as if he were going to explode, but he held back, giving her a moment to adjust before burying himself deep inside.

Jesus. Don't push . . .

"I-I'm n-not sure this is going to work," she said anxiously. "M-maybe when you're a bit smaller?"

A chuckle rumbled from his chest through the pain. He would explain some of the intricacies of the matter later. "Trust me, love. We will fit perfectly." But admittedly he'd never been with a maid before. "You might feel some pain for a moment." He looked into her eyes. "All right?"

She nodded, but looked a little less certain than before.

He held her gaze the entire time, giving her silent encouragement, as he sank a little deeper. Inch by excruciating inch.

The sensation of her body wrapped tightly around his cock was nearly too much. He had to fight against the urge to thrust, knowing how good it would feel. The tight, wet heat gripping him. Milking him. Every muscle in his body was rigid with tension as he tried to hold back, as he tried to go slow. It felt so good.

But he would make it perfect for her, damn it.

Almost . . .

There. The point of no return. Looking deep into her eyes, he felt his chest contract and gave the final push.

She gasped, and her eyes widened with pain, but she didn't cry out. The stoic look on her face gave him the perverse urge to smile. "It will get better, my love, I promise. Try to relax."

She shot him a look as if he were crazy. "I don't think that's possible."

But then he kissed her and proved that she was wrong.

Anna felt a sharp pinch as he entered her and wanted to cry out in pain. But she could see him struggling and bit it back, knowing how badly he was trying not to hurt her. It wasn't his fault God had made him so . . . oversized. It must make things terribly uncomfortable—

Wait. He was distracting her with his kiss, but she thought she'd felt . . .

There it was again. A twinge. A twinge that felt nice. *Very* nice. In fact, it felt amazing. Her body had softened around him and the pain had subsided. Now she could feel him. Hot and hard, filling her in a way that she'd never imagined.

And then he started to move. Slowly at first. Sinking in and out in long, smooth strokes.

She gasped as each thrust reverberated through her body. It felt as though he were claiming her. Possessing her in the most primitive way possible.

It felt incredible. She had to move with him, lifting her hips to meet his thrusts, taking him deeper. Harder. Then faster.

She clutched his shoulders, drawing him closer. Wanting to feel his weight on top of her. Their bodies seemed fused together. Skin to skin. It was so hot. Her body so achingly heavy.

Passion gripped her in its shimmery hold. Sensations fired inside her. Building. Coiling. Concentrating in that most feminine part of her. He felt it, too. He was like steel under her fingertips, his muscles tense and flared, ready to explode.

But it was the look in his eyes that sent her over the edge. Intense. Penetrating. Dark with not just desire but also with emotion. Reflected in those golden-amber depths, she saw the love that burned in her own heart.

He loved her. He might not realize it yet, but she did.

He held her to him, not letting her turn away as he thrust into her again, burying himself as deep as he could go, and held her there.

Something powerful and magical passed between them. A connection unlike anything she'd ever imagined.

Her breath caught high in her chest as sensation took hold. For one moment everything seemed to stop. Her body held at the very peak of ecstasy, balanced on the heavenly precipice.

She let out a sharp cry as the first spasm of release sent her careening over, shattering into mindless oblivion.

"That's it, love, come for me." He started to move again, pounding into her with fierce abandon. "Oh God. You feel so good. I can't . . ."

With a deep groan of satisfaction that seemed ripped from his soul, he drove into her one last time. His body stiffened, then shuddered as his release caught the tiding wave of her own. His face was fierce and beautiful, primitive in its passion.

When the last sensation had flickered to an end, he collapsed on top of her, their bodies still joined. All she could hear was the heavy sound of their breathing and the fierce pounding of their hearts.

She wished she could stay like this forever, but too soon he rolled off her, breaking the connection.

Cool air swept over her flushed, damp skin, making it prickle with gooseflesh. She was conscious of her nakedness but too spent to move. Her limbs were like jelly. But she had no cause for embarrassment; Arthur wasn't looking at her.

He stared up at the ceiling, still breathing unevenly but ominously quiet.

Shouldn't he be saying something?

She bit her lip, wondering what he was thinking. It had seemed wonderful to her, but what if—she felt a pang—she'd disappointed him?

At last he turned his head to the side to look at her. Lifting his hand to her face, he gently swept the hair back from her face. Seeing her uncertainty, he smiled—a lopsided, boyish smile that wrapped right around her heart and would never let go. She knew she would never forget how he looked at this moment.

"I'm sorry, I don't know what to say. I've never . . . I've never felt anything like that."

She beamed back at him, unable to hide her joy. "Really? I didn't have anything to compare it with, but I thought it was wonderful."

"Aye, it was." He bent down and gave her a tender kiss. But when he lifted his head to look at her again, his gaze had clouded. "I'll never regret what just happened, Anna, but for your sake I wish it hadn't."

Anna felt a flicker of unease, hearing the unmistakable air of warning, but she pushed it aside, refusing to let anything cloud the moment.

Instinctively, she tucked herself against him, nestling under his arm and resting her head on his shoulder. "I'm glad it did," she said.

Now they were bound together and nothing could break them apart.

Arthur gazed down at the tiny, naked woman snuggled in his arms and felt his heart catch. What they'd just shared had been unlike anything he'd ever experienced. He'd had more than his fair share of women, but swiving for him had always been about sating lust. He'd see to a woman's pleasure and she would see to his with one goal in mind—release. Once accomplished, that was the end of it. He didn't linger. And he sure as hell didn't want to hold her in his arms and wish that they could stay like this forever.

Compared to what had just happened with Anna, what had come before seemed almost mechanical—as if he'd just been going through the motions to get the prize.

But with Anna, the prize had been the experience itself. The pleasure was in the exploration, in the discovery, and in the details. It was in the way she responded to his touch—the arch of her back, the press of her hips, and the little sounds that came from her lips. It was the look in her eyes when he slid into her, the flush that spread over her cheeks as she neared her release, and the way her head fell back and lips parted when she finally found it.

He hadn't been able to look away. He usually avoided eye contact, but with Anna he'd sought the connection. He wanted the closeness.

He rested his cheek on the top of her head, savoring the silky softness of her hair. She was so sweet and beautiful. And so damned trusting. A fierce swell of protectiveness rose inside him. And something else. Something warm and tender and powerful. Something he'd never thought was meant for him.

He'd thought himself different. That he didn't need anyone. That he was happy being alone. But he'd been fooling himself. He wasn't different at all. He needed her. Wanted her. Loved her with a ferocity that surprised him.

Maybe he could find a way to explain. To beg her forgiveness. Maybe there was hope . . .

Ah hell. A knot fisted in his gut as he pulled himself back to reality. Who was he fooling? She would never forgive him. How could she, when he was here to destroy all that she held dear?

He loved her, but it didn't change a damned thing. It would only make what was to come more painful. When he finished what he'd come to do, there would be no chance for them.

He loved her, but his loyalty was to Bruce. He had a mission to complete, not only for the king but for his father.

In a different time—in a place uncomplicated by war and feuds—they might have a chance. But not here. Not today.

Yet he wished . . .

God, how he wished it were different.

She peeked up at him from under her lashes. "I'm sure we aren't the first betrothed couple to anticipate the wedding night."

The stab of guilt deepened. That was the problem: There would be no wedding night. Not when she discovered the truth. He was an arse. A dishonorable arse. What could he have been thinking?

He knew exactly what he'd been thinking. That he wanted her more than he'd ever wanted anything in his life, and that he'd do anything to hold on to her. Consciously or unconsciously, he'd wanted to bind her to him in a way that could not be undone. Not even by deceit and betrayal.

It was desperate. It was selfish. It was wrong. It would only serve to give her more cause to hate him. But it was done, and he could not change it even if he wanted to.

"Nay," he said. "Not the first, but under the circumstances we should have waited." He drew her against him, his voice as fierce as his hold. He was a selfish bastard, but he swore when this damned battle was over he'd give her a choice. He would fight for her—for them—if she would let him. "I will come back to you, Anna. If you want me, I will come back."

She smiled up at him, so guileless and innocent. So trusting. "Of course I want you. Nothing will ever change that."

He wanted to believe her. More than anything in the world, he wanted to believe her. But her words would soon be put to the test.

Twenty-one

"What's wrong with you, Anna? You seem unusually quiet this morning. Did you not sleep well?"

Anna gave her sister a sharp glance, wondering if Mary suspected something. It was hard to tell. Her sister wore a serene expression on her face, one befitting the morning's sermon that they'd just heard.

Anna had no idea what it had been about. She'd been too busy playing back every second of what had happened last night. She was sure there was something horribly sinful about thinking of such things in a chapel, but Anna had so much to do penance for already, she figured the added damage to her soul was incremental.

She smiled as the memories returned. No doubt it was even more of a sin to be so happy about sinning, but she *was* happy. She loved Arthur, and he loved her. Last night had proved it.

She hadn't returned to the chamber she shared with her sisters until very late. Or early, depending on how you looked at it. She'd stayed curled up in his arms for as long as she'd dared, but eventually she'd been forced to return to her room.

The hours she'd spent in his arms had been some of the most contented of her life. In the protective bower of his embrace, the war, the chaos and the uncertainty of the world right now, didn't exist.

In the cold light of day, however, it all came back.

Today was the twelfth day of August. Three days before the truce ended.

It was the war that was troubling her, she told herself. If Arthur had seemed unusually pensive or if his words had held the edge of warning, she told herself it must be the war. With what was to come in the next few days, the loss of her virginity before the wedding should be the least of her worries.

But why had he talked about not coming back?

She had to stop this. "There's nothing wrong," Anna said firmly. "I slept well." Like the dead actually, for the four hours or so of sleep that she'd gotten.

"It must have been quite a book."

This time there was no mistaking the dry tone in Mary's voice.

"It was," Anna assured her, unable to hide her blush. Though she often read late in one of the mural chambers to avoid disturbing her sisters, Mary obviously had guessed the truth.

They were following a little behind the rest of her family as they crossed the courtyard from the chapel to the Great Hall, where they would break their fast. Most of the men, however, were already out in the yard practicing. The clang of swords and cacophony of voices grew louder as they drew near. Reflexively, she scanned the mail-clad forms looking for . . .

There. Her heart lurched just to see him. Arthur stood on the other side of the stables with his back toward her. It was near the place where they had the straw buttes set up, so she figured he must be practicing with his spear.

His brother Dugald stood nearby. Unlike Arthur, however, Sir Dugald wasn't alone. He was tossing a short spear back and forth, spinning it in the air, with three pretty young serving maids looking at him as if he were a magician, hanging on his every word.

One of the girls was standing in front of him, and he was attempting to show her how to catch the spear, but her immense breasts were getting in the way of his arms.

The two brothers couldn't be more different. Dugald was a loud braggart, the kind of man who wasn't happy unless he was the center of attention and surrounded by as many women as he could hold. Arthur was quieter. More solid. A man content to stay in the background.

Mary rolled her eyes at the display and turned away, climbing the stairs into the Hall. Anna raced up after her, glancing over her shoulder one more time.

Sir Dugald laughed at something one of the girls said. Anna couldn't hear his reply, but she swore it looked as if he'd said, "Watch this."

He lifted the spear in his hand as if to throw it, shouting to Arthur at the same time. "Arthur, catch!"

Before Anna realized what he was going to do—before the scream could rise from her throat—the spear was spinning in the air, hurled right at Arthur.

They were standing so close together, Arthur barely had time to turn at the sound of Dugald's voice before the spear was on him. At the last second, he snatched it out of the air with one hand. In one fluid motion, he brought it down across his knee, snapped it, and tossed the pieces back at his brother, his face dark with rage.

A memory pricked.

An icy breeze washed over her skin. She'd seen something like that only once before.

The blood drained from her face. Anna covered her gasp with her hand and sank back against the wall of the entry, her heart pounding in her throat.

It was just like that night in Ayr. The night she'd been sent to fetch the silver for her father and walked into a trap. The knight who'd rescued her had done the same thing.

The spy.

Nay, she told herself, horror creeping up her spine. It couldn't be. It had to be a coincidence.

But the memories twisted in her mind, confusing her.

It had been dark.

She'd never seen his face.

He'd spoken in low tones to disguise his voice.

But the size—the height, the build—was right.

Nay, nay, it couldn't be. She covered her ears and closed her eyes, not wanting to see. Not wanting to think about all the reasons it *could* be. His cryptic warnings. The feeling that he was hiding something. His initial attempts to avoid her. Her uncle Lachlan MacRuairi's look of recognition.

Her stomach knifed.

The scar. God, not the scar. But the star-shaped arrow mark on his arm fit with the injury to the knight who'd rescued her.

Bile rose in her throat.

Mary must have realized she wasn't behind her and had come running back to the entry, where Anna stood like a poppet of rags, sagging against the wall.

"What is it, Annie? You look as if you've seen a ghost."

She had. Dear God, she had. Anna shook her head, refusing to believe it. The room started to spin. "I-I don't feel well."

Without another word, she raced up the stairs to her chamber, barely pulling out the basin from under her bed before she emptied the meager contents of her stomach, purging her heart along with it.

Arthur glanced around the Great Hall as he made his way into Lorn's solar for the night's war council. He frowned, not seeing her. Where the hell was she? The vague feeling of concern that he'd felt on not seeing Anna this morning had grown worse as the day went on.

Alan said she wasn't feeling well. A stomachache. But given what had happened last night, Arthur didn't know whether to believe it.

Was she upset?

Did she regret what had happened?

Guilt ate at him. What had he done?

He forced his mind away from Anna and concentrated on the task at hand. Time was running out. King Robert and his men were planning to attack in less than four days, and he still hadn't discovered anything useful.

He entered the room behind Dugald—who was in as foul a mood as he'd ever seen him—and gathered around the table with the rest of the high-ranking knights and the members of Lorn's *meinie*.

A few minutes after the men had gathered, Lorn made his entrance. But this time he wasn't alone. His father, the ailing Alexander MacDougall, was with him.

Arthur's pulse spiked. If MacDougall was here, perhaps this was important.

The Lord of Argyll took the thronelike wooden chair usually occupied by his son, leaving Lorn to pull up a smaller chair beside him.

When the room had quieted, Lorn drew out a folded piece of parchment from his sporran and spread it out on the table.

Arthur stilled, recognizing it immediately. He bit back a foul curse. *The map.* Or more accurately, *his* map. The one he'd drawn for the king and passed to the messenger. It must have been intercepted before it reached Bruce. *Damn,* he wished he'd thought to mention it when he'd met with them last.

The men drew closer, trying to get a better look. "What is it?" someone asked.

Lorn's mouth fell in a hard line. "A map of the area

around Dunstaffnage." He flipped it over. "And the numbers of men and supplies we have readied."

There were a few angry mumblings as some of the men realized what that meant.

Dugald leaned closer, studying the map with enough intensity to make the hair on the back of Arthur's neck stand up.

There was nothing identifying about the document. The handwriting was minimal, and as for the drawing . . . Dugald had never paid much attention to Arthur's "scribblings," except to make fun of them. He had nothing to fear. But still his brother's interest made him uneasy.

"Where did you get it?" Dugald asked.

"It was taken off an enemy messenger my men intercepted a few weeks ago," Lorn replied. "But from the accuracy of the numbers, I suspect there is a traitor in our midst."

Murmurs of outrage and anger buzzed across the room, which Arthur joined.

"Unfortunately," Lorn added, "the messenger was unable to identify him."

"How can you be sure, my lord?" Arthur asked.

A knowing smile curved Lorn's mouth. "I'm sure."

Meaning the messenger had been tortured.

Lorn scanned the faces of the men around him—the inner circle of his command. "Keep your eyes out for anything unusual. I want this man found." He flattened the map with the palm of his hand. "But his map has proved useful. I have a plan to beat the usurper at his own game."

Arthur stilled, trying not to show his excitement. Perhaps he was finally going to have something to report to the king.

"What do you mean?" Alan asked.

"I mean we are going to turn his tactics against him. Bruce has achieved victories against much larger forces by fighting battles on his terms—choosing the right place and terrain to attack, striking hard and fast from places of concealment, using the same kind of tactics used by our ancestors for generations. *Highland* warfare. I'll be damned if I let a Lowlander beat me at my own kind of war." He paused to a chorus of agreement. "We aren't going to sit here and wait for him to lay siege to the castle as he expects; we're going to attack him first."

Everyone started talking at once. Arthur forced himself not to jump into the fray, waiting to hear the rest. But he knew this was big—monumental, in fact. Lorn was right: the king wouldn't be expecting an attack. Not with a fortress like Dunstaffnage to hole up in.

Lorn quieted the room with a movement of his hand. "Hold your questions until I tell you the rest." He edged the map forward on the table, enabling the men gathered in front of him to see it better. "Bruce and his men are coming from the east, following the road from Tyndrum." He pointed to the far edge of the map. Arthur's skin prickled, sensing something important. Lorn moved his finger along the road, stopping at the Pass of Brander. Arthur's stomach sank with dread.

"To reach Dunstaffnage they will have to cross through the mountains here. At the long narrow pass of Brander. This is where we will attack. We will position men here, here, and here," he said, pointing to three high ridges above that would be nearly impossible to see due to curves in the road.

Arthur bit back a curse as the room exploded in excitement. It was the perfect place from which to wage a surprise attack. The MacDougalls would surprise Bruce from above, descending on the marching army in a narrow gap where the king wouldn't be able to take advantage of his superior numbers.

"When?" Dugald asked the loudest.

"Our reports put Bruce at Brander early on the fourteenth."

Treacherous bastard.

The room fell quiet. "But the truce doesn't expire until the fifteenth," Alan said carefully.

Lorn's eyes narrowed. "It is the usurper who has chosen to ignore the code of warfare, not I. Bruce is marching on our lands. He is the one to break the truce."

A self-serving rationale if ever Arthur had heard one. But no one attempted to argue with him.

"Alan," Lorn continued, "you will leave with the main force of the army tomorrow and be in position by nightfall, just to be sure."

Arthur wasn't surprised to hear that Alan would be in command. The steep gullies and demanding terrain would be difficult for even the younger warriors to navigate.

"You will hold the castle, my lord?" he asked.

Lorn shot him an angry glare. "My father will hold the castle," he corrected. "I will take a fleet of galleys with the rest of the army and command from here." He pointed to the place where the River Awe flowed into Loch Awe. "Thus, after we surprise them from above, we'll attack from ahead as well."

Striking Bruce from two directions.

It was a brilliant plan. Not only was it the perfect location from which to launch an attack, but by striking first—and before the truce expired—Lorn would have surprise on his side.

A barrage of questions followed, but Arthur was already focused on the task ahead of him. He needed to warn the king as soon as possible, without alerting Lorn that his plan had been compromised.

He would have to risk trying to get a message out tonight. Then, in the excitement and chaos preceding the attack, he would be able to slip away.

For good.

A knot fisted in his gut. The moment he'd dreaded, but knew was inevitable, had come. The time to say goodbye.

The time when he was supposed to slip back into the shadows and disappear without a word. It was what he did. What he'd always known he would have to do. He just hadn't expected it to be so damned hard.

It felt cowardly to leave without explanation. To let her discover the truth on her own. He wanted to prepare her. To tell her he loved her and hadn't meant to hurt her.

To tell her he was sorry. To tell her he was hers if she still wanted him.

But he couldn't. He would ride out tomorrow, letting her think he was one man, and when he returned, it would be as another. She would hate him.

Though he doubted there was a chance in hell for them, when it was all over he vowed to find her and try to explain. If she would listen.

It can't be true. It can't be true. Anna refused to believe it. But she couldn't shake the doubt that had wormed its way into her gut and wouldn't let go. Her plea of illness had not been feigned. Doubt was twisting—festering—inside her, making her weak with it.

All day long she'd sought the quiet refuge of her bedchamber, trying to convince herself that it wasn't possible. That he couldn't deceive her like that. But there were too many questions. Questions that couldn't wait until morning. Tomorrow could be too late. Mary and Juliana had returned to their chamber a short while ago to inform her that the men were readying for war.

War. Fear twisted in her chest, the need to find him taking on a desperate edge.

Her gown was dusted with Squire's hair and wrinkled from a day of lying on her bed, but she didn't waste the time to change it. After splashing water on her face, rinsing her teeth, yanking a comb through her tangled hair, and asking her sisters to keep an eye on the puppy, she made her way to her father's solar.

Expecting to find the men locked up in their war council, she was disappointed to see the open door. The sound of voices, however, drew her inside.

Her father stood beside Alan, leaning over a piece of parchment spread out on the table. He glanced up as she entered the room. "Ah, Anna, you are feeling better?"

"Aye, Father, much better." She tried to hide her disappointment at finding them alone. Arthur must have already retired to the barracks for the night. What was she going to do? What excuse could she find for seeking him out this late?

"Is there something you needed?" Alan asked, watching her with a concerned look on his face. His gaze dropped to her hands, which she realized were twisting in her skirts. "You seem upset about something."

If only he knew.

Oh God, he *should* know. Her stomach sank, realizing she should tell them both her suspicions.

But she couldn't. Not until she was sure. Her father . . .

It hurt her to admit that her father's anger wasn't always rational. She couldn't be sure what he would do.

But she had to tell them something. "It's the war. Mary told me the men are readying to leave tomorrow."

"There's no reason for you to worry, Anna. You, your mother, and sisters will be safe here."

"I don't think that's what she's worried about, Father," Alan said with a wry smile.

He was right. Anxious to find Arthur, Anna started to back away. "I didn't mean to disturb you." She glanced down at the parchment on the table. "You are obviously busy, I'll leave you—"

She stopped with a startled gasp. Her eyes landed on the piece of parchment. A piece of parchment she recognized. Although now that it was finished, it looked different. It no longer resembled a sketch. Now it looked like a map.

A map. What did this mean? If Arthur had been drawing a map for her father, why wouldn't he have said something?

He'd been trying to hide it.

Heart drumming with inexplicable dread, she took a few steps closer. Trying to control the quivering in her voice, she said, "That's an interesting map." Her throat was too dry, her words coming out in a rasp. "Where did you get it?"

"Some of our men intercepted it off an enemy messenger," Alan answered. He traced his finger over the finely etched lines. "It really is quite good. The detail is magnificent."

All Anna heard was "enemy messenger." The blood drained from her face, her worst fears seemingly confirmed.

He's a spy.

"What do you know of it, daughter?"

Anna's gaze snapped to her father's. She opened her mouth to speak the words that would condemn him, but they froze in her throat.

She couldn't. She couldn't do it. Not before she gave Arthur a chance to explain.

"Nothing," she said quickly, lowering her eyes, unable to meet his gaze.

Alan was looking at her strangely. "Are you sure you are all right, Annie? You don't look so well."

She didn't feel so well. She felt dizzy. As if the room were spinning around her, or the floorboards had just been jerked out from beneath her feet. She swayed and then took a step to steady herself. "I-I think I'd better return to my room."

Alan came forward, concern written on his face. "I'll take you."

"No." She shook her head furiously, tears burning tight

in her eyes. "It's not necessary. I'm fine. Finish what you were doing."

She fled before he could stop her.

Feeling as if she were suffocating, she quickly made for the *barmkin*. The cool night air slapped her with relief as soon as she opened the donjon door. She inhaled deeply, filling her lungs and trying to even her quickening breath. She clutched the wooden railing at the top of the stairs like a lifeline, allowing the fresh air and the soothing canopy of the black, starless night to calm her racing heart, her racing breath, and most of all her racing head.

A few of the men patrolling the *barmkin* wall were staring at her, but she was too upset to care.

Upset? Nay, poleaxed. Crushed. Horrified. Her head still spinning with disbelief.

She was trying to decide what to do. Whether to march across the yard, knock on the barrack door and demand to see him—to Hades with propriety—when the door to the barracks opened and a group of soldiers came out, dressed in full armor.

Her heart lurched, realizing one of them was Arthur.

They were heading toward the stables.

He was leaving. *Leaving.*

Her fingers squeezed the railing until splinters bit into her hands. She stared at him, her chest burning with pain, a small part of her still not wanting to believe it.

As if sensing the heat of her gaze, he glanced up and jarred to a halt midstride. Their eyes met across the torch-lit darkness.

He said something to one of the other men, then broke off from the group to walk toward her.

Drawing a deep, uneven breath, Anna started down the stairs, meeting him at the bottom.

Her breath caught when she saw his face.

It can't be true. How could he look at her with such concern and be planning to betray her?

"What's wrong?" he asked. "I was worried when I didn't see you earlier."

He reached for her, but she twisted away. She couldn't let him touch her. It would only confuse her further.

"I need to speak with you."

The stiffness in her voice alerted him. His gaze slid to the stables where the men had disappeared. "I don't have much time. They're waiting for me."

"You're leaving . . . without saying goodbye?"

The small tic below his jaw gave him away. It spoke of guilt.

"It's a night patrol only. I'll be back in a few hours."

"Are you sure? Didn't you warn me that you might not come back?"

His eyes scanned her face, and he seemed to realize something was truly wrong. Aware of the men patrolling around them, he took her arm and drew her toward the garden tucked around the far side of the tower, where they could not be overheard.

Turning her around to look at him, he gave her a stern look. "What's this about, Anna?"

She lifted her chin, hating that he made her feel like a recalcitrant child. "I *know*."

"What do you know?"

A sob rose in her chest but she tamped it down. Her words came out in a rush. "I know the truth. I know why you're here. I know you were the one who saved me in Ayr. I know you're working for *them*." She practically spat the last, unable to say it. He was working for her family's mortal enemy.

His face was still—too still, his features schooled in perfect impassiveness.

Her heart sank. Tumbled. And crashed to the floor. The lack of reaction was more damning than a denial.

"You are overwrought," he said calmly. "You don't know what you're saying."

"Don't you dare!" Her voice shook, the emotion burning in her chest erupting in anger. "Don't you dare lie to me! I saw you catch the spear this morning and break it over your knee. I've seen something like that only once before. Surely you remember coming to my rescue that night? A rebel spy pretending to be a knight? You took an arrow in your shoulder for it." She wanted to rip off his mail and force him to deny it. "It's the exact same place you have a scar."

She paused for a denial, half-hoping for an explanation, but silence filled the dead air between them.

"I saw the map, Arthur. The map you let me believe was a drawing. It was taken off an enemy messenger." She eyed him challengingly. "Perhaps I should call my father and let him decide."

His mouth thinned in a white line. He grabbed her elbow and brought her closer to him. "Lower your voice," he warned. "Just an accusation like that could get me killed."

She sobered, her anger dissolving a little, knowing he spoke the truth.

He steered her toward a stone bench and set her down. "Don't move."

She bristled at the order. "Where are you going?"

He gave her a hard look. "To tell them I will be delayed."

Twenty-two

Think! Damn it, think!

Arthur took his time in the stable informing the men of his delay, while trying to calm the fierce rush of blood pounding through his veins. But every primitive instinct of self-preservation had kicked in, in response to the danger.

The worst had happened. He'd been discovered. Anna had figured out the truth.

He cursed his damned fool of a brother for tossing that spear—which had very nearly succeeded in skewering his head—and himself for being so careless with the map.

His mission had just gone to shite, and unless he could think of a way to explain, there was every chance he wouldn't live to see another sunrise. He couldn't think about what his failure might mean to Bruce. If he didn't warn them, they would be marching into a trap. A MacDougall victory could turn the tides of war once more.

Though Arthur didn't sense anything, his hands were on his weapons as he exited the stables, half-expecting Lorn's soldiers to be waiting for him. But Anna hadn't gone to her father. Yet. She was waiting for him on the bench where he'd left her.

He breathed marginally easier as he strode back across

the courtyard, but still wasn't sure what he was going to say.

It wasn't just his mission and his life at stake. If there was ever going to be a chance for them, he needed to make her understand.

She didn't look at him as he approached but stared silently out into the darkness, her face a pale mask of anguish.

He sat down next to her, never having felt more helpless. He wanted to take her into his arms and tell her it would be all right, but he knew it wouldn't. He'd betrayed her. It didn't matter that it couldn't have been helped.

"It's not what you think," he said softly.

Her voice was thick with emotion. "You can't imagine what I think." She turned to him, her big blue eyes blurred with unshed tears, and he felt a stab of pain in his heart so sharp it made him flinch. "Tell me it isn't true, Arthur. Tell me it's all a mistake. Tell me you aren't what I think you are."

He should. What was one more lie on top of so many? He could try to deny it. Maybe he'd even be able to convince her. But he didn't think so. She *knew*. He could see it in her eyes. And if he lied to her now, he would never have a chance to make her understand.

For them to have a chance, he had to tell her the truth.

He looked into her eyes. "I never meant to hurt you."

She made a sound, a whimper of pain like that of a wounded animal—a fluffy, little kitten caught in a bear trap.

He couldn't help himself. He reached out to touch her, but she jerked away.

"How can you say that? You used me. You *lied* to me about everything that was important." Tears seeped from the corners of her eyes, streaming down her cheeks. "Was any of it real? Or was making me care for you part of the plan?"

"What happened between us was real, Anna. You were never part of the plan. You were never supposed to be involved. This isn't about you."

"What is it about, then? Robert Bruce? The feud? Your father?" He clenched his jaw and she sucked in her breath. "It *is* about your father. You blame my father for his death." She pulled back. "This is all some horrible, twisted attempt at revenge. Because your father died in battle you want to see my family destroyed, is that it? What do you plan to do, kill my father to avenge the death of yours?" She drew up in horror. "My God, you do."

Arthur's teeth gritted together. She made it sound petty. Simple. Yet it was anything but. Anna was blinded by the love she had for her family from seeing the reality of what was happening around her. He hated being the one to force her eyes open, but he didn't have a choice.

"It's your father that is going to destroy your clan, Anna, not me. Robert Bruce has done what none thought possible. He's the best chance Scotland has of winning its freedom from the English. He has won the hearts of the people. But your father's hatred and his pride have prevented him from seeing it. He'd rather see an English puppet on the throne. But the MacDougalls are standing alone, Anna— even Ross will submit."

Her spine went rigid. "My father is doing what he thinks is right."

"Nay, your father is doing whatever he can not to admit defeat. Do not mistake what this is about, Anna. Your father will see you all destroyed rather than accept losing."

He could see the outrage burning on her cheeks. "You don't know anything about my father."

She tried to get up, but he grabbed her wrist and held her down. "I know too much about your father. I know exactly what he'll do to win."

She tried to free her arm. "Let go of me."

"Not until you hear all of it." He wished to hell he

wasn't the one to disillusion her, but he knew he couldn't protect her from the truth any longer. "I didn't tell you everything I saw the day my father was killed."

"I don't want—"

"But you will," he bit in. "Even if you don't want to hear it. I stood on that hill and saw everything, Anna. My father had yours at the point of his sword. He could have killed him, but he offered him mercy. Your father accepted terms—agreed to surrender—and then when my father turned his back, he killed him."

Anna gasped, her eyes wide with disbelief and horror. "You're wrong. My father would never do something so dishonorable."

Arthur pulled her toward him and forced her to look in his eyes. "I was there, Anna. I saw and heard everything but could do nothing to stop it. I tried to warn my father, but it was too late. Lorn heard me and sent men after me, but I hid in the forest for a week. By the time I came out, it was too late to change his story. I wouldn't have been believed."

He could see her panic. Feel her heart fluttering wildly against his. She was fighting to hold on to any thread to preserve the illusions she had of the man she thought her father to be. "You must have misinterpreted what happened. You were too far away."

"I didn't misinterpret anything, Anna. I heard every word."

He was wrong. He had to be wrong. Didn't he? Her father had a bad temper, but she knew the kind of man he was.

She turned harshly away from him. "I don't believe you."

The pity in his eyes cut deeper than glass. "Ask him yourself."

She didn't say anything, refusing to listen.

"Your father will stop at nothing to win, Anna, nothing. Hell, he even used his own daughter."

She stiffened, his accusation stinging. "I told you the alliance with Ross was my idea."

"That's not what I'm talking about. I'm talking about using you as his messenger."

She sucked in her breath. He knew about that? Oh God, had she unwittingly given him information? "When?" she breathed. "When did you find out?"

"Not until a few weeks ago—unfortunately." His face turned fierce. "Damn it, Anna, do you know how much danger you were in?"

"Aye, but I never imagined the source." *From you.* He was the enemy, spying on her and doing what he could to . . .

She stared at him as all the terrible ramifications came tumbling through her mind. Suddenly, she jerked back in horror. *No, not that. Please.* Her stomach turned. "Why did you insist on accompanying me north, Arthur?"

"To keep you safe."

"And to prevent the alliance with Ross?"

He met her stare unflinchingly. "Aye, if necessary."

Pain lashed her heart so hard she choked on a sob.

"It's not what you think. I didn't plan for that to happen."

The pain lashed inside her. She felt raw—bleeding. "And I'm supposed to believe you?"

His jaw clenched. "It's the truth. What happened in that room was because I was half-crazed with jealousy, nearly out of my mind at the thought of losing you. I'm not proud of what I did, but I swear to you it wasn't planned."

"It just happened, is that it? And what about last night? Did that just happen too?" Her voice shook with the emotion flaying inside her. "How could you, Arthur? You knew what was going to happen eventually, and yet you let me believe that you cared for me—that you planned to marry me. But it was all a lie."

How could she have been so foolish to have given herself to a man who was planning to betray her. To betray them all?

"Nay," he said roughly, forcing her to look at him. "It wasn't a lie. None of it was a lie. I—" He hesitated, as if the words didn't fit in his mouth. "I love you, Anna. Nothing would make me happier than to marry you."

For one foolish moment, her heart leapt as she heard the words she'd longed to hear. Words that should have made everything perfect, but instead made it feel even more wrong.

He was cruel. Telling her what she so desperately wanted to believe. He was probably just trying to manipulate her so she wouldn't turn him in.

Turn him in. Oh God, what was she going to do?

She had a duty to tell her father what she'd discovered. But if she did, she had no doubt what would happen: Arthur would die. And if she didn't, Arthur would take whatever information he'd learned while spying on them and give it to their enemies.

It was an impossible choice, but even after all that Arthur had done, she knew that she couldn't be the one to put the noose around his neck. One man could not defeat an army.

"You honestly expect me to believe you love me?"

He stiffened, but held her gaze to his. "Aye, I do. Perhaps I don't have any right to do so, but it's the truth. I've never said those words to anyone and never thought I would. But from the first moment we met I felt something special—I know you felt it, too—a connection I couldn't resist."

"What you felt was lust," she said, throwing his words back at him. His mouth tightened. She knew she was pushing him, but she was too hurt and angry to care. "How can you expect me to believe you love me, when you've lied to me from the first moment we met?"

"What would you have had me do? I couldn't very well tell you the truth. Do you think I wanted this to happen? Bloody hell, you were the last person I wanted to fall in love with."

Anna flinched. Was that supposed to make her feel better? Though hearing how reluctant his feelings were for her stung, his words rang of truth.

"I tried to stay away," he pointed out, his frustration taking a toll. "But you wouldn't let me."

"So this is my fault? Is that it?"

He sighed, dragging his hand through his hair again. "Nay, of course not. Even if you had avoided me, I would have fallen in love with you from afar. I was drawn to you the first time I saw you. Your warmth. Your vitality. Your kindness. You're everything that I didn't know was missing in my life—that I didn't think was possible for me. I never wanted that kind of closeness until I met you."

Despite her every intention not to be gulled by him again, she felt a pang in her heart.

He cupped her chin in his hand and tilted her face to his. "I know I can't expect you to believe me, Anna, but I hope you'll try to understand that I did the best I could under impossible circumstances. I was doomed to betray you before we even met."

Her eyes raked his face, looking for signs of deception but seeing only sincerity. She wanted to believe him, but how could she with what he meant to do? Even if his feelings for her were real, he still meant to betray her. He was on one side and she was on another. He wanted to kill her father.

She wrenched her face away, fearing her own weakness. When he looked at her like that all she could think about was kissing him, and how good it would feel to let him put his arms around her and pretend it would be all right.

"How can I believe you care for me when you are here spying on us to destroy my family, and to exact some kind of revenge on my father? If you really loved me, you wouldn't do this."

His eyes glittered hard in the darkness, as if he wanted to argue with her but recognized the futility. "What would you have me do?"

"I'd have you put aside your quest for vengeance." She looked up in his eyes, knowing that she was about to ask the impossible, but also knowing that it was the only way for them to have a chance. "I'd have you choose me."

Arthur stilled. Damn her for doing this to him! For forcing him to choose.

She'd asked for the one thing he could not give. He couldn't put aside his honor and loyalty—even for her.

His face turned to granite. "I took an oath, Anna, pledging my sword to Bruce." And to the Highland Guard. "To go against that would be to go against my conscience and everything I believe in. Despite what you may have cause to believe, I am a man of honor."

Duty, loyalty, and honor were what had brought him to this point.

"But this isn't just about honor, is it?" she challenged. "It's about revenge. You want to see my father destroyed."

His jaw hardened. "I want justice."

Her big eyes gazed up at him, luminous and pleading, eating into his conscience. She put her hand on his arm, but it might as well be fisted around his heart. "He's my father, Arthur."

He felt his insides squeeze. Her soft plea penetrated more than it should. How did she do this to him? Twist him up in knots with the urge to do anything to please her.

But he couldn't. Not this.

For fourteen years his life had centered on one thing: righting a wrong. He'd been waiting too long to meet Lorn face-to-face across the battlefield. He could no more deny his vow for justice for his father than he could deny his feelings for her.

"Do you think I don't know he's your father? Do you think I haven't spent every day of the last two months wishing differently? I didn't want this, damn it."

Her eyes glistened with tears. "I think you made that clear. Your feelings for me are an inconvenience."

His fists clenched. "That's not what I mean."

"There's no need to explain. Believe me, I understand." The bitterness in her tone made her feelings clear. She stood up from the bench and walked a few steps into the courtyard, staring aimlessly out into the darkness. "Go," she said tonelessly. "Leave before I change my mind."

He couldn't believe it—she was going to let him go. For a moment, he felt the flicker of hope. It had to mean she still loved him. She was putting him before her family by letting him go. And he had to go. He didn't want to leave her like this, but he had to get word to the king.

He came up by her side, took her elbow, and gently turned her to face him. She looked so young and fragile in the moonlight, her face a pale oval of alabaster. "I swear to you I will return as soon as I am able."

She shook her head, not breaking her trancelike gaze. "You made your choice. If you leave now, I don't want you to come back." Finally, she looked at him. Her gaze never wavered. "I don't ever want to see you again."

The finality in her voice cut like a blade.

"You don't mean that." She couldn't mean it. It was her anger speaking. But the stubborn set of her chin sent a flash of panic surging through his veins. He knew that look. He pulled her hard against him, knowing he had to make her see sense. "Don't say something you'll regret."

She gasped at the contact. "What are you doing? Let go of me!" She pried at his chest, trying to wrench free.

But her struggle only increased his sense of panic. He

had to make her see. How could she deny this? Didn't she feel the energy snapping between them? The heat? They were meant to be together.

He was out of words and out of time. So he kissed her, capturing her mouth with his in a fierce, desperate embrace. She stilled—no longer struggling, but going limp in his arms.

No. Damn it, no.

Her lack of response only increased his sense of urgency. He kissed her harder, deeper, forcing her lips apart, searching for something that he feared was slipping through his fingers.

Her lips were warm and soft, and tasted like honey, but it was all wrong.

She doesn't want this.

He stopped.

What the hell am I doing?

He released her with a curse, staring at her in horror. He'd never done anything like that in his life. The thought of losing her was making him lose his mind.

"God, Anna, I'm sorry." His voice was rough and uneven from the harshness of his breath.

He deserved the way she was looking at him—as if he were scum beneath her heel. "I never thought you were a brute. But it seems you are well placed with your usurping king. You just take what you want."

"Anna, I—"

"Just go," she said bitterly. "The best thing you can do is go. You've done enough damage already." Her eyes met his, challenging. "You didn't honestly think I could ever forgive you for this, did you?"

It was a confirmation of his worst fears. He'd been a fool. He'd let his emotions color his perception of reality. Because he wanted her so badly, he'd let himself believe a future could be possible. But there had never been a chance for them. She would never forgive what duty, honor, and loyalty demanded he do.

His gaze locked on hers, searching for any sign of weakness, but her eyes met his, cold and unflinching. The lack of tears, of anger, of emotion, left no doubt. It was over. God, it was really over.

He'd always known this moment might come, but he'd never expected to feel such helplessness and despair. He'd never expected it to hurt like this. He felt as if he were being ripped to shreds inside and there wasn't a damned thing he could do about it.

"I love you, Anna. I will always love you. Nothing will ever change that. I hope one day you will understand that I never meant to hurt you."

Unable to stop himself, he reached out to touch her cheek one more time. But she jerked away from him as if he were a leper, and his hand fell to his side.

"Goodbye," he said, and then with one last look that he would have to hold on to for a lifetime, he turned and walked away.

He would never forget how she looked at that moment. Small. Alone. Achingly beautiful, with her long golden hair tumbling around her shoulders in shimmering waves and her delicate features cast in the opalescent glow of the shadow of the moonlight.

So fragile she could shatter like glass.

But resolved. Painfully resolved.

His chest felt as if it were on fire, the burning intensifying with every step. He felt as though he were walking through the fires of hell, the weight of each footfall sheer agony. He couldn't quiet the sensation that it was wrong to leave her like this. That if he didn't do something right now it would be too late. He made it halfway to the stables before he turned around.

But it was too late. She was already gone.

He glanced to the top of the stairs leading to the donjon

tower, catching a glimpse of golden hair streaming out behind her like a banner before disappearing behind the door.

When it closed, it seemed as if something inside him had closed as well. For good. It was a part of him that should never have been opened in the first place.

This was what he got for letting himself get involved. He was meant to be alone. He should never have forgotten that.

He tried to ignore the emptiness burning in his chest. He had to stop thinking about her. He needed to focus on the task at hand. But images of her face kept flashing through his mind. Haunting him. Distracting him.

He entered the stables, quickly readying his horse. Volunteering for the night patrol was proving doubly fortuitous—not only would it serve as an excuse for him to get out of the castle, but it also meant he didn't have to waste time returning to the barracks. His important belongings he had on him: his mail and his weaponry. The extra clothing and few personal items he could leave behind.

His plan had changed. He needed to leave for good now—even if it meant Lorn learned his plan had been compromised. Anna learning the truth had left him no options. He could not risk the chance that she would change her mind.

He spent no more than five minutes in the stables. All he could think about was getting out of there and putting distance between them. It was better this way, he told himself. He'd been fine on his own before; he'd be fine again.

He didn't make it out of the stables. His senses alerted him, but not in time. Once again his emotions had distracted him. Though this time it wouldn't have made any difference.

He opened the stable door to find himself surrounded. John of Lorn and his son Alan beside him were flanked by at least two dozen guardsmen with swords drawn.

Arthur's jaw clenched against the gut-stabbing pain. He couldn't believe it. Anna had given him up.

Perhaps he should have expected it, but he hadn't thought her capable. He'd underestimated her love for her father and overestimated her love for him.

It shouldn't feel like so much of a betrayal.

But it did.

Lorn lifted an indolent brow. "Going somewhere, Campbell?"

"Aye," Arthur said casually—as if he didn't have armed men surrounding him. "I'm joining the team on the night's patrol." He glanced around meaningfully, not having to feign his outrage. "What is the meaning of this?"

Lorn smiled, though his expression held no humor. "I'm afraid you are going to be detained for a bit. There are a few matters we need to clear up."

Arthur took a step forward. He heard the slink and clatter of mail as the guardsmen around him responded to the perceived threat, lifting their swords and closing in tighter around him.

But it wasn't necessary. He was trapped. He might be able to fight his way through two dozen men circled around him with swords poised at his neck, but the gate was already locked for the night. He wouldn't be able to get past it before the entire castle was roused.

There was no way out.

His gaze flickered to Alan, but he would get no help from that direction. His gaze was as hard and unrelenting as his father's, albeit without the glitter of steely malevolence.

Every instinct urged him to fight. To pull his sword from its scabbard and take a few of Lorn's men with him. But he forced himself to stay calm. Not to do anything foolish. His mission had to come first. If there was a chance in hell that he could escape to warn Bruce, he had to take it.

Maybe he could talk his way out of this. He couldn't be sure how much she'd told them.

"Can it wait?" he said. "The men are waiting for me."

"I'm afraid not," Lorn said. With a wave of his hand, two of his strongest men stepped forward to grab Arthur by the arms. "Take him to the guard room. Search him."

Ah hell. There would be no talking his way out of this.

He'd forgotten about the note. The message he'd planned to leave in the cave for the king tonight. A small slip of paper folded in his sporran with three words that would seal his fate: *Attack, 14th, Brander.*

Although perhaps his fate had been sealed two months ago. The moment he'd come face-to-face with the girl he'd rescued in an ill-fated attack. The girl who could unmask him.

With a fierce battle cry that tore through the night, Arthur let instinct take over. *Bàs roimh Gèill*—Death before Surrender. He fought like a wildman, taking five men down before he fell beneath the pommel of Alan MacDougall's sword.

As blackness closed over him, he knew it wasn't over yet. And it was about to get worse.

They wanted him alive.

Twenty-three

Her heart shouldn't feel as if it were breaking.

Anna wanted him to go. He'd lied to her. Betrayed her. Used her. He wanted to destroy everything that was important to her. How could he think there would ever be a chance for them?

He'd even tried to turn their passion against her. As if a kiss could make her forget what he'd done. She'd hated him at that moment. Hated him for sullying something that was beautiful and pure.

She told herself this was what she wanted. But when he'd turned his back on her and walked away, the ice in her heart started to crack.

He was leaving. *Leaving.*

She would never see him again.

Oh God. She held herself stone still, not daring to move, but her insides started to shudder. She felt as if she were a thin pane of glass being battered by a violent storm of emotions. On the surface strong, but in reality fragile. One hard blow and she would shatter into thousands of tiny pieces.

After what he'd done, she shouldn't feel like this. It shouldn't hurt so much. The pain. The burning. The despair. The feeling that her heart was being ripped out of her. The intensity of emotion seemed like weakness. She was strong. Where was her pride? She was a MacDougall.

But right now all she felt like was a girl who was watching the man she loved walk away from her forever.

Unable to bear it a moment longer—and fearing what he would see if he turned around—she ran. Ran as fast as she ever had up the stairs, until she reached the safety of her chamber. There, careful not to wake her sleeping sisters, she collapsed on her bed, pulled the covers over her head, and crumpled like a poppet of rags. Only then did she let her emotions break through in silent sobs that seemed wrenched from her soul.

Sensing her distress, Squire curled up beside her. She hugged the puppy to her, the warm, furry ball of unconditional love her loyal companion during the long, miserable night.

I love you.

She couldn't get the words out of her head. He'd sounded so sincere. But he'd lied about everything else, so how could she believe him? Even if it was true, it shouldn't matter.

Over and over she replayed what had happened in her mind, recalling every word of his explanation—justification—whatever it was he was trying to make.

It was bad enough that they were on opposite sides of a war, but did he honestly expect her to understand that he had to destroy her clan? Kill her father, the man she admired most in the world? All for some kind of revenge?

Justice, he'd called it.

She didn't want to listen to his explanations or understand his reasons. Nor did she believe the horrible lies he'd spouted about her father for one moment. Her father could never have killed a man so dishonorably.

He'll do anything to win. She pulled the pillow tighter around her ears, wanting the feathers to block it out.

Ask him, Arthur had challenged.

She didn't need to ask him; she knew the truth.

But Arthur had been so certain about what he'd seen . . .

Anna slid out of her bed as the first rays of dawn spilled across the floor. After hurrying through her morning ablutions, she slipped past her sisters on her way out of the chamber.

She knew exactly what she was going to do. She was going to prove Arthur wrong. Then she'd be able to put this behind her and stop the miserable aching in her heart.

The trestle tables had yet to be set out, and some of the men were still stirring from their pallets in the Great Hall, as she rushed to her father's solar. Though it was not yet an hour past dawn, she knew her father would be up. He barely slept when readying for battle.

She heard his voice as she neared the entry. "I don't care how long it takes, I want to know the names."

"I don't know how much more he can—"

Alan stopped abruptly, seeing her enter the room. One look at his face and she knew something was wrong.

Her father was seated behind the table, his henchman, the captain of his guard, and her brother Alan standing before him. His gaze narrowed angrily upon seeing her. The others seemed to look away, almost as if they were avoiding meeting her gaze.

Thinking her father's anger was because of her interruption, she bid a hasty retreat. "I'm sorry. I will return when you are done."

"Nay," her father said. "I want to talk to you. We're finished here." To Alan he said, "No more excuses. Get me what I want. Whatever it takes."

Alan's mouth fell in a thin line, but he nodded. Anna felt a prickle of unease when he left the room without a word or even a glance.

She took a seat on the bench opposite her father, folding her hands in her lap. The intensity of his gaze was making her vaguely uncomfortable. He was angry, and it wasn't about the interruption.

"If you have something to tell me, you are too late."

Her heart sank. "T-tell you?"

He pulled a folded piece of paper from his sporran and tossed it on the table before her. A chill swept across the back of her neck when she recognized the map. "Aye," he said. "Like where you'd seen this before."

Shame flooded her cheeks. How had he found out?

He answered her question for her. "Your reaction. Looking for him right away confirmed the source."

Had her father been watching them the whole time? Nay, maybe in the courtyard, but he couldn't have seen them in the garden—it wasn't visible from the Hall. Yet he'd obviously seen enough.

"I expected better from you, Anna."

She bowed her head, his disappointment cutting sharply. She had no excuse. She wanted to say she hadn't been sure, but she had. The moment she'd seen the map, she'd known he was a spy. "I'm sorry, Father. I wanted to give him a chance to explain."

Her father's voice was as biting as a whip. "And did he 'explain' to your satisfaction?"

She shook her head. Though she knew she had a duty to tell him everything, the words were still difficult to say. Arthur was gone, she reminded herself. "He is loyal to Bruce." She paused, peering up at him cautiously. "He said that Bruce has won the hearts of the people. That he is Scotland's best chance to be free of English tyranny for good. And that we are going to lose and should submit."

Her father's face turned red with rage. "And you believed him? Arthur Campbell would have said anything to gain your sympathy. You foolish girl, he was using you to escape. We will never submit and we will *not* lose."

She wondered at his certainty and bit her lip, hesitating to mention the rest. Her father was angry enough with her.

But she had to put this behind her. "He claims that he was there when you killed his father and saw the whole thing."

The slight flicker in his gaze could have been anything, but her heart stopped.

"That's impossible," he dismissed. "I don't know what he saw, but Colin Mor and I had fallen away from the group. We were alone when we fought. In any event, I have never denied that he fell by my sword. Or that my victory for our clan was the cause of the Campbells losing their lands around Loch Awe. If Arthur Campbell harbors vengeance for that, it cannot be helped—but it is no excuse."

She forced herself to look at him, though she hated herself for repeating Arthur's accusation. "He said that his father had you at the point of his sword, offered you surrender, that you accepted, but then killed him when he turned away."

This time the flicker in his eyes could not be misinterpreted. Nor the tightening in his jaw or the white lines around his mouth. He was angry.

Angry, but not outraged the way he should have been.

The blood drained from her face. *Oh God, it's true.*

The horror in her expression seemed to annoy him. "It was a long time ago. I did what I had to do. Colin Mor was growing too powerful. Encroaching on our lands. He had to be stopped."

Anna felt as if she were looking at a familiar stranger, seeing the real man for the first time. He was still the father she loved, but he was no longer a man who could do no wrong. A man whom she did not question. He was no longer a god. Nay, he was frighteningly human. Flawed and capable of making mistakes. Big mistakes. Hideous mistakes.

Arthur was right. There was nothing her father wouldn't do to win. Even the good of the clan would not stop him.

"You have little cause to judge, daughter. You who

would let a traitor to your clan walk free." His voice grew so hard it shook. "Do you know what kind of harm he could have done?"

He was right. She'd chosen to let Arthur go free, even knowing he could harm her clan, because she could not bear the thought of being the instrument of his death. "I didn't want to see him hurt. I . . . I care for him." She stopped. Suddenly, the tense he'd used struck her. Her heart pounded. " 'Could have'?" she asked.

Her father's mouth was clamped tight, the whiteness of his lips stark against his ruddy, angered face. "You are fortunate that I was able to mitigate a disaster. My men surrounded Campbell when he tried to leave last night. He carried a message with him that proved his guilt." His eyes flared dangerously. "A message that would have ruined everything."

Anna couldn't breathe as horror pounded her. Fear laced around her heart and squeezed. "What have you done with him?"

"It's none of your concern."

Tears burned the back of her throat. Her eyes. Panic seized her lungs. She could barely get the words out. "Please, Father, just tell me . . . is he alive?"

He didn't answer right away, but watched her with a cold, assessing gaze. "For now," he said. "I have some questions for him."

She closed her eyes, exhaling with an overwhelming sense of relief. "What will you do with him?"

He eyed her impatiently. Clearly, he didn't like her questions. "That depends on him."

"Please, I must see him." She needed to make sure he was all right.

He looked outraged by the request. "So you can let him go again? I don't think so." He clenched his mouth angrily. "It would serve no purpose. The man is dangerous and can't be trusted."

"Arthur would never hurt me," she said automatically, then realized it was the truth. He loved her. Deep down she'd known it. It didn't change anything in the past, but perhaps it could the future. Her heart squeezed. If he had a future. "Please?"

Her pleas fell on deaf ears, his dark-eyed gaze hard and unyielding. "Arthur Campbell is no longer your concern. You have done enough damage already. How can I be sure that you will not try to find some way to help him?"

The protest died in her throat. Truth be told, she wasn't sure either. The fear that clutched her heart when she thought of Arthur imprisoned made her realize that her feelings for him were not so easy to put aside.

"I did not expect this from you, Anna." The disappointment in his voice cut to the bone. Worse, she knew it was deserved. But she felt trapped—caught between two men she loved. He dismissed her with a harsh wave of his hand. "You will be ready to leave within the hour."

She sucked in her breath. "Leave? But where?"

"Your brother Ewen is marching ahead of the army with a large force of men to bolster our defenses at Innis Chonnel; you will go with him. Once we have sent King Hood to the devil, you will visit my cousin the Bishop of Argyll on Lismore. There, you will have time to think about what you have done—and where your loyalty lies."

Anna nodded, her tears coming harder. Clearly he didn't trust her and wanted her gone from the castle while he was away.

She knew she'd gotten off lightly. Her father's punishment could have been much more severe. But she couldn't bear the thought of leaving Arthur not knowing what was to become of him.

"Please, I'll do anything you ask. Just promise me you won't kill him while I am gone." She choked on a sob. "I love him."

"Enough! You are trying my patience, Anna. Your tender feelings for the man have made you forget your duty. Only the knowledge that I might bear some of the responsibility for asking you to watch the man has spared you from a far greater punishment. Arthur Campbell is a spy. He knew the risk he took when he chose to betray us. He's going to get exactly what he deserves."

Arthur no longer felt a thing. He'd passed the point of pain hours ago. He'd been beaten, whipped, and had every finger in his hand broken by the thumbscrew. But he could taste the blood. The sickly, metallic scent filled his mouth and nose as if he were drowning in it.

His head hung forward, his hair—wet and caked with blood and sweat—shielding his gaze from the men around him. There'd been as many as a dozen to subdue him at some points throughout the night. Now, as the sunlight pierced the narrow arrow slits of the guard room, there were only three.

He was chained to a chair, but restraint wasn't necessary. He wasn't a threat to anyone anymore. His right arm had been twisted so hard it had popped out of the socket. His left hand hung useless at his side, every finger crushed one by one in excruciating slowness.

To think he'd laughed when he'd first seen the device. The small steel vise looked so unthreatening—certainly nothing that would compel him to tell them what they wanted.

But he'd quickly learned how something simple could exact terrifying amounts of pain. More pain than he'd ever imagined. He'd been one screw turn from telling them everything they wanted to know. He would have told them anything to make it stop.

"Damn you, Campbell, just tell them what they want to know."

Arthur eyed Alan MacDougall through the clumpy veil of sodden hair. Anna's brother stood near the door as if he couldn't wait to get the hell out of there, his face strained and bloodless. It almost looked as if he were the one being tortured. Lorn's heir did not have the stomach for this.

But his henchman did. Arthur had the feeling the sadistic bastard could go on like this for days.

Arthur could no longer speak, but he made a croaking sound and moved his head in a partial shake. Nay. Not yet. He wouldn't tell them yet. But he no longer said never.

His head snapped back as the bastard hit him again with his chain-wrapped sledgehammer of a fist.

"Their names," he demanded. "Who are the men who fight in the secret guard?"

Arthur no longer bothered to feign ignorance. They didn't believe him. Anna had unknowingly doomed him. Lorn was certain that he knew at least one member of the infamous "phantom" guard because of what had happened in Ayr a year ago when he'd come to her rescue and the recent attack.

He couldn't blame her for that. Nor, it seemed, could he blame her for turning him in. Sometime during the night— in between the beatings and the whip—he'd realized from the questions being pelted at him that he'd probably been wrong. If she had betrayed him, she hadn't told them much.

He sensed the bastard's fist going back again—a black spot on the edge of his consciousness. Instinctively, he braced himself for the blow, though he knew it wouldn't help. From his size and the power of his punch, the henchman could have come from a long line of blacksmiths.

A knock on the door, however, gave him a moment's reprieve when Lorn's henchman was called away.

Arthur slumped in the chair, trying to force gulps of air through his watery lungs. He had at least one broken rib, perhaps more.

"They'll kill you if you don't tell them," Alan said.

Arthur took a moment to respond, trying to pull together enough strength to speak. "They'll kill me anyway," he croaked.

Alan didn't look away, although from the way he winced, Arthur feared his face looked as bad as it felt. "Aye, but it will be far less painful."

And quicker.

But Arthur had failed in so many ways already; he was determined to salvage what he could of this cursed mission. If he could go to his death without revealing the names of his brethren, he would die with some semblance of honor.

Still, it would be a Pyrrhic victory at best when his failures were so catastrophic. He'd lost everything. Anna. The chance to destroy Lorn and get justice for his father. And the chance to alert the king of the threat. Bruce and his men would be walking right into an ambush, and he wouldn't be able to warn them.

He'd fail them, just as he had his father.

Being beaten to a bloody pulp, flayed to within an inch of his life, and having his fingers crushed one by one had kept his mind from wandering beyond the four stone walls of his prison. But in the small breaks, he feared the other consequences of his capture.

Lorn loved his daughter. He wouldn't hurt her. But he had to ask. "Anna?"

Alan gave him a solemn look. "Gone."

His stomach dropped.

Seeing his horrified expression, Alan hastily added, "She's safe. My father thought it better that she be removed from the castle until—"

He stopped. *Until I'm dead,* Arthur finished for him.

Air filled his lungs again. She'd only been sent away. But then he remembered. "Not . . . safe," he managed. With the battle coming, Bruce would have war bands all around them, closing in.

The grim line of Alan's mouth suggested he didn't disagree. But like Arthur, he'd been powerless to stop it.

"My brothers?" Arthur asked. Dugald and Gillespie might be his enemies on the battlefield, but he didn't want them to suffer for his choices.

"My father had no cause to believe them involved. They were questioned briefly, and appeared just as surprised as the rest of us." He paused, his gaze confused. "Why did you save my life? You didn't have to."

Arthur shook his hair away from his face to meet his gaze. "Aye, I did."

Alan nodded with understanding. "You really love her."

He didn't say anything. What could he say? It didn't matter anymore.

The door opened and Lorn's henchman came back in the small room, a rope in his hand.

Arthur's heartbeat spiked, an instinctive response to the danger.

"It's time to go," he said. "The men are ready to march."

Arthur steeled himself, knowing his time was at an end. He'd won. They would kill him now. One small victory in a bitter sea of failure.

"He's to be hanged, then?" Alan said.

The henchman smiled, the first hint of emotion Arthur had seen on his ugly, grizzled face. "Not yet. The rope is for the pit."

The relief that crashed over Arthur told him he wasn't quite as ready to die as he'd thought. After what he'd just been through, the dank hole of a pit prison would feel like heaven.

"Maybe the rats will loosen his tongue," the henchman laughed.

Or a living hell.

The blast of terror that shot through him gave him a primitive burst of strength. He thrashed against the steel of his bindings like a madman. His bruised, shredded skin crawled with the sensations of the rats covering him.

He had to get away.

But he couldn't. Chained and wounded, he was no match for the guardsmen who dragged him from the guard house to the adjoining room. In the end they didn't bother with the rope, but just tossed him in.

Dark.

Squeaking.

Falling. Reaching.

A hard, bone-shattering slam.

And then—blissfully—only blackness.

Twenty-four

"Ewen, I'm afraid I'm in dire need of a moment of privacy," Anna said, feigning a chagrined blush.

"Already?" He looked at her as if she were five years old. They were deep in the forest, near an old burial cairn, not two miles from the castle. "Why didn't you go before we left?"

She shot him a glare that told him she didn't appreciate him talking to her as if he were their mother. "Because I didn't have to go then."

He scowled. "We'll stop when we reach Oban; it's only another mile or so."

Anna shook her head. "I can't wait that long. Please . . ." She begged in a high voice, wiggling around in the saddle a little to emphasize the urgency.

Her brother muttered an oath, then turned to put a halt to the score of guardsmen who'd accompanied them on the roughly thirty-mile journey to Innis Chonnel—a journey that would be made much more swiftly by boat, but her father, before he'd sailed from the castle with his fleet, had decided it would be too dangerous.

"Hurry up, then," Ewen said impatiently. "One of my men will accompany—"

"That won't be necessary," she interrupted hastily. *It*

would ruin everything. "I . . ." She didn't have to fake the blush this time. "I fear I ate something this morning that didn't agree with me. It may be a while."

Her brother looked properly mortified by her sharing of the too-personal details of a subject that shouldn't be mentioned at all. Anna was appalled at herself for the nature and depth of her duplicity, but she needed as much time as possible to get away.

She had to get back to the castle. She couldn't explain it, but ever since she'd left her father's solar this morning, she hadn't been able to shake the overwhelming sense of foreboding. Perhaps it had been triggered by something her father said, but she knew something was wrong—terribly wrong. The feeling had only gotten worse as the castle faded into the sunlight behind them. She didn't know what she was going to do; she just knew that she had to do something.

They might not have a future, but she didn't want him to die.

Since her father had left the castle just before they did, this was her chance.

Mustering as much dignity as she could—given the humiliation of having roughly twenty men watching her tread off to relieve herself—she accepted the aid of her brother's squire to slide down off her horse, handed him the reins, and walked regally into the dense canopy of trees and bracken. The moment she was out of sight, she picked up the edge of her skirts and started to run.

It would take her about ten minutes to run back to the castle from here. How long it would take her to talk her way into the guard room where the prisoners were housed, she didn't know. But she hoped she could reach it before her brother realized she was missing. It wouldn't take Ewen long to figure out where she'd gone. And unlike her, he would be on a horse.

She raced through the trees, running parallel to but out

of sight of the road, trying to make as little sound as she could. But the dry leaves and branches littering the forest floor made silence impossible.

She heard a sound behind her and wanted to howl with anger. How had they discovered her missing so fast? She ducked behind a large rock, hoping to hide, but found herself lifted off the ground from behind.

"Let go of me," she said, trying to twist free. As she was expecting it to be her brother or one of his men, when she turned and found herself looking into the steely-eyed gaze of a brutish, nasal-helmed warrior, the blood drained from her body. She let out a cry of alarm that was muffled by his hand.

"Shush, lass, I don't want to hurt you."

His fearsome visage didn't inspire a lot of confidence. He was built like a mountain, with rugged, rough-hewn features to go along with his bulk.

She forced herself to still, pretending to believe him, then as soon as he relaxed, she kicked him as hard as she could with the edge of her booted heel and shoved her elbow as deep as she could into his leather-clad chest, wincing when she connected with the bits of steel.

He let out a grunt of surprise, but never loosened his hold enough for her to free herself.

She gazed back at him in frustration again, and she stilled—this time for real. There was something familiar about him. Nay, not about him, but about his attire.

She sucked in her breath. The blackened helm, the black leather *cotun* studded with mail, the strangely fashioned plaid . . .

It was the same distinctive warrior's garb worn by the handsome warrior in Ayr and by her uncle. This man was part of Bruce's secret guard.

A fact that was confirmed only a moment later. "I don't think my former niece believes you, Saint."

Anna gazed in stunned surprise as Lachlan MacRuairi emerged from the trees alongside another warrior.

"Saint, Templar," he motioned toward her, "May I present the Lady Anna MacDougall." He waved off the man holding her. "You can release her. She won't scream unless she wants to see her brother and his men killed."

Anna rubbed her mouth as soon as she was free, trying to return the sensation. She looked around. "There are only three of you."

The men looked genuinely amused by her comment. "Two more than we need," the third man said. He was slightly smaller of stature than the other two men—she was beginning to think being a muscle-strapped giant was a requirement for becoming a member of Bruce's secret army—and beneath the shadow of his nasal helm his grin was both good-natured and friendly.

Templar, her uncle had called him. What a strange name. He was far too young to have fought against the infidel. The last crusade was over thirty-five years ago.

And he'd called the man who'd been holding her Saint. They must be *noms de guerre*—war names—she realized.

Ranger! That was what the handsome man in the forest had called Arthur. Was that his war name?

"What are you doing here, Uncle?" It felt strange to call someone only ten years or so her senior *Uncle*. He didn't look much older than Arthur, though he must be three or four and thirty.

"Perhaps I should ask the same thing of you. Why did you flee from your brother and his men?"

She wasn't surprised that he hadn't answered her. He'd either been scouting the area or watching the castle. As they were very close to the coast, she figured he'd come by boat. Lachlan MacRuairi was a seafaring pirate to the bone.

"You are supporting Bruce's attack against my father from the sea," she said, guessing at his purpose.

He shrugged evasively. "Now, tell me, Lady Anna, why I find you running through the forest."

"I need to return to the castle."

"Why?"

She bit her lip, debating what to tell them. But she knew she didn't have much time. They'd delayed her too long already. She'd be hard pressed to make it back to the castle before her brother caught up with her. Perhaps they would give her a ride?

"Do you have horses nearby?" she asked.

MacRuairi frowned. "Aye."

She exhaled. "Good. I shall need your help to get back to the castle. I need to make sure Arthur is all right." None of the men reacted. Nor should they, she supposed. They didn't know she knew the truth. "I believe you call him Ranger."

MacRuairi swore. "He told you?"

She shook her head. "It's a long story. I figured out the truth. Unfortunately, I wasn't the only one. My father knows as well."

He swore again, this oath a vile expletive that even her father rarely used. "Then he's dead."

"Nay," she said, taken aback by his vehemence. "Imprisoned. My father is questioning him."

MacRuairi spat, a look of raw hatred coming over his dark features. "Then he'll wish he was."

What did he mean?

Reading her confusion, he said, "I've been on the other side of your father's 'questions' before. He has rather persuasive and inventive methods of exacting information. If Ranger isn't dead already, he soon will be."

Her stomach turned at what he was suggesting. "My father wouldn't—"

It wasn't the grim expression on his face that stopped her protest, but the memory of the partial conversation she'd heard upon entering her father's solar. A conversation that now made sense. *Get me what I want. Whatever it takes.*

Oh God. Anna nearly buckled over, feeling as if she were going to be ill. Her father was torturing him. She knew such things happened, of course, but it was an ugly side of war that she didn't like to think about. Nor did she like to think of her father being involved in such cruelty.

"We need to help him," she said frantically, tears pricking her eyes.

Her heart slammed in her chest when she heard a shout go out a short distance away. "Anna!"

She looked at the three men in panic. "They're calling for me—we have to go *now.*"

MacRuairi shook his head. "There's no need for you to come. We'll take care of it."

"But—"

He cut off her protest. "If you come with us, they'll follow. It will be easier for us to help him if they don't suspect anything. Return to your brother and continue on your journey."

"But you might need my help." And she wanted to see him for herself. "How will you get in the castle? How will you find him?"

MacRuairi's mouth was set in a grim line. "I know where he is." She shivered, knowing from the way he said it that he'd been there himself. But it was the haunted look in his eyes that chilled her blood.

God, what had her father done to him? And what was he doing to Arthur?

"You've done enough," he said. "If Ranger is alive, he'll have you to thank for it."

If he's alive. Anna bit back her tears and nodded, knowing they were right. The best way for her to help Arthur was to let them go without her. But it didn't make watching them disappear into the trees any easier. She wanted to go with them.

He's alive, she told herself. He had to be. She'd know if he wasn't. A part of her would have died as well.

As soon as they were out of sight, she started to run back in the direction from which she'd come. When she drew near a small stream, she answered her brother's calls. She would have some explaining to do, but considering the subject matter she didn't think her brother would be inclined to question her too heavily.

Now, all she could do was pray for a miracle. For that's what it would take to rescue Arthur from the virtually impenetrable Dunstaffnage Castle before it was too late.

Arthur let them come. Honing his senses on each scamper and squeak, he let the rats get close enough to catch, then was able to snap their necks with one hand against his leg. Which, as he had only one working hand, was fortunate. Unfortunately that hand was attached to a dislocated arm, so every movement was excruciating. He'd tried to pop the arm back into his shoulder by himself, but he didn't have the strength or the leverage.

Being eaten alive by starving rats wasn't the way Arthur had hoped to die, but he didn't know how much longer he could fend them off. Each time he passed out, their gnawing bites would wake him. But he'd lost a lot of blood, and with each hour that passed he was getting weaker and his senses were dulling. Soon he wouldn't wake at all.

He thought he must have killed fifty of the disgusting creatures already, but there were hundreds of them down here. He shuddered. When they'd held the torch to the hole to drop him in, the entire floor had been swarming in them.

With the hole closed up it was pitch-black in the pit. He was dependent on his senses, which were slowly fading.

His eyes started to close. He was so tired, he just wanted to relax for a . . .

"Ah!" He let out a sharp cry of pain, snapping back to

attention as razor-sharp teeth sunk into his ankle. He kicked, sending the rat flying.

He supposed he had Dugald to thank for his lasting this long. Those hours spent in the dark storage outbuilding had taught him well. He knew what to listen for and how to anticipate the rats' movements.

But his reactions were slowing. More were escaping his grasp, and more of their teeth were finding his hand. He knew he couldn't last much longer.

They wouldn't come for him until the battle was over. As he'd lost track of time hours ago, he didn't know when that might be.

Damn. It wasn't just the horror of the swarming rats that was driving him mad, but the knowledge that his friends were out there marching into a trap and he couldn't help them.

He'd failed. *Failed.* He closed his eyes, wanting to blot out the bitter truth. The heaviness bore down on him. It was getting harder to resist the pull, the drag toward the blissful darkness of unconsciousness. He was so tired.

This time his eyes stayed closed.

Nothing could wake him. Not the rats, and not the blast of thunder that sent the guards running to the gate a few minutes later.

Someone was shaking him.

"Ranger! Ranger! God damn it, wake up! We don't have much time."

Who was Ranger?

His eyes snapped open, only to close again as the beam of light from the torch pierced his skull like a dagger.

He was Ranger.

But how . . . ?

He opened his eyes again. Slowly this time, letting them grow adjusted to the light.

MacRuairi.

He could see the relief on the other man's face. "I wasn't sure you were alive."

Arthur's mind felt dull and sluggish. "I wasn't sure either."

MacRuairi shuddered, and even in the torchlight Arthur could see that he didn't look well. His face was gray and his eyes flickered around anxiously. He almost looked panicked. "Let's get the hell out of here. Can you walk?"

Arthur nodded, trying to scoot himself up to a sitting position. He was careful not to look down. The torch was keeping the rats away for now. "I think so."

"Good, I wasn't looking forward to trying to carry you out of here."

He held out his hand, but Arthur shook him off and managed to struggle to his feet. "You're alone?" he asked.

MacRuairi's gaze flickered over him, quickly assessing the damage. His mouth hardened as he realized the reason for Arthur's refusal of aid. "Nay. Saint and Templar are with me. Hawk wanted to come, but someone needed to stay with the fleet. You didn't hear the blast?"

Arthur shook his head. "Is that how you got in?"

MacRuairi helped secure the rope around his waist and between his legs. Arthur's legs trembled like those of a newborn foal, but he managed to stay upright.

"Nay, but it's good for a distraction." MacRuairi grabbed hold of a second rope and quickly climbed up. Then he hoisted Arthur up with the rope, which wasn't easy as he was virtual dead weight on the other end. But MacRuairi, in addition to being as mean as a snake, was as strong as a bloody ox.

The sense of relief that hit Arthur to be out of that hell-hole was nearly overwhelming. He felt like bawling like a babe. MacRuairi unwrapped the plaid he was wearing and handed it to him. Arthur had forgotten he was naked. He accepted it gratefully, securing it around his waist and shoulders as best as he could with his mangled hand.

"The stench of rat shite will eventually wash away."

Arthur was surprised to see the hint of compassion in the other man's gaze. Suddenly, he realized why MacRuairi had looked so close to panic down there. He'd known what it was like. He must have been through something similar. "And the rest?" Arthur asked.

MacRuairi turned sharply away, as if the chip in his icy armor annoyed him. "The rest takes longer."

Or never. Arthur heard the unspoken words.

"How did you find me?"

"The lass told us you'd been taken prisoner. I figured out the rest."

The lass . . .

"Anna?" he asked, his voice sharp with disbelief.

"Aye, it was fortunate we caught sight of her." MacRuairi explained how they'd been scouting the area and checking the burial cairn in the woods to make sure he hadn't left any messages when they heard a group of riders nearby. They'd glimpsed Anna and had followed her when she gave her brother and his men the slip.

Arthur was shocked. "She tried to escape?"

"Apparently she wanted to make sure you were all right."

He muttered an oath. Thank God she hadn't been the one to find him. He never wanted her to know what her father had done to him. It was too much reality. Let her hold on to some illusions.

But knowing that she cared enough to come find him meant a lot. More than a lot. He owed her his life. It also gave him hope.

"Ah hell," MacRuairi muttered with disgust. "You've got the same silly-arse look in your eye as MacSorley. We don't have time for this. I'll tell you the rest later." MacRuairi wrapped one arm around Arthur's waist, careful to avoid his injured shoulder, and helped him walk to the door. He knocked twice in quick succession, then once slowly. The door opened.

"Damn, Viper. I was about to go in after you." Magnus "Saint" MacKay took one look at Arthur and winced. "You all right, Ranger?"

Arthur tried to smile but faltered at the sting of pain. "I've been better, but I'm damned glad to see you. How did—"

A loud boom thundered through the night air, cutting off his question. *Night* air. Jesus, the attack! "What time is it?"

"A little after midnight," MacKay said.

"I have information for the king—"

"Later," MacRuairi said. "We don't have time. That was our distraction. If we want to get out of here, we'll have to hurry."

With MacKay on one side and MacRuairi on the other, they carried Arthur from the antechamber and into the guard room. A quick glance down told him what had become of the guardsmen. Unfortunately, none of the three bodies was that of his torturer. The henchman had marched with Lorn.

Yet one more reason he hoped to hell they got there in time—and another debt to pay.

They exited the tower housing the guard room into the cover of darkness. The courtyard was deserted, though he could hear a commotion coming from near the gate. Instead of heading in that direction, however, they started up the rampart.

Arthur realized what MacRuairi had planned. On the far side of the rampart opposite the gate and overlooking the loch, they secured three long ropes to the parapet. Normally a guard would be walking the perimeter, but the blast had diverted him to the gate.

Arthur glanced down into the darkness and grimaced.

"We'll have to fix your shoulder first," MacRuairi said.

He turned him around, grabbing hold of the top of his arm. He handed Arthur his dagger. "Ready?"

Arthur put the wooden hilt between his teeth and nodded. The pain was extreme but quick. After a moment, he was able to roll his shoulder freely in the socket. "You've done that before?" Arthur said.

"Nay," MacRuairi said, a rare smile on his face. "But I've seen it done. I guess you're lucky I'm a quick study."

With his arm back in position, Arthur was able to shimmy down the rope with their help. When they were all safely on the ground, MacRuairi led them to a dark section of the outer wall. Arthur looked down, noticing a few stones had been removed, leaving a hole beneath. They'd burrowed their way in.

"This is the oldest section of the wall," MacRuairi explained. "The rocks almost crumble out."

He must have done this before, Arthur realized. Gordon was waiting for them on the other side.

"What took you so—" He took one look at Arthur and stopped. "Ah, hell, Ranger, you look like shite."

"So I've heard," Arthur said dryly.

They took time to repair the wall in case they ever needed to use it again, and a short while later they were running along the shore. About a half-mile away from the castle, they found the small skiff that MacRuairi had hidden in a cove.

"You need to get me to the king. As fast as you can," Arthur said. Already he could see the first light of dawn softening the night sky on the eastern horizon. With the seaway to Brander blocked by Lorn's fleet, they would have to ride. "I hope we make it in time."

"What is it?" MacKay said, sensing the urgency. "What have you found out?"

As they sailed west, slipping through the barricade of ships where Loch Etive met the open sea at the Firth of Lorn, Arthur quickly explained Lorn's treacherous plan—

both the details of the ambush and of planning to attack before the end of the truce.

Gordon swore. "The treacherous whoreson."

MacKay echoed his sentiments in far more colorful terms, then added, "The king won't be expecting it."

"Aye," Arthur added. "Lorn has chosen his place well." He explained the narrow pass and steep-sided gully of Ben Cruachan.

"I know the place," MacRuairi added. "The scouts will be hard pressed to find them."

"Which is why we have to warn them."

MacRuairi shook his head grimly. "They are marching at first light. Even if we get there before they reach the narrowest part of the pass, it won't be easy to turn three thousand troops around. This entire area is dangerous."

"They won't need to turn around," Arthur said. "I have a plan."

His three fellow guardsmen exchanged looks.

"What?" he asked.

It was Gordon who said what they were all thinking. "You aren't in any condition to fight. We can get the message to the king."

Arthur grit his teeth together. "I'm going." Nothing would stop him from fighting. If he had a chance in hell of facing Lorn on the battlefield, he was going to take it.

"You'll only slow us down," MacRuairi said bluntly. "You don't look strong enough to sit a mule, let alone travel at the pace we're riding. And how the hell are you going to hold the reins with that hand?"

Arthur shot him a venomous look. "Let me worry about it."

MacRuairi met his gaze. After a moment, he nodded. "We'd better find something for you to fight in."

They made it in time, and Arthur didn't fall off his horse—although he'd come embarrassingly close.

With MacDougall's men already in position, they'd been forced to flank around them from the south. They caught up with the king less than a mile from the pass.

The king didn't give way to temper very often, but he did so when Arthur informed him of Lorn's plan.

He swore and called Lorn every vile name under the sun. "By the rood, how did we miss this?" he demanded of no one in particular, but each of the warriors felt blame for what could have been a disaster—including the king. He knew better than to trust in the code of chivalry.

"They're hiding high in the rocks on a steep hillside," Arthur said. "It would be easy to miss them if you aren't looking for them."

From the looks MacLeod was giving the scouts, Arthur knew—understandable or not—there would be hell to pay.

"You said you have a plan?" the king asked.

"Aye." Arthur knelt down and drew a map in the ground with a stick. "We can beat Lorn at his own game. A few hundred men are positioned here." Arthur marked the position halfway up the hillside. "The rest of his army will attack at the mouth of the pass, as you are trying to flee—catching you from above and from below." He pointed to a place a little above Lorn's men. "If you send a group of men above them, Lorn's men will be trapped. When the ambush fails, Lorn will be overwhelmed."

Bruce frowned. "Are you sure we can get men up there? From what you describe, the terrain is steep and treacherous. If they discover us before we are in position it will not work."

"My Highlanders can do it," his brother Neil said. "They know this ground."

"You're sure of it?" Bruce asked.

"Aye," Neil said. "They fight like lions but they move like cats."

"I'll lead them," Arthur said. "I know the terrain well."

Neil was still one of the most formidable warriors in the kingdom, but he was fifty and not as fleet-footed as he once was.

Bruce's gaze swept over him and Arthur could read his uncertainty. Though he'd washed most of the blood and filth from him before donning his borrowed battle garb, wrapped his hand and wrist, and ate and drank enough *uisge-beatha* to put color back in his face, he knew he still looked like he'd been chewed up and spit out by a rabid beast from hell.

Before the king could deny him, he added, "I can do it, sire. I look worse than I feel."

It was a lie, but not much of one. The knowledge that he was close to the reckoning with Lorn had invigorated him.

"You've earned the right, Sir Arthur," the king said. "Without your information, this could have been a disaster." Arthur knew the memory of Dal Righ, two years before, where Lorn had sent him fleeing for his life, was still too fresh on Bruce's mind. Bruce called forward one of his youngest but most trusted knights, Sir James Douglas. Douglas's chief rival, the king's nephew and former turncoat Sir Thomas Randolph, was with MacSorley in the west, readying the sea attack should it be necessary. "Douglas, I want you to go with him." He motioned to one of the other warriors. Gregor MacGregor, Arthur's original partner in the Highland Guard, stepped forward. To him he said, "Arrow you're in charge of the archers." To Arthur he ordered, "Take as many men as you need."

"Better toss some MacGregors in there, Ranger," MacGregor said to him, as the king turned to confer with Neil and MacLeod. "We can't let the Campbells claim all the glory."

Arthur managed a smile. God, it was good to be back. Good to jest about the ancient blood feud between the MacGregors and Campbells that had once made them bitter enemies. "That's just like a MacGregor, wanting credit for a Campbell's hard work."

"I need something to impress the lasses with," MacGregor said.

Campbell laughed. MacGregor didn't need anything to impress the lasses; his face did it for him—it was also a subject that provided plenty of fodder to prod him with. "If you want help with that pretty face of yours, I can send you to the guy who did this." He pointed to his own.

MacGregor winced. "The bastard was thorough, I'll give him that."

"I'll make sure to compliment him for you when I catch up with him," he said dryly. They both knew that would not be a long conversation.

Neil had finished with the king and pulled Arthur aside as he was going to ready the men. "Are you sure you're all right, Arthur? Everyone would understand if you don't feel up to it. You've done enough already."

I would understand, he meant. Arthur could see it in his brother's face. But they both knew this wasn't the end. "I'll be fine," he assured him, "when this is done."

Twenty-five

Arthur's plan worked. With Douglas, MacGregor, and a small force of his brother's men, he led the war band to a place high on the slopes of Ben Cruachan above Lorn's lying-in-ambush clansmen. As Bruce's army came marching through the narrow pass below, the MacDougalls unfurled a hail of arrows and rolling boulders down on the "unsuspecting" soldiers.

But the MacDougall "surprise" attack was met by another. The MacDougall warriors gazed up in horror as Arthur and his men let unfurl a hail of arrows of their own and descended on them like wraiths.

Having lost the element of surprise, and the strategically important higher ground, the MacDougall ambush became a rout. Trapped from above and below, the men were crushed. When Lorn launched his frontal attack at the mouth of the pass, instead of confronting an army in disarray, he was met with the full force of Bruce's powerful army.

Arthur raced down the steep mountain, joining in the fray, cutting through the swarm of battling soldiers with one purpose in mind: finding Lorn. He caught sight of Alan MacDougall across the hillside, rallying his men and valiantly attempting to wage another charge. But valiance wouldn't be enough. He hoped for Anna's sake that Alan recognized this before it was too late.

The narrow funnel of the pass took away some of Bruce's advantage in numbers, but it wasn't long before Lorn's attack collapsed. Arthur reached the front line just as the MacDougall vanguard started to break.

At the head of his army, fighting alongside his closest knights and the members of the Highland Guard, King Robert ordered pursuit of the fleeing clansmen. In the frantic attempt to retreat to Dunstaffnage, many MacDougalls were cut down or drowned while trying to cross the bridge over the River Awe.

They'd won! The MacDougalls' attempt to best Bruce had failed, and the king had his revenge for Dal Righ. The hold of the most powerful clan in the Highlands had been broken.

Victory was sweet, but it wouldn't be complete until Arthur found Lorn.

In the chaos of the retreat, he scanned the fleeing clansmen for his enemy. He was glad to see Alan MacDougall leading a contingent of his men to safety.

Catching sight of MacRuairi near the bridge, he made his way down to him.

"Where is he?" Arthur didn't need to say who.

MacRuairi spat and pointed south to the mouth of Loch Awe. "He never left his *birlinn*—the bloody coward directed the battle from the water. As soon as the men started to retreat, he fled down the loch."

Arthur swore, refusing to believe that he could have come so far to be denied the chance for justice at the last moment. "How long ago?"

"Five minutes, not more."

Then he still had a chance. But he would need MacRuairi's seafaring skills if he was going to try to catch him. Lorn had three castles on Loch Awe, but the newest—and most heavily fortified—was Innis Chonnel, the former Campbell stronghold. That's where he would go.

Arthur's gaze fell levelly on MacRuairi. "Feel like a race?"

The man known as one of the most feared and menacing pirates on the sea smiled—at least it was supposed to be a smile. "I'll gather the men; you find the boat."

Arthur was already running down the edge of the river toward the harbor. This was one race he didn't intend to lose. John of Lorn would not escape his fate this time.

All Anna could do was wait. But not knowing what was happening beyond the thick stone walls of Innis Chonnel Castle was pure torture.

Her heart tugged. Nay, not torture. It was nothing like what Arthur was going through. She couldn't bear to think about it, yet it seemed she could do nothing else. Imagining what was happening to him . . . Not sure whether he lived or died . . .

It was madness! How was her uncle going to get into the castle, let alone rescue him?

I should have gone with them. Then at least she would know. But her uncle was right: she would only have led her brother back to the castle.

The hours passed slowly. When not on her knees praying in the small chapel, she tried to keep herself busy.

With most of her father's soldiers called to battle, only a small force of guardsmen—perhaps a score—had been retained to hold the castle. When her party had arrived the evening before (with no more false trips to the stream), Anna had organized the men into preparing the chambers, freshening the Great Hall, and inventorying the stores.

Innis Chonnel Castle had been built about the same time as Dunstaffnage. Though not as grand, it shared a similar construction. The square-shaped fortress was built upon a rocky base on the southwestern end of the island. The high,

thick stone walls surrounded a small courtyard. Two
square towers had been built into the corners, the large one
serving as the donjon and the second as the guard house.
Between them was the Great Hall. Other smaller wooden
buildings, housing the barracks, armory, stables, and
kitchens, had been built against the walls.

It was strange to think that this had once been Arthur's
home. She'd always enjoyed visiting this castle with her father, but now it felt strange. It felt as if she shouldn't be
there. As if she were an intruder.

She knew it was ridiculous. Castles changed hands all
the time in war. But with what he'd told her . . .

Anna was torn. Torn between the father she still loved
though no longer idolized and the man whom she should
hate but couldn't.

She didn't want to understand why Arthur had done
what he'd done, but she did. She could understand the loyalty that drove him because it drove her as well. Loyalty to
king and country. Loyalty to clan and family.

Aye, she especially understood that.

Arthur was a Highlander. Blood for blood was the Highland way. He would feel it his duty to avenge his father's
death. But she knew it was more than vengeance. A part of
him was still that little boy who'd watched his father die,
believing he should have been able to prevent it. Justice.
Revenge. It was also atonement.

But understanding did not bring any answers. What
could she do when loving one meant losing the other?

After a restless night, she spent the day after her arrival
in much the same way as the first—praying and trying to
keep herself busy so she wouldn't think about what was
happening beyond the thick walls. If her fears for Arthur's
fate weren't enough, there was also the battle being waged.

The world as she knew it could be ending right now. The
men she loved could be lying dead or wounded, and yet
here, in the protected confines of Innis Chonnel on the iso-

lated isle on Loch Awe, everything appeared normal. The bright sunlight still shimmered off the softly undulating waters of the loch, the birds still flew, and the damp wind still ripped through her hair as she paced the courtyard.

She caught sight of Ewen exiting the square donjon. "Any word?" she asked, though she already knew his answer. She would have heard the call go up if anyone was approaching.

He shook his head. "Nay, not yet."

She knew the wait was hard on her brother too, albeit for different reasons. He wanted to fight. But if he blamed her for his banishment to Innis Chonnel while the battle waged on, he did not show it.

She chewed on her lower lip. "I wish I knew what was happening."

He smiled. "I do as well. But as soon as there is anything to report—"

"Ships approaching, sir!" The call came from one of the guards in the high tower.

Anna followed her brother as he raced up the stairs to the ramparts. She could just make out the three square sails bearing down on them from the north. They were coming fast.

"It's father," Ewen said, his voice despondent.

A chill of foreboding ran down her spine. "What is it? What's wrong?"

Ewen didn't bother to try to hide the truth from her. "He would only be coming here if it were necessary."

Necessary. Her heart dropped. Meaning if he were in retreat.

They'd lost!

She wobbled a little, her legs suddenly feeling like jelly. Gripping the stone edge of the rampart with her fingers to steady herself, she watched the ships approaching and prayed for another explanation. Anything but that Bruce had won.

She squinted into the sunlight, seeing something else. "What's that?" she said, pointing just beyond the oncoming ships. "Behind them?"

But Ewen was already shouting orders. "Attack! To your positions!"

The men sprang into action, while Anna, unable to look away, watched in stunned horror as the ships approached. Her father's men didn't seem to be aware they were being chased.

"Behind you!" she shouted, trying to warn them. But the wind carried her voice away.

Ewen shouted up to her. "Anna, get away from there. It isn't safe. Go to the tower and bar the door."

Mutely, she nodded and did as he bid. Once inside, she raced to her second-floor chamber to look out the small window. As the donjon tower was on the southern corner of the castle, she couldn't see the boats until they'd nearly reached the landing area.

Heart in her throat, she watched as the battle broke out right below her.

She could see her father at the rear of his men, shouting orders, as the ship of enemy warriors—

She stopped, her heart catching with a fierce, thudding jolt. She blinked. No, it wasn't a dream. Her heart squeezed as a hard swell of relief rose inside her.

Arthur was alive.

He was dressed in unfamiliar battle garb, his hair and face shielded by a nasal helm, on the surface unrecognizable from the other warriors around him. But she knew it was him.

Thank God.

Then, suddenly, the full import of his presence hit her. Horror washed over her, clinging in an icy embrace. If he was here, it was for one reason.

She raced to the door, knowing she had to do something. She had to stop him. She couldn't let him kill her father.

* * *

The moment Arthur had been waiting for was here. Somehow it seemed fitting that the final reckoning would take place on the small island of Innis Chonnel, in the hulking shadow of the castle that had once been his home.

The race had been close, but in the end Lachlan MacRuairi had given proof that his reputation was well earned. Hiding in the black hole of the bright sunlight, he bore down on Lorn's retreating ships undetected, catching up with the three *birlinns* as they neared the landing.

Only then did Arthur launch a barrage of arrows on the unsuspecting MacDougalls.

MacRuairi had gathered forty of his pirate clansmen, which given the roughly three times as many MacDougalls should have been an uneven fight. But MacRuairi's men were more than up to the challenge. Brigands, cutthroats, ruffians—that was describing them generously—the MacRuairis had earned their reputation as the greatest scourge of the sea.

But they fought just as fiercely on land.

The MacRuairi warriors were already jumping out of the boat—swords raised, letting go a cry of "For the Lion"—as MacRuairi pulled their purloined ship up to the landing on the heels of the MacDougall ships. Arthur was right there with them, leading the charge.

Lorn had positioned his men at the end of the jetty, expecting to easily cut down MacRuairi's men as they attempted to reach land.

But the MacDougall warriors weren't any match for the vicious onslaught of their kinsmen. Though both clans were descended from sons of Somerled—the Norse king who'd ruled the Isles over 150 years ago—they'd battled often over the generations for supremacy. The MacDougalls had won after Largs, growing in favor with the Scottish kings, but assimilation had taken them farther away from their Viking roots. The MacRuairis fought like the barbarians that they had been not so long ago—that most might still call them.

They broke through the wall of MacDougall soldiers easily, sending the battle onto the rocky shores of the island.

With only one arm—not to mention his weakened condition—Arthur was at a disadvantage. But while nowhere near his normal fighting abilities, he managed to hold his own. Plowing determinedly through the clansmen, he kept his eye on Lorn the entire time.

Lorn was at the rear of the battle, in the protective circle of his men. One of whom was his henchman.

Arthur's blood rushed in anticipation.

The MacDougalls were being pushed back, and it soon became clear that Lorn's superior numbers were not going to win the day.

Locked in a fierce sword fight with one of the MacDougall clansmen—a man he unfortunately knew—Arthur heard the cry for retreat.

He swore, knowing that he had to stop Lorn and his bloody henchman before they reached the safety of the castle gates.

He wouldn't come this close and be denied.

With a renewed burst of energy, he deflected a blow from his opponent and, using the force of it, spun his sword around under him and delivered a death strike.

Lorn—still protected by his henchman—was racing the fifty feet or so to the castle gate.

Not this time.

Arthur drew the attention of a few of MacRuairi's men, telling them what he wanted them to do. He fought his way toward Lorn, the men following behind him. They created a hole in the protective circle around Lorn, cutting him and his henchman off from the group. Once Arthur was through, MacRuairi's men spread out to form a barrier behind him.

If Lorn wasn't a few dozen feet from the safety of the castle walls, Arthur would have enjoyed this particular death more. But as it was, he was forced to dispatch the henchman quickly. For all the man's skill at torture, he was no match for Arthur—even one-handed.

At last he turned to Lorn, catching up with him not ten feet from the gate. Lorn's men were so busy defending themselves that no one was able to come to his aid.

Arthur could see the rage in his eyes as Lorn lifted his sword to his. "How did you escape?" he demanded incredulously.

"Surprised to see me?"

Lorn's eyes flashed murderously. "I should have killed you."

"Aye, you should have."

"You are the reason for this disaster. You betrayed my plans to the murdering whoreson."

"King Robert," Arthur prodded, circling him like prey. "I would say you should get used to saying it, but you won't be around long enough."

And with that he swung.

Lorn was prepared for the blow and managed to deflect it—albeit barely, his entire body shaking with the effort. John of Lorn, once one of the most feared warriors in the Highlands, was no longer a threat. Age and illness had taken their toll. It wasn't cowardice but illness that had kept him on the loch and at the back of the battlefield. Lorn's damned pride prevented him from admitting just how sick he was.

Arthur's second blow brought him to his knees. He held the tip of his sword to Lorn's neck, the mail coif no match for the sharp steel of Arthur's sword.

The sun flashed off the older man's helm—just as it had that day fourteen years ago when Arthur had watched from afar as his father held the blade to this same man's neck and offered him mercy.

It was the moment he'd been waiting for. Anticipation should be surging through his veins. The taste of victory should be sweet. His muscles should be clenched, ready to drive the blade forward.

But he felt none of those things.

All he could think about was Anna.

If he did this, he would forever be to her the man that Lorn had been to him: the man who killed her father.

Perhaps her forgiveness was more than he had a right to hope for, but if he killed Lorn he'd destroy whatever chance remained.

What honor was there in killing a man too sick to fight? His father had his justice. Lorn was finished. His defeat at Brander had crushed whatever hope he'd had of stopping Bruce.

Anna was right. Killing him now would be nothing more than revenge, and he wanted her more than he wanted whatever fleeting moment of satisfaction killing Lorn would give him.

Well, maybe more than fleeting, but he wanted her more all the same.

From beneath the steel visor of his helm, Lorn's gaze burned into his. "What are you waiting for? Just do it!"

Mercy. His father's last lesson; though he'd forgotten it until now.

"Submit to the king, and I will let you live."

Lorn's face contorted in rage. "I'd rather die."

"And what of your family? What of your clan? Would you have them die, too?"

His eyes blazed with raw hatred. "Better than to submit to a murderer."

"You'd see your daughters die for your damned pride?" Arthur could feel his temper rising. He knew Anna. She would never go against her father. Family was everything to her. "Give Anna your blessing. I'll keep her safe. You know as well as I do that you are done. But your clan can live on in our children—in your grandchildren."

Lorn's rage had turned frenzied. Veins bulged at his temples, his eyes were glazed with madness, and his face was beet red. He let go a string of vile oaths, spittle foaming at the edge of his mouth. "You will never have her. I'd rather see her dead!"

"Father!"

Arthur heard the anguished cry behind him. Anna. He turned instinctively.

Giving Lorn his back. Just as his father had done before him.

Twenty-six

Anna reached the courtyard just as Arthur brought her father to his knees.

Oh God, she was too late!

She ran faster.

Ewen and the other men were attempting to defend the castle with carefully aimed arrows through the slits in the curtain wall, ready to lower the gate just as soon as her father and his men retreated inside.

The guardsmen at the gate were so focused on watching what was in front of them, they didn't see her slip past them.

"My lady!" one of the men called after her. "You can't—"

She wasn't listening. She darted a few feet beyond the gate, but didn't make it far. The enemy soldiers had formed a line, separating Arthur and her father from the rest of the fight. When she attempted to run past them, one of the men caught her.

"God's blood!" he said, lifting her feet off the ground. "Where do you think you're going, lass?"

She opened her mouth to scream at the terrifying-looking ruffian to let her go, but then she heard Arthur speak and stilled in the soldier's arms.

She couldn't believe what she heard.

Arthur held a sword at her father's neck, at the very point of achieving the vengeance and atonement that had driven him, and offered him mercy. Offered her father a chance to save them all. A chance that after what he'd probably done to him, her father didn't deserve. A chance for a future.

He loves me, she realized. *He loves me enough to put aside his quest for vengeance.*

But if Arthur's words had filled her heart, her father's eviscerated her.

I'd rather see her dead.

She recoiled, wrenching out of her captor's hold. Shock and horror made her cry out.

He didn't mean it.

But she knew he did. He would rather see her dead than married to the enemy, even if she loved him. His harsh refusal of Arthur's offer shattered what was left of her illusions.

But her cry was a mistake. A mistake more horrible than she could have imagined.

Her voice should have been lost in the heavy din of battle. No one should have heard her. But Arthur did. He turned at the sound of her voice, and the world seemed to stop.

Dear God in Heaven. Beneath the shadow of his helm the sight of his beaten, ravaged face made her stomach clench and bile rise to the back of her throat.

But the worse horror was yet to come. Out of the corner of her eye she saw her father's sword flash.

"No!" She took a step forward, but the man caught her before she could advance. "Watch out!" she screamed.

Blind spot. She was his blind spot. But she couldn't let him die for it.

Arthur spun, swinging his sword around to deflect her father's death blow with enough force to rip her father's sword from his hand and send it flying through the air.

Arthur raised his sword over his head.

Anna turned away, shielding her eyes from the horror of what was to come. He was going to kill her father, and after what he'd just done she couldn't blame him.

She waited for the sickening thud of death.

But the silence seemed endless. It was so quiet that she realized the battle around them had stilled as well.

"Go," she heard Arthur say. "You have five minutes to take your men and daughter from this castle."

Her gaze shot back to her father—her father who was still alive. Arthur had lowered his sword and moved away from him. Her father had gotten to his feet, his face a mask of rage and defiance. "You're a fool."

"And you're lucky that your daughter means more to me than your foul life. But I assure you, the king will not feel the same. Leave on your own or leave in chains. It matters not to me, but leave you will."

As if to bolster his words, a cry came from above. "Ships, my lord. A half dozen of them, headed this way."

Bruce.

Her father didn't hesitate. Gathering his men, he ordered Ewen to evacuate the castle and bring whatever weapons he could carry.

The man holding her released her. She ran forward, but Arthur was already walking away.

He and the other Bruce warriors—she recognized her uncle among the group—moved to the side to let the MacDougalls pass.

Her uncle didn't look too pleased with the arrangement, but after a quick but harsh exchange of words, he and Arthur stood silent.

Arthur wouldn't look at her.

Why wouldn't he look at her? She wanted to go to him, but he looked so remote. So distant.

Her heart squeezed with doubt.

She'd always thought he would be the one to leave her.

But he stood like a sentinel: solid, stalwart, and true. A man to count on. A man who would stand down dragons and crawl through the fires of hell.

"Come, Anna. It's time to go." Ewen had come up behind her, attempting to steer her away by her elbow.

"I . . ." She hesitated, her eyes flickering to Arthur as if expecting—hoping—he would say something.

Ewen gave her an uncertain look as he moved off with his men.

Her father must have caught the exchange. "Don't do it, daughter. Don't even think about it."

Her gaze fell on her father. The man she'd loved her entire life. A man who was far more complex than she'd realized. It was hard to reconcile the loving father with the man she'd seen here today, though she knew they were one and the same.

For a moment, she wanted to go back to being that little girl who'd sat on her father's knee and looked at him as if he were a god. To go back to when things were simple.

If she'd ever doubted Arthur's love, she could no longer. Not after what he'd just done for her.

"I love him, Father. Please."

She saw the flash of hurt before her father's gaze hardened. "I'll hear no more of this. Make your choice. But do not be mistaken. Go to him, and I will never see you again. You will be dead to me."

Tears sprang to her eyes, burning her throat. "You don't mean that."

But he did. "Choose," he demanded angrily.

Tears streaming down her cheeks, Anna started to walk to the boat where her brother waited for her.

Arthur turned away, unable to watch her leave.

He'd listened to every painful word of her conversation with her father. Damn Lorn for doing this to her! For making her choose between them. It didn't have to be this way.

Arthur had tried to give him a way out, but the bastard wouldn't take it.

He almost wished he'd killed him. Almost. But when he'd heard Anna say that she loved him, he knew he'd done the right thing. Even if it meant he had to let her go.

Unfortunately, the pain of parting wasn't any easier the second time around. His chest burned. Every muscle in his body felt teased on a razor's edge, reverberating with tension and restraint.

He wanted to stop her from getting on that damned boat. To tell her she belonged with him. To tell her he loved her.

To ask her to choose him.

But he wouldn't make it harder on her than it already was. He wouldn't tear her apart even further. One look at her stricken face when her father had given her his ultimatum was enough to see the terrible toll it was taking on her.

"I'm sorry, Ewen. Tell Mother—" Her voice broke. "Tell her I'm sorry. But I belong with him."

He jolted still, clearing his ears, refusing to believe he'd heard her right. Slowly, he turned and saw her hugging her brother.

Hugging him goodbye.

Arthur couldn't breathe.

Stepping away from her brother's embrace, she turned and ventured a look in his direction. The uncertainty in her gaze sent a hard twinge through his chest that broke every last thread of his restraint.

He was at her side in a few long strides. His voice rumbled with the effort to constrain the emotion surging in his chest. "Are you sure? You don't have to do this. I'll protect you and your family as best I can, even if you go."

She smiled, tears shimmering in her eyes. "The fact that you would do that is exactly why I am sure. I love you. If you still want me, I'm yours."

Oh God, did he want her. Forgetting the dirt and

grime that clung to him—not to mention the stench of the battlefield—Arthur pulled her in his arms with a sigh of relief that tore from the deepest part of him. From the place he'd never thought to open again. He rested his cheek on the top of her head, absorbed the golden, silky warmth and fragrance of her hair, and held her tightly against him, too moved to speak.

But he didn't need to say anything. The way she slid her arms around him and rested her cheek against his *cotun* said it all.

She'd chosen him. He couldn't believe it. He'd never thought to feel like this. Never thought that this kind of happiness was meant for him.

But his joy was tempered by the knowledge of how difficult this must be for her.

Reluctantly, he released her. She gazed up at him, the sunlight caressing her beautiful features in a soft, golden light. Light that spread through him like a warm embrace. He felt a fierce tightening inside him. He was a lucky man.

Realizing he still hadn't answered, he lifted one corner of his mouth. "If you didn't guess, that was a yes."

Her smile made his heart catch.

He'd thought he was meant to be alone, but now he knew he'd only been waiting for her. Together they would face whatever challenges and obstacles life threw at them.

Including her father. Arthur held her against his side as Lorn strode down to the jetty to take his place among his men.

He could feel Anna wobble as her father walked past where they stood without giving her another glance.

Arthur squeezed her to him tighter, wanting to protect her from this. The bastard was breaking her heart.

"Father," she cried softly.

Lorn turned to look at her with an icy glare. But he wasn't as unaffected as he wanted to be. There was real pain in the older man's eyes. "There is nothing more to be said. You made your choice."

She shook her head. "I choose to love you both. But my future is with Arthur."

Lorn gave her a long look, and for a moment Arthur thought he might relent. But he flattened his mouth and turned to leave without another word, pride dooming him once again. He was only hurting himself, cutting her off like this. Anna was the light—the glue—that had held everyone around her together. Without her, their life would be a little darker. Arthur ought to know; he'd been there.

He wished he could save her from the pain or take it for himself, but all he could do was stay by her side as her father and clansmen sailed away from her.

When they disappeared from sight around the bend in the loch, Arthur tipped her chin to look into her eyes. "I swear I will make sure that you never regret this."

Through the shimmer of tears, she gave him a wobbly smile. "I won't. It's the only decision I could make. I love you."

He leaned down and gave her a soft kiss. Her mouth was even sweeter and softer than he remembered. "And I love you."

He wanted to say so much more, but the rest would have to wait. Reinforcements would be arriving at any minute. "Which is your room?" he asked.

She blushed, looking embarrassed. "The top chamber overlooking the loch."

He should have guessed. "That was my room."

Her eyes widened, and she said hurriedly, "I'll move—"

He shook his head, cutting her off. "Stay, I shall know where to find you." He liked thinking of her in his room.

He glanced over her shoulder, seeing the ships drawing near. "Go. There are some things that I must attend to. I'll find you when I'm done."

She reached up to cup his face. "Your poor face."

He winced. "I know it looks horrible."

Guilt filled her eyes. "God, Arthur, I'm sorry."

He shook his head. "None of that, lass. It's over. We can't change what happened in the past; all we can do is live for today and plan for the future."

A future that only a moment ago looked grim now blossomed with hope.

He watched her go, knowing how damned close he'd been to losing her. But now that he had her, Arthur swore that he would never let her go.

Arthur didn't keep her waiting long. Anna heard the soft knock on the door barely half an hour after the ships departed.

Bruce's men had not stayed long. Still, it was strange, watching from the tower window as the courtyard filled with enemy soldiers.

Nay, not enemy. In choosing Arthur she'd also chosen Bruce, though it would take some time, she expected, to come to terms with exactly what that would mean. For now, she was just trying to get used to the idea that she didn't know when—or if—she might see her family again.

In refusing to submit to Bruce, her father would have no choice but to follow the path that John Comyn, Earl of Buchan, had taken months earlier to England. She suspected her mother, brothers, and sister would soon follow.

But no matter how difficult her decision, Anna knew she'd made the right one.

The blind love she'd had for her father was that of a child—a child who thought he could do no wrong. But her love for Arthur was that of a woman. A woman who understood that people—even those you loved—made mistakes. Forgiveness was part of loving.

She opened the door and her heart slammed against her

chest just seeing him there. His large frame filled the doorway, and he had to duck as he entered the room.

The small chamber suddenly felt very small—and very warm. The fresh scent of soap filled the air. He'd bathed and changed from his armor and was wearing a clean shirt, tunic, and hose. Borrowed, she suspected, from one of her departed clansmen.

It wasn't the visceral awareness, however, but the boyishly uncertain look on his face that made her throw herself into his arms and bury her face against his broad, warm chest.

She felt the deep sigh of relief go through him, as he wrapped his arms around and held her.

"You're all right?" he asked.

She nodded, resting her chin on his chest to look up at him. "You were worried?"

A lock of damp hair flopped across his forehead. "Aye, more than I wanted to be."

"I made my decision, Arthur. I meant what I said. It might not always be easy, but I'll not regret it."

Her brother Alan was right. She deserved a man who would love her as fiercely as she loved him. Who would stand down dragons and crawl through the fires of hell for her. Arthur had done that, and she would never let him go.

She paused, easing back in his arms a little. "Thank you for what you did. I know"—her voice caught—"I know it couldn't have been easy."

His face clouded, but only for a moment. "I'll not regret it." He repeated her words back to her with a wry smile. "Sparing your father's life was a small price to pay for the happiness I've received in return."

She bit her lip. "But what about Bruce? Won't he be angry that you let him go?"

He grimaced. "Probably, if your former uncle's reaction was any indication. But the king owes me a few favors; I think I may have just called them in. As long as your father leaves Scotland, he will likely understand."

Likely. Suddenly, she realized she could feel only one hand on her back. She moved out of his embrace and looked down to see that his left hand was wrapped in heavy bandages. She hadn't noticed before because he'd been wearing gauntlets.

"What happened to your hand?"

"It's broken," he said, matter-of-factly.

Their eyes met and he answered her unspoken question. One look at his beaten face was all it took to tell her how it happened. Her heart stabbed. "What else?"

He shrugged. "A few ribs. Some bruises and cuts. Nothing that won't heal." There was something in his eyes that told her differently. "It was no more than I deserved for what I did to you."

"Don't," she said, shaking her head adamantly. "Don't say that. What you did was awful, but I would never have exacted such punishment." Tears sprang to her eyes. "We have not had a very easy time of it, have we?"

He cupped her chin, shaking his head. "Nay, love, but I promise that will change. No more lies. No more secrets." He smiled crookedly. "You know the most dangerous of them, anyway."

That he was part of Bruce's secret army. "Why do they call you Ranger?"

There was a moment of awkwardness when he looked around the room for somewhere to sit and realized there was only the bed. But he sat down on the edge, indicating for her to sit beside him. She noticed that he was careful to keep a few inches between them as he explained.

He'd been forced to leave training before the others to take his place as a spy. The decision to use war names had been made in his absence. Some of the names had been taken from jokes among the men, and others—like his—were derived from their skills.

"So I was right," she beamed. "I thought you would make a perfect scout."

He laughed. "Aye, though I wasn't happy about it. I was trying to hide my abilities, but you seemed to have other ideas."

She was beginning to have other ideas now. She leaned a little closer to him, letting her breasts brush against his arm. "What will happen next?"

He seemed to be holding himself very still. "Right now, I think I'd better leave. I shouldn't be here alone with you like this. Not without a priest."

She laughed, and put her hand on his thigh. The heavy muscles flexed under her palm. "I don't think I want a priest here with us."

His jaw clenched—actually, most of the muscles in his body seemed clenched. "I meant until after we are married."

"I rather think it's too late to stand on ceremony, don't you?"

"I didn't come up here to—" He stopped. "Damn it, Anna, stop that." He covered her hand with his, stopping her exploratory little dip down his thigh. "I'm trying to do this right."

"Do you mean you didn't do it right before?" She blinked with exaggerated innocence.

He gave her a scolding look. "You know that's not what I meant. It was bloody damned well perfect."

No more teasing. When she looked up at him again, she did so with all the love in her heart. "Please, Arthur, I need to feel that way again."

She needed the closeness. Needed the connection. Needed to know that everything was going to be all right.

Her eyes flew open. "Unless you aren't able. I forgot—"

He stopped her with a searing kiss that tore through her soul. "I'm able, damn it."

And he proceeded to show her in painstaking detail just

how able he was. Slowly, deeply, and tenderly, with all the love that was in his heart. And when the last shudders of pleasure had faded from her body, when he held her naked body to his bruised and battered one, Anna knew that in the arms of this strong, steady warrior she'd finally found her peace.

Epilogue

Dunstaffnage Castle, October 10, 1308

Peace felt good—for Scotland and for Anna. Less than two months after her father's defeat at Brander, Bruce had won the battle for Scotland's nobles. Her grandfather, Alexander MacDougall, had submitted after a short siege of Dunstaffnage Castle, and the Earl of Ross had submitted a few days ago.

That Bruce had allowed Ross to live, forgoing punishing the man responsible for the capture and ongoing imprisonment of his wife, daughter, sister, and the Countess of Buchan, was a testament to his desire to see Scotland—and its nobles—united.

For the good of Scotland. Anna had to admit the philosophy impressed her. The man himself . . .

Well, she was trying to keep an open mind. Years of allegiance did not switch in a matter of weeks. But what Bruce had planned for today would do much to change her mind. She knew how much it would mean to Arthur.

Her gaze swept over the Great Hall, across the sea of celebrating clansmen. Some were familiar, but most were strangers. It would take time, but Anna vowed she would know them all.

This would be her home. For his loyalty and service to Bruce, Arthur had been made keeper of Dunstaffnage Castle. His next mission, too, would keep him close. He'd be spending the next few months surveying the entirety of Lorn and Argyll and mapping his findings.

Arthur slid his hand over hers and gave it a gentle squeeze. "Are you happy, my love?"

She lifted her gaze to the man seated beside her at the dais, the man who only this morning had become her husband. Tears of joy filled her eyes as she looked upon his handsome features, which bore only faint traces of his ordeal. "Aye, how could I not be? You've finally made an honest woman of me, and perhaps I shall be able to look Father Gilbert in the eye again."

He laughed. The deep, rich sound, so much freer now, still had the power to send tingles of warmth skittering all over her. "I told you I should have left earlier."

Her lips turned down in a pout. "I was cold."

"I offered to put another blanket on the bed before I went."

"I didn't want another blanket," she said with the same stubbornness that had gotten her in trouble in the first place. She'd wanted him.

She'd grown used to sleeping beside him at Innis Chonnel, and it had been difficult the past month when she'd returned to Dunstaffnage. Sneaking around wasn't nearly as warm and cozy. And of course, the biggest problem with sneaking around was the potential for discovery—which was exactly what had happened last week when Father Gilbert caught Arthur leaving her room.

He gave her a long, heated look. "You won't need any blankets tonight."

Despite the fact that her innocence had been lost many times—and in many illuminating ways—over the past two months, she blushed.

He bent closer. "Do you think they'll notice if we leave now?"

The soft whisper of his breath in her ear made her shiver. But it was his hand moving possessively—determinedly— down her thigh that sent soft bolts of heat pulsing between her legs.

The brush of his finger reminded her of his tongue. And if she remembered his tongue, she would have to remember his mouth. And if she remembered his mouth, she would remember the way he'd woken her this morning—her wedding day, the irreverent brigand!—and made her weep with pleasure.

And then she'd remember how she'd paid him back for the devilry by teasing him with her tongue. She'd remember the delicious salty taste of him. The velvety-soft column of hot flesh sliding deep and deeper into her mouth. How she'd milked him hard, drawing him with the suction of her mouth and circling the plump, heavy head with her tongue, until he was begging for release. How he'd finally lost control, holding her head to him as he pulsed deep in her mouth, his deep guttural cries of release ringing in her ears.

Her body melted with the sweet warmth of arousal. Suddenly, she startled, remembering where they were.

She swatted his hand away, hoping no one had been watching. Her eyes were half-lidded, for pity's sake! She was supposed to be keeping him distracted, not the other way around. "We can't leave. Not until—" She stopped, realizing she'd almost said too much. "We're the guests of honor."

He frowned, looking down to the end of the table where there were a few empty seats.

Nails to the cross! Her pulse spiked with panic. He'd noticed. Of course he'd noticed; there was nothing the too-observant man didn't notice.

She grabbed his hand. "Come, we should dance."

He frowned, not moving. "Is something wrong, Anna? You're acting odd."

Her eyes widened. "Of course not. I just wish to dance."

A wry smile turned his mouth. "I'm afraid you'll need to give me a few minutes."

"Why . . . ?" He glanced down to his lap and her cheeks heated, seeing the heavy bulge. It seemed she hadn't been the only one remembering.

She glanced down the opposite end of the table to where Gregor MacGregor sat. He gave a subtle shake of his head and she turned back to her husband.

He was frowning again. "Are you sure it's not . . . I know you miss your family."

A bittersweet smile played upon her lips. "I do, but it doesn't mean I'm not happy. And my grandfather is here."

She nodded toward the MacDougall chief, who sat a few seats away beside the king—or where the king had been sitting a minute ago.

After the fall of the castle, her mother and sisters had been permitted to follow her father and brothers into exile, but Bruce wanted her grandfather's support. Whether he would earn it from the old warrior, she did not know, but she was glad to have at least one member of her family here on her wedding day.

And of course she had Squire. One day she'd force Arthur to tell her how he'd managed to sneak the puppy out of the castle when it was under siege. She'd blubbered like a fool when she saw him, having to explain to a confused Arthur that she was happy. He'd claimed to regret it every day since when the besotted puppy followed after him, but she knew he didn't mind half as much as he pretended to. Accepting—nay, trusting—affection came easier to him now.

That Arthur had gone to such efforts to see to her happiness had moved her beyond words.

When he'd done the same with her brother Alan the day

before the castle fell and her family had fled to England, she'd been nearly inconsolable with joy. Seeing her brother, knowing that he did not agree with her father's decision and would not cut her off completely, was more than she could have hoped for. Alan was loyal to their father, but that loyalty did not come at the expense of his love for her.

Aye, she had much to thank her new husband for.

"And what of you, Arthur? I know you must be disappointed that not all your fellow guardsmen could be here."

Anna had not been told all the details about Bruce's elite guard, nor did she ask, knowing that secrecy was what would keep her husband safe. But she knew they were the most elite warriors in Scotland—the best of the best in all disciplines of warfare. She'd always suspected there was something special about Arthur, but she'd never imagined how special.

She'd figured out a few of their identities as well. Her uncle. The two men with him who'd helped to free Arthur— Gordon and MacKay. The ridiculously handsome Gregor MacGregor, who'd been part of the attack all those months ago—his face was one that was hard to forget. And it seemed she was correct to suspect that the fierce-looking Islander Tor MacLeod was one as well, as was the wickedly charming Norseman Erik MacSorley. Both men had been seated near the king with their wives, although now only the women remained.

She might not know all the details, but she knew enough to understand how important these men were to him— even if he didn't.

But he would.

He shrugged as if it didn't matter to him. "There is peace in the north, but along the borders there is still unrest. I'm sure they would have been here if they could. Gordon is to be married soon; perhaps I will see them all then." He paused. "There is much to do before the king holds his first parliament next spring." His gaze traveled to a table just below the dais. "I'm glad my brothers could be here. It's the first time all of us have been in one room in years."

Sir Dugald and Sir Gillespie had submitted along with her grandfather and Ross; surprisingly, they seemed to harbor little ill will toward Arthur. But from the expression on Sir Dugald's face as he argued with Sir Neil, the same could not be said of Dugald's feelings toward his elder brother.

"From the looks of it, maybe it could have waited a few more."

He chuckled. "They've always been like that. Fierce rivals even when they were lads. I think that's why Dugald allied himself with the English for so long—so he wouldn't have to follow orders from Neil. They'll work it out. Eventually."

Anna could see him start to look around the room again. "Are you ready to dance?" she asked anxiously.

He lifted a brow. "I'm ready to go to bed."

Unconsciously, her gaze shot to Gregor MacGregor again. Much to her relief, this time he nodded.

When she turned back to Arthur, however, his eyes had narrowed. "Do you mind telling me why every time I mention bed, you look at MacGregor?"

She blushed.

"Are you going to tell me what this is about?" he demanded angrily. "You're up to something—and don't try to tell me you're not, I can feel it."

She lifted her chin, annoyed by his perceptiveness. "I thought I was supposed to be your blind spot."

"You are," he gave a sharp wave of his hand, "but he's not."

It wasn't easy trying to surprise someone who picked up on every nuance, noticed every detail, and sensed every thing around him. He'd even noticed the changes in her body before she did—informing her that they had better move up the wedding or their child was going to be very large for two months early.

She gave him a smug look. "You're jealous." She let her gaze slide back down the table, taking a long, considering look. "He's quite handsome, your friend."

Arthur's scowl only grew darker. "He won't be so pretty much longer if you keep looking at him like that. And you're stalling."

She gave up in a huff. "Very well, but I wanted it to be a surprise."

"*What* to be a surprise?"

A short walk outside the castle gates later, he discovered the reason for the subterfuge. Standing in a clearing before a single standing stone with the orange halo of the setting sun behind him, King Robert the Bruce stood in full kingly regalia. Flanking him, spread out like an iron wall, their features masked by the darkened nasal helms, were the other ten members of Bruce's secret guard.

Arthur stopped in his tracks, giving her a swift look of incredulity. "Did you have something to do with this?"

She shook her head. "It was King Hoo—" She stopped at her husband's look. "King Robert's idea," she amended, though it still didn't fall easily from her tongue. "My mission was to distract you." She made a face. "A mission it seems I failed."

He pulled her into his arms and kissed her. "I think you succeeded admirably."

She beamed. "Go. They're waiting for you."

Arthur was finally going to have the ceremony he'd never had. The one denied him by his role as a spy. These men were a part of him, just as she was. She folded her hand over her stomach. And soon, as their babe would be.

He gave her another kiss. "I won't be long."

"I'll be waiting for you." *Always*. Just as he would always come back to her. The man who'd once looked at the door as though he wanted to leave had found the place he belonged. And in a world where peace was as fragile as a sliver of glass, Anna had found her rock.

She watched him walk toward the others, a fierce swell of pride and happiness filling her chest. When he reached the others, she started to walk away.

She'd made it only a few feet beyond the circle of trees, however, before two women stopped her.

"Where are you going?" Tor MacLeod's wife, Christina, asked in a hushed voice.

Anna tried not to be awed by her beauty, but it was impossible. Christina was as exquisite and refined as a faerie princess—especially compared to her terrifying-looking husband. He looked torn out of the pages of some ancient Norse myth. "I . . . I thought I was not supposed to watch."

The second woman smiled. Though not in the same realm of beauty as Christina Fraser, there was something calm and pleasing about the brash seafarer Erik MacSorley's wife, Elyne. Anna had been shocked to discover she was the daughter of the Earl of Ulster, a close friend to the English king. But she was also sister to King Robert's imprisoned wife, Elizabeth. Another divided family, it seemed.

"We're not," Elyne said. "But that's not going to stop me. I didn't get a chance to see my husband's. I wouldn't miss this for anything."

"Won't they be angry?" Anna asked.

Christina gave her a saucy grin. "They'll get over it. Besides, I want to see what kind of marking they give him."

Anna gave her a perplexed look. "He already has one. It's the lion rampant. I thought all the men had one."

"They do," Christina answered. "But they decided to add to it after the spider in the cave. Have you heard the story?"

Anna nodded. The story of Bruce's spider in the cave had already become legend.

"To honor the occasion, Erik decided to add a band around his arm like a torque," Elyne said. "It looks like a spider web. Because he's a seafarer, he incorporated a *bir-*

linn." She smiled. "Once the other men saw it, they all decided to get one." She laughed, rolling her eyes as if to say, *Men.*

"Come." Christina grabbed her hand and dragged her back through the trees. "It's begun."

Together, the three women watched from the shadows as Arthur kneeled before the king, taking his rightful place among his fellow guardsmen—and friends.

Steadfast, the sword the king gave him said. Anna couldn't agree more.

AUTHOR'S NOTE

The Battle of the Pass of Brander was a key battle of the Wars of Scottish Independence. It stands not only as an example of the shift in Bruce's war tactics (he ambushes the ambushers), but also harkens the precipitous fall in fortune of the MacDougalls and a shift of power in West Highland politics to another branch of descendants of Somerled, the MacDonalds, and to the Campbells, who were to profit from the MacDougalls' misfortune.

There is some disagreement among historians as to the time of Bruce's Argyll campaign, when John of Lorn fled to Scotland, and the fall of Dunstaffnage Castle. I went with the more conventional date of the summer of 1308, but some have argued that the final capitulation of Argyll did not occur until 1309.

Although I give a fictional account of the battle, I incorporated many of the actual events, including John of Lorn commanding his men from a *birlinn* in the loch as he was thought to be still recovering from the illness that had necessitated the truce the year before. When the attack failed, Lorn was said to have retreated down the loch to one of his castles.

But one detail of the battle in particular gave me the idea for the story, when I read about a scout who was supposed to have warned Bruce of the ambush, thereby saving the day. It sounded like the perfect job for my elite scout, Arthur Campbell.

The character of Arthur Campbell is loosely based on "Arthur of Dunstaffnage," the brother (or possibly the cousin) of Neil Campbell. As his designation suggests, he was appointed the constable of Dunstaffnage Castle after the war. This fit in nicely with my MacDougall heroine—although Anna is a fictional character and the name of Arthur's wife (if any) does not survive. Interestingly, however, a betrothal agreement between Arthur and Christina (MacRuairi) of the Isles did exist, though they were never married.

What also fit in nicely is that Arthur—along with another brother, Dugald—was said to have been aligned with the English for a time, later coming over to Bruce.

"Arthur of Dunstaffnage" is probably not the Arthur who is the progenitor of Clan MacArthur. It seems most likely this Arthur was from a different (and possibly senior) branch of the family, the Campbells of Strachur (the sons of Arthur). But there is plenty of confusion and different theories about the MacArthur lineage, including a direct descent from King Arthur. An old Highland proverb says, "There is nothing older, unless the hill, MacArthur, and the devil."

Neil Campbell was one of Robert the Bruce's most important and loyal supporters. Indeed, Neil would eventually marry the king's sister Mary when she was released from her cage above Roxburgh Castle (around 1310). As was common for an age with so many widows and widowers, Mary would wed again on Neil's death. Readers of the first book in the series, *The Chief*, may be interested to know that her second husband was Alexander Fraser, Christina's brother.

An interesting aside about Neil gives a little color to the age: Neil's first wife was said to have been a daughter of

Andrew Crawford. Neil and his brother Donald, who had been made guardians of Crawford's two daughters, decided to take the sisters for wives—literally—by abducting them.

John of Lorn, also known as John Bacach (lame John) and John of Argyll, was a key figure in West Highland politics, responsible not only for Colin Mor Campbell's death at the Battle of Red Ford, but also for the death of his kinsman Alexander MacDonald, Lord of Islay (Angus Og's brother).

Allied with the Comyns by marriage, Lorn suffered greatly for his loyalty to that family and his hatred of Bruce—which, given Bruce's murder of the Red Comyn, was probably understandable.

Lorn's use of female messengers was my invention, but the frustration with messages gone astray is not. A number of letters from the period survive, including a recently deciphered letter from the sheriff of Banff to Edward II, where he complains of messengers being killed.

Similarly, Lorn's frustration at being left alone to deal with Bruce and the difficulty in garnering support from the local barons is based on surviving correspondence from Lorn to Edward II, where he claims to have been forced to truce with Bruce because he was ill and the "barons of Argyll give me no aid." (*Robert Bruce*, G.W.S. Barrow, Edinburgh University Press, Edinburgh, Scotland, 2005, pg. 231.)

The source of Lorn's illness does not survive. The heart attack and subsequent heart problems were my invention that happened to go along with his propensity to have violent fits of temper. Similarly, the source of the debilitating illness that hit Bruce in the winter of 1307 is also not known. Although some historical rumor had it as leprosy, the latest supposition is that it might have been scurvy. Whatever the cause, it hit the new king hard—reputedly nearly killing him. Bruce was supposedly carried into battle at Inverurie by his men.

The brooch Lorn wears in Chapter Two, reputedly ripped off Robert during the Battle of Dal Righ, is still in the hands of the MacDougall chief and made an appearance as recently as fifty years ago. However, some experts have suggested that the brooch in question dates from a later period.

The Battle of Red Ford happened differently than the way I portrayed it. Rather than an ambush, Colin Mor and John of Lorn met near a burn that fed into Loch na Streinge (later called *Allt a chomhla chaidh*, the burn of the meeting). Discussion degenerated into argument, and then into battle. The MacDougalls were outnumbered, and it looked as if they would lose, until Great Colin was shot and killed by an archer from behind a boulder.

The extent of Campbell power around Loch Awe before the war is not known, but as Colin Mor was made Ballie of Loch Awe circa 1296, presumably it was not insignificant. Although it is believed that the Campbells held Innis Chonnel Castle prior to the MacDougall possession known to have existed in 1308, historians aren't certain. At the time of the novel, however, it was in MacDougall hands. In a letter to King Edward, Lorn mentions three castles in his possession on Loch Awe.

The hatred between Bruce and the MacDougalls was rivaled by that of their kinsmen the Comyns. The "harrying of Buchan" following the Battle of Inverurie (Hill of Barra) on May 23, 1308, which takes place in the beginning of the book, appears to have been one of the few times Bruce let vengeance reign unfettered. The destruction was so great that it allegedly took years to recover and was talked about for generations.

By contrast, King Robert did indeed accept the submission of William (Uilleam II), the Earl of Ross, without reprisal for Ross's role in the capture—and subsequent imprisonment—of Bruce's ladies (his wife, daughter, sisters, and the Countess of Buchan). Not long after Ross's submission, his son Hugh (Aodh) was married to Bruce's sister Matilda.

Alexander MacDougall, Lord of Argyll, is said to have been too old and infirm at the time to fight at Brander. He submitted to Bruce after a siege of Dunstaffnage Castle, attending the king's first parliament in March 1309 at Ardchatten, but later followed his son into exile, where he died in 1310.

As usual, some of the castles mentioned in the book are also known by different names. Auldearn Castle is also known as Old Even, and Glassery (Glassary) Castle as Fincharn.

Medieval rat torture was far more gruesome than I suggest. A cage with a rat underneath would be placed on the stomach of the victim and heated from above. The rat, in an attempt to get out, would eat a slow hole into the gut of the victim. Charming (and perhaps providing a little too much "color" of the age)!

Finally, readers of the third book in my Campbell trilogy, *Highland Scoundrel*, might note the connection of Arthur's sword to Duncan's, which was engraved with the word *Steadfast* and had been passed down through the generations from the time of Bruce. Although my invention, it was indeed customary to engrave swords and pass them down.

Not enough? Make sure to check out my website, www.monicamccarty.com, for more information and "picture books" of some of the places mentioned in the books.